PAINT IT BLACKMAIL

By the same author:

The Art of Danger (John Kite Book 1)
Pictures To Die For (John Kite Book 3)
Killing Art (John Kite Book 4)

Praise for the first John Kite novel, *The Art of Danger*

"I can't tell you how much I enjoyed it. A treat. I'm a fan. A hugely entertaining story.' Characterisation is superb." (*Crime novelist E V Seymour)*

"Well paced page turner with good characterizations. Looking forward to reading more of his work." *(Amazon, US Reviewer)*

"Raymond Chandler's Philip Marlowe reinventing himself as a 21st Century English Art Investigator" *(Amazon UK reviewer)*

"Excitement plus! I highly recommend it" *(Amazon, France, reviewer)*

"Plot had some very cool twists" *(Goodreads reviewer)*

"I was entirely hooked by the plot line and read it pretty much at one sitting." *(Amazon UK reviewer)*

"Brilliant read. Strong characters" *(Goodreads Reviewer)*

PAINT IT BLACKMAIL

Stuart Doughty

To TESSA and JULIET

This action crime thriller is the second in a series about investigator John Kite whose speciality is recovering stolen artworks. To find out more about the books, the author and get an introductory and exclusive FREE story… join the Readers' Club by going to: https://stuart-doughty.com/free-download

Chapter 1

Don't think I'm a smart alec if I say I can spot suspicious behaviour at a hundred paces. It's not that hard. You only need use your eyes. Plus a particle of grey matter.

The three people in the museum were a classic case. As out of place as a child's paint-by-numbers canvas would be in the National Gallery.

First up, they looked nervous. Nobody looks *nervous* in a museum. People look amazed, fascinated, bored, studious. They chatter, laugh, yawn. They're overwhelmed, hungry, foot-sore. They hold hands, they kiss, they take selfies, they take notes. They buy souvenirs, they get lost, they look for the toilet. They point at things and say 'Wow, look at that!' They do all that and more but what they *don't* do is stand around fidgeting like they're waiting for a cue. And most of all, visitors look at the exhibits. The three people I was watching were giving as much attention to the displays as you give to the scenery in the Channel Tunnel.

I was in the British Museum in London, that vast granddaddy of a museum. I wasn't having a day off. I was there to do some research and was on my way home. I'd gone through the Great Court, the huge central space that's always thronged with the world's tourists, and into the King's Library. It's the oldest part of the museum, built in the early nineteenth century for George III. You don't get many kings popping in to borrow a book these days, but the old library houses ancient treasures from all around the world: Egypt, Babylon, Rome, Persia, India, Japan. Irreplaceable exhibits of incalculable value.

As soon as I saw the nervous threesome, I stopped heading for the exit and doubled-back round what's called the Piranesi Vase. It's not really a vase at all. It's nearly twelve feet tall, so tricky to get flowers into. More of a bathtub on legs. It's Roman, second century, if you're interested.

Anyhow, the Vase was good cover so I lurked behind it and watched the suspects: two men and a woman. One man was in a wheelchair. He was in his forties, average build, average looking. What wasn't so average was he was wearing some kind of work clothes with reinforced patches on the knees. The kind I've seen worn by carpet fitters. Now, inclusivity and diversity may be watchwords when hiring these days, but I can't imagine many wheelchair users have jobs as carpet fitters.

The woman was also forty-ish, blonde, and in an all-purpose dark skirt and jacket. Also work clothes, I thought. The sort of thing worn by a hotel receptionist, an accountant, an optician. Almost anybody.

The other man was roughly my age, early thirties, and he was wearing a grey suit with a pale blue shirt but no tie. So far, so bland, but what didn't fit was he had a walking stick. It looked new, unused. Which was not surprising because he didn't need it. He walked normally. In tight little circles. But a walking stick is a potential weapon. Like those Victorian sword-sticks and walking cane rifles.

A walking stick is also the kind of thing which, with a bit of play-acting, you could get past security scanners. And however efficient the security staff are they're not going to scan a wheelchair either. If the stick was a weapon, the wheelchair could be a Trojan horse. A neat, covert way to carry armaments or explosives into the museum.

Wheelchair Man was trying to extract something stuck in a pocket of his coveralls. And he was having trouble. He plainly wanted to stand up to get better purchase. But if he wanted to maintain the deception of disablement he couldn't do that. I saw his frustration.

Something was about to happen. But what? A terrorist attack? The three suspects were white, British-looking, ordinary, verging on dull. But enough ordinary-looking kids went out to join ISIS.

I looked around for museum security staff. There weren't any. I had to get closer. I moved away from the Piranesi Vase, went past the Rosetta Stone and tucked myself in behind the Discobolus, the huge Roman statue of a nude sportsman holding a discus.

Tourists continued to tour. A school party trailed noisily after their teacher. No one but me even glanced at the threesome.

The fidgeting from the three increased. Wheelchair Man shifted in his seat and finally extracted the package. He passed it to the woman. The three of them looked at each other and I got the impression of throat-clearing. That they were about to go into action.

I itched to intervene. But until they *did* something I had to wait.

Another school party appeared. Excitable, fractious, misbehaving.

Then the man in the wheelchair stood up – with no physical difficulty. He reached down and took something from where it had been secreted under the seat of his wheelchair. A heavy claw hammer.

That was it. I took off and ran towards him.

I was only thirty feet away but the school party leader, trying to subdue the children, called them all into a circle. Suddenly a jostling mass of thirty twelve-year-olds was between me and the suspects. I tried to push through but was caught up in a Sargasso Sea of kids chattering, comparing worksheets, passing round sweets, sniggering at the Discobolus's huge and well-defined genitals.

Wheelchair Man lifted his hammer and held it poised above his head. He was static for a moment and looked like a figure in a Soviet propaganda sculpture, symbolising achievement in construction or something.

'Stop!' I yelled at him.

Which both frightened and excited the schoolchildren. They broke ranks and got in my way even more.

Wheelchair Man brought his hammer down onto a display cabinet containing four-thousand-year-old Egyptian clay tablets incised with hieroglyphics.

But he did it in a strangely measured way, almost slow motion. It reminded me of those elaborate outdoor clocks where mechanical figures strike bells to mark the hours. And his aim was off. The hammer dented the hardwood frame, but the glass stayed whole.

I burst out of the tangle of children to see the man with the walking stick upend it and solemnly bring it down on another cabinet. Once again, the action was stylised, theatrical. A lump of bird's-eye maple was gouged off the edge of the cabinet, but the glass held. The woman unfurled the package she'd been given by Wheelchair Man. It was a home-made banner which said something about repossessing native artefacts. And I thought, yes, if you wanted to protest about the UK holding antiquities which 'belong' to other nations, then this gallery of the British Museum was a good place to do it. The woman began to intone a convoluted statement about government policy and cultural imperialism.

I reached the man with the hammer as he raised it for another blow. I caught his arm as it came down towards the cabinet and wrenched his wrist through three-quarters of a circle. He cried out in pain and dropped the hammer. Then my right fist went straight into the middle of his face. He staggered back, blood pouring from his nose, and crumpled to the floor. He made no attempt to get up.

People screamed. People shouted for help. People ran for the exit. Others calmly took out their phones and began to film. Somewhere an alarm sounded. Teachers led their children away.

I moved towards the man with the stick. He saw me coming, moved away from the exhibits and slashed at me with the stick, sabre-style, but he only hit my shoulder. He should have aimed for my head. And he was far too slow with a follow-up. I grabbed the walking stick, wrenched it from his grasp in a single action and sprang towards him. He looked terrified and retreated. But he was again too slow. I punched him hard: twice in the stomach, once to the jaw and he joined his friend on the ground.

I heard a smattering of applause and a cry of 'Go, Rambo!' I turned and saw I had an audience. A group of tourists had lined up to watch. Did they think this was regular entertainment in the museum? Like jousting at medieval castles?

The woman ditched her banner and picked up her friend's walking stick. 'Leave us alone,' she shouted at me. 'You've ruined everything, you bastard.' Charming. Sorry to have spoilt your day, madam. Why not go and smash your own house up? Then she swiped

Paint It Blackmail

the stick at me like she was dispersing bees. I seized it from her hand and snapped it in two under my foot. But the woman still came forward. She was furiously angry. 'How dare you?' she said. 'How dare you?' And aimed a surprisingly powerful slap at my face with her hand. I felt a sting as her ring grazed my cheek.

I caught her arm and twisted it behind her back. She squealed in pain but she was rummaging through her bag with her other hand and pulled something out of it. Then I heard the hiss from an aerosol can and I was instantly blinded. Pepper spray. I let go of the woman, turned away, and pulled a handkerchief from my pocket to wipe my streaming eyes.

As I doubled over, I heard one of my fan club shout, 'They're getting away.' Through stinging eyes, I saw the three attackers at the far end of the room heading towards the next museum gallery. Someone else shouted for me to go get them and thrust a bottle of water into my hands. I up-ended the bottle over my face, rubbed my eyes, blinked half a dozen times, then set off in pursuit.

I ran out of the King's Library, through a wide vestibule with its grand stone staircase, and into the next gallery, which is devoted to North America, then into the next, which is Mexico. The attackers ran to where more stairs led down to the Montague Place exit, the museum's back door. If you're trying to escape, it's better than the front. The back has no steps, no wide courtyard to cross before you get to the street. I rushed after them and got outside to see the three getting into a car. Even before the doors were shut, the car was moving and accelerating fast.

I was about to chase after it. But then I thought about the wheelchair. If they were terrorists, had they left an explosive? They hadn't seemed intent on causing damage in the museum so maybe what I'd seen was a diversionary tactic. Terrorists in Afghanistan will set one bomb off then, when crowds of rescuers have gathered, detonate a second, much deadlier one.

So I ignored the escaping car and ran back into the museum.

In the King's Library museum staff had materialised in large numbers. Some were making phone calls. Some were examining the damaged cabinets. But they were all ignoring the abandoned wheelchair. In my nightmare scenario it had lethal potential. For me. For many others. For priceless artefacts.

'The wheelchair,' I yelled. And heads turned. 'Has anyone checked it?' And they looked at me like I'd escaped from a secure institution for the maladjusted.

I got to the wheelchair, knelt down to examine it, then lay on the ground and looked underneath. I was hardly breathing, dreading to find wires and a battery, fearing to touch it in case there was a mercury tilt fuse or anti-tamper. I checked it inch by inch but I could see nothing. Surprised, but finally persuaded it was safe to move, I gripped it and turned it on its side. There was nothing underneath except a clip screwed beneath the seat which had held the hammer. Apart from that modification, it was a hundred per cent wheelchair.

Huh! An anti-climax. I guess it's better to overreact than not react at all, but I felt irritated. I was irritated because I had no idea what the three were up to. I went to one of the museum's mahogany benches and sat down to work things out.

I hadn't seen the demonstrators' banner properly but one of the phrases the woman uttered was, 'Give people back what is theirs.' So I assumed they were campaigning to get some artefact taken from the British Museum and sent back to whichever country it had originated from. Like the Greeks have lobbied for decades to have the Parthenon statuary, or the Elgin Marbles as they're known, sent back from London to Athens. But the demonstrators weren't Greek. The woman was the only one who had spoken and she sounded as English as warm beer and cricket matches.

If you go to the trouble of organising a protest it's a bit stupid – well, a complete failure really – if no one knows what the protest is about. That was the first thing that baffled me: what the hell did they want? Second, the demonstration itself was kind of stylised, almost theatrical. They only *pretended* to smash things up. Very considerate. But weird. Third, the people involved were nervy, amateurish and timid. Fourth, they were physically weak, not fighters or combat trained. Fifth, they ran away as soon as the heat was on. Political protesters almost always want to stick around, get arrested and plead their case in front of TV cameras. I'd never seen a demonstration defeated so easily.

And lastly – the oddest bit of all – an expensive car was standing by to whisk them away to safety.

Had I mistaken some charity or arts event for a demo? No. The man had a hammer. They were there to cause trouble.

My eyesight was returning to normal and I noticed something on the floor near the wheelchair. It was an old printed label, of the stick-on variety. Once it had been fixed to the wheelchair frame but the adhesive had dried and it had fallen off when I turned the chair over. The label said: BROOMFIELD CARE HOME. There was a phone number and an address in Ruislip.

I put the label in my pocket.

Just as the police arrived.

I would have liked to slink away and get on with work. But I'm an ex-cop and I know the routine. And the hassles. I don't want to make it harder for the lads than it already is.

Fifty minutes later I was still there. I'd given my statement and contact details, but I hadn't mentioned the address label. Well, it might be nothing. And if it was something, I didn't see why I shouldn't have the advantage. You can't spoon feed them, can you?

I was about to leave when there was a further kerfuffle.

A TV news crew arrived panting. Literally. Not because it was hot breaking news, but because they'd run in all the way from the street, run upstairs to the Egyptian mummies on level three because they'd misheard the location, then run all the way back down again.

I said 'crew.' In fact, there was only a cameraman who doubled on sound and a reporter. She was a good-looking young black woman with well-coiffed hair and perfect make-up, but had mud all over her spike-heeled ankle boots. An earlier story must have been something agricultural out beyond the M25. I saw her speak to one of the museum staff who pointed in my direction. She then beamed a smile at me and came right over.

'So, you're the hero of the day,' she said, extending a hand, twinkling her eyes.

I smiled back but shook my head and wrinkled my nose. 'I don't like things in museums to get damaged, that's all.'

'Would you mind if I asked you a few questions on camera?'

I hesitated. I work freelance but I'm not into publicity. Friends tell me I should have a better website, write a blog, join Twitter, resuscitate my Facebook page, get ten thousand followers on Instagram and so on. But I hate all that. The idea of posing for a selfie with my torso oiled in front of the Tate Gallery or – even worse – New Scotland Yard makes my skin creep. Not that I don't look good with my shirt off. My body's had five-star reviews from various girlfriends – one even said I looked like a young Bryan Ferry – but if I wanted to be a model I'd join an agency.

Within seconds the cameraman had set up his tripod in front of me, the reporter had thrown her jacket on the floor, was fluffing her hair with one hand and holding a microphone in the other. In spite of my dislike of publicity there was no way out. Well, I suppose I could have stamped my foot and refused but… life's too short, isn't it?

The way TV interviews work is that, while you continue talking sensibly and to the point the reporter will meet your eye, smile and nod encouragingly. This has a beguiling, almost hypnotic effect, drawing you on to say things you didn't want to say or hadn't even thought about before. Then you take a half second's pause for breath and their next prepared question comes in hard. So, after a minute of me describing what had happened, I took a breath and the reporter jumped in:

'Was it a terrorist attack?'

'So…' Everyone being interviewed starts their answer with a 'so.' I don't know why. I don't know why I did. But I did. 'So, that was my first reaction. But now I'm not sure…'

'You said they had a hammer with them.'

'Yes, but they didn't attack anybody with it. They hardly even attacked the exhibits.'

'What were they campaigning for? What did they want?'

'So…' Done it again. It gives you time to think… 'Well, that's the puzzle. I'm not sure. They mentioned British cultural imperialism. I suppose they were claiming the British Museum holds items they want returned to foreign nations…'

'Were they supporting what Prime Minister James Fresnel once called "cultural repatriation"?'

'I guess, but the Prime Minister never actually backed the idea.'

'Maybe the demonstrators were trying to make the Prime Minister think again. Which country were they from?'

'I don't know. They didn't say…' I looked at the banner where it still lay in a heap on the floor. I'd never seen it stretched out clearly enough to read.

Then my phone went off. The ringtone is straightforward. No rock. No comedy. No animal sounds. But it is persistent and I was secretly relieved.

'I'm sorry,' I said, scrabbling in my jacket pocket for the phone.

'Cut it, Nick,' said the reporter to the cameraman. Then back to me, 'They'll only use twenty seconds. So we've got plenty.'

I answered my phone without checking who was calling and told whoever it was to hold on.

'Thank you so very much.' The reporter and I shook hands, she flashed another beautiful smile and turned away, ready for the next assignment.

'Mr John Kite?' said a cultured male voice on the phone.

'Speaking.'

'I'm calling from Number Ten Downing Street. The Prime Minister would very much like to speak to you this evening.'

Eh? What? Was this a wind-up? One of my ex-colleagues having a laugh? Then I had one of those mad, illogical thoughts. Just for a second you think something is true even though you know it cannot possibly be. For a crazy moment I imagined the PM had heard what I'd said. That in some freaky way the interview had been live. But of course it wasn't. And he hadn't. But because I'd been speaking about him only seconds previously, the coincidence was uncanny. I felt rattled. Like it was a dream.

'The Prime Minister? Are you sure?'

'My name is Tom Daubeney. I'm one of the Prime Minister's private secretaries. I assure you this isn't a scam. Though I understand your caution.'

But they would say that, wouldn't they? If it was a scam. Like when they phone to tell you your computer isn't working properly.

'Why does the Prime Minister want to talk to me?'

'I'm not sure of the exact nature of his enquiry but he will want to use your expertise in some way.'

'My expertise...?' What did they know about me?

'Your expertise as a Detective Inspector at Scotland Yard. I know you were in the specialist firearms command SCO19 and later transferred to the Art and Antiques Unit. You left the Metropolitan Police three years ago to work as a freelance investigator. Recently you have worked for Geneva Toto Insurance and Maskelyne Global Insurance on matters of recovering stolen art.' He paused a moment. 'Have I passed the test, Mr Kite?'

'Yes. Sorry to have...'

'No matter. I quite understand. Are you available this evening? Seven o'clock.'

'You mean... he wants to phone me then?'

'No, no...' I heard amusement in the secretary's voice. 'He wants to talk to you in person. At Number Ten. Is that convenient for you?'

'Seven o'clock?'

'Yes. At Downing Street. How would you be with that?'

Gobsmacked is how I was. But there was no way out.

I saw the attractive reporter speaking to the police and I wandered out of the museum in a daze.

Had someone stolen a painting from Downing Street? From Parliament? From the Queen? What the hell could the Prime Minister want to speak to me about?

Chapter 2

A mate of mine reckons a quarter of all art sold at auction is 'wrong.'

That is, suspect. Either stolen or fake or illegally trafficked or misattributed or inaccurately described. Maybe it's carelessness, maybe it's ignorance, maybe it's a wilful con. But sure as hell there's a lot of 'wrong' stuff about.

And that's why I'd been at the British Museum in the first place. I'd been hired to help check whether a picture was wrong or right. This is not what I normally do. I call myself an art detective, but that doesn't mean I'm an art *expert*. I'm not a scholar. I don't spend hours looking at pictures under a lens to judge whether a picture is by Rubens or by one of his students. What I do is recover stolen art from the criminals who stole it.

But I'd had my arm twisted to do something I don't normally do. My client was a guy called William Havers. He's some kind of trader or broker in the City. So therefore stinking rich, as well as a bloke who likes to be always right. He had bought a picture which the dealer told him was by John Sell Cotman. Cotman's not a name on everyone's lips – he was a nineteenth-century painter of the so-called Norwich school – but his stuff is valuable and collectable. Havers said he'd got the picture cheaply and along with the painting he had been given a photocopy of a page from an exhibition catalogue to show provenance. He said he had never questioned before whether the picture was genuine or not, but he'd taken out a new insurance policy and his insurers had whacked up the premium when they saw the name Cotman. If he was going to pay what they were asking he wanted to be sure it was actually by Cotman.

I told him straight off that he should go to a specialist or one of the major auction houses. But he didn't want to. He wanted me. All I had to do, he said, was check the photocopied exhibition page. Was that genuine or not? If it wasn't, then he would assume the picture wasn't genuine either. I asked why he couldn't do that himself. He was far too busy, of course. People like him didn't spend time researching in museums. They get others to do it for them. I pointed out that checking the freebie he'd been given – the catalogue extract – wouldn't prove anything either way about the picture. Havers argued it would. He said if the copy of the catalogue page was wrong it meant the picture was wrong too: otherwise why would it have been offered? After all, a photocopy of an old auction catalogue page isn't expensive to get hold of.

There was a kind of logic to this argument and, to give Havers his due, I had heard of cases where a piece of fake provenance was given as a freebie to bolster the worth of a dodgy picture.

Even so, I felt uneasy. But he offered me double my normal daily rate and said a friend of a friend of his knew a contact of mine who is high up at Scotland Yard and they'd recommended me. The contact wasn't someone I wanted to let down, so I felt under pressure. Thanks a bunch, friend of a friend of a friend.

Then as a final persuader – well, more of a cosh on the head really – he let slip, casually, that he knew something about my past which I thought only two or three others in the world knew. The threat was implicit: if I didn't do what I wanted he would spread this embarrassing information around. It was blackmail. I could have resisted further but I prefer to take the easier course if there is one. Life's hard enough without finding extra battles to fight. I said yes.

At the British Museum I discovered that the exhibition of Cotman pictures was genuine enough. It was in 1822 in Norwich. I saw the original catalogue and there were several Cotman pictures listed. But the page William Havers had been given was a complete invention. The dealer had forged a fictitious catalogue page to include *Wherries on the Yare*, which was the title of Havers' picture. A wherry, by the way, is a traditional Norfolk sailing boat, and if you don't know what the Yare is... well, there's always Google. The fake page was carefully printed in the right fonts and looked the business. But the text didn't match the original in the museum. *Wherries on the Yare* was never in that Norwich exhibition.

I had met Havers only once and viewed the watercolour briefly. It looked like a good nineteenth-century piece but, as I said, I'm not an expert. If it wasn't genuine, it was in the style of Cotman. Perhaps by one of his sons or students or the bloke round the corner who brought the coal. What screwed it up for Havers was the dealer had tried too hard. They weren't content with lying about who painted it. They wanted to try to *prove* it was by who they said.

I wasn't sure what my client's reaction would be when I told him what I'd discovered, but William Havers would have to wait. My mind was on the call from Number Ten. Whatever James Fresnel, the Prime Minister, wanted to discuss – and I couldn't imagine he wanted my take on policy matters – I wanted to be prepped. So I did some quick research. About him.

When Fresnel was appointed there was much coverage on the correct way to pronounce his surname – with a silent 's', as you know – and the fact it came from a scientific French forebear who'd invented a special kind of lens. (Don't ask.) There was also a lot of space devoted to his unusual education – unusual for a British prime minister, that is – a state school and a university that wasn't seven hundred years old. He'd not gone to Oxford or Cambridge but to the excellent University of Manchester, founded as recently as 1824. But what made the media go bananas was something which cut this prime minister out from all his modern predecessors.

He was an Arts person. At university he hadn't read economics, law, politics or even business administration. He'd studied history of art. And even as a student he collected paintings, hanging them in his student flat in suburban Manchester like the camp guy in *Brideshead Revisited* hung them in his Oxford rooms. As an MP and junior minister he'd lobbied successfully for more cash for art education. As PM he'd amazed many by increasing grants to the Arts Council, started schemes to promote British art and support British artists. Not only that, he seemed to have a strong grip on the economy, social policy, education and foreign affairs.

The consensus was he was a breath of fresh air, a revolutionary wind of change and his approval ratings soared. Inevitably, even the brightest, most brilliant prime ministers or presidents get ground down by the daily attrition of their job and never deliver quite what they promised. So it was with Fresnel, but even his detractors accepted he was an intelligent and well-meaning safe pair of hands, if not the star that people had expected.

Time was getting on. I had to get over to Downing Street. But what to wear? A suit? A tie? I generally dress casually, but not too casually. I don't want to look like a cookie-cutter undercover guy, so I avoid leather jackets and jeans. I like a bit of colour, a bit of brightness. Nothing flamboyant, but I try to look, well… interesting, I suppose. Not like your typical cop.

In the end, all I did was put a clean shirt on. One with a dark blue and red print. I put back on the green jacket I'd worn at the museum and forgot about the tie. Well, even prime ministers often don't wear ties.

Then I worried again about the phone call from Downing Street. Yes, the caller knew my CV well, but anybody in the police could have discovered that. In fact it was the kind of stunt coppers or ex-coppers might set up for mates. Gradually I convinced myself the phone call was wrong. Like Havers' picture. A scam. A hoax. I ransacked my memory as to who could be behind it. Clem from the Arts and Antiques Unit? Mark from SCO19? Ryan from years back at Wanstead?

Anyway, at five-to-seven I walked up to the security gates at the entrance to Downing Street and expected to be greeted by a guffaw, a punch on the shoulder and a cry of 'Got ya!' followed by the offer of a drink because I'd fallen for such an obvious trick.

But when I gave my name to the officer and showed some ID it was received with nothing more than a 'Thank you, sir' and I was let through.

No hoax then. Blimey.

Paint It Blackmail

It's maybe a twenty second walk from the outer security gate to the door of Number Ten. Long enough to savour the experience. Short enough not to become carried away by a sense of self-importance. The street was deserted. No press opposite the front door. No official cars. It was still daylight, just, but the early autumn weather was overcast. From my gloomy pavement angle the street looked much like any other eighteenth-century terrace in London.

As I approached the doorstep, the Downing Street cat appeared from nowhere and when the door was opened the cat shot in ahead of me. The man on the door gave it a muttered greeting before bidding me good evening.

So I knew my place.

While I waited for someone to escort me to the meeting I watched and listened from the wings to the machinery of government in action. A small group of people at the far end of a corridor were talking together. They saw me and the group moved away to an office. A young woman rushed out of another office holding a sheet of paper calling, 'Clare! You've left the last page.' A woman further down the corridor stopped and turned. Phones rang, people were typing, people were arguing. I heard a voice: 'I need him now, Robin!' And a twenty-something man ran out of an office and disappeared into another.

I'd expected the meeting to be in a conference room, but I was led upstairs past the famous pictures of previous prime ministers. I was going to the Flat. Was this because my mission was special? Or because it was insignificant and could be dispensed with while the Prime Minister's wife cooked spaghetti for dinner?

There are two flats in Downing Street. Number Ten and Number Eleven. Number Eleven's is larger and has been used by prime ministers with a young family – Tony Blair and David Cameron – while Margaret Thatcher, whose children were grown-up, and Theresa May, who had no children, lived above Number Ten.

The current PM, James Fresnel, has two children of school age so he commandeered Eleven while his Chancellor uses Ten.

'Mr Kite! Welcome, John. Thank you for coming,' Fresnel said as I was shown into the flat. There was no sign of his wife and children. Nor of any spaghetti. Apart from a loosened tie and an undone top button he looked and sounded much like he did on TV. Impeccably tailored suit. White shirt. Perfectly combed hair.

'Apologies for the delay. I was having a set-to with the Foreign Secretary about our new Environment Bill. Told me it didn't go far enough and I was cowardly.' He broke off as he saw my raised eyebrows. 'Yes, it's no secret. Rory Featherstone's greener than the Greens. He's gone vegan now. I told him he was in the wrong party.' He laughed. 'Anyway, back to you. Sorry to drag you up to the garret but what I want to talk about is absolutely confidential. Not a word to be breathed outside this attic.'

'I understand,' I said. Long ago I'd signed the Official Secrets Act.

'What I'm going to ask you to do has nothing to do with Parliament or the government or even politics. Nevertheless, the future of my position as Prime Minister depends on how successful you are in this mission. This may sound melodramatic, but I'm serious. Your actions, your achievements, will decide whether or not I remain Prime Minister.'

Fresnel fixed his eyes on me. It was a stare I'd seen on TV. Both reassuring and persuasive. I opened my mouth, but I couldn't think of anything to say. My brain whirled. What on earth was I being asked to do? I desperately tried to play it cool.

'I'm... intrigued,' was all I said. Then I worried I should have been more enthusiastic, more gung-ho. Maybe: 'Yes-sir! Right-on! With you all the way!' But Fresnel seemed happy with my reply and carried on with no demur.

'There are a couple of others joining us, so I'll wait for them before bullying off.' Then he looked at me again. 'You seem a bit surprised, Mr Kite, but there's no need to be. If you don't mind me saying, you look a very capable young guy and I'm sure it will all be in a day's work for you.'

All in a day's work? I'm not fazed by confronting a villain with a gun, but facing the nation's leader who had some life-changing problem for me to sort out made my stomach somersault. Perhaps the Prime Minister has been given the wrong data. Perhaps I'd been

Paint It Blackmail

confused with someone else. I recalled a story where two contributors to different TV programmes at the same studio had been mixed up. An expert on birds of the Amazon rainforest had been interviewed on Chinese economic policy while a Chinese professor from the LSE had been questioned on Amazon avians. Maybe the Prime Minister saw me twitching because he said:

'Have a drink. Red or white? Or beer?' He held up a couple of bottles. I asked for a glass of white wine. 'Government issue, of course, but it beats your Tesco plonk any day. Not that Tesco isn't a fine purveyor of comestibles – if you're planning a blog or a tweet, or a lawsuit.' He laughed.

I took a gulp of the wine. And very pleasant it was. I sat down and gazed around the flat, trying to take in and remember the details of this once in a lifetime visit. But though my eyes moved around they saw nothing. My brain was overheated, racing through a hundred possible scenarios as to what my mission could be.

I thought bizarrely of those 'snobbery with violence' novels from the early twentieth century. Dead male authors that no one reads nowadays. John Buchan and co. A confident, stiff-upper-lipped agent is sent off to give the Hun or the Bolsheviks a bloody nose with little more than a British passport and his public school tie to protect him. If the Prime Minister was asking me to act against some criminal, I suppose it wasn't a million miles from those novels of a hundred years ago. Except I'm not a spy or secret agent.

The wine was hitting the spot and relaxing me when a man came in who I recognised as Chris Spanswick, Minister of Defence and Deputy Prime Minister. He was my height – six-two – but wider and heavier than my hundred and ninety pounds. Burly is what Spanswick is. On TV his clothes look too small and I saw his jacket cuffs were closer to his elbows than his wrists. We shook hands and, even though my hands are large and powerful, they were engulfed by his meaty, rough-skinned fingers. What used to be called workman's hands. In his youth he'd toiled in one of the last remaining Yorkshire coal mines. Spanswick took a beer and said, 'Ready when you are, Prime Minister.'

'Waiting for Tanya, Chris,' said Fresnel.

'Oh. Sorry.' Spanswick said, like his wrist had been slapped. He raised his eyebrows at me and looked at his watch.

Spanswick had been an MP for nearly thirty years, an old school, career politician who had sat in Parliament through wars, terrorist attacks, the banking crisis and the virus disaster. He had been everywhere and got the T-shirt. He was down-to-earth, cast-iron reliable and loyal.

The door opened again and in came a woman whose whole bearing, style and appearance screamed of power. And cool. She was also aloof, and her aloofness screamed *'noli me tangere'*. Sorry for the Latin. But I had to do it at school and, well, it sticks... like being a Catholic, I suppose. Not that I am one. Anyway, I know you know what it means. But if you don't... well, you know where to look it up.

'Not late, am I?' she said, looking concerned but checking the time.

'Forty-five seconds early,' said Spanswick with a grin. 'You had time for another meeting on the stairs coming up.' He laughed and gave her a friendly, but forceful, punch on the shoulder.

The woman smiled a carefully neutral smile which humoured Spanswick but made it clear she resented being treated like a rugby team-mate. The Prime Minister introduced her as Tanya Brazil from the Cabinet Office. A senior civil servant from the department that supports the PM and calls itself the corporate headquarters of the government.

I found myself staring. It was strange that someone so senior – yet so attractive and only thirty-something – had no public profile. But I'd never heard of Tanya Brazil, never seen a picture of her. Where had they been hiding her? And her surname. Brazil. How good was that? If she became a spokesperson, the tabloids would dream up a caption that was both witty and raunchy, and she would push the government up the polls on her own.

British politicians and civil servants are not style icons. The British way is often baggy clothing masking a lumpy figure with wayward hair and wayward teeth. Comfort always trumps fashion. For men and women.

But Tanya knew how to dress and had the self-confidence not to mind looking sexy. She was wearing a conventional combo of dark jacket and above-the-knee skirt, but the cut was tight and flattering and made the most of her slim figure. Under her jacket, in place of the usual creased cotton blouse, was a clingy pale silk number. Like those attractive young female politicians in France or Italy who get all the coverage in *Paris Match* and *Grazia*. She had poise. Shedloads of it.

I was still gazing at her when she looked at me and our eyes met. I gave a little smile. She didn't return it. She just said:

'I saw that brawl you were in.'

One of the tourists had posted video online.

'It's going viral.' She made it sound like you could actually catch something from watching it.

'Any news who was behind it, Prime Minister?' said Spanswick.

'The Met Commissioner is reporting back tonight,' said Fresnel. 'But first indication is they're all clean skins. Not only that, it's not clear what they were campaigning for.'

'They wanted all the good stuff shipped back to Africa, Asia, Australia wherever,' said Spanswick. 'Like someone I know suggested once.' He quirked an eyebrow, including me in his ribbing of the Prime Minister.

'I didn't *suggest* it,' said the Prime Minister with sudden annoyance, 'as you very well know.' He turned to me. 'You may remember the incident, Mr Kite. I merely *referred* to what certain campaigners were asking for and coined the phrase "cultural repatriation." That was eight years ago and nobody's ever bloody forgotten it.'

His actual words had been that 'he understood the campaigners' motives' in wanting to return certain artefacts in UK museums to their countries of origins. But this casual remark had caused an apoplectic fit in the museums and galleries community. Leading curators pointed out the whole point of a museum was to be universal, to offer a panorama of world cultural history and not be nationalistic. Fresnel never mentioned the subject again and in interviews it remained a no-go area. But times change. The painstaking work to return artefacts looted by the Nazis to descendants of the owners has continued for decades. Perhaps it's that which has inspired national groups to want something similar. Perhaps people want to reclaim their own history and don't understand why they have to travel to western Europe or the US to view it. Whether the Prime Minister liked it or not, 'cultural repatriation' was on the agenda.

'In any case, the protesters' banner was gobbledegook,' said Fresnel. I was thrown for a moment. I'd been so dazzled by the phone call from Number Ten that I'd never actually walked across to read the wording on the banner. The Prime Minister went on, 'Whatever it all meant we've a lot to thank Mr Kite for. A defender of our national heritage. Well done, John.'

Spanswick smiled and nodded then turned to anecdote. 'I was in that very room at the museum not a few months back. My son was doing a scene there.'

'He's an actor?' I said.

'No, location manager. For the films and so on. I went along for a look-see. Anyway it's beautiful stuff they've got there, beautiful stuff. Well done, son. You know how to use your fists, I'll give you that.'

Tanya kept her attention on the PM. She sat upright. Her back was as straight and perpendicular as Nelson's Column. She had a long neck and controlled her body like a model or a dancer does. She sat to attention while us three men sat casually. Untidily. Almost lolling. Fresnel was leaning back, one arm over the back of his chairs and playing with a pen, rotating it between his thumb and first two fingers. Spanswick was slouched with his feet up on a stool. I was hunched forwards, elbows on the table, hands under my chin, my body language trying to signal how hard I was concentrating. Tanya did nothing. Just sat. Still. Graceful. Her body spoke a language I'd never learned.

'To business,' said Fresnel. 'You know I have form as an art lover, Mr Kite. Some may hold it against me, but I don't care. Anyway, the problem I want your help with concerns a picture I recently purchased.' He indicated a framed picture on the kitchen sideboard.

'A delicate oil sketch by Vanessa Bell of her friend Duncan Grant, dated 1937. And on the back is attached a brief letter from Bell to Grant mentioning the drawing and making comments about it. I got it for a bargain price but as time went by I began to think my bargain was too much of a good thing. In fact, I now think it's a fake. I think I was conned.'

I jerked upwards from scribbling notes. My heart sank. It was another Havers case.

'That's an odd coincidence,' I said, with a pasted-on smile, trying not to sound as uneasy as I felt. 'It was something similar that took me to the British Museum today.'

All three looked at me.

'Extraordinary,' said Fresnel.

'What were you doing there, son?' said Spanswick.

I explained briefly about the Cotman commission.

'Who was your client?' said Fresnel. 'Anyone we should know?'

'Though if it's confidential, Mr Kite, we understand of course,' said Tanya Brazil, gracefully rotating her head to include the two men either side of her. Her poised demeanour reminded me of a heron, long-necked and watchful on a river bank.

I waved aside her civil service regard for data protection. 'A man called William Havers. He works for a bank in Canary Wharf.' All of them shook their heads. Which was good. I'd thought for a second Havers had blown his mouth off to someone and recommended me. But even so... shit. This was going to be embarrassing. I was here under false pretences but the PM had high hopes. How diplomatic could I be?

'I'm afraid you may have got the wrong idea about me, Prime Minister. In spite of the little commission I did for Mr Havers I'm not an art expert. Not someone who can give an opinion on authenticity or authorship. What I do is hunt for stolen pictures, usually on behalf of insurers, and try to get them back. I'm not a connoisseur, just an investigator. A detective. You probably have far more knowledge of art and artists than I do.'

Fresnel looked upset. 'You're saying you can't do this for me? Won't do it?'

'You could easily find someone better qualified than me.'

'But you did the job for Mr Havers.'

'Not exactly, Prime Minister. All I did was research a page from an auction catalogue. I didn't give any judgement on his painting. Also, he stuck a gun to my head.'

'A metaphorical one, I hope,' said Fresnel.

I smiled. It wasn't a shooter, but the gobbet of information he had about my youth was still a bloody big persuader. No, I wasn't a teenage drug dealer, rent boy or child pornographer. It was something about my father. How Havers discovered it I don't know.

'This is a bugger,' said the Prime Minister.

'Damn right,' said Spanswick, shuffling in his chair, preparing to leave.

'Prime Minister,' I said, also shifting about, 'can you not go back to the dealer about this picture? Query the authenticity?'

Fresnel shook his head. 'It'd be all over the media in a flash. Stupid headlines, childish cartoons. It needs to be kept under wraps. That's why you're here. We heard you were the numero uno. The go-to man. How can we persuade you?'

Shit. What was I doing? Telling the PM to fuck off isn't a good career move. Trouble was, in a list of experts on the paintings of Vanessa Bell I come about 5,943rd. I'd taken Havers' job because, in the last resort, I'd earn good money for a few days' work and the outcome wasn't of national importance. If I screwed up the Prime Minister's commission I might as well move to Antarctica.

Then Tanya Brazil did the heron act again, turning her head around as if looking for prey and fixed her intense gaze on me again.

'Mr Kite. We understand your modesty in terms of expertise, but the Prime Minister wanted this job handled by someone outside the establishment, someone whose hands were not tied by bureaucracy. Someone who could act independently and decisively. An individualist. A lone wolf, if you like.'

'Someone who could beat up the dealer with no questions asked,' said Spanswick with a grin.

Tanya wasn't amused by Spanswick and turned back to me.

'Mr Kite, you seemed ideal for the Prime Minister's purposes and my sources thought so too. Time is of the essence and your appointment has been approved at the highest level. If you cannot accept this commission then very well, but I personally would be disappointed if you said no.'

Her eyes stayed fixed on mine, unblinking, for three, four, five, six seconds. I felt like a minnow in a pond, about to be gobbled by the heron.

'As for recompense,' said Fresnel, 'in spite of the economic situation we can rustle up more than just loose change for you. And we could also add a dollop of alphabet soup.'

'The PM means an honour,' said Spanswick, checking his watch again. 'MBE or some other bollocks.'

Jesus. Was I being blackmailed again? I looked back at Tanya. She was still looking at me. Wow. Some eyes she had. Green like emeralds. Persuasive. Mesmerising. The more she looked, the more I felt I couldn't disappoint her.

There was no way out. I agreed to take the commission and there was relief around the table.

'If the picture's a forgery you want your money back, Prime Minister?' I said.

'Exactly.'

'You want him punished? Arrested for fraud?'

'Whatever the police and Crown Prosecution Service decide. But of course no violence.'

'At least not that we get to hear about,' said Spanswick with a laugh.

'And utmost secrecy,' said Fresnel. 'That's important.' Then he stood up and the rest of us did the same. 'Chris and I have duties elsewhere,' he said fastening his collar and tightening his tie. 'So I suggest you and Tanya put your heads together for half an hour and come up with a stratagem. Here are the dealer's details.' He handed me a handwritten A4 sheet. 'I thought this was safer than email.'

'Read it then eat it,' said Spanswick, laughing as he heaved himself to his feet. 'Or wipe your arse with it.'

'Thanks for the input, Chris,' said Fresnel. 'You'll need the picture and the letter, John. Please take them.' He indicated where they were. 'And report to Tanya. Tanya, keep me briefed, please.'

'Yes, Prime Minister,' Tanya said.

'Good to meet you, John.' Fresnel shook my hand, smiled broadly but gave me the hard stare as well. 'Next time we meet I'll expect to see unequivocal proof of authenticity – or a large refund.'

Shit. I was on a hiding to nothing.

Chapter 3

After Fresnel and Spanswick left, Tanya said we should leave the flat and go to a meeting room. I followed her down to the ground floor. Through corridors, past offices. I heard laughter, arguments, phones, a cheer, someone shouting 'Arsehole!'

Invariably, I walk quickly. And even in her heels, so did Tanya. Always in front. Not only poised but athletic. We went down to a basement then walked through corridors that could be in any administrative building anywhere. There was no glamour, no indication of the power that was wielded here. We came to a door labelled BRIEFING ROOM A and Tanya led me inside. I laid the Prime Minister's picture on the table and we sat opposite each other. I took out my laptop and leaned back in the chair. Then I thought better of it and sat up straight. Poised. Like Tanya.

Then I thought about the name of the room we were in.

'Are we in the Cabinet Office?' I said.

'Part of it.'

'So this is…'

'Briefing Room A. Yes. Where COBRA meets. But don't get excited. The room's just a room.'

'No nuclear button.'

She gave a weak smile but didn't bother to answer.

Even so I looked around. Cabinet Office Briefing Room A. The dull designation had provided a thriller-style acronym for the room where the country's most vital decisions were taken. About war. About terrorism. About economics. About the recent pandemic.

Once again, I felt the pressure mounting.

I opened my laptop and started an email.

'What are you doing?' she said.

'Making an appointment to see the dealer. David Pilcher.' It seemed an obvious first move. 'I'll pretend I'm interested in buying something.'

'What will you do when you meet him? You won't really beat him up?' If this was her dry sense of humour her face didn't show it.

I smiled. 'Not always a good opening gambit.' I finished the email and sent it.

'I'm sorry you feel we've misjudged you, Mr Kite. But Chris Spanswick came up with a job description which the Prime Minister liked. He said they wanted 'an operator'. And you have friends in high places. I was impressed.'

'Who did you speak to? Who got me into this?'

'I'm afraid I can't say.' A sentence she must have used many times before. Secrecy was second nature to her. She made no apology for it.

'This room bugged, or something?'

Her faint smile again.

'Was it Leo Somerscales?'

'I cannot confirm or deny.'

'Come off it,' I said, leaning towards her, my arms on the table again. 'I've taken a job I shouldn't have done. But I'd like to do it on my terms. I'm not a civil servant and I've been around the block a few times You can be open with me.'

Her eyes widened. Her face flushed. The first sign of emotion I'd seen from her.

'There are ways of doing things, Mr Kite.'

'We're supposed to be working together, so you might treat me as something like an equal. And you can drop the mister for a start. Call me John.'

She met my gaze and breathed in hard but said nothing.

'Or just Kite will do. If you prefer.'

She nodded. 'Public school habit,' she said. 'But of course you went to one, didn't you?' She paused briefly. 'I was sorry to hear about your parents… the car crash and all that. And how you had to pull out of university as well. Very sad.'

Jesus! They'd obviously vetted me thoroughly. Then she looked contrite.

'Sorry. I didn't mean… It all came out in a rush.' She had the honesty to look embarrassed. I think she'd been trying to build bridges.

'Doesn't matter. But make sure you don't circulate my file to every department in Whitehall. Some things in my past I'd prefer to keep to myself.'

All she said was, 'Oh?' Which I took to mean they hadn't found anything. Then she looked at me in a different way from before. Interested. Like that piercing gaze she sent my way in the PM's flat. 'Something in your past… Was that the gun Mr Havers held to your head? The thing he blackmailed you with?'

'Sorry. No comment.' It was my turn to give her a hard smile.

She realised she'd gone too far. There was a pause while we both retrenched. My laptop pinged with a reply from David Pilcher. He'd be delighted to meet me to show me his stock. I bet he would.

'Do you want to come with me to see Pilcher? The dealer.'

'Do you want me to?'

'I thought you'd want to. So you can stop me beating him up. Or haggle with him over the refund. Or make him sign an affidavit. Though the picture might be squeaky clean and the Prime Minister worried over nothing.'

'Is that possible?' She gave the picture a stern look, daring it to speak up for itself.

I shrugged. 'No idea. I wasn't bullshitting when I said I wasn't an expert. But I'll do some research tomorrow.'

Tanya picked up the painting and held it at arm's length. It was in an impressionistic style and showed a man sitting outdoors in a garden chair with a sketchbook on his knee.

'I like it,' said Tanya, coming to a decision. 'It's sensitively done.'

'Yes, it's a good painting all right. But that's not the point.'

'Yes, of course. Sorry. I'm trying to do what you said you couldn't do. And I'm certainly no expert.' She put the picture back on the table. 'Where's the dealer based?'

'Broadway.'

She made a disapproving, or maybe a disappointed face.

'In the Cotswolds.'

'I know where it is,' she said. 'I thought he'd be in London.'

'This guy deals online. You can do that from anywhere.'

She checked her phone diary.

'It would need to be afternoon. Say four o'clock. There are things I can't shift. How do we get there? Trains to the Cotswolds are hopeless.'

'I can drive.'

She nodded.

'I'll tell him four o'clock.' I tapped another email and sent it.

There was a knock, the door opened and a face I recognised looked in.

'Mind if I join you? Just to catch up on the PM's picture.'

'Come in, Lyle,' Tanya said. 'Meet John Kite. Mr Kite, this is Lyle Brabant, Minister for Education.' I stood up and we shook hands. Brabant was good-looking but more wiry than he appeared on TV – almost gaunt – and his face was perma-tanned as a result of his work in the tropics. He'd been an MP for only five years but was already in the Cabinet. Critics said he owed his rapid promotion to his close friendship with Fresnel which started when they were both students in Manchester. Brabant had studied medicine and after qualifying as a doctor joined Médecins Sans Frontières. He'd done good work against terrible odds in the shittiest places on the planet. Then through skilful self-promotion, a face that cameras loved and an ability to deliver a killer sound bite with charm, he had become a media star. He'd also made headline-grabbing speeches about world health at Davos but his jump into mainstream politics had been a surprise. Nevertheless I liked the quote that he – or some sharp PR person – had trotted out. He said, 'I want to move from being a *wunderkind* as a doctor to being an *enfant terrible* as a politician.' Clever.

'The PM asked me to join you in the flat, but something came up at the last moment.' Brabant had piercing eyes but, above them, an almost permanently creased brow. He turned to me. 'So you're going to save the PM's bacon?'

'I'll give it my best shot,' I said.

'Excellent. The PM's always had a thing about art. The flat we shared had all sorts of stuff over the walls.'

'Was that in Manchester, at university?'

'That's right. In Rusholme.'

'Sounds like something you do after work. Rush-home,' said Tanya. A joke. I smiled with relief.

'Rusholme's in south Manchester,' I said. 'On the way to Withington and Didsbury. It's curry house mile. Hundreds of Asian restaurants one after the other.'

'That's right,' said Brabant. 'You know Manchester well?'

'Went there for a day once.'

He looked wrong-footed and Tanya gave me a questioning look. But I know places. Everywhere. It's one of my special skills. No one ever believes me. Until they encounter it. Since I wasn't going to elaborate, Brabant changed subject and picked up Fresnel's picture.

'Exhibit A,' he said, looking at the painting. 'I've seen it before, of course, and I rather like it.'

'As Mr... er, John has said, whether it's good or not isn't the point,' said Tanya with a quick glance in my direction.

'I suppose so,' said Brabant laying the picture down. 'So what's the plan?'

'We're seeing the dealer tomorrow,' said Tanya.

'Four o'clock,' I said, checking my inbox. 'He's just confirmed.'

'Good,' said Brabant. 'The sooner it's sorted the better. The PM's more worried than he lets on.' He picked up the piece of paper on which Fresnel had written the dealer's name. 'Pilcher... Pilcher, the filcher.'

'Fresnel's not saying Pilcher *stole* the picture. Just that it's not as described,' said Tanya.

'Yes, of course.' Brabant stood up. 'Good luck, Mr Kite.' We shook hands and he walked to the door. 'Oh, Tanya, about the man you call the Salesman – sorry to talk shop,' he looked at me then back to Tanya. 'I raised it in Cabinet and the security services agree. He'll be given forty-eight hours to leave the country.'

'Excellent. What changed your mind?' Tanya said.

'Oh... events,' he said and left the room.

I looked back at Tanya to see if she would elaborate on the enigmatic and intriguing conversation. But of course she didn't. 'Well, anything else?' she said, collecting her papers and iPad by way of closing the meeting. 'Let's hope we can get everything sorted out amicably tomorrow.'

I looked at her. 'You think it's that simple?'

'You don't?'

'The Prime Minister's making a big thing of it.'

'I suppose he doesn't want his reputation as an art connoisseur ruined.'

I shrugged. 'Maybe.'

My dubious tone of voice made Tanya looked up. She put her iPad back on the table and resumed her formal pose. Straight-backed, hands on the edge of the table.

'What's worrying you?'

'Odd coincidences,' I said.

There was only a split-second's pause before she said, 'You mean between the Prime Minister's case and William Havers'?' Tanya was always on the ball.

'Yes. They don't feel like coincidences.'

'But there's no connection between them.' She paused. 'Is there?'

'Not that I know of.'

'No doubt you'll investigate.'

'No doubt I will. One other thing before I go... that protest at the Museum. Do you know what they were campaigning for? I never got a look at their banner.'

'Didn't you watch the news item?'

I shook my head.

'I know people who would have recorded it and sent copies to all their contacts. But maybe you're being interviewed every week.' She gave a little smile. Which was nice. 'I'll play it to you.' That was nice, too. She searched for the news item and clicked play on her iPad.

The piece started with a short introduction from the reporter, who I now learned was called Lucy Bladon, then I was interviewed and it cut to phone footage of the attack which had come from one of the tourists. It ended with a close-up of the banner and a piece to camera by the reporter.

When I saw the banner I understood what Tanya and the Prime Minister meant about it being gobbledygook or a joke. It read: *Trastivenia Liberation Front Demands UK Return Stolen Artefacts.* And Lucy Bladon made much of the fact that no one knew where Trastivenia was. She had recorded herself googling the name and showed the search results to camera. There *were* no results.

I turned to Tanya, bemused.

'Is she right?'

'Of course. No such place exists. The FCO press office has been besieged. I thought you might have got something from the demonstrators.'

'There wasn't time for conversation. Has nobody worked out what Trastivenia is?'

'You haven't seen all the stuff online?'

'I'm not a social media fan. I don't want to tell the world what I had for dinner or who I shagged last night.'

A wry smile from Tanya. 'Ah… these things in your past… But have a look. People are posting all the time.'

She turned her screen towards me and I was amazed. The internet was flooded with theories about who or what Trastivenia might be. Spanish speakers pointed out it meant 'Trasti is coming' but no one knew who Trasti might be. A Norwegian chef called Trasti had been found who ran a hotel. Italians suggested a misspelling of Trasteverina, which refers to a female occupant of the Trastevere area of Rome. English-speaking crossword addicts pointed out Trastivenia was an anagram of 'Invite a star.' But who was the star? A celebrity or a heavenly body? Was it an astronomical warning? An omen? Was there a religious message?

It gives me a laugh when social media go bonkers in this way. It also makes me sad so many people can spend so much time chasing their tails.

'The name's also unknown to Interpol, MI6, CIA, and every European police force,' Tanya said.

'On the surface it looks like they were clowning around. A piece of street theatre. But I'm sure it wasn't.'

Tanya looked at me, serious. 'You think it was political?'

'It's got to be.'

Tanya gave me her intense stare again. 'Go on.'

'It didn't feel like a political demo at the time. The three of them were middle-of-the-road working people. Their clothes were conventional, not freaky, not "look at me I've a point to make". No funny hats, buttons or campaign badges on their jackets. The reason I noticed them was they looked uncomfortable and nervous. Political agitators are usually extrovert, outspoken, boiling over with self-righteousness.'

Tanya nodded.

'They also had a fast car standing by to drive them away.'

'So what do you think was going on, Kite?'

I looked at her. 'You've given up on John then?'

She was momentarily thrown. The use of my surname must have been accidental, so she improvised. 'Well, John's such an ordinary name, isn't it?' Perhaps she only mixed with aristocrats called Giles, Septimus or Tristan.

'As I said before, plain Kite is fine. What do I think is going on? There must be a connection to what Fresnel called "cultural repatriation"?'

'That off-the-cuff remark has been an albatross round his neck for years.'

'But there's a new wave of interest now. If he stopped pretending he never said it and instead pushed forward with the idea… if he sent stuff back to Greece, Nigeria and wherever, he'd win a Nobel Prize.'

Tanya considered a moment. 'Quite possibly. But he'd lose the next election.' She gave a wry smile. 'Westminster is the place where any Greta Thunberg-type idealist ends up doing exactly what their party whips tell them.'

'That's why I was surprised Lyle Brabant went into politics.'

Tanya raised her eyebrows. 'You're not the first to think that.'

'If the demonstrators were trying to make a serious point, why didn't they stick around to get their message across?' I said.

'Because you jumped in. All we have on the video is the warm-up act, the lead-in. They never got to deliver the punchline.'

She had a point. 'Yes, the woman was angry when I intervened. Incensed I'd rained on her parade.'

I paused and fingered the scratch on my cheek caused by the woman's ring. Tanya noticed.

'Battle scar?' she said. 'I saw it in the interview. The light caught your cheekbones.'

I've always been rather proud of my razor-sharp cheekbones and felt strangely pleased she'd watched so attentively. 'I've had worse,' I said. Then I watched her eyes surreptitiously scan my face for other marks. Though, if I wasn't such a modest guy, I could imagine she was admiring my dazzling sky-blue eyes as well. I have got other physical scars but they're only visible when I take my clothes off. I have some mental ones, too. But I keep the mental ones covered up 24/7.

'The banner said s*tolen artefacts*,' I said. 'You've no idea what artefacts and who stole them?' Tanya shook her head. 'But this messing about in the museum must be just a beginning.'

'The beginning of what?'

'A way of getting attention. But what they want attention for… I don't have a clue.'

'Something serious?'

'Definitely something serious and we must stop them before things run out of control.'

Tanya's brow creased. 'Shouldn't you leave it to the police?'

'They don't have enough people. It'll get logged but won't be followed up. From the police point of view the level of crime is low, or even non-existent. What can they charge them with? Criminal damage? Just about. Disorderly conduct? Possibly. But no one's been hurt, nothing's been stolen. The police have no motive to investigate.'

'Over to you then. Once you've sorted the Prime Minister's picture you can investigate Trastivenia. He might give you a knighthood then.'

Chapter 4

Next morning, I had a taste of what it must be like to be an actor. The tourists' videos of my intervention at the museum had been posted, re-tweeted and viewed countless times with tens of thousands of likes. I personally was the subject of much comment. Reviews of my 'performance' ranged from 'vicious' to 'brave' and from 'sexy' to 'wooden' (for the interview I gave to Lucy Bladon). Take your pick. I didn't know whether to be embarrassed, angry or flattered.

Unsurprisingly, there were no startling revelations about the meaning of Trastivenia, just increasingly bizarre and unlikely explanations. I expected the three demonstrators to take advantage of the public interest they'd stirred up and I looked for a follow-up statement or manifesto. But there was nothing. The Trastivenia group seemed shy, frightened of revealing themselves.

Everyone's intrigued by the apparently inexplicable. The human psyche loves a puzzle. And so it is with me. I better not say the Prime Minister's picture was a dull case to work, but it was the museum demo which obsessed me. There had to be an explanation and I wanted to be the one to unravel it.

And the label from the wheelchair was burning a hole in my pocket.

Even so, I couldn't neglect the Prime Minister. Before I began to chase down Trastivenia I emailed my art world contact, Gus Lamport, and asked for any info he had on David Pilcher. Gus had bought and sold pictures all his working life and knew anyone who was anybody. He knew plenty of nobodies, too.

Then I drove into West London and dropped the Prime Minister's picture off to be examined by an expert in that period. She promised to report back later in the day and I headed out to Ruislip.

Ruislip is not the most exciting of London suburbs. Until about 1900 it was mostly farmland but then the Metropolitan Railway – in search of more passengers to fill their trains that ran through the area – promoted the area as a desirable place to live and houses sprouted like weeds after rain. What began as a semi-rural paradise, dubbed *Metroland* by the salesmen, quickly grew into a fully-fledged suburban sprawl of tens of thousands of almost identical houses.

The Broomfield Care Home stood out by being larger and more modern than the houses which surrounded it. It had been built only twenty years ago, when opening a care home seemed a good way to make money. Times have changed.

The walled grounds were spacious and pleasant. Roses climbed over pergolas, but the garden was deserted: the autumn weather was bright, but too cold for patients to sit out. I pressed the front doorbell and waited in the porch. Through the glass doors I saw staff hurrying past. One or two acknowledged my presence and made signs which I interpreted as: please wait a minute. Inside people were no doubt dying, having fits, needing help to go to the toilet. I could wait. And I did. For eight minutes.

The door was unlocked by a flustered, pink-faced but smiling carer of Malaysian origin who apologised for the delay. On a table, next to a dispenser for hand sanitiser, was a school-type exercise book with hand-drawn columns down the page. I signed in with my time of arrival and took a squirt of sanitiser. The place was clean, brightly painted and tidy but it suffered from the curse of care homes: that ever-present whiff of industrial strength air-freshener which masks the much more unpleasant smell of bodies, mass catering and urine.

'If you put down who you're visiting, please.' The care assistant indicated the column I had left blank.

'I'm not visiting anyone. I've come because I think you've had one of your wheel-chairs stolen,' I said.

She looked baffled and I showed her the label I'd found at the museum. She hadn't seen the news item so looked even more baffled as I explained what had gone on. As I spoke there was a high-pitched scream from down the corridor. Then another. And another. The cries sounded gut-wrenchingly desperate. As if some horrific torture was in progress. I tried to carry on but kept glancing down the corridor expecting some fiend of hell to appear. All the while the care assistant was quite unmoved, listening to what I wanted. Finally I had to ask what was going on.

The carer smiled reassuringly. 'It's Mrs Plastow,' she said, as if the name explained everything. I started to explain my mission again but she held up a hand to stop me in a this-is-above-my-pay-grade kind of way and said, 'Come to manager. This way.' Then she led me along a corridor and waved me through the open door of the manager's office. Then she disappeared towards the sound of the screaming.

The manager looked up from her computer screen. She was a tense-looking woman in her forties and, although clearly busy, pushed her reading glasses on to her forehead and cheerily wished me good morning. She was apparently used to strangers being ushered in with no explanation. Her name was Becky Wynyard and she hadn't seen the news item either. As I explained what had happened, her gaze alternated between me and her screen and she continued occasional typing. But she was listening too and said she had no knowledge of a wheelchair being stolen.

'Does each patient have their own?' I said.

'Not at all. Some patients are ambulant. Some are ambulant with walkers or frames. We encourage patients to try to walk even when they say they can't. It keeps the body more flexible. Helps prevent sores. Wheelchairs are a last resort.'

'And none of the wheelchairs is missing?' I said as screaming started up again in the distance. Was someone having a tooth pulled without anaesthetic?

Becky Wynyard saw my concern and glanced briefly out of the door. 'Sorry about that. It's Mrs Plastow. She's 104. Only mild dementia but a violent temper. She overreacts to minor problems. No sugar in her tea, too much sugar in her tea. That sort of thing. Wheelchairs… It would be hard to tell immediately if one's gone missing. Some are owned by the home, some by the patients. Inevitably they get mixed up; the staff sometimes just grab the nearest.'

'The patients don't notice?'

Becky Wynyard smiled and shook her head. 'Many of them are beyond noticing anything much.' Wynyard picked up the card I'd given her and gave it a dubious look. 'You said you're not with the police.'

'No. But I am working for the government.' It was something I'd never said before. I hoped I didn't sound pompous or a bit of a prick.

'For the government?' Her tone was even more doubtful and she gave me a look over the top of her reading glasses which were now back on her nose.

'Yes. I'm a Special Advisor.'

She raised her eyebrows, still unconvinced. 'Advising on… what?' She removed her glasses from her face, held them in a hand and looked at me waiting for an answer.

She was giving me a hard time. Like a schoolteacher I remember. But this was no time for modesty. I returned her gaze eyeball for eyeball and leaned towards her. With precise articulation, a hint of a smile on my lips, a slight quirk of an eyebrow, I tried to give the impression that confidential matters were involved and, while I couldn't reveal everything, she could trust me implicitly. 'You know that James Fresnel, the Prime Minister, is particularly interested in the arts. I am advising him on various security matters which are art-related. That was why I was in the British Museum at the time of the demonstration. Because of my Scotland Yard background, a senior civil servant in the Cabinet Office asked me to pursue this enquiry alongside the police so the Prime Minister can be kept abreast of all developments.'

It was flannel and I wasn't sure I was making complete sense. But at that moment the Malaysian carer came into the office.

'Sorry, Becky. It's Mrs Plastow. I cannot understand her.'

'What's up?'

'She say she got wrong newspaper. *Daily Express*. And she does not like. She wants cartoon dog.'

'Cartoon dog?' said Becky, taking off her glasses, spraying them with lens cleaner and wiping them with a tissue..

The carer shrugged helplessly.

'She means Fred Basset,' I said with a chirpy smile. 'It's a cartoon strip in the *Daily Mail*. Been running since before I was born.' You might think I knew the cartoonist personally.

'Yes, of course,' Becky smiled at me. 'Thank you.' She turned back to the carer. 'I remember there was some problem at the newsagent this morning. I'll come and explain. Excuse me, Mr Kite.' The manager got up and hurried out.

With a quick look into the corridor I slid into her seat. I minimised the email she'd been writing and looked into Explorer. I found a folder labelled Residents, then sub-folders and sub-sub-folders. I found Accounts, Medication, Care Plans… then I heard footsteps. I brought the email back on screen and was in my chair just before the manager came back in.

'Sorry about that,' she said. 'Actually it was fortuitous because, when I talked to her about the newspaper, she complained about something else. She didn't like the wheelchair she'd been put in. Says it's not hers.'

'So her own chair could be the missing one?'

'I think so. She described her own chair pretty well. It's got a big scratch by the seat and there's tape round one of the arm-rests. I think she's right. Patients with dementia can experience lucid spells.' She put her reading glasses back on, used the mouse to find something on the computer and said: 'You're not related to Mrs Plastow? You didn't know it was hers?'

'I've never heard the name before.'

Becky Wynyard then looked at the file she'd brought up on screen. 'No... we don't have you down here. There's only one contact name for Mrs Plastow.'

She was back to the doubtful looks again. 'I suppose you're going to ask me now to tell you all about her family.' She scrolled down the open file.

'It would be helpful if you did. Invaluable in fact.' I smiled my best smile.

'Can you prove to me you're working for the Prime Minister?'

Who was this woman? Rosa Klebb? I thought my Fred Basset intervention had won the day for me. I took out the card Tanya had given me from Tom Daubeney, the PM's secretary. The Get Out Of Jail Free Card, she called it. 'Call this guy. He's at Number Ten. He knows me.'

Becky took the card, read it carefully and had the phone in her hand when another carer hurried in.

'Sorry, Becky. It's Mr Grant. I think we're losing him.'

Becky put the phone down and stood up.

'Excuse me, Mr Kite, once again...'

As soon as she was gone, I moved back into her seat behind the desk and looked at the open file of residents' details. There was a home address for Mrs Plastow and details of a next of kin, a daughter called Barbara Turner. The information was thin. But it was all I was going to get.

I left the manager's office and went out to my car.

Twenty minutes later I was outside the centenarian's home in East Finchley. It's an older part of London than Ruislip, closer to the centre, but it's been cut in pieces by main roads: the Great North Road, the North Circular Road. It's a mixed area now, lots of flats, both high- and low-rise, as well as houses of many styles and dates. Mrs Plastow's was a small nineteenth-century house at the end of a terrace; it looked uncared for, but not totally abandoned. There were signs that somebody was, or had recently been, living there.

The front garden was full of weeds, but someone had recently trimmed back brambles by the front gate so you could get in with becoming entangled. The front door Yale lock didn't have the coating of verdigris and tarnish that years of disuse produces. And when I looked through the letterbox there was no pile of unsolicited mail on the carpet. Mrs Plastow had been in the care home for five years and her daughter, in her late seventies, had an address over a hundred miles away in Shropshire. Who was using the house?

There was a single lock on the front door and my electronic pick quickly opened it. The interior had that distinctive old person smell, different from the chemical odours at the care home. Here it was the sad combination of old, tired and dusty things. Clothes, books, furnishings. There were yellowing prints on the walls and yellowing books on the shelves.

I opened a cupboard and found a cache of toys from the middle of last century: Ludo, Snakes and Ladders, Cluedo, Totopoly – a horse-racing game – a game called Halma and some Meccano.

Among the vintage books, some bright and shiny ones caught my eye. Art books. They were much newer than anything else in the house, none more than ten years old. And what really interested me was they were all on the same topic: Vanessa Bell, Duncan Grant and the Bloomsbury Group. Some were coffee table books but there were also academic works. One or two looked like what specialists call *catalogues raisonnés,* volumes which attempt to list all known works by an artist; serious stuff. I picked up one of the Vanessa Bell books and flicked through it. In one of the pages a torn piece of paper had been used as a bookmark. It marked a painting of Duncan Grant by Bell. It wasn't the Prime Minister's picture, but it was similar.

I felt a familiar tingle run through me. The feeling I get when something significant turns up. And this discovery was potentially game changing. It suggested the British Museum demo was linked to the Prime Minister's painting.

This was exciting, but what did it mean? How could a 104-year-old woman in a care home be connected to the Prime Minister?

Then in one of the bedrooms I found something newer and fresher than anything in the rest of the house. A modern, vibrant smell. Deodorant, perfume, make-up. There was also a backpack on the floor and some clothes on a chair. Clothes for a girl of twenty or so. The bed had been recently slept in and a T-shirt nightdress lay discarded on the pillows. On the bedside table was another book about Grant and Bell. This one was about Charleston, the house in Sussex where they lived for many years.

In the bathroom was a sponge, toothpaste and some shampoo and conditioner – *Harvest Gold: to enhance your natural colour.*

There was a rational explanation for what I'd found. The backpack owner was a tenant of Mrs Plastow's, a postgrad student researching Vanessa Bell and Duncan Grant. Simple. Logical. And certainly possible. But it would be another odd coincidence.

I explored the rest of the house, found little else of interest and reverted to an old standby tactic: search the rubbish. I went out of the kitchen door to the garden and found the wheelie-bin. I opened the lid, pulled out the single black plastic bag inside and tipped it upside down. There was little more than wrappers, packaging and tea bags. Whoever the girl was, she wasn't into home cooking and seemed to be living off takeaways, toast and soup.

Then a piece of paper caught my eye. It was a handwritten note that had been screwed into a ball. I picked it up and smoothed it out. Written on the back of an advertising flyer for a kebab shop was a message in ballpoint.

Hope the conditioner's the right kind. Hayden will be in Orange Street from 11 o'clock for 5 mins only. Don't miss him. And say Trastivenia so they know you're with me.

Trastivenia.

My excitement redoubled.

Logical explanations went out of the window. The girl wasn't a student of art history at all and I'd got right to the heart of the mysterious demonstration.

Chapter 5

Harvest Gold. Orange Street. They go together well.
There is only one Orange Street in London. It runs from Haymarket into Charing Cross Road behind the National Gallery and the National Portrait Gallery. Was another demonstration planned? The shampoo girl was out of the house. It was an even bet that whatever was happening was happening today. At or before 11 o'clock. I checked the time. 10:14. I would have to travel fast.

I chucked the rubbish back in the bin, closed and bolted the back door to leave it as I'd found it and exited through the front. I was in my car and doing sixty within seconds. It was a thirty limit but I knew where most of the cameras were and hoped there were no cops around. Problem is, speed itself isn't much use in central London. There's too much other traffic in the way. What's more important than speed is knowing the shortcuts, the rat-runs, the back-doubles, the way the cab drivers go. Luckily, I do. And I used every one, which helped me bypass traffic lights and tailbacks. It was a longer route, but a quicker one. Even so, it would be touch and go to get there in time.

At six minutes to eleven I was hurtling down Gower Street. The tricky junction at St Giles was mercifully clear and I was into Monmouth Street, narrow, slow, touristy and always dreadful at Seven Dials. But then I was across it and over Long Acre and into St Martin's Lane. Now two hard decisions: where the hell do I dump the car and which gallery do I head for? The National Gallery and the National Portrait Gallery are side by side.

The second question was answered for me. As I careered down St Martin's Lane, I saw a police car with flashing lights and siren heading up from Trafalgar Square. It stopped outside the Portrait Gallery where two other patrol cars, an Armed Response Vehicle, an unmarked police car and an ambulance were already blocking most of the road. The officers exited their vehicle at speed. I ditched my car in the lea of the patrol car, adding further to the bottleneck. But I hoped nobody would notice. Or they'd think I was with the cops. As I went to the door of the Portrait Gallery, a second ARV screamed to a halt. The officers steamed out with their Heckler and Koches at the ready and ran into the gallery.

I sprinted after them, tucked in close behind, and slipstreamed them through the fast-gathering crowd. The incident was still ongoing. The scene had not been secured. I could hear a female voice declaiming loudly and male voices demanding that she stop. Me and my unknowing escort ran towards the cacophony and burst into the gallery where the ruckus was.

A petite, serious-looking young woman of about twenty was standing in front of a sixteenth-century portrait of Ann Boleyn and making a speech. She looked like many girls her age in jeans, T-shirt and a fashionably over-sized bright green cardigan. But it was her hair which stood out. Chrome Yellow, a painter might have called it. Or Straw. But I knew it was Harvest Gold. The shampoo girl. The young woman staying in Mrs Plastow's house. She was speaking well and confidently, much better than the woman at the British Museum had managed. She was talking about ownership of artworks, saying many of the pictures on display should be returned to their rightful owners. These owners were often foreign countries, she said, and she mentioned France, Spain, Italy, Germany, Austria... and Trastivenia.

Up till now the onlookers had been listening more or less in silence, apart from the odd jeer or joke. At the mention of Trastivenia, the crowd erupted into laughter and ironic cheers. They knew about the British Museum event and were up to speed on the online debate. But the girl handled her audience well and ad-libbed a response, stressing that, 'if things have been stolen, they should be returned.'

A uniformed sergeant moved towards the woman. 'Once again, madam, I must ask you to stop what you're doing. You're causing a disturbance. And we don't want any of these pictures to get damaged. If you don't stop, you will be arrested.'

The woman carried on with her speech.

I overheard police radio chatter and it seemed they were waiting for a female officer to arrive. The woman would have to be physically restrained and they were playing things by the book. The other officers looked frustrated at the delay and started to clear the gallery of onlookers. This had the opposite of the desired effect. The crowd had been good natured but now they started to argue with the police and take the young woman's side. For no very good reason, except that's what crowds do.

'Ask the artist. He'll tell you this belongs to Trastivenia,' the woman said, holding the frame of the portrait. There was laughter from the crowd.

'Don't touch that,' shouted one of the gallery staff.

'Hands off. Don't touch,' repeated several police officers.

'Can't you arrest her?' said the gallery person.

'All in good time, sir,' said the sergeant.

It had turned into a show. Twenty phones were recording, including my own.

Then there was noise behind us. *Clump, clump.* Running feet. At last the female officer had arrived. The constable burst in, panting in her stab vest, with baton drawn. There was ironic applause from the onlookers. She looked bemused by her reception and by what was happening in front of her.

'Last chance,' said the sergeant to Harvest Gold.

The young woman glanced at her watch and I remembered 'Hayden' was only going to be in Orange Street until 11:05. It was now 11:03. Time to quit. She reached into a bag that was slung over her shoulder, pulled out a handful of leaflets and flung them into the air. It was a great piece of misdirection. As they fluttered down, everyone in the crowd made a grab for one and the woman did a disappearing act. She ran to the corner of the gallery and slipped through a door I hadn't noticed. It was one of those gib doors – a hidden door which has no visible frame or architrave and is disguised to look like the wall around it. I'd seen a similar one in the British Museum's King's Library the previous day. The woman did a perfect vanishing act, going through the door like she was in a Penn and Teller magic show.

Officers rushed forward to follow her, but they were hampered by the crowd which was moving in the same direction to pick up the leaflets. And the woman had prepared her exit. The secret door was locked from the other side. In stately homes and palaces these hidden doors lead to narrow passages and stairs which were designed so servants could move around the building without disturbing the owners. The young demonstrator must be heading for an exit somewhere.

I turned and ran towards the main door of the gallery, leaving behind a Keystone Kops scenario as officers tried to prise open the escape hatch door.

I raced out of the main entrance and turned left towards Orange Street. As I rounded the corner of the building, I saw the woman with the bright straw-coloured hair coming out of a rear entrance. She vaulted easily over a stainless steel railing and ran towards a smart saloon, another BMW, its engine running and parked where it shouldn't be on double yellows at the junction of Orange Street and Irving Street.

I ran past the statue of Sir Henry Irving, the actor after whom the street is named, and chased after her.

She got to the car and opened the back door. I was close enough to hear her call out the Trastivenia codeword to the driver and, as happened at the British Museum, he set off even before she'd closed the door. I sprinted harder, within touching distance of the car now. As it approached Charing Cross Road it tried to edge out in front of a red double-decker. But, in an argument between a twelve-tonne bus and an automobile, the bus generally wins. And so it did now. The getaway driver had to stop for a few seconds which gave me time enough to catch it up, yank open the door and jump into the front seat.

The driver – serious muscle, hard-faced, a pro – was putting his foot down as I got in. The car lurched forward as he gaped at me. Then his eyes went to the front again, realised he was about to smash into a delivery van, and swung the wheel hard to the right.

'What the fuck you doing?' he said, pulling a gun from his clothing and aiming it at me.

The Harvest Gold girl screamed, 'It's a gun!'

Yeah. I thought it was. A Smith and Wesson M&P9, to be precise.

I made a grab for the weapon, forcing his gun hand up against the roof of the car. Which made driving difficult. Too bad. I banged his wrist repeatedly against the roof, but the car was so damned luxurious. There was too much padding over the metalwork for it to hurt him and make him drop the weapon. With both my hands around his one hand, the inevitable happened. He took his other hand off the wheel to fight me and the car careered wildly. Harvest Gold screamed again. He put a hand back on the wheel to straighten up and I took one hand off his gun to punch him in the face. He recoiled. The car veered again, scraping the side of a truck to our right.

Then I banged his gun hand hard on to the headrest behind him. The gun dropped to the floor behind us and out of peripheral vision I saw Harvest Gold jump up on to the rear seat as if a snake were loose in the back.

I had no seatbelt to hold me back but the driver was still buckled into his. I knelt on the seat, got an arm round his neck and reached for the gear change. He took his hand off the wheel again and sent a couple of meaty blows to my middle and to my face. I wrenched harder at his neck and with one hand pushed the lever to Park. The transmission didn't like it. It made a complaining noise and the car decelerated fast, but not fast enough to stop it crashing into an Audi.

The airbags deployed.

The girl in the back opened a door and ran.

One of the patrol cars from the gallery stormed up behind us while one of the ARVs boxed us in from the front.

Chapter 6

Ten minutes later, the incident at the National Portrait Gallery had gridlocked half the West End.

The driver had been arrested and I was sitting in the back of the police patrol car behind the wrecked getaway BMW. I was with DI Liam Bolt, a scruffily dressed but twinkly-eyed detective. He was under forty, but already losing most of his hair. I recognised him from the previous day as the officer who attended the British Museum. And fortunately, with his copper's eye for a face, he remembered me. He'd watched me being interviewed on TV and fancied the reporter.

'Be my guest,' I said. 'But I didn't get her number.'

'Pity.' He studied the card from Tom Daubeney, trying to prove I was who I said I was.

'Anyone could get these printed,' he said, bending it between his fingers. I'd only had the card a few hours and it was getting dog-eared already.

I shrugged. 'I could tell you a guy to call. Foreign and Commonwealth Office. He'll vouch for me.'

Bolt wrinkled his nose. 'Nah. I don't need to renew my passport at the moment.'

'How about someone in the job? Well, ex job.'

'What rank?'

'Assistant Chief Constable.'

His eyebrows shot up. 'Flash bugger. How have you got him in your pocket?' Bolt's tone was half wary, half impressed.

I couldn't reveal too much. 'I worked with his daughter once and I fund certain events.'

'So he's in your wallet as well as your pocket?'

'Nothing to worry the Complaints Commission, otherwise I wouldn't be telling you.'

I gave him the number. He stepped out of the car and called. In a couple of minutes he was back.

'Are you some kind of crazy millionaire?' Bolt said.

'I had an inheritance once. As for crazy, well, I refused psychological counselling many years ago... but you can make your own mind up.'

'Well... the Assistant Chief Constable – or Archie, as I think you call him – said to give you every assistance. So I will. What do you want to know?'

'The car they escaped in at the British Museum. How far did you track it on CCTV?'

'They switched vehicles in Kentish Town. We lost them after that.'

I nodded. The transport side of the demos was highly professional. 'This car is a similar BMW. And I reckon this one will be the same.'

Bolt was puzzled. 'How do you mean?'

'Rental car, hired under a false name.'

Bolt was surprised I knew.

'Just a guess. But thanks for confirming it.'

Bolt made a face. Impressed, though not wanting to admit it.

'I'll give you something in return,' I said. 'The girl with the bright hair who got away is connected to a woman called Margaret Plastow.'

More raised eyebrows from Bolt as he made a note. 'And where can I find her?'

'You can't. At least not to interview. She's 104, demented and in a care home.'

'Thanks, mate.' His voice was deadpan.

'It was her wheelchair they used yesterday.'

'Wheelchair... Another hot lead, Kite.'

I shrugged. 'Best I've got. Except to say there's a kind of enigma.'

'Hey, don't go all Bletchley Park on me.'

'The enigma as I see it is the protests are political, aimed at the Prime Minister in some way, or at the government. But they're not politicos or activists doing it...' I looked to Bolt for agreement.

'Right. None on our watch lists had anything to do with yesterday's spectacle.'

'They're being run by amateurs. But they've got some serious professional help. Like the guy with the shooter today. That's the enigma.'

Bolt nodded his head as if he knew what the hell I was talking about and was considering it seriously.

'Well, keep in touch,' he said.

'I'm happy to pass anything on to you *pro bono*.'

'I can hardly wait.'

'In return for a *quid pro quo*.'

Bolt gave me a look. 'We generally speak English back at the station.'

'*Touché, mon brave*.' I grinned and left DI Cynical-but-Amusing in his car and headed back to the Portrait Gallery. I wanted to see the leaflets the girl had thrown into the air. I got there as staff were sweeping busily to get the room ready to reopen. I grabbed one of the flyers from the floor just in front of the broom.

'Put it in a bin when you've read it,' the cleaner said. 'Or take it home. Please.'

The folded A5 leaflet was a bizarre piece of comedy writing. It was a pastiche of all those campaigning flyers that exhort us to vote for a party or donate to a charity. It proclaimed the right of even an insignificant, unknown state like Trastivenia to reclaim its own treasures back from UK museums and galleries; it praised the Trastivenia government's approach to the arts; it also encouraged tourists to visit the island and provided a map of where it was.

Coupled with what I have to call the 'performance' at the gallery, it was all an elaborate joke. Surreal. The kind of thing you might see in *The Simpsons* or *Family Guy* or, I think, the old *Monty Python*. But the joke had a definite political purpose. At the bottom of the back page was a slogan: DON'T STEAL ART. GIVE IT BACK WHERE IT BELONGS.

Much of the flyer's text read like an April Fool jape but, the more I read, I decided it wasn't an hilarious one. Whoever had written it had struggled for ideas and tried to give it a kind of reality by inserting a number of 'facts.' My eye came to rest on a passage about the supposed leaders of the country. The President of Trastivenia was named as someone called Earl Scott Zukov and the Vice President as Sky Richards. There was something odd about the names. Richards and Zukov. British and Russian. Not impossible. But unusual. And what about Earl Scott Zukov? Another unlikely set of names.

I got the feeling whoever had written this nonsense was trying hard to fill up space. The names sounded contrived. Like some of those James Bond names. Pussy Galore, Plenty O'Toole, Mary Goodnight. *They* were tongue-in-cheek, but what about these?

Word games aren't what I'm best at. But I know someone who's ace. Clark Munday. He's an IT geek with an IQ of 170 who claims his parents named him after Superman, Clark Kent. This may or may not be true but Clark had grown up to be a fan of Marvel comics, the movies they inspired and all things techie.

His day job is in the fraud and investigation department of Maskelyne Global Insurance which was where I'd first come across him. He works strange hours to suit himself and, if he gets engrossed, it's sometimes all night.

When I called he answered at once. I asked if he was up for some freelance work and he said he was. I explained what I was doing, working for the government. Then I threw him the two names I was puzzling over.

'Are you asking if I know them?' he said.

'I don't think they're real people.'

'I'm on good terms with many people who are not real.'

I laughed. 'I don't want to know about your private life. What I'd like you to do is… wrangle them. See if they mean anything.'

'Translate them? Spell them backwards?'

'Anything you like. It's all a long shot. Like people have been playing with the word Trastivenia to try to unlock some secret meaning.'

He burst out laughing. 'Yeah. The meaning of Trastivenia. Looks like bollocks to me. And the meaning of life. Bollocks too, I guess. Though according to *The Hitchhiker's Guide to the Galaxy* the meaning of life is 42.'

Clark was hard to stop once he got going.

'This Sky Richards... That a woman?'

'I guess.'

'Though wait a minute,' he said. 'There's someone called Sky in that musical, *Guys and Dolls*... What's he called?'

'I don't do theatre. Especially musical theatre.'

'You're missing out... Sky *Masterson*. And he was a Guy not a Doll.'

'OK... Could be either sex. Very modern. Can I leave it with you?'

Of course I could. Clark is happiest working alone and I was behind schedule. Before I went off to Broadway with Tanya Brazil, I had to do some research on Vanessa Bell and Duncan Grant. To earn my 'loose change' from the Prime Minister.

Vanessa Bell was the sister of the novelist Virginia Woolf. Her husband was an artist and critic, Clive Bell, but their relationship was on-off and for many years they lived apart. Vanessa was also the companion, partner and sometime lover of the homosexual artist Duncan Grant. For many years they, and sometimes Clive Bell, lived in an unusual ménage of friends, lovers and family at a house called Charleston near the Sussex coast. It's a confusing story, but that's the Bloomsbury Group for you.

Vanessa Bell painted Duncan Grant on several occasions and there are many letters between the two of them which are available online from the Tate Gallery library. The Prime Minister's dealer had included with his picture a copy of a letter from Bell to Grant. But it would have been comparatively simple for Pilcher, the dealer, to invent a letter and forge Vanessa Bell's handwriting in the same way as someone else had forged the Cotman auction catalogue page.

Paint It Blackmail

I went to the Tate Gallery Archive and found there was no exact original of the Prime Minister's letter. This didn't surprise me. The handwriting and phrasing were comparable to those in the archive, but not exactly the same. I was sure as I could be that the letter was a forgery and I was surprised that the Prime Minister – a self-confessed art tart – would have been deceived.

As for the picture itself, it wasn't recorded anywhere in the archive at the Tate, but that didn't mean it was not genuine. At the Tate was a helpful lady with unruly auburn hair and the beautifully old-fashioned name of Matilda who wore beautifully old-fashioned clothes too. She was in her early sixties, but the clothes and hair made her look like one of those young, red-haired, pale-complexioned models used by the Pre-Raphaelites. She kindly agreed to keep looking through the archive to see if she could find any reference to Fresnel's picture.

I left the Tate and returned to the specialist I had left the painting with earlier that morning. She said the quality of the painting was good and it looked to be of the right date. The paint the artist used and the board it was painted on was also right. But none of this proved it was genuine. And none of this proved it was fake. And the expert's verdict was confusing. First, she said it wasn't the work of Bell, then she changed her mind and said it definitely was. Then she came to a final decision and said she couldn't decide either way. That's the trouble with art experts. They used to be indecisive, now they're not quite sure.

As with the Cotman, the so-called Vanessa Bell sketch was in the same style as her work and done at a similar date. But without laboratory tests, radiography, pigment analysis, second opinions, third opinions, committee meetings and a majority vote no one would swear it was or wasn't by the named artist.

And it's as hard to prove a picture is *not* by a certain artist as to prove it is.

Finally, before going off to the Cotswolds, I remembered I had to call William Havers. I expected outrage, fury, and a decision to prosecute the dealer for fraud. But when I gave him the verdict on the auction catalogue page, he took it calmly.

'Win some, lose some,' he said. I hadn't heard him in a philosophical mood before.

'Just because the catalogue page is fake it doesn't mean the picture is,' I said. 'Cotman had sons. They were both painters and they're collectable. It could be by one of them. I've a dealer friend, Gus Lamport, he could take a look…'

'Thank you for your positivity and optimism. But I don't agree. If the picture wasn't wrong there'd be no reason for the dealer to give me a fake catalogue page. I'll transfer your fee straightaway. Many thanks.' He ended the call in his usual abrupt way.

And then, on cue, an email arrived from Gus Lamport himself in answer to my query that morning. He wrote:

Pilcher is a sad case. In his pomp he had a fine gallery in Kensington Church Street. Good pictures. Very knowledgeable and reliable but he suffered some catastrophe around the millennium. Rumours are: he was fencing stuff from the Isabella Stewart Gardner heist, buying altar pieces the Mafia had nicked from Italian churches and (possibly more likely) that he gave information which led to the arrest of those responsible for the Whitworth Gallery, Manchester robbery 2003 and was half killed for his trouble. Pilcher retreated to darkest Cotswolds and ran an antique shop. He's off my radar now and I suspect off most people's.

The heist from the Gardner Museum in Boston was in 1990 and is notorious as one of the biggest ever art robberies. It's still unsolved and the pictures have never been recovered. All sorts of criminals have been suspected of a connection, even the IRA, but it's unlikely Pilcher had enough clout to be involved. The Manchester robbery was more intriguing, both from the point of view of the location – the city where both Fresnel and Brabant went to university – and also that it was a quirky theft. A Van Gogh, a Picasso and a Gaugin were stolen from the Whitworth Gallery, Manchester and after a tip-off were found stashed in a graffiti-daubed, disused public lavatory. With the pictures was a scrawled note which claimed the pictures had been stolen to highlight 'woeful security' at the gallery.

The Manchester robbery reads more like a drunken student stunt than anything else. I checked the dates and both Fresnel and Brabant had left university by 2003. But if Pilcher was based in Manchester around that time it was possible Fresnel knew of him.

I looked Pilcher up on the Police National Computer – I shouldn't have access, but if you don't tell, nor will I – and found an entry. He'd been cautioned four years previously by West Mercia Police for what was tantamount to attempted fraud. Cautions, like art experts' opinions, are unsatisfactory things. The police reckoned an offence had taken place, and Pilcher would have to acknowledge guilt for the caution to be issued, but there had been no prosecution. Even if all the stories about Pilcher were untrue, he seemed an unlikely dealer for the Prime Minister to buy art from – unless *he* had been woefully naïve.

Chapter 7

I called Tanya to check she was still good to go. She was and I agreed to pick her up from Whitehall. Then, like all freelancers, I had to mention money. 'Am I working for Queen and Country solely for the honour or do I get paid as the PM said?'

'We're making you a SpAd,' she said.

'Sorry?'

'Special Advisor. There's a contract in the pipeline.'

SpAd to the PM. That could look good on a CV. On the other hand it could look like a typo.

Parking anywhere near Westminster is a trial but I found a slot off Victoria Street near Westminster Cathedral and jogged round to the Cabinet Office at 70 Whitehall. I was surprised to see a van parked on the double yellow lines outside. An armed officer was standing by, but he seemed to be guarding the van not sending it on its way. As I got closer, I recognised the van's maroon livery and the discreet logo on the doors of Tabard & Spurgeon, the specialist art transporters.

As I waited for Tanya in the entrance, a procession of three porters in traditional brown coats came from inside the offices carrying carefully wrapped paintings. Being taken for cleaning or restoration I supposed.

Tanya appeared exactly thirty seconds before our arranged time and we hurried out to the car. Today she was in a shortish skirt with a Burberry kind of pattern and what looked like a fine cashmere tank top over a cream blouse and smart heels. As before, she walked at a cracking pace. I asked her about the pictures being carried out.

'Government Art Collection,' she said. 'They move them around different offices. Happens all the time. Some new ministers make a big thing of it. They complain the pictures in their department are too dull, too traditional, too *brown*. They want something more modern, more vibrant, more *purple*. They should spend their energy on their portfolio instead of redecorating.'

As we reached the car she said, 'Would it be a bore if I sat in the back?'

'You want to pretend I'm your chauffeur?'

'Don't be like that,' she said. 'I need to read a stack of things and I can spread out over the back seat.'

Her Smythson leather case was bulging and she had more document files under her arm. I opened a rear door for her. Chauffeur-like.

And for the entire journey we didn't speak. She read and made notes, occasionally sending a text or email. Was Tanya stand-offish with everyone? Why was she so stiff and rigid? She was the person who recommended me so she must believe I could do the job. Perhaps I'd disappointed her. Was it the clothes I wore? Not as chic as hers, of course. Didn't like my face? I've never had trouble with women before in that department. Perhaps it was my sense of humour. Didn't like being ribbed? Well, that was my style.

I looked in the mirror. I couldn't see her face because she was looking down at documents but the low autumn sun highlighted the waves in her long, dark brown hair and, in the V-neck of her top, there was the sparkle of jewels. An Edwardian pendant. There was something a bit Edwardian about her, too, and her straight-backed style. I found it alluring.

The journey was easy. Up the M40 as far as Oxford then on to the A44. Scenic but always slow. We reached Broadway on time. Its High Street is exceptional but it's not my favourite Cotswold town. Stow-on-the-Wold and Chipping Camden are equally pretty and historic but somehow friendlier, cosier. Broadway is too aware of its own attractiveness. It doesn't engage, it's unemotional. Bit like Tanya.

But that was unfair. I think she considered sorting out the PM's problem painting was a waste of time, a frivolous diversion from serious things like governing the country.

Pilcher's house wasn't in the stunning sixteenth-century heart of Broadway but in a late twentieth-century development that lies on the edge of town. Some of the properties have a token facing of Cotswold stone but, apart from that gesture, it's an estate of dull, mean architecture that could be anywhere.

I stopped outside Pilcher's house. Nearby, a gleaming new BMW stood out from the other five and ten year-old hatchbacks in the road. The driver was behind the wheel on the phone. It looked similar to the cars at the British Museum and the Portrait Gallery and I gave it a hard look, wondering whether to approach the driver. Then I had doubts. Surely it couldn't be connected to the demonstrators, not out here in the Cotswolds? I didn't want to overreact. Like when I thought the wheelchair was an explosive device. Didn't want to make Tanya think I was paranoid. Then she suddenly looked up from her papers.

'We're not there, are we?' she said.

'Yes, milady,' I said, with an attempt at a cod Cockney accent. But she didn't seem to get the Lady Penelope *Thunderbirds* reference.

'Where are all those lovely honey-coloured buildings, that posh hotel, the…'

'The Lygon Arms. It's back there. I've just driven past it.'

She looked around. 'This is depressing. And it's where he lives?'

'You can sell beautiful pictures from any old slum.'

'I suppose.' Then she leaned forward and leaned an elbow on the back of my seat. I got a waft of expensive perfume. 'If you're supposed to be Parker…' I saw a glint in her eye. She had got the *Thunderbirds* reference. '…Where the hell's your satnav?'

'I don't need one.'

'Why?'

I sighed. People never believe me when I tell them.

'I've got a highly-developed spatial sense. I was born that way. I can look at a map once and remember it. I always know where I am, where to go.'

'My parents had a dog like that. Could find its way home from anywhere.'

My head whipped round and she saw I was annoyed. People always take the piss when I tell them.

'Sorry,' she said. 'That was rude.'

I shrugged. 'People have said similar before.'

'And you didn't kill them?' There was another twinkle in her eyes. Tanya was making a joke. She had opened up.

I smiled. 'Only repeat offenders.'

She smiled again. 'Oh, by the way, there's been another Trastivenia thing.'

'At the National Portrait Gallery? Yes, I know. I was there. Chased the blonde. Disarmed the guy with the gun. Gave a lead to the police.'

She turned to me and she said nothing for several seconds as her brilliant green eyes drilled into mine. Her face showed incredulity, then amazement, then a kind of wonder and, finally, reassurance that she'd hired the right guy.

'Someone that didn't know you might think you were showing off,' she said, as a faint smile hovered over her mouth.

We got out of the car and I gave another glance at the BMW down the road. Feeling pleased I was making an impression on Tanya, I dismissed my worry about the car and decided it was a taxi waiting to pick up someone going to the airport for an expensive holiday.

We went to Pilcher's front door. A car was parked in front of his garage. I knocked and rang the bell, but there was no answer. I tried again.

'He did confirm the time?' said Tanya.

'Yes.'

'It was today?'

I gave her a look. 'His car's here.'

I looked through the letterbox. Everything seemed normal.

'Let's try the garage. Or round the back.'

There was a side door to the garage which was unlocked. I pushed the door open and called Pilcher's name. No answer.

Inside the garage were the remnants of the antiques shop he'd once run. They weren't proper antiques, more vintage stuff. What used to be called curios. Or old junk. Only one step up from the stock of charity shops. It was all dusty and unloved.

We moved to the back door of the house, which was also unlocked. It led into the kitchen.

I called Pilcher's name again. All was quiet.

'It feels bad, breaking in,' Tanya said in a whisper.

'We haven't broken in.'

'It's still spooky.'

'There's no need to whisper,' I said. Entering premises uninvited isn't exactly spooky, but it always makes me tense, makes my stomach flutter. Bit like before you start a marathon or before an exam at school.

We looked around. There were some unwashed utensils in the sink and on the hob was a saucepan of water with some potatoes in, ready to be boiled. There were carrots in another pan and the oven was on. I opened the oven door. Inside, half-cooked – though I'm no expert – was a home-made pie.

'Steak and kidney?' I said.

'Smells like it,' Tanya said. 'Pastry looks good. Better than mine.'

I called his name again and we went ahead into the dining room and then to the front sitting room. There were some large pieces of eighteenth- and nineteenth-century furniture, antiques bought in better times, and they dwarfed the modest rooms. The walls and paintwork had once been stylishly decorated but hadn't been touched for years. There were pictures on the walls, but they looked like leftovers from his dealing days, not things he loved. There was still no sign of Pilcher.

Upstairs there were three bedrooms. The largest had a small en suite with one toothbrush on a shelf above the wash basin. So Pilcher lived alone. The second bedroom looked unused and the third was full of old pictures. Many were the kind you can get in a job lot of four for a hundred quid at auction. A corner of the room was laid out as an artist's studio. There were five or six canvases in different styles, some nearly complete, some begun and abandoned. There were also shelves of art books. I searched among them and pulled out one of the books on Vanessa Bell I'd seen at Harvest Gold's house. I flicked through the pages, found the portrait of Duncan Grant and put the book down on a work table so Tanya could see.

'You think that's the inspiration for the Prime Minister's picture?' Tanya said.

'Only if Pilcher forged it,' I said.

Tanya reacted to this with raised eyebrows then said, 'Where is he? Out shopping?'

'And leave the doors unlocked and dinner in the oven?'

'But why isn't he here?' Tanya sighed and checked the time, not best pleased.

We went back on to the landing and stood in silence for a minute or so, wondering what to do. I was as irritated by the no-show as Tanya. Nothing suggested it was the house of a Mafia associate or a man who fenced internationally important stolen art. Just an elderly guy at the bottom of the heap, at the fag-end of his once successful career. Had something or someone from his past caught up with him? Just today, before we arrived? An impossibly wild coincidence. And there was no evidence of a break-in. No signs of a struggle. Everything was calm and peaceful. Like they said the Mary Celeste was.

Then Tanya said, 'Do you think he'd mind if I used the loo?'

There were two half-open doors leading off the landing: a family bathroom and a separate lavatory.

'Go ahead.'

She walked to the loo door and turned back to me.

'You don't have to stand guard.'

Dismissed, I went downstairs, walked into the kitchen, picked up a copy of *Antiques Trade Gazette* from the table and wandered into the garden.

In a couple of minutes I heard the lavatory flush and the door open. I heard Tanya's footsteps go to the adjacent bathroom.

Then she screamed.

There was the sound of a scuffle, another cry from Tanya, a thump on the floor and feet racing down the stairs. I was running into the hall as a man was pulling open the front door and tearing out. I raced after him. He leaped over the low hedge at the front of the property and dived into the BMW which was waiting with its engine running and passenger door open. The car pulled away fast, its door still open and even as I ran into the road it was doing fifty.

I clocked its number then ran back into the house where Tanya was in the hall, looking pale.

'I went to wash my hands. He was in there... And so is Pilcher.'

I went upstairs. Lying in the bath full of water was the naked body of a man aged about seventy. There were no wounds or visible injuries on his front. I donned latex gloves and pulled his body forward. There were no marks on his back either. But he was undoubtedly dead. And the bath water was still tepid.

I pulled off the gloves and went out to see Tanya who was standing on the landing, examining a graze on her wrist. 'Did he hurt you?' I said.

'It's nothing,' she said. 'He pushed past and knocked me to the floor. Just a bit of a shock.'

'Of course. Want to sit down, or something?' I put a tentative hand on her shoulder and she jumped at my touch. 'Sorry.' Her cashmere or whatever felt luxurious and soft under my fingers.

Tanya looked down, staring hard at the faded twist carpet, which may once have been a bright cornfield colour, but which now looked like post-harvest muddy stubble.

'I guess you're used to all this,' she said, putting on a smile. 'Bodies, and so on.'

'No one ever gets used to it. Not coppers. Not soldiers. Not doctors.'

We stood silently on the landing, a few steps apart, Tanya gazing at the carpet, me staring into space trying to make sense of what had happened. I thought about the Prime Minister and had a brief fantasy image of James Fresnel acting like Henry II with Thomas Becket, calling up MI5 in a rage and ordering a wet job to rid him of this meddlesome dealer. If only. Maybe one day somebody will write the story.

'Let's go downstairs and I'll phone the police. They'll want statements.'

Tanya nodded. As we went down, she said, 'Did you get a look at the man?'

'I didn't see his face, but he had a tattoo on the back of his neck.'

'Yes!' She looked at me as she remembered. 'You're right.'

'It was one of those Egyptian things,' I said. 'The what's-it…? The all-seeing eye.'

'The Eye of Horus. It's meant to be a good luck charm.'

I nodded, remembering I'd walked past examples in the British Museum only the previous day. 'Eyes in the back of your head. I could do with some of those.'

Tanya smiled. Then she jumped as her phone's jarring ringtone broke the silence of the house.

'Tanya Brazil…' She listened and began to walk away from me. As she reached the kitchen I heard: 'We shouldn't be talking about this, Hayden. The meeting was entirely informal. The PM may have been genial in your meeting – he's a polite person – but that doesn't mean that…' And her voice faded away as she walked through the house and out of the back door.

Hayden. The driver who picked up Harvest Gold. It wasn't a common first name. But perhaps I'd misheard what Tanya said.

I reported the death to the West Mercia police then I decided, like Tanya, to get on with the day job. I phoned the helpful Matilda in the Tate Archive. Had she made any progress in tracing the Prime Minister's 'unrecorded' picture? She apologised but she was a member of the gallery's security and safeguarding team and since the demonstration at the British Museum they had been instructed to review the Tate's preparedness in case any similar event occurred there.

'Health and Safety trumps everything,' she said, her light, delicate voice making her sound like she was sixteen not sixty.

'Don't I know it,' I said. Except in my line of work.

I went to the car to get my laptop and outside I heard Tanya still on the phone. She'd gone into the garage to prevent the whole of Broadway hearing her talking tough about whatever secret thing she was discussing. I couldn't make out any words but what came through loud and clear was the rhythmic click-clack of her heels on the concrete floor as she paced up and down. The speed of her pacing told me she was laying down the law in no uncertain terms.

Back inside I opened the laptop, intending to trace the car in which the murderer had escaped but my phone rang. Surprisingly, it was Tom Daubeney from Number Ten. He was in a sunny mood.

'Having a nice time in the Cotswolds? Grand weather for a trip to the country.'

'Yes… Not bad for the time of year.'

'And all going fine so far, the PM says. Everything under control.'

'Well, early days…'

'Of course. I quite understand. Now the reason I called is the Home Secretary would like a word…'

God. Surely, not another problem picture.

'…Nothing formal, just to introduce himself.'

'Well, that's good of him.'

'You may know there's a big review of the police service coming up so he's open to any thoughts from serving or retired officers. And with your experience, he'd be pleased to listen if you have any pointers, suggestions for improvement, that kind of thing.'

'How long as he got?' I laughed. 'I'll make a list.'

'Well… I'm sure he's got time enough…'

'No. I'm only joking. Yes, I'd be flattered.'

'He suggested lunch tomorrow. Wilton's, one o'clock. If that's OK, I'll text you the details.'

I said it was hunky dory and the text followed immediately. I have always had a healthy cynicism and a hard-working crap filter but the sudden exposure I was receiving in social media and on TV had raised the settings to max. What did the Home Secretary want? Thoughts on the police service? I don't think so. He was bombarded with those every day of the week.

Then Tanya came back in.

'Why does the Home Secretary want to buy me lunch?'

'What?' Her mind was still on her troubling phone call so I told her what Daubeney told me.

She made a puzzled face and shook her head. 'He's got two kids at university. Maybe he wants career advice – one of them wants to do what you do.'

I gave her a dubious look. 'How does he know what I do?'

She thought for a moment then nodded in agreement. 'True. But all I'll say is the food's good at Wilton's.'

'But there's no such thing as a free lunch.'

'True again,' she said. 'Do you want me to find out what's up?'

I shook my head. 'You've more important things to do.'

I turned back to my laptop and she watched me tapping in the registration of the getaway car. She looked concerned. 'You didn't hear anything of my phone call?'

'I guessed it was secret.'

Tanya chewed her lip. Looked at me. 'Does that mean you didn't hear anything, or you heard everything but won't tell anybody?'

I smiled. 'I only heard the odd word. But whatever it is, I reckon you think it's more important than this bloody picture.'

Tanya smiled wanly. 'If you knew what it was you'd agree with me.'

I looked up at her. 'Who's Hayden?' I said.

Tanya wheeled round sharply to face me. 'You said you only heard the odd word.'

'Hayden was one of them. And Hayden was also the name of the getaway driver at the National Portrait Gallery this morning. I saw the name written on a note at the girl's house.'

Her eyes were large and once again her gaze was penetrating. She'd have made a good interrogator. 'How on earth…?' Tanya was amazed.

'I followed a lead I got from the British Museum. It took me to the house. I saw the note. I went to the Portrait Gallery. So tell me. Who is Hayden?'

Tanya's tone was an icy blast. 'Forget you heard the name. Forget you heard me on the phone. That conversation never happened. Never mention it again to anybody.'

Chapter 8

Neither of us spoke for several seconds, but each of us flicked our eyes towards the other then flicked them away again, not knowing the next thing to say. I guessed Tanya was wondering how much of a liability I was and whether she could trust me. I was wondering the same about her. Had she come to Broadway to keep an eye on me? Was this case really about the Prime Minister's picture or was it all a front, a blind? Cover for a deeper operation I would never get to know about.

Then we heard a car approach at speed and come to a halt outside. There were blue flashing lights. I had to break the silence.

'What are you going to say to the police? You obviously can't mention the Prime Minister.'

Our eyes met and she held my gaze for some seconds. Then she went on in an urgent whisper: 'I know... I'll pretend the Prime Minister's picture is mine. I hired you in the same way as Havers did. I've come to complain and ask for my money back.'

'But why have we travelled together?' I was whispering too.

'I was going to come on my own. You said it was dangerous. You've come as backup. Muscle... an enforcer... whatever you call it. Besides, we've done nothing wrong, and if the shit hits the fan the PM will have to have a quiet word with the Chief Constable.'

I nodded. I couldn't fault her quick thinking. She gave a little smile and somehow a bond between us was established.

It was dusk when we left Pilcher's house. After the clear blue skies there was now a chill in the air. Maybe, further north, the first frosts of autumn.

'Do you mind if I sit in front?' said Tanya as we left the house.

'It's what the passenger seat's for,' I said. 'And it's too dark to read now.'

As we drove I looked across at her. She was sitting in her usual position: straight back, knees tight together, legs angled towards the door, hands folded in her lap. Still perfectly poised. Finishing school stuff.

After several miles of silence she cleared her throat and said, 'What do you make of it?'

'What do *you* make of it?'

'You're the professional.'

'And you've a brilliant brain. First class degree from Oxford. MBA. Fluent in three languages. Top job in Whitehall and still only thirty-three.'

'You've looked me up?' She was taken aback.

'I look everybody up. It's what I do. Ask me some questions or throw me some ideas and I'll bat them back to you.'

'OK… How was he killed? Strangled? Drowned? Injected with a rare poison?'

'There were no marks on the body. No marks around his neck. There was no water on the bathroom floor. The man with the tattoo didn't look wet either. No signs of a struggle. I think he died of natural causes.'

'A heart attack?'

'Or a stroke. It's first impressions, of course. They'll need a post mortem.'

'You think he was having a bath and the Eye of Horus man came in and…'

'…And scared the shit out of him.'

'Maybe he was a drug dealer. Some deal had gone wrong and the cartel wanted revenge?'

'Pilcher's place didn't feel like a dealer's house. No bags. No scales. No equipment.'

'OK… Now it's your turn.'

'It looks professional, certainly. A two-man job and a car standing by. But I'm not sure what the Eye of Horus man wanted.'

'Maybe it's nothing to do with art. Nothing to do with the PM's picture.'

'Except, why did someone who looks like a full-time thug and bully-boy burst in on Pilcher the very day after the Prime Minister hired me to go and see him?'

Tanya looked at me, her face puzzled and concerned.

'Another odd coincidence, you'll agree,' I said. 'Except it's not a coincidence; it's cause and effect.'

'Cause and effect? God.' She paused. 'So who sent the two heavies, and why?'

I had half an answer, but I still wasn't sure if I could trust Tanya completely. Not sure how much I could trust anyone close to the Prime Minister. So I said, 'Pass.' And I changed the subject to something uncontroversial. 'You're not going back to the office now?'

'No, I'll work at home this evening.'

'Tell me where you live and I'll take you there.'

My offer surprised her. 'Oh… that's kind. I live in…' She broke off, her habitual self-control melting into an almost girly enthusiasm. 'Now here's a chance to test you. On your route-finding skill.'

'You didn't believe me earlier?'

'Well, no.'

'People often don't.'

'But I suppose, testing your skill… It's a bit cheeky.'

'I can do cheeky.'

'I don't doubt it.' She was opening up.

'"Test Your Skill". That's what those fairground sideshows said when I was a kid. Shooting ranges, and so on.'

'I suppose you were a crack shot even then.'

'Just because I was in SCO19 doesn't mean I'm an Olympic marksman. So, go on. Test away.'

'What should I tell you?'

'If you live in London, give me the street and I'll find it. If you're further out, tell me the village or town. Or if we're going for gold, give me a grid reference.'

'Right. But I'll have to look that up.' She opened Google on her phone and I saw a map of Great Britain. She played around with the screen for a while then said.

'Here's the grid reference for where I live. SU968868. That's as close as I can get with this little screen.'

The UK's National Grid is based on map squares of one hundred kilometres. Each of these squares is subdivided into squares of one kilometre and then are further divided into squares of a hundred metres. Just fifty-five of the big squares cover the whole of the UK and each one has a two-letter designation, so it's no great shakes to remember those. Narrowing down a location to a specific area takes a little more effort; partly memory, partly an ability to visualise the mapping in my head and zoom in. But mostly I think it's instinct.

I was silent for a few seconds as I computed everything.

'Should I be timing you?' Tanya said.

'If you like. But here's what I know. Grid square SU covers a chunk of southern England. From the Channel up to south west London. That's easy and I'm not surprised you live there. The first two numbers – 96 – put you south of the Chilterns, the fourth and fifth – 86 – put you west of Heathrow. Put them together: 96/86... That kilometre square is just outside the M25. Buckinghamshire. Between Gerrards Cross and Slough... It's a village called...Farnham Royal. No, that's 96/85. You live in Hedgerley.'

'Bloody hell,' she said.

'Then the fine-tuning with the northings and eastings, they're the third and sixth numbers: 96-*8* 86-*8*. So it's 8 in both cases. It's a rural area. Not many streets, not many houses, but there's a new development, I think. I remember the odd sort of horseshoe shape from the map. Don't know what it's called. Detached executive-style houses, four and five bedrooms. That kind of thing?'

'Yes, it's called Misbourne Croft. Shouldn't you be running GCHQ instead of catching art thieves?'

'If GCHQ want to find a place they look at a computer. It's quicker.'

'How do you do it?'

'I was born this way.'

'You never get lost?'

'Not if I'm sober.'

She gave a chuckle. 'I see why you're interested in architecture. Shapes. Spatial awareness. Topography. Why didn't you continue with it?'

I said nothing. Just smiled.

'Gotcha,' she said. 'One of the secrets that vetting didn't reveal.'

I still said nothing. Kept driving, looking straight ahead.

Then Tanya said, 'I suppose that man Havers discovered the reason. Was that the metaphorical gun he held to your head?'

I smiled. 'You think I'm wasted. What about you? You ought to be in the security services.'

Her answer surprised me.

'I nearly was. In my graduation year I applied for MI5 as well as the Civil Service. Both accepted me. I chose Whitehall.'

'No regrets?'

She laughed quietly. 'People who say they have no regrets are usually lying. Or easily satisfied.' She paused for a beat. 'How did Havers find out stuff about you?'

'I don't know. But I want to find out and plug the leak.'

'Sounds like someone could be in for torrid time,' she said with a smile in her voice. Then she continued in the same light, almost teasing tone. 'The reason you chucked your university architecture course. I wonder what it could be…'

I said nothing for a moment, then, to get her on side, to get closer to the truth, I took her bait.

'I'll tell you, Tanya, if you tell me something comparable. Your life story. And who Hayden is.'

Tanya didn't react. She just said, 'Another time.'

She'd opened up. But only so far. A sidelong glance showed me she hadn't moved from her charm school position. Maybe it was camouflage. To fool adversaries into thinking she'd be a walkover in a conflict. But beneath her demure exterior she was as tough as any hairy-arsed bastard in the civil service.

I drove in silence for several miles. Then the phone rang. A London number, but not one I recognised. I looked at Tanya.

'Someone for you?'

'Means nothing to me,' she said.

'The Ambassador of Trastivenia?' I said, which produced an appreciative but decorous snort from Tanya. I switched the phone to speaker and picked up. 'Hello, it's John Kite.'

It was a woman's voice, roughly my age. 'Mr Kite? This is Carly Havers. William Havers' wife.' He had never mentioned he was married. I did a big eyebrow raise in Tanya's direction.

'What can I do for you, Mrs Havers?'

'You did some research for my husband about a picture?' I agreed I had. 'And you said the picture was a fake. I'd like to know what qualifications you have to decide such a thing.'

'First, I didn't say the picture was fake. I only said the catalogue page Mr Havers asked me to check was a fake. Second, I wouldn't have taken a commission to judge the picture's quality because, as you imply, I have no such qualifications.'

'Oh.' Mrs Havers was taken aback. She paused. 'In that case my husband is an even bigger shit than I thought he was.'

Tanya and I swapped looks that each said 'Blimey!'

'Could you tell me a bit more, please Mrs Havers? What's the problem exactly?'

'My husband and I are going through a divorce. My solicitor has been assessing my husband's assets and estimated the Cotman picture at £300,000...'

'That would certainly be a fair price for a genuine Cotman.'

'He's had the picture for several years and always regarded it as genuine,' said Mrs Havers. 'If it's judged a copy or fake then I lose £150,000.'

I sympathised and apologised, though all I'd done is what Havers asked me to do. I also gave her Gus Lamport's number – which I got Tanya to read out for me. If Gus couldn't help her persuade the

Paint It Blackmail

divorce lawyers the picture was genuine then he would know someone who could.

The call ended and Tanya said, 'What a bastard. He hired you as part of a plot to save money in the divorce settlement.'

'He stitched me up, conned me. Like he tried to con his wife. I argued at the time that having a fake catalogue page didn't affect whether the painting was good or not. But he didn't care. He wanted ammunition to throw at his wife's solicitor.'

I drove on without speaking but seething with anger. I'd wanted to refuse Havers' commission like I'd wanted to refuse the Prime Minister's. And there were alarming similarities between both jobs. Was the Prime Minister also trying to con me? Trying to get some sort of evidence that the Vanessa Bell picture was not genuine when he knew conclusively it was. If so, it was extraordinary. He'd told me my actions would decide whether or not he remained Prime Minister. What was going on?

I looked sidelong at Tanya and wondered how much I could say. She was my employer, not my partner, not my DS. I worried about speculation getting back to Whitehall and Downing Street. As we left the M40, not far from Hedgerley and Tanya's place, she turned towards me. 'You've gone quiet. What's bothering you?'

'I don't think it's stuff I should share with you.'

'Hey,' she said. 'You made the point yesterday we were working together. Told me not to be so formal, so fuddy-duddy, so stick-in-the-mud...'

'I didn't say that.'

'It's what you meant. So it's your turn. Spill.'

'What's said in the car stays in the car?'

'Yeah. Of course.' She'd answered automatically but then the ramifications of what I'd said hit her and her tone hardened. 'What are you going to say?'

'I'm worried about the similarities between Havers' case and the Prime Minister's. Both bought pictures they thought were good. Then they both had sudden doubts. Or they *say* they did. And both were given an extra, an add-on, which was meant to prove the authenticity of the pictures but is actually doing the opposite.'

'Another odd coincidence.'

'Exactly.'

I drove into her village and found the modern estate she lived on. In the horseshoe-shaped road I calculated which house was hers. I discounted those with lights on, those with more than one car in the drive and those with children's trampolines in the garden.

'This yours?' I said stopping by a detached three-bedroom house with a Prius outside.

'Very good,' she said. 'Now go on.'

I turned the engine off. Undid my seatbelt and eased myself down in the seat. Tanya unbuckled herself but otherwise didn't move.

'These add-ons – the letter and the catalogue page – are both fakes. Forgeries. Because of that we are supposed to draw the conclusion that the paintings are copies or fakes, too. But that doesn't follow.' I paused a beat. 'There was no evidence of forging pictures at Pilcher's house. There was some painting gear and half-finished pictures, but it looked more like his hobby than anything else.'

'Not skilful enough to forge a good artist?'

'I doubt it. Now, Mrs Havers implied her husband only had doubts about their picture when they were getting divorced. He knew the catalogue page was fake before he gave it to me. Its only purpose was to influence a solicitor's decision.'

Tanya's brow furrowed. 'If Fresnel is trying the same scam he knew the letter stuck on the back was a fake before he gave it to you.'

'But the painting is probably absolutely genuine.'

'God, this is terrible.' Tanya put a hand to her mouth. 'The Prime Minister lying and cheating.'

I gave her a look. 'I'm sure he won't be the first. Or the last.'

'But it's over something so silly. A picture. Not a great state secret or major policy. And Mr Pilcher has died.'

'He may not have even bought the picture from Pilcher. He may have used him as a patsy. Set him up as a fall guy. Had we ever spoken to Pilcher he would have put on a convincing display of regret, sorrow, apology, promises of paying the PM back etc., etc.'

'Because he'd been primed to say all that.'

'*Paid* to say it, I assume. And Fresnel could tell anyone who was interested that the picture was a copy or a fake. And he'd still get to keep it. That was the whole point of sending us on this wild goose chase.'

'Jesus... Why would the Prime Minister do something like that?'

'I have absolutely no idea.'

'And if the Prime Minister knows his Vanessa Bell picture is genuine, what has happened to make him want to pretend it isn't?'

A good question.

'How many people knew we were going to see Pilcher today?' I said.

'Maybe... a dozen or so within Downing Street and the Cabinet Office. Possibly more.'

'Had any of them got a motive to stop us talking to Pilcher?'

Tanya was aghast. 'What?'

'His death must be linked to us going to see him. Somebody didn't want Pilcher to play his role and tell us the Prime Minister's picture was fake. Somebody knows it's genuine. And they also know the Prime Minister is lying to us.'

Chapter 9

We sat side by side in silence. Then Tanya shivered again and wrapped her jacket more tightly round her. With clear skies, the evening was getting colder. I started the engine again and ran the heater. 'Are you all right?' I said. 'Is your hand OK where you fell?'

'I'm fine. But it's ghastly. Frightening. Pilcher died because he was going to tell us a lie.'

I nodded. 'It means the Prime Minister's picture is far more important than we thought.'

'Poor Mr Pilcher. And that thug with the tattoo…' Tanya shuddered again. But she breathed in hard, lifted her head up and said, 'It's horrendous, but I suppose it's also… sort of exciting.' She turned to me. 'That sounds terrible. But I'm a bit of an adrenalin junkie.' And she gave the first proper smile I'd seen her give. Warm. Companionable. 'Though it's all so worrying I don't know whether I'll sleep tonight.'

I smiled back, wondering who, if anyone, she normally slept with. I looked down and saw the street lights shimmer on the tights covering her slim thighs. Legs still at the forty-five-degree slope. How often did she open those tightly closed legs?

We chewed the fat about the case for another half hour. We talked about the Trastivenia issue and wondered if that eccentric protest had any connection with Pilcher. Tanya was rattled by the idea of Fresnel using me for some kind of fraud and her mood grew darker again. My world view was more cynical than hers. I was angry I'd been fitted up.

'Look,' said Tanya later, as she got out of my car into the cold. 'The windows are all steamed up. My neighbours will think we've been up to something.'

Chance would be a fine thing.

Next morning, the first phone call I made was to Mrs Havers. If the Prime Minister was playing the same trick as Havers, there had to be a link between them. It was also possible that the link was the source of Havers' information about my past. My father had been a criminal and when I got to know what he'd done it pushed me away from my architecture course and into the police. But I had only ever told the truth about him to two people. One was India, my first girlfriend at university, and the other was Rochelle Smith, a private investigator I had worked with. If someone else had assembled a dossier on my background then my whole career could be in danger. I wanted to find out how Havers knew what he did.

'Mr Kite, what can I do for you?' Carly Havers said, sounding brighter than the previous evening. 'I was watching breakfast news. Wanted to catch the latest on this Trastivenia palaver.' I could hear TV sound in the background.

'I'm sorry to call so early and I won't keep you long. This may sound an odd question, but does your husband know the Prime Minister?'

Mrs Havers spluttered a laugh. 'That's certainly from left field. No, I think I can say categorically that William has never met the Prime Minister.'

'Thank you, Mrs Havers.'

'Is that all you wanted? Can I get back to the mysteries of Trastivenia?' Her tone once again was light and jolly.

'There was one other question.'

'Well, I am Miss Popular. Go on then....'

'When I agreed to act for your husband he persuaded me to work for him by revealing that he had certain information about my past.'

Carly Havers laughed. 'Sounds just like William. That's always how he does his best deals. Would you call it blackmail or something?'

'I was interested in how he may have got the information.'

'Is it financial information? Social misdemeanours? Romantic liaisons?' She laughed, or rather chuckled, in a throaty kind of way.

'It's a legal thing. A police matter concerning my father.'

'Police? We don't move in those kinds of circles, darling. Although William does play bridge with a detective from Scotland Yard. Handsome kind of guy. Shawn, he's called.'

'Would you have a last name for me?'

'Well, as I said, policemen don't feature on my Christmas card list. But I could probably find a surname.'

'That would be extremely helpful, Mrs Havers.'

'And what's in it for me?' Her tone was part jokey, part flirty.

'Well, my budget for information is limited…'

Carly Havers laughed again. 'Just buy me a drink sometime.' I heard the TV sound increase in volume. 'They're playing that video of the fight in the museum again. I must say you look a handsome kind of fellow, too… Oh! That must have hurt… But I want to listen to the studio discussion. Bye for now.'

And the call ended.

In spite of what Carly Havers had said, I began double-checking for any links between the Prime Minister and William Havers. Havers was brought up on the edge of London in suburban Kent, the Prime Minister spent his early years on the Suffolk/Essex borders, Constable country. Possibly the inspiration for his love of art. The Prime Minister's state school and northern university education was very different from Havers' public school and Cambridge. It seemed unlikely they shared any friends from student days. Their work history was also diametrically opposed. Havers was into banking as soon as he graduated. Fresnel pursued politics. Fresnel holidayed almost exclusively in Europe in places with big art and architecture credentials. Havers was into scuba diving and holidayed in the tropics. Fresnel had turned out occasionally for the House of Commons cricket team and had a season ticket for Tottenham Hotspur. Havers had no apparent interest in team sports but skied every year and was a keen bridge player, on the board of the English Bridge Union.

There's the old trope about 'seven degrees of separation' which claims you can be linked to anyone anywhere in the world through seven interconnecting friends. It didn't seem to work for Fresnel and Havers. So I turned my attention to Pilcher.

Gus Lamport's email had mentioned Pilcher's connection to Manchester, but Pilcher was a man who left few traces behind him. I spoke to the Greater Manchester Police, to people at the regional newspaper and TV station, to the University of Manchester and to the Whitworth Art Gallery itself.

I did eventually find a trace of Pilcher's existence. An article in the *Manchester Evening News* from 2001 mentioned Pilcher's art stall in the Levenshulme Antique Market. Levenshulme is barely a mile from Rusholme, where Fresnel and Brabant shared a flat. It was credible, even likely, that Fresnel had visited Pilcher's stall, but impossible to prove. There was no evidence they had ever become acquainted.

I was getting frustrated with my lack of progress when Clark Munday called.

'Where are you?' he said. 'I thought you'd be round first thing.'

'I thought you might be busy,' I said. I'd almost forgotten I'd asked him to wrangle the names on the Trastivenia leaflet.

'Up to my eyes. I've been here all night. But come over now. Or whenever.'

I got in the car and drove. The Maskelyne Global office where Clark works is in an uninspiring office tower near St Paul's Cathedral. Some offices have great views of the cathedral but his, on the eleventh floor, is on the wrong side. It's more of a workshop than an office, a den even, and it hadn't changed since I was last there. Blinds permanently closed, lighting faded right down so the lamps hardly glowed. More screens than in a TV news director's gallery.

He must have been doing several all-nighters because it was messier than I remembered. There was a half-eaten Domino's pizza, an unopened tuna and sweetcorn sandwich from Pret, unwashed mugs, used teabags lying on a paper plate with a piece of cold toast, two Costa cups and an empty packet of Cadbury's Giant Chocolate Buttons. On the floor round his waste bin was a halo of scrunched-up napkins, paper bags, wrappers. Stuff he'd aimed at the bin, but which had missed the target. Clark was never a sportsman.

The air quality would make a health inspector call for breathing apparatus. But opening the windows brought in traffic noise. Which was a red line for Clark.

Clark looked wan and undernourished, but then he always did. 'Pale and interesting,' as a Victorian woman writer might have described him. And in spite of the lack of sleep he wasn't tired. In fact he was buzzing, jumping. Maybe he'd taken something. At any rate he laid aside the vegan burger he'd been nibbling at and kicked straight off with no intro, talking fast.

'Working on a railway robbery?' Clark said as I walked in.

This threw me completely. I wrinkled my brow and gave him a WTF look.

'You said you were doing a SPAD,' he said.

I nodded. Where was he going with this?

'Signal Passed At Danger.'

'What?'

'It's when a train driver goes through a red light by mistake. Obvious potential cause of major disaster. What's that got to do with stolen art?' Clark was a transport nerd with an extreme knowledge of railway systems.

'I'm a Special Advisor – S-p-A-d for short – for the government.'

Clark gave an impressed kind of look but mostly seemed relieved I wasn't encroaching on his transport territory. 'So if you're a SpAd, then I must be an AsSpAd or maybe better a SpAdAd. Assistant to a Special Adviser or Special Adviser's Adviser.'

'Whatever you like,' I said as he got on with bringing images up on his screens.

'I found a copy of your Trastivenia brochure online. So I checked it all. The landscape pics were taken from random tourist board websites, as I'm sure you guessed. If you want to know where they're of...'

'No thanks. I'm fine.'

'OK. They've inserted the fictitious island of Trastivenia to the north of Sumatra in the Andaman Sea. Nicely done. Brightness, contrast, hue and colour saturation all match. The original map shot isn't from Google, isn't even digital. It's copied from a printed atlas. Which is perverse. But maybe you can use that. I dunno. North of this crazy place Trastivenia there's part of Myanmar. Modern atlases often put Burma, its old name, in brackets after it. This map has Burma with no mention of Myanmar. Which suggests it's antique. Well, forty, fifty years old or more.'

'Nice one, Clark.'

'There's more.'

'I was hoping so.' Clark scowled. He didn't like jokes at his expense.

'So, what you asked about. Those names. I played around with them. Chopped them up. Swapped them around. Reversed them. Anagrammatised them.'

'Yes...?' I had to say something.

Clark held up a hand. 'Give me a chance. I came up with about a hundred variations on these two names. Stuart Z. Kissovo, Cy L. Shader, Richard S. Scott ... you know the kind of thing. I ran all the variants through Facebook, LinkedIn, Twitter, Pinterest, Instagram and had hits with... wait for it...' Clark liked playing to the gallery sometimes. *'Richard Zukovsky* and *Scott S. Earl.* They're real people. Combined anagrams of Earl Scott Zukov and Sky Richards'

'Great. Fantastic. Well done, Clark.'

Clark shrugged. 'People's vanity...' He tutted. 'Couldn't resist putting their own names in the frame. Making themselves supremos.'

'So who are these two?'

'They're listed as directors of a company called Morphic Motivational.' Clark quirked his eyebrows and gave me a you-must-be-joking look. 'That could be a cover for anything. Their registered office is at Trieste House in Farringdon. Suggestive, you'll agree.'

'Trieste. Trastivenia. Yeah,' I said. 'Suggests they didn't break sweat inventing names.'

Chapter 10

It was good work from Clark. He suffered from self-doubt and to get the best out of him you had to stroke his ego. Critical comments made him shut down. He accepted my plaudits eagerly but pretended not to.

I took a bagful of his rubbish to the bins in the basement as a thank you present.

On the way out of the Maskelyne Global offices I stopped in reception. Something on the TV that played silently there had caught my eye. Over a shot of Foreign Secretary Rory Featherstone speaking in the Commons, the scrolling tickertape of breaking news told of a Chinese diplomat being expelled from the UK. I stood and read the text of Featherstone's speech and wondered if this was the man Tanya had discussed with Lyle Brabant – the one she called the Salesman. If so, what kind of things had the man from Beijing been trying to sell?

On screen, Featherstone spoke well, but his appearance conformed to my general rule on British politicians: baggy clothing, wayward hair. I wondered whether he took his green credentials so far as to buy clothes from charity shops.

Trieste House is an older London tower block. Off Clerkenwell Road. Built in 1976, according to a stone by the main door, laid by a forgotten and presumably dead junior government minister. The concrete was rain-stained, ceramic tiles were missing from the cladding, metalwork in the porch over the entrance creaked ominously in the wind. It may have once housed a blue-chip company but was now rented to numerous firms. By the hour, possibly. They were the kind of businesses that put economy before public display, the kind that mostly operate online, the kind that don't expect or encourage callers.

There was a guy at the front desk sitting behind a sign which read CONCIERGE. I doubt he knew what the word meant because he showed no interest in checking me out or even checking me in. His main tasks were probably no more than taking in deliveries and locking the front door at night. I scanned a board listing the building's occupants and saw Morphic Motivational was on the fourteenth floor.

'Where are the stairs?' I said to the desk man.

'Lift is working,' he said. His accent was east European. Maybe Latvian, Lithuanian.

'I'm impressed. But where are the stairs?'

'Round the side.' He waved lazily and looked at me as if I were a freak.

I always use stairs if I can. It beats going to a gym. And in a strange building it's a way to get a feel of the place. To see what you wouldn't see inside a lift cage. People are naturally lazy. They avoid stairs. So stairways become hideaways, sanctuaries, places of assignation.

I jogged upwards, noting bits of litter and dust in the corners where the cleaner's brush hadn't penetrated. On the fourth floor a man in his forties was talking urgently to his phone. When he saw me he looked embarrassed and turned towards the wall. Like I'd caught him in some gross indecency. Insider dealing? Or just dealing? Don't know, don't care. On the ninth floor a young man was finishing rolling a joint. He saw me, gave a sheepish grin and hurried up the stairs ahead of me. On the eleventh floor an Asian woman and a white man, both in their late twenties were pressed close together whispering and looking into each other's eyes. They reacted and broke apart but the interruption I caused was only momentary. As I turned the corner at the next landing I saw the woman put her arm round the man and pull him closer. What was the story there? Splitting up? Getting together? Pregnancy crisis? I jogged on.

At the fourteenth floor I came through the stairwell fire door and it banged noisily behind me. A broken closer spring. Stairs are neglected by maintenance crews as well.

Morphic Motivational shared the floor with several other businesses. Lights were on at Morphic and their door was open. I went in. The diminutive reception area had a desk and a display of promotional literature, but the desk was unoccupied. Behind it, a corridor led to offices.

'Mr Zukovsky. Mr Earl,' I called out. No answer. Everything was quiet. Not even the patter of fingers on a keyboard. I called again. Nothing. It was like I was back in Pilcher's house. I walked along the corridor and looked into the first office. A desk and chair. Bland décor. Unused. Unoccupied. I went to the next. Same bland décor. Unused. Unoccupied. I went to the next. Same bland décor but bigger in size. Post-its. Pens. A4 pad. Invoices. Computer powered up. A jacket hung on the back of the desk chair. But no jacket owner. I went to the next. Same bland décor but bigger again. Computer. Packed shelves. Wall chart. More Post-its. And it was occupied all right. There were two people, two men. Both lying on the floor. Both dead.

Both had been shot. Cleanly. Efficiently. By people who knew what they were doing and had done it before. There was no sign of panic, of trying to escape. The men had fallen to the floor where they stood. It was an execution.

The dead men were of similar age – forty-ish – but of different appearance. I put on latex gloves and without disturbing the scene I searched for ID. The men's wallets told me the balding one with the beer belly, jeans and the Alan Turing T-shirt was Richard Zukovsky, while the smaller, fitter-looking guy in a striped cotton shirt and trousers to match the jacket on the chair back was Scott S. Earl. They were the directors of the little firm; probably the only staff.

I looked around the office. There was a wall chart from a computer equipment group, one of those given away free as advertising. Zukovsky had used it as a mixture of work planner and diary. A yellow Post-it was stuck to a date three weeks previously and written on it was *Julia Frobisher* and the single word *Art*. The name meant nothing to me, but I took a photo of the sticker to check her out later.

On the shelves was spare computer equipment, cables, drives, monitors. Some box files of paperwork. A photo of a wife and children and other personal knick-knacks. And there was something odd. A large book. It was the only book in the place. An old, well-used hardback, badly rubbed at the corners, its spine crumbling away. *Philips School Atlas*, it was called. I opened it at random and a loose page fell out. It was part of a map of South East Asia, including a section of Burma below which a neatly drawn imaginary island had been inked into the ocean. Trastivenia. Then inside the cover I found 'Mary Turner Form 4B' written in beautifully neat, old-fashioned, italic handwriting. Mrs Plastow's daughter. It looked as if the inspiration for Trastivenia had been a bored schoolgirl's doodle from sixty years ago which the dead men had digitised and printed. Not a capital offence. Writing silly things about a non-existent island wasn't something worth dying for. I don't think the authors of *Treasure Island* and *Gulliver's Travels* got murdered for their pains.

I left the offices depressed. This brutal double murder was in a different style from the timid demo at the British Museum, and the exuberant production number at the Portrait Gallery with the vivacious Harvest Gold girl. I'd been right when I told Tanya something serious lay behind the Trastivenia nonsense, but how serious did it have to be to justify these killings?

I went to the stairs and started to go down when I realised the floor I was on, the fourteenth, was the top floor of the building. Above it was only lift machinery and the roof. Remembering how we'd surprised the Eye of Horus killer in Broadway I wondered if the same could happen twice, the roof being a potential escape route for the murderer. As were the stairs. I thought again about the man I'd passed coming up who was having the intense conversation. No. He wouldn't have lingered.

Nevertheless, I went up the stairs. On the next floor I came to double doors with NO ENTRY EXCEPT AUTHORISED PERSONNEL and HIGH VOLTAGE – DANGER OF DEATH signs. The lift machinery. I carried on up and the stairs narrowed. There was a final flight which led to a door to the roof. This door was also splattered with signs warning unauthorised personnel to keep out and in big red letters: DOOR TO BE KEPT LOCKED AT ALL TIMES.

It wasn't, of course. A padlock hung uselessly open on its hasp, the bolts were not fastened, a Yale-type lock had long ago been prised off. I pushed the door and it opened easily. Immediately I saw the reason for the vandalism. Cigarette ends littered the area outside the door and some addict had even positioned two folding chairs in the lea of an air extraction intake. Extra comfort for the unofficial smoking area and the man I'd seen with the joint lower down was taking full advantage, puffing away.

There was no sign of the man who was having the intense phone call and I was about to return when I caught a slight movement on the far side of the roof. Lying together on a blanket were the couple I'd seen on the stairs. His hand was up her skirt and hers was between his legs. So that was their story. I left them to it.

I went downstairs. In the ground floor entrance hall I walked around looking for two different things. The first I found quickly. CCTV cameras. As I'd assumed, they were positioned over the main door and also over the lift doors.

The second thing I couldn't find. So I went to the front desk, to talk again to the disinterested man who sat there. He was in his late twenties, casually dressed and clearly a recent immigrant. As I'd thought, the CONCIERGE sign promised more than he delivered.

'Do you have a certificate of public liability insurance?' I said.

'Eh?'

I repeated my request and added, 'Public buildings are required to hold such insurance and display said certificate.'

He gave me a look and disappeared under his desk. I could hear things being moved, papers being searched, drawers being opened and closed. After a minute or so he resurfaced with a framed ten-by-eight certificate and handed it to me. I glanced at the details and handed it back.

'Is the building manager in?' I said.

'What?'

'The guy in charge of running this place. Security, safety, maintenance.'

'What do you want?'

'I work for the government. I'm engaged on a survey of office premises. Checking systems are in place for any kind of terrorist incident as we've had in recent years.'

'Are you expecting such thing?'

'I'm expecting to talk to the manager.'

He gave me a dirty look, picked up a laminated sheet of phone extensions, and pressed numbers into an internal phone.

'Mr Capenhurst. Man to see you. From government... about terrorism.'

He turned to me. 'He say, are you MI5?'

'If I was I'd hardly tell you, would I?'

He relayed this to Capenhurst. There were some grumbling noises from the other end of the phone. Then the concierge said, 'He say OK. But he's very busy.'

'Thank you.'

'Next floor. Room 1008. You can use stairs.'

Mr Capenhurst was so busy there was perspiration on his forehead and more staining the armpits of his dark blue shirt. This may have been due to excessive weight not excessive work. He could certainly lose thirty pounds.

'Now what's all this about terrorism?' he said, bustling about his office, moving an industrial pack of paper towels from a seat so I could sit down.

'Just a pretext,' I said. 'Sorry.'

He left the paper towels where they were and turned to me.

'What did you say?'

'I need access to your CCTV recordings. I'm investigating the outrages in the British Museum and at the National Portrait Gallery. I believe those involved may have come to this building. To an office on the fourteenth floor.'

'No way, Jose,' said Capenhurst. 'On your bike, whoever you are.'

'You know there's a serious breach of fire regulation at the top of the stairwell?'

'What?'

'And your Public Liability Certificate was not displayed as it should be.'

'What fire regulation?'

'The door to the roof on the top floor should be locked at all times, but it isn't. There's evidence that many people use the roof for smoking, sunbathing, and even illicit sex. If that door is permanently open it creates an airflow down the stairwell, which in the case of a fire breaking out would be a source of oxygen to feed the flames.'

He sighed a tired bureaucratic sigh. 'I know about that. As soon as the lock's replaced some bastard goes and unscrews it.'

'It would be a pity if the owners of the building, or even worse the insurers, got to know about this flagrant breach.'

'What is this? Blackmail?'

'I need a favour. And I happen to know one of the executives at the company which insures this building. Fiona MacIver, she's called. At Maskelyne Global. Call her if you don't believe me.' I took MacIver's card from my wallet and put it on his desk.

'Fucking hell.'

'Give me what I want and I'll not say a thing.'

'Why should I trust you?'

'You'll just have to, won't you?'

'We only keep CCTV recordings for four weeks. What date do you want?'

'Let's try from yesterday afternoon till an hour ago. Just the camera that covers the lifts.'

'Are you really with MI5?'

'No. But I am working for the government. I can give you a number to call if you want to check.'

Without being too precise, I explained what I was investigating and Capenhurst's hostility quickly waned. People can be surprisingly helpful when they're asked to contribute specialist knowledge. He took me to the CCTV control room, efficiently selected the material I wanted and fed it to a preview monitor.

'I've not given you this. OK?' he said. 'I've never met you.'

'Of course not.' I handed him my card. 'Any problems, call me.'

Then he left me.

Paint It Blackmail

I watched the material at speed. There were surprisingly few visitors to the office block but I quickly saw somebody I recognised. If the Harvest Gold girl was unmistakeable because of her hair, this man was equally distinctive because of his. His hair was black not blond, but he had a snow-white streak running across the top. In horses it's called a blaze. It looked like he'd painted bleach across his head in some post-punk fashion, but his two-tone hair was entirely natural. I knew this because he used to work for me. His name was Spenser Duggan; about ten years older than me, he'd once been a Detective Constable. I discovered he was on the take and I flagged him up to the anti-corruption branch. They investigated but he resigned before disciplinary action could be taken and went to ground. That was six years ago. What he'd been doing since I didn't know, but I guessed it was criminal, and almost certainly violent.

There are few people who make me feel uneasy to be near. Spenser Duggan was one of them. Even before I realised he was bent I was wary of him. His eyes often carried some unspecified threat, his body language was defiant, his remarks could be needlessly malicious. I even went to the trouble, on some pretext, of rearranging the seating in the office so I could keep a better sight of him.

There was another man with Duggan on the CCTV who was wearing a denim jacket with metal studs on the back. That had a familiar look, too. As they stood in the entrance hallway waiting for the lift I zoomed in as far as possible. On the back of the second man's neck was a tattoo. The Eye of Horus.

They were both capable of pulling a trigger.

On video I watched them go into the lifts, then I zoomed in further to see at which floor they got out. The lift stopped at floors five, eight, eleven and fourteen. I fast-forwarded the video to watch them come out twenty-three minutes later. Then I reversed it to check on which floor they'd got into the lift. The indicator showed it had stopped at floors fourteen, nine, seven and four. Fourteen was the only floor the lift had visited both times they were in it. Morphic Motivational was on the fourteenth floor.

I was out of Trieste House as quickly as if it had been ablaze and jogged back to my car while I called DI Liam Bolt. I told him about the bodies and the CCTV and he suggested in his sardonic way that I might take a few days' holiday so he could catch up with all the work I was sending his way. Very amusing. But had he got anything for me in return for all the public service I was doing? The registrations of the car outside Pilcher's house and the getaway cars used at the British Museum and the National Portrait Gallery had been checked. The cars were all the same type, new BMWs, and they were all rentals. None were from the same depot, but all had been hired in false names. So Pilcher's murder was somehow linked to the two demonstrations and presumably to Hayden, whoever he, she or it was.

The person who might know more about the two dead men at Morphic Motivational was young Harvest Gold, since she'd been handing out leaflets they designed. So I headed back to Mrs Plastow's house in East Finchley.

On the way I drove past Lancaster House and saw a van in a familiar smart maroon livery parked outside. It was the specialist art transporters Tabard & Spurgeon. I pulled into the side as a procession of porters in brown coats carried wrapped paintings out of the main door of the government offices. Another ministerial request for new office décor. I got out of the car and watched as the back of the truck was opened and the porters carefully placed the pictures inside. I caught a glimpse of another twenty or thirty artworks, securely fastened in place and beautifully protected, almost gift-wrapped, in bubblewrap and corrugated fibreboard. A whole new look for some department on the way.

At Mrs Plastow's there was no answer when I rang the bell and no sign of life inside. Had the girl left town? Once again I opened the front door and went inside. Once again I called out. Nothing but silence. This was becoming a habit. After Pilcher and the two bodies at Trieste House I didn't want to find another corpse. I toured the whole house room by room, including the bathroom and toilet. No blondie. This time an empty house was indeed empty of bodies, alive and dead. The girl's things were still there, much as they had been earlier, but she'd changed her clothes and there was more rubbish in the bin. So at least she'd returned safely after running out of the car in Charing Cross Road. I assumed she'd come back later.

I moved my car to a position about a hundred feet from the house where I had a clear view of any comings and goings and settled down to wait. Cloud had been building all day and a dull late afternoon became a gloomy early evening. The street lights came on. The house remained dark and deserted.

My phone rang.

'John, darling? Hi, it's Carly Havers. Are you anywhere near the West End?'

I explained that unfortunately I wasn't.

'I'm in a little bar in Great Queen Street while Miles parks the car. We're going to Covent Garden. A new ballet by someone I've never heard of. Sounds a bit grim, to be honest, but Miles is such a fan. You wanted to know about Shawn?'

'Yes. Have you got a last name?'

'I raided William's briefcase. I thought if he's stitching me up then I've a right to go through his things.'

'Sounds fair,' I said.

'Exactly. I borrowed one of his credit cards, too, for a rather lovely outfit I saw online. Now, has this policeman – Shawn – got evidence against William for something? Can he get him heavily fined or put away in prison?'

'No, it's about a different thing altogether.'

'Shame. Anyway, darling, the man's name is Shawn Cussons.'

'Thank you. You don't know his rank, I suppose?'

'Not a clue. I only met him once. Hefty kind of man who looks at you as if he's taking a statement and waiting for you to make a slip. Going to chase him up, are you?'

'Something like that. Thank you very much indeed, Mrs Havers. I'm sorry I can't buy you a drink to thank you.'

'Another time, darling.' I heard a voice shouting her name across the bar. 'Oh, gosh, Miles has stormed in saying we must get going. Curtain's up in five minutes.' There was the clink of her glass as she swallowed the gin and tonic that I owed her. 'Well, don't get into trouble, Mr Kite. You looked so powerful in that video from the museum. And such a lovely, juicy sort of voice. If ever I get tired of Miles, I may come knocking. Bye, darling.'

I guessed Miles might get tired of Carly Havers before she got tired of him.

I waited some more, then two hours after I arrived a car approached and stopped outside. Spenser Duggan got out, his white streak unmistakeably bright under the street lights. He let himself into the house with a key. But the house remained dark.

I stayed in the car. Surely he wasn't working with the Harvest Gold girl? Though, just because the young woman was attractive, bright and spoke well to an audience, it didn't mean she couldn't be a criminal.

Then I thought of the scream of surprise she gave when the driver produced a gun as we careered up Charing Cross Road. There was genuine terror in her voice and deep shock. It was the last thing she'd expected.

Another thirty minutes passed. Night fell. Nothing happened in the street. Nothing happened in the house.

Then another bright thing shone out from the end of the street. Two bright things. I saw a swaying lamp and a head of bright blonde hair reflecting light from the streetlamps. The Harvest Gold girl was on a bicycle.

The lights in the house were still off. Duggan had secreted himself in the house and was lying in wait for the girl. I had to warn her. I jumped out of my car and ran towards her as she cycled up to the house.

'Hi,' I called. 'We met this afternoon.' A dumb kind of opening and I cringed as I said it. She'll think I'm trying to pick her up. 'In the car,' I went on, 'at the National Portrait Gallery.'

She gasped. 'You!' And dropped her bike in the front garden and ran to the house.

'Don't go in. There's a man in there. He's dangerous.'

'Fuck off.' She turned to me in disbelief and sneered as she searched her bag for the key. 'Go away, copper, or whoever you are.'

The front door of the house was opened from the inside.

Paint It Blackmail

She heard the noise of the lock, whipped round and saw Duggan standing there. She screamed. Duggan made a lunge, but she was quick and lithe. She danced out of his reach and grabbed her bike. With the bike in her hands, she jumped over the small hedge at the front of the property, swung herself into the saddle and was away, pedalling hard down the road.

Duggan and I both raced to our cars and started after her. He'd parked facing her direction of travel so had an advantage. I turned round quickly and closed the gap with Duggan but there were parked cars on both sides. No space for me to overtake.

Duggan was clearly unknown to the girl. But who was he working for? For Hayden? Whoever that was. The girl had run off after the car crash in the West End but they wanted her back.

The girl cycled fast, taking risks, pushing her luck. She was sometimes on the road, sometimes zipping on to the pavement to avoid parked cars or to cut a corner. We zig-zagged behind her through the suburban streets, me a few feet behind Duggan. The girl was heading for the A1, the main artery of north London. Not a great place for cycling. But maybe she was counting on it being traffic-clogged as usual. Maybe she thought a bike could outpace a car.

She reached the main road and chanced her luck again to squeeze into the southbound traffic. But she gambled too much and had to brake, skidding sideways to avoid a Number 43 bus: it knew who was boss on that stretch. Duggan reached the same place and hardly slowed, forcing his way in front of a Nissan. This produced a long blast on the horn from the driver he'd cut up. I edged into the traffic flow two cars behind. Ahead I could see the girl pedalling hard. She bounced the bike up on to the pavement which was clear of pedestrians and gained herself more space than on the crowded roadway. It was the start of the downhill section that goes all the way to Archway. Easy pedalling for her and she was gaining speed, opening up a lead on Duggan and myself as we crawled towards red traffic lights.

When the lights turned green Duggan roared ahead with me on his tail. As we came down the hill I caught sight of the girl. She was stuck by The Woodman pub, unable to get across Muswell Hill Road.

Then she found a gap and was off again, speeding down the pavement on the steepest part of the hill. Duggan chased her. I chased Duggan.

Half way down the hill I saw the girl jump off her bike, throw it against some railings, and disappear. It was Highgate tube station. Duggan had seen her too. He stopped his car by the tube entrance, got out and ran after her. I stopped behind him and followed him in. He kept on running. I chased after him. He'd killed Earl and Zukovsky. I couldn't let him kill the girl.

Ahead of both of us bright blonde hair bobbed as she went through the ticket barrier at speed and ran down the long escalator that leads to the trains. She was fifty feet ahead of Duggan, who was the same distance ahead of me. She disappeared from view into the tunnel leading to the platform. Duggan and I followed. He was still running but he was struggling, panting hard. I was so close behind I could see sweat glistening on his hair.

I raced on to the platform and was surprised at the size of the tightly packed crowd. Maybe a hundred, a hundred and fifty passengers waiting in various stages of frustration. There must have been a delay on the line. Blonde hair had disappeared completely, her slim, youthful body slipping through the standing passengers, hiding away from her pursuer.

Duggan surged forward, barging through the crowd, forcing people who were looking at phones or reading books to make room as he came past, knocking a bag from a woman's hand, a magazine from someone else's. People shouted after him, bawling him out for his rudeness. I followed in his wake, surfing the turbulence he'd caused, gliding through the gaps he'd opened up.

Then the crowd solidified again. My way forward was blocked. Duggan had stopped his charge. Where was he? And where was the girl? I moved to the platform edge for a better view, scanning the crowd for the two distinctive heads of hair. One black, one blonde.

I heard the next train approaching, rumbling through the tunnel. Still I had no eyes on the girl.

Then there was a scream. I saw movement in the crowd. And I saw the head of corn-gold hair. She was struggling with someone. It had to be Duggan. I heard her shout, 'Get off me!' and scream again. Louder than the noise of the approaching train. The crowd surged again. An eddy formed. A hollow space like the middle of a whirlpool. People were avoiding two struggling people they didn't know, shunning an argument they didn't want to be part of.

I saw Duggan grab hold of her, but she forced herself away. He made another lunge at her. She twisted away nimbly and her plume of golden hair floated out towards the tracks. He thrust forward again, she pirouetted and then to my horror I saw her body teetering on the platform edge. She took a step to right herself, but her foot found only air. Her arms flailed. However deft and agile she was she couldn't save herself. She over-balanced and fell sideways on to the track.

Then the train burst clattering out of the tunnel pushing a gust of dusty air before it.

I ran towards where the girl had disappeared. She'd fallen on to the rail nearest the platform, not the central high voltage rail. But there were only seconds before the train would be on top of her. No time to scramble back up to the platform. The train was eighty feet away, its headlights shining brightly. I saw its illuminated destination sign: Mordern via Bank. I saw the horrified driver's face. I heard its frantic whistle. I heard the sound of its brakes: a deafening, squealing, banshee scream.

The only place of safety in such a situation is under the central electrified rail that powers the trains. It's elevated a few inches higher than the two running rails and underneath it there's a concrete trench along its length. A desperate last resort, a refuge in dire emergency. 600 volts runs through the central rail. Touching it is almost certain death.

'Get under the rail,' I shouted to the girl. She looked at me but didn't respond. Was she badly hurt? Dazed? The train was barely forty feet away, its brakes screaming.

I jumped on to the track in front of her. I rolled myself into the shallow trench under the high voltage rail and made a grab for her. 'Under here!' I yelled, getting hold of her beautiful hair in one hand

and the strap of her shoulder bag in the other. I yanked hard. She slid under the electric rail and into the oily trench.

A fraction of a second later the train was over us.

'Don't move!' I yelled above the noise of the train. 'Don't move. Don't move. Don't move.'

I held her head down in the trench as the train screeched over us. I felt the ground tremble as hundreds of tons of train and human cargo rattled inches above us. The brakes shrieked and the train whistle still rang out. Sparks fell on us from the electric pickup as it slid along the live rail over our heads. The wheels locked and the train skidded along the track, a deafening scream of tormented metal on metal.

Chapter 11

When the train finally stopped, the noise of its wheels and brakes was replaced by screams from horrified passengers, urgent commands shouted by station staff and wailing alarms.

I looked at the girl.

'Are you hurt?' I said.

Our eyes met. She shook her head. 'Don't move,' I said. 'Lie still.'

Her golden hair was two inches below the high voltage rail.

Forty minutes later, the PA system was apologising for delays on the Northern Line 'due to an incident at Highgate station.' The power had been switched off, the train had been moved clear and neither of us had any visible injuries.

Our faces and clothes were grimed with oil and dirt. The girl's hair was streaked with pitch-black grease. Like a negative version of Duggan's hair.

We were being led to an ambulance. 'Tell me exactly what happened,' I said. 'Did the guy push you? Was he trying to kill you?'

'He wanted me to go with him. When I said no, he tried to grab me. I struggled and then I tripped.'

'Why did he want you to go with him? Do you know him?'

'Never seen him before tonight. He said he was going to take me to my mum.'

'Where is your mum?'

'At home, I thought. Who is the guy? Do you know him?'

'He's a criminal. His name is Spenser Duggan.'

Then her eyes became more focussed, more intent. The determination and self-assurance I'd seen at the National Portrait Gallery returned.

'And who are you? You were fighting the man in the car.'

'My name's John Kite. I'm an investigator. Not the police.' I paused. 'What's your name?'

She hesitated. I saw her weighing up the odds. Was I a danger to her? How could I be? Shit. I'd saved her life. But I saw her mind working it out.

'My name's Zoe Oxenhope.'

I handed her my card. 'Here's my number. Would you give me yours?'

'Why?'

'I'd like to ask you some questions. About what you were doing in the National Portrait Gallery, what you want to achieve, who you're working for. And about the demo at the British Museum. About who Hayden is.'

'How do you know about Hayden?'

'I came across the name. You can trust me. I've been investigating a case for the Prime Minister, believe it or not.'

She reacted abruptly to this, more shocked than I could have imagined. Her reaction was strange and complex: a mixture of surprise and excitement. Her eyes lit up with what looked like hope.

'The Prime Minister…' she repeated. 'Really?' I could see her mind whirling.

'What is it?' I said.

'Nothing,' she said, and she suddenly switched off. As if I'd intruded on a private matter. She said no more and looked at the ground..

We'd reached the surface. The ambulance waiting for us was parked behind my abandoned car. Another traffic snarl-up I'd helped to cause. Duggan's car had gone.

'Look,' I said to Zoe, 'I'm not going to hospital. I feel perfectly fine. That's my car parked there. I want to move it before it's towed away.'

She looked towards my car. 'I feel OK, too,' she said.

'Don't let me stop you going for a check-up. They'll offer counselling, that sort of thing. It could be useful. But I would like to talk to you. When you get home. Wherever that is.'

She nodded as the paramedic helped her into the back of the ambulance. I thanked the crew for their help but explained I was refusing any further attention. They were reluctant to let me go. But I insisted.

'All I need is a shower,' I said, and got into my car. Then I called Bolt. He ought to know I'd witnessed an attempted murder. His phone went to voicemail, so I left a message. Then I thought about calling Tanya. We needed to speak to Fresnel. Just as I pressed her number there was knocking on the side window. A uniform asking me to move? No. Zoe was standing there. I was surprised – and pleased. I lowered the window.

'I said I didn't want to go to hospital either. I've had enough therapy and counselling. I'm sick of it.'

I nodded. 'I can understand. I know a bit about therapy.'

This caught her interest and emboldened her to ask, 'Are you really working for the Prime Minister? You've been to Downing Street and that?'

I said I had.

'Cool. Can we go for a drink then? I'm spitting feathers.'

I smiled. 'Of course. What about your bike?'

'It's alright. Someone's nicked it anyway.'

She opened the door and got in. 'Is there anyone you want to call?'

'I'll call my mum. When we get to the pub.'

'How old are you?'

'Old enough to drink.' She spat out the words.

'I wasn't doubting that…Twenty-one? Twenty-two?' I guessed older on purpose to make her feel better.

She gave me a resentful look. 'Nineteen.'

Asking someone's age always causes offence. Unless they're over 85; then they expect congratulations for living so long.

'You did your speech well… In the National Portrait Gallery,' I said. 'And you fooled everyone by going through that secret door.'

She gave me a cagey look, wondering if I was buttering her up. Which of course I was.

'You were on to it pretty fast.'

'That's my job, I guess. Was this Trastivenia thing your idea?'

She smiled at me for the first time. 'Did you like it?'

'It was wacky, alright. And complicated. I don't know if your message got across. Not sure anyone knows what you're campaigning for.'

'But that's the point. We wanted to tease people. Get the idea of Trastivenia going viral. Everybody tweeting about what the fuck it was all about. And then we drop the bombshell.' She smiled again and her eyes gleamed and glistened. I could tell she felt superior having to explain her strategy to someone who hadn't got it. And she looked confident, seeing visions of triumph and glory for her cause.

'And what *is* it all about?'

She smiled teasingly. 'I might tell you. But only if I think I can trust you.' And then she clammed up.

We were close to one of my favourite London pubs, The Holly Bush in the middle of Hampstead, but we were both grubby and I settled for one lower down on Haverstock Hill. It would be less busy.

I got pints for both of us: ale for me and a Leffe Blonde for Zoe. She swigged half of her drink quickly then took out her phone and called her mother. The call started casually. I heard Zoe thank her mother for the shampoo and conditioner then things got more serious and she wandered away into a quiet corner of the pub near the lavatories.

Bolt called me back and I gave him more on what had happened. I also passed on Zoe's name. Then I said: 'Now it's my turn for a bit of tit for tat.'

'*Quid pro quo.*'

'You see, you are a linguist after all. I'm trying to track down a CID officer called Shawn Cussons.'

'Do you know what rank or where he's stationed?'

'All I have is the name. He might even be retired.'

'No trouble. I'll get back to you. Saw that sexy reporter, Lucy Bladon, on TV again last night. You sure you don't have a number for her?'

'I'm sure, Liam. She was interviewing me, not the other way around.'

The call ended and I looked around for Zoe but couldn't see her. Her drink was still on the table. Some minutes passed and I became uneasy. Had she done a runner? I walked across to where she'd been talking to her mother. I thought about checking the ladies to see if she was there, but instead, I hurried out of the pub and went round to a dead-end alley at its side. In the pub's wall were two small windows with frosted glass. One for the gents, one for the ladies. The window to the ladies was wide open. A woman washing her hands saw me looking in and immediately went to close it. The window was six feet above the ground and only a couple of feet square. But Zoe was slim and athletic. Another bit of escapology to rival that at the National Portrait Gallery.

I cursed. Her mother must have warned her against talking to me, frightened of repercussions. Perhaps she'd heard about the deaths of Zukovsky and Earl and was uncertain which side I was on. I wondered how involved in the plot the mother was. Then I thought about the woman at the British Museum. She had blonde hair too. She would be the right age to be Zoe's mother.

Then I heard a phone ping. The sound was coming from the end of the alley which dog-legged behind the pub. I walked round. There was wind-blown litter, a splatter of old vomit and a smell of piss. There was a stack of empty beer kegs and sitting on one of them was Zoe.

'Do you want to finish your drink?' I said.

'My mum said I shouldn't talk to you. A car's coming for me.'

'She's sending a taxi?'

'No. It's the people we're working with.'

'Is that Hayden? Can you tell me who they are?'

'I'm not supposed to. Mum doesn't want me to tell anybody anything. She didn't like me coming to the pub with you. She's even got me to turn off the location thing on my phone so no one can find me.'

I smiled. 'It's the signal from the phone's transmitter that's tracked. The software settings make no difference.'

Zoe thought a moment and realised her mum's mistake. 'Yeah... course. Stupid.' She paused a beat. 'How do you know about them, anyway?'

'I hoped you'd tell me about them. And you said them. Is Hayden a company? A business?'

She shrugged. 'It's a name they use. It was one of them texting. Saying he'd be here in five minutes.'

There was a double horn blast from a car on the road.

'That'll be them. I'd better go. Thank you for... you know.'

'Don't mention it. Just... look after yourself. You've got my details. If you need help, call or email.'

Zoe went to go, then turned back to me. 'When did you have therapy?'

I smiled. 'I refused it. I was about your age. Both my parents had been killed in a crash.'

'God.'

I shrugged. 'What about your therapy?'

'That was because of my parents too.'

'In what way?'

She shook her head and walked away. 'See you.'

'Call me. Any time. I can help you,' I said, watching her saunter off down the alleyway. After she turned on to the road, I ran down to the corner of the alley and peered round the brickwork, keeping close to the wall and out of sight of any surveillance from the road. I watched her walk to where a car was parked at the roadside. It wasn't a BMW like the other escape cars but a Jaguar. A door was opened from inside and she got in. I watched the car drive southwards down Haverstock Hill.

I ran to my car and followed them. It was surprisingly straightforward. They were not in getaway mode and kept to the speed limits. I stayed close, but not too close, with at least one other vehicle always between us. They went south-east, skirting the City of London and under the Thames through Blackwall Tunnel. Then it was the South Circular and on to the A23 and M23. Were they going to Gatwick Airport? Fleeing the country? A real getaway job? No, they passed it by and then headed off into the Sussex countryside. Traffic was thin so I had to hold further back. They turned off the main road and onto a narrow country lane. No street lighting, of course, so I held back even further. After a couple of miles the Jaguar slowed and disappeared into a drive. I slowed down too and came to the imposing gateway of a substantial country house. A bronze plate fixed to one of the brick entrance piers bore the name Birchfield Place. I watched a pair of fancy wrought-iron gates close automatically on the Jaguar then I drove on a short distance until I found a place to stop. Then, before I did anything else, I texted the Jaguar's registration to Clark who might still be at work. I assumed it was a rental like the others but at the insurance company he had instant access to almost all automobile details. Maybe he could dig down and find more information than I could.

I was between Lewes and Polegate. Significantly, the nearest village was Firle, close to Vanessa Bell and Duncan Grant's house, Charleston. I opened my laptop and made a search for Birchfield Place. The property was available to let and was listed on one of the more upmarket 'country cottage' websites at £7,000 a week rental. And that was low season. No way was it a cottage. Set in five acres of land, it had eight bedrooms, six bathrooms, three reception rooms, a library, an indoor pool and all the rest. Who was renting this luxurious hideaway and why was Zoe being taken there?

I indulged myself for a few moments, feasting my eyes on the period details of the late eighteenth-century house but was dragged back to the matter in hand by a call from Clark, who was still in the office. The Jaguar, to my surprise, wasn't a rental.

'It's government property,' said Clark.

'What?'

'I can't get any more detail. It's either a government pool car or for the use of a particular minister. Better be careful, Kite. You could be playing with fire.'

Chapter 12

I have a lockable metal toolbox in the back of the car which is bolted behind the rear seat. From it I took out a Maglite, a pair of miniature binoculars, wire-cutters and my house-breaking kit. I stowed them in a small backpack and set off to Birchfield Place.

I didn't bother to go back to the ornamental gates. From the road, I climbed over a barbed wire fence into a field. Then I walked through barley stubble to the six-foot brick wall that ran round the perimeter of the Birchfield Place estate. I hoisted myself to the top of the wall and examined the house through binoculars. The Jaguar was parked by the front door, alongside another car. Lights illuminated the front of the property but the garden was mostly dark. I saw the usual intruder alarm but no evidence of CCTV coverage.

I went over the wall into the garden and tested for security lighting with a few careful steps. Nothing was triggered by my movement so, keeping low and in the unlit area, I scuttled to the centre of the garden for a better view. Lights were showing downstairs and on the top floor, but half the house was in darkness. Some curtains had been drawn but I trained my binoculars on rooms where there was a clear view in. I couldn't see Zoe, her mother or anybody else. I moved back to where it was darkest and followed the wall to the back of the house. There were lights in a kitchen and what looked like a breakfast room. But I still had no visual on any occupants. I saw a PIR by the back door and hesitated, not wanting to spotlight myself.

Then I heard an eery, hollow thumping sound coming from the darkness to my right by a one storey extension. I switched on the

Paint It Blackmail

Maglite and turned round. A dog was lying in a large kennel, looking at me expectantly. His tail, beating on the kennel's wooden floor, was making the spooky sound. As I watched, he got up, yawned, stretched and went straight to the back door, his movement activating the security light. He seemed friendly enough and I followed him to the door. There was still nobody visible inside, so I opened the door. The dog bounded in and I followed. The dog went to its food bowl, which was empty, sniffed and licked it then came straight back to me. It looked up and nudged me with its nose. Then it made some snuffling and whining sounds, nudged me again and seemed about to bark. I couldn't let it do that.

I opened the big retro-style fridge and found a supermarket 8-pack of jumbo sausages. I thought of the Fred Basset strip: dogs and sausages always go together in cartoons. But in real life I think it's different. Also in the fridge was a half-eaten steak pie and a pack of Ardennes pâté. I scooped the pâté out of its plastic container and dropped it in the dog's bowl with the steak pie remains. He began to gobble greedily. My friend for life. Or at least while I was in the house.

As I turned away from the dog something on the kitchen table caught my eye. Sticking out of a supermarket plastic bag was a vintage child's toy. It was a faded and dog-eared cardboard box labelled JOHN BULL PRINTING KIT. I pulled it out of the bag and saw written on the box in ink, with neat penmanship: *To Barbara, Love from Auntie Gladys. Xmas 1952.* I opened the lid. The toy was exactly what it said. A printing kit. There were hundreds, thousands, of small rubber letters, like pieces of type. The idea was to slot these letters, backwards of course, into grooves on a wooden block, then press the block on to an ink pad and then on to a piece of paper. Hey presto! You could print a message. Mind-bogglingly slow and fiddly. Just like five hundred years ago in Caxton's time.

It seemed to have been brought in recently and I remembered the vintage children's games at Margaret Plastow's house. Mrs Plastow's daughter was Barbara Turner; it had to be her Christmas present. Why would Duggan want an old child's game?

Leaving the dog scoffing, I emerged from the kitchen into a hallway. There was TV sound from one room and occasional male conversation, but the TV made it impossible to make out more than a few words. The doors of other downstairs rooms were open, but they were either dark or unoccupied. I started up the stairs, hoping the old timber wouldn't creak. It did, but not enough to be heard above the TV.

Upstairs were bedrooms, all unoccupied. Two of them had male clothes in so they must belong to the men I heard below. I moved up to the top floor where I'd seen lights from outside. There were five doors leading off the landing, only one of them was closed and, significantly, a key protruded from the lock. I moved to the door and listened for voices. Then I heard a lavatory flush followed by the sound of an internal door opening and then closing.

Then I heard Zoe's voice.

I turned the key and went into the room. Zoe was there with the woman I had fought with in the British Museum. Both women jumped up in shock and spoke simultaneously.

'John!' said Zoe.

'You again. What do you want?' said the woman who had struck me.

I hushed them and closed the door. 'Never mind what I'm doing. It's time you told me what the hell you're up to.'

'I'm saying nothing,' said the woman. 'You should go. Leave us alone. Stop interfering. You're ruining everything.' She was still as angry as she had been in the museum. Now I saw her next to Zoe, it was clear they were mother and daughter. And she was younger than I had first thought; definitely under forty.

'This is the man who saved my life. We owe him,' said Zoe.

'The more people that know, the more trouble we'll be in.'

'Hey, hey...' I waved my Maglite at them to quieten them down. 'You'll be in a hell of a lot more trouble soon if you don't stop working with the criminals and killers downstairs.'

'We've got to tell him, Mum' said Zoe. 'We're in the shit. This is my mum, by the way...'

'Helen Oxenhope,' her mother said. I nodded to her.

'And John's working with the Prime Minister.'

This got her mother's attention at once. 'Do you know about our letters?' she said.

'What letters?'

'Letters to the Prime Minister. That's how it all started. That's why we're involved with this lot.'

I sat down on one of the single beds. 'I think you'd better explain from the beginning,' I said. 'How are these criminals involved with the Prime Minister?'

'They're not. They're employees, drivers, toughs… They work for this Hayden group. They're all supposed to be helping us with our campaign,' said Zoe.

'And they have,' put in Helen.

'Up to a point,' said Zoe with heavy sarcasm. 'I don't call being kidnapped and locked up here very helpful.'

'They didn't kidnap us.'

'Virtually. That thug with the weird hair chased me for a mile then almost got me killed. And they're not really interested in what we want. They've got their own agenda.'

'Hang on. Go back to your letter to the Prime Minister? What did it say?'

'It was about the painting.'

'Which painting?'

'The picture of Duncan Grant by Vanessa Bell,' said Helen Oxenhope.

'The Prime Minister's painting?' This was extraordinary.

'The one he's got, yes,' said Helen Oxenhope. 'But the point is…'

'Did these villains get hold of the letters you sent to the Prime Minister?' I said.

'*They* didn't. Somebody else did.'

'Who? Someone in Downing Street? In the government?'

Zoe looked at her mother and Helen Oxenhope looked at me. 'I can't say. We were told to keep it absolutely secret.'

'You can trust me,' I said.

'That's what everyone says. Why should I believe what you say?' said Helen.

'He's working for the Prime Minister, mum,' said Zoe.

'But is he for us, or against us?' Helen gave me another suspicious glance.

I was getting frustrated at the lack of clarity. 'Tell me what you want and I'll tell you whose side I'm on.'

'We want back what is ours and to let the Prime Minister know the truth,' said Helen, still not giving a straight answer.

'What the Prime Minister said years ago about sending stuff back from British museums to wherever it originally came from gave Mum the idea for this daft Trastivenia stuff,' said Zoe.

'I felt it was something to latch on to, a way of referencing the debate. Some friends of mine printed leaflets. We thought they were funny…'

'These friends…' I said. 'Richard Zukovsky and Scott Earl?'

'Yes. Two guys who have a little IT company. I met them…'

'So have I. But I'm afraid they're both dead.'

'My God! No.' Helen Oxenhope put her hands to her mouth. There were tears in her eyes. 'I don't believe it.'

I looked at her as her daughter hugged her tightly.

'How do you know them?' said Zoe.

'I don't. I just found their bodies. They'd been shot. By Spenser Duggan and another man. Duggan is the man who was chasing you. The man who nearly killed you.'

'God…' said Zoe. 'All our fault.'

'It's not our fault,' Helen said, with tears running down her cheeks. 'They didn't deserve that, but it's not all our fault.'

Zoe and her mother sat side by side, their arms around each other, silent and distraught. They were realising that in starting the Trastivenia business they had made the biggest mistake of their lives.

'The leaflet was their idea,' said Zoe looking sick. 'Richard was trying to get a sideline as a comedy writer. He's sent stuff to radio and TV. It was all meant to be fun. They said humour would attract people to our grievance. An off-the-wall way to draw attention to our case, they said.'

'You still haven't explained what you're campaigning for,' I said. 'What's your grievance? What's your case?'

'We want to get back what was ours. What was stolen from us,' said Helen.

'What was stolen from you?'

'The picture, of course. That's why we wrote to the Prime Minister in the first place. The picture by Vanessa Bell. He stole our picture and we want it back.'

Chapter 13

I could hardly believe what they'd said. My brain was rapidly reassessing everything concerning the Vanessa Bell picture, Pilcher's death, William Havers and the charade of Fresnel hiring me and the farce of our trip to Broadway.

'I thought you knew,' said Zoe to me at last.

'How could I?'

'You said you were working with the Prime Minister.'

'I am, but…'

The door crashed open behind me. Duggan was standing there with a heavy-set man at his side in a red T-shirt. The Jaguar driver.

'Detective Inspector fucking Kite,' Duggan said. 'Never had you down as a dog lover. I was looking forward to that pâté.'

Red T-shirt looked shocked. 'He's a copper?'

'Not any longer,' said Duggan. 'Inherited some money, or so the story is. Ponces about as a freelance art detective now. After he got me suspended.' He moved closer to me and I saw he was holding a heavy wooden club. 'Come to apologise after screwing me around?'

'There was no fit up, Duggan,' I said. 'It's only because your brief was bent that you didn't get sent down for longer. Why are you holding these two women?'

He slapped the cosh against his palm in a menacing way. 'We're helping them get what they want. And we're protecting them too,' said Duggan.

'Bollocks. It's unlawful imprisonment.'

'We're assisting with their campaign.'

Paint It Blackmail

'Bollocks. You're pretending to do that and using them to hide behind. Let them go.'

'It's not my decision,' said Duggan with a calm smile, like he was awaiting an email from the CEO.

'No,' I said. 'It's my decision.' And I swung the Maglite hard at the knuckles of his hand holding the billy club. The torch is tough and metallic, it's designed for military or police use and with its batteries has a useful weight. Duggan's crushed fingers reacted by reflex and the stick dropped to the floor. I uppercut him with the Maglite under his chin and he stumbled backwards. I swept his stick up from the floor in my left hand and used it to slash sabre-like at red T-shirt's head. Then, tossing the Maglite behind me, I put both hands on the billy and used it as a pike to ram first into Duggan and then into his sidekick. I had a couple of inches of height and probably thirty pounds advantage against Duggan. Red T-shirt was beefy, but undisciplined. I was fitter than either. Using my height and strength I swung the heavy stick from side to side as frantically as I could. They retreated under my assault and I drove them back to the landing, far enough to give me the space I needed. I snatched the key out of the far side of the door, stepped back into the room, slammed the door shut, leaned hard against it and turned the key. A nanosecond after the lock clicked home the door shuddered as the two big men charged it.

The lock would hold for a few minutes, but no longer.

I went to the window and lifted the sash. In typical late eighteenth century fashion, the top floor of the house had dormer windows. The roof itself was a squat affair. The tiles didn't reach the edge of the house but sloped down to a flat, lead-lined area behind a parapet. This flat roof section provided a walk way round the house.

'Let's go,' I said, climbing out of the window.

'We can't,' Helen said as the door creaked and groaned under the assault.

'For God's sake, Mum,' Zoe said, following me out on to the leads and holding a hand out for her mother.

'No. It's too dangerous,' Helen Oxenhope said. 'And if we leave now we'll never get our picture back.'

'They're not interested in your stolen picture,' I said. 'You said so yourself, Zoe. They've got another agenda.'

Zoe went back inside to try to coax her mother out. 'Please, Mum. John will help us get it back.'

'We're safer here.'

Another heavy charge against the door made it bend inwards. The architrave was already cracked opposite the lock. I reckoned it would last a couple of minutes, tops.

'Mrs Oxenhope, Zoe… it's your last chance,' I shouted. 'Come on.'

'They're criminals. We're not criminals,' Zoe said, holding her mother's arm trying to drag her to the window.

'But they're helping us get what we want. We've got to stay. There's no option.'

'Mum!'

Helen Oxenhope stayed where she was and Zoe turned to me. 'I can't leave her. If she won't come, you go. Help us from the outside.'

As Zoe begged her mother to leave one last time, the lock gave and the door crashed open.

'Call me,' I shouted to Zoe as I disappeared on to the roof and Duggan and Red T-shirt careered into the room.

I scurried around the edge of the roof looking for a way down. I'd gone round three sides of the rectangle and was wondering if I'd got myself in a place from which there was no exit when I saw an iron service ladder. It was screwed to the brickwork of the house and led vertically down to the flat roof of a one-storey extension. It was old and rusty, but I didn't hesitate and swung a leg over the parapet. I'd only gone two rungs down when one of the retaining screws pulled out of the wall and the ladder swayed back. I took my feet off the rungs, clamped them outside the ladder sides and slid down to the roof below.

As I landed, Duggan and Red T-shirt appeared above me. Red T-shirt climbed on to the ladder and immediately gave an anguished cry. His weight had torn out a second screw and the upper section of the ladder swayed back, two feet from the wall.

'Spenser!' the big man yelled. 'Help me. Hold the ladder.'

'Just get yourself down there, Craig. You big wuss,' Duggan said. He was more interested in using my dropped Maglite to scan the flat roof to find me. The beam lit me up, still looking for a way to the ground. Duggan pulled a gun and I squeezed behind a buttress as he aimed and fired. The bullet kicked up gravel from the flat roof and I heard Helen Oxenhope scream from inside the bedroom.

I leaned over the roof looking for a place to jump and saw a dark box-like shape on the ground beneath. A useful landing zone. I swung my legs over the roof and dropped easily on to it. The dog's kennel.

Duggan had come down the iron ladder himself on to the flat roof and, as I ran through the garden and vaulted over the brick wall, he fired twice. But it was dark and the range was too long for accuracy with a handgun. I heard the bullets zip into trees. I reached the car and drove off. But after a short distance I stopped. I checked nobody was hunting me and got my scanner from its metal box in the back of the car. I wanted to get some tracking information on Zoe's phone. There was only one signal coming from Birchfield Place, but it was an anonymous burner. I'd seen Zoe's phone in the pub. A high-end smartphone with a pink backplate. I guessed Duggan and Craig had forcibly removed both Zoe's phone and her mother's before I'd arrived.

As soon as I was on a main road, I called Tanya. She answered curtly.

'You're still at work,' I said.

'How do you know?'

'The way you answered. Brusque. Efficient. You don't let personal things intrude into office life.'

'Well... I suppose I don't.' She sounded thrown by what I said.

'Has no one mentioned that before?'

'Well...' She sounded even more thrown.

'I'm not complaining,' I said. 'Just pointing it out.'

'You mean, like for future reference? Thank you.' She paused and her tone relaxed. 'So... how are you?'

'You're alone?'

'At the moment, yes...'

'I'm driving up the A23 having just been shot at by an ex-police officer I used to work with.'

'Jesus. What's going on?'

I gave her a summary of the last few hours. But I didn't mention Hayden. The word had a bad effect on her, made her frightened and suspicious and she clammed up. I would wait until I had specific names.

She said, 'They claim the Prime Minister stole the Vanessa Bell picture from them? When was this?'

'Don't know. But it explains why he wanted to pretend it was a fake or copy. And there's this government car involved as well. It's crucial we talk to the PM as soon as possible.'

'I've been trying to fix something since we got back from Broadway.'

'Is he being evasive?' I said.

'No. But he's under pressure. I've never seen him so tense.'

'A revolt in the cabinet?'

'That's part of everyday government and he copes fine. But there was a long one-to-one the other day with people I didn't know. People outside government. I asked Lyle Brabant about them and he said it was a party funding discussion so nothing I should be involved with.'

'Did you believe him?'

'Why do you say that?'

'If the Prime Minister lied to us about that painting, he could certainly lie about other things. More important things.'

There was a long pause. And her tone of voice changed. 'Yes, I think that could be a fair assessment of the situation.'

I twigged at once why her tone had gone formal. 'Someone come into the room?'

'That's correct. I suggest we reconvene this conversation at an early opportunity.'

'Later this evening?'

'I've probably got a window around then. We could assemble at the… the Grid. I think you know that place.'

I smiled to myself. 'Grid Reference SU968868. An excellent choice. Say ten o'clock?'

'That's good for me. Thanks so much for calling.'

She wasn't a bad actress, Tanya. I could see her as an undercover agent.

I dropped into my house first. Uxbridge isn't far from where Tanya lives and I needed to clean off some of London Underground's grease, dirt and oil as well as the mud, brick dust and dog hair from Birchfield Place.

Showered and in fresh clothes, I was at Tanya's house by 10:15. She was still in office clothes, but had at least condescended to ditch her heels. The inside of Tanya's house surprised me. Everything was painted white, there were white blinds on the windows and the hardwood flooring was in pale limed oak – as near white as timber can be. But there were no carpets, no rugs, nothing on the walls and the house was almost empty of furniture.

'Just moved in?' I said.

'Been here a year. Sorry it's so bare.'

Bare was an understatement. 'It feels like an art gallery – before they've put any pictures in,' I said. 'Plenty of potential though.' The kitchen looked unused. Oven, fridge, freezer, microwave, toaster; all gleamed in showroom condition. A sparkling food processor even had the manufacturer's tag still dangling from it. One room had a glass and chrome dining table and four matching, never sat-upon chairs, one still with plastic wrapping on its legs. Another room had a solitary desk and swivel chair. The living room had a large TV and a beautiful six-seater sofa. Nothing else. No books. No music. No art.

I wandered round the bare, echoey rooms, surprised that someone with Tanya's vivacity and personality could live like this.

'Always at the office?' I said.

'Well, sort of,' she said. 'Embarrassing isn't it?'

I shrugged. 'Everyone has different lives. Makes different choices.'

She opened the nearly empty fridge and took out a bottle of Chablis. She expertly removed the cork using one of those 'waiter's friend' corkscrews that confuse many people and poured two large glasses. Very large glasses. There was little left in the bottle when she put it down.

I saw she'd put a plaster on the wrist she'd hurt in Pilcher's house. The plaster was small and neatly applied but on Tanya it somehow looked gross and out of place. We sat side by side on the plush sofa. I was glad I'd changed my clothes otherwise I would have been forced to sit on the floor. Though I probably would have been too grimy even for that.

'So what's going on?' I said. 'This secret meeting.'

'It wasn't officially secret, but nothing's being said about it and no one knows what's going on. Even the diary secretaries.'

'Who was involved?'

'Just the Prime Minister, Brabant and a third party.'

'Brabant's Education Minister. Surely education isn't top secret.'

'I don't think it's about education. Fresnel and Brabant go so far back he often gets involved in things which are not part of his brief. The PM trusts him totally.'

'You mean like…' I groped for the right word. 'What did they call it when Elizabeth the First had special mates as ministers?'

'Favourites. Yes, it's a bit like that. I think Brabant himself would rather be more independent. He gets flak from other ministers and in the press.'

'Who were Fresnel and Brabant seeing?'

'Nobody knows. The guys arrived by the back door. Through the garden gate from Horse Guards so few people actually saw them.'

'And nobody knows what they were discussing?'

'Just lots of rumours.'

'Like…?'

'Rumour number one: because of the museum and gallery demos Fresnel has done a U-turn on "cultural repatriation" and is going ahead to send back items from national collections.'

'So the Greek Ambassador was on the phone straight away about the Parthenon stuff?'

Tanya gave me a sardonic grin. 'Bullseye. Plus other ambassadors. And people from the Louvre, the Rijksmuseum, galleries in Berlin, Brussels… not to mention gallery people in the

UK. But it's almost certainly not that. The person he was seeing didn't look the type somehow.'

'You've seen them?'

'Only in the corridor. One principal and two assistants. Or minders. They were brushing past trying to avoid eye contact.'

'And they didn't look like museum people?'

'Not at all. The principal's suits and shoes were too expensive. His shirt was hand-made.'

I quirked an eyebrow. 'You got all that from a brush past?'

'I can tell,' she said with a look that dared me to doubt her judgement. I bet she could tell. Her taste in clothes was impeccable and she had a forensic way of looking at things. She would have been a good detective as well as an agent.

'I'm glad I've never asked you to analyse my clothes,' I said with a smile.

She came back immediately. 'But your clothes are perfect for you. They're you, exactly.' I looked at her, startled she'd already studied me in sufficient depth to break down my character traits and critique my clothes. Then she realised she'd betrayed an interest in me over and above the purely professional. She blushed, pulled her legs tighter together and sat up even straighter on the sofa.

I smiled at her embarrassment but chose to ignore what she'd said and went on quickly. 'So what's the second rumour?'

'That they're American and Swiss drug firm people. Fresnel is going to privatise the National Health Service.'

'There'd be barricades on the streets.'

'Yes, certainly. But the clothes thing sort of matches. They're rich players. And not British. The third rumour is a privatisation of local government.'

That sounded even crazier. 'How would that work?'

'Don't know. It's a new one on me. And I can't see how it would save money. Councillors are unpaid anyway. Unless he was planning to abolish a whole section of local government and run it centrally.'

I took a gulp of the wine and lay back on the sofa. She also leaned back then pushed her legs out straight in front of her and flexed her toes. I could see bright red nail varnish through the tights which she habitually wore. She toyed with the emerald pendant round her neck.

'You do relax occasionally then?' I said.

She smiled. 'Of course.' Then I saw a pang of guilt cross her face. An innate concern that relaxing while discussing work was wrong. So she sat up again and resumed her upright pose, with legs together and drawn hard up to the sofa. 'What do we do next? Are you going to rescue the women from that house?'

'The mother wouldn't come with me. She seems to believe Duggan and co can help her cause.'

'But what does Duggan want? Or the people that Duggan is working for – what are they trying to do?'

I shrugged and shook my head. 'That's top of tomorrow's list.' I finished the glass of wine and put the glass on the floor. I stood up. 'I'd better be going.'

'Another drink?' Tanya stood up too.

'Better not. I won't be fit to drive.'

Our eyes met and we smiled at each other. Then I moved to the front door, opened it and turned back to Tanya.

'It's depressing, isn't it? A prime minister stealing a picture. Secret meetings with anonymous people.'

Tanya moved towards me until she was right in front of me. 'More than depressing. It's frightening.' I looked at her and I saw the fear in her eyes. I reached towards her and put my hands on her shoulders. Unlike the time at Pilcher's house she didn't flinch and to my surprise she put her hands on my waist and moved a step closer.

'I expect you'd like to stay,' she said brightly, as if offering an invitation to tea.

Formal. Cool. Unexpected.

She smiled and our eyes met and held together. I moved my hands to her waist and was about to lean forward and kiss her when she said, 'But you can't. I'm sorry. I'm pretty tired and if any of these rumours get out, I'll be called in to help firefight. If nothing happens overnight, I'll make sure I'm in the office by six thirty. So tonight's not a good night.'

'I understand, of course,' I said. I took my hands from her waist and unconsciously echoed her formality by standing straight-backed in a nineteenth century kind of way.

I was flummoxed by her double reversal of expectation and hardly knew whether to shake her hand, kiss her hand, or click my heels.

Chapter 14

Next morning, I checked newsfeeds and social media and found the leak Tanya had worried about had happened. In fact it was more a flood than a leak. More a dam collapsing. A tidal surge. A tsunami of scare stories, supposition, conspiracy theories, rumours and rumours of rumours.

Several different and indeed conflicting policies were reported as 'being under serious consideration for early implementation by the Prime Minister'. First up was the old chestnut of "cultural repatriation" which he had never put forward as a policy. Long lists of exhibits were suggested in the press for surrender to overseas territories. The Parthenon sculptures and frieze topped the list, followed by the Nigerian Benin bronzes, quantities of Chinese ceramics, Japanese prints, Italian statuary of the Roman period, Indian carvings, Egyptian mummies and sarcophagi, most of the Inuit and other native American collections, all Australian aboriginal items, objects collected by Captain Cook and other explorers from Pacific islanders and thousands more artefacts from all over the country. Pundits claimed there'd be little left in our museums apart from Turners, Constables and the Great Bed of Ware. If you're wondering, Ware is a small town in Hertfordshire. The sixteenth-century bed is an interesting monster, but if the Parthenon scores 10 for all-time cultural importance the bed might scrape a 1.

The second rumour was that the Royal Navy was to be disbanded. Or alternatively that the Royal Air Force was to be closed down. Or possibly they were to be combined. Destroyers scrapped but aircraft carriers kept on, presumably.

The third rumour was the 'definite plan' to privatise the NHS. Not surprisingly, privatising the NHS was the trending subject and some commentators appeared to think it had already been agreed in a deal with either 'American pharma-cartels' or 'Russian oligarchs' or 'Saudi businessmen.' Fresnel was attacked on all sides for allowing such a deal, even though Downing Street categorically denied all the rumours.

The local government scheme Tanya talked about didn't get a mention. Perhaps that meant it was a definite runner.

The National Portrait Gallery demo also brought more criticism, that even an art-loving Prime Minister was unable to protect the nation's heritage. There was more satire, making fun with Trastivenia, several commentators suggesting it as a suitable place for the PM to retire to, but also more in-depth discussion of what the demos were really about. Conspiracy theory merchants dreamed that Fresnel had organised the demos himself as a way of diverting attention from his planned privatisation of the NHS.

Enough nonsense. I needed facts. I turned to the Oxenhope family. Their surname was thankfully unusual and search results popped up quickly. Zoe's mother, Helen Oxenhope, who was even younger than I thought – only thirty-six – ran an art gallery in the North Yorkshire coastal village of Staithes. It's a pretty, almost Cornish-type, fishing village which has a reasonable tourist trade in the summer months.

Helen Oxenhope's maiden name was Turner. Her mother was Barbara Turner and her grandmother was Margaret Plastow. That explained the wheelchair at least. Helen was born in Brighton on the south coast but her parents then made a significant move. To the village of Firle. Near Vanessa Bell's house, Charleston, and Birchfield Place, where Helen and Zoe were incarcerated.

I checked census returns for Firle, which didn't take long because the village is so small and found that the Turner family were living in the village at the same time as Margaret Plastow, though not at the same address. Now I was getting somewhere.

I looked at the British Museum video again. There was a likeness between the two men and Helen Oxenhope. Were all three related? I went to Oxenhope's Facebook page and there were pictures of her two brothers. They were the two men I had fought at the museum. It was a family affair.

Living in such a small village it was likely that Margaret Plastow knew the Bloomsbury set at Charleston. Her daughter, Barbara Turner, was born in 1945 so she could have known them too. Vanessa Bell died in 1961 and Duncan Grant lived until 1978. But the killer question was where did the Prime Minister fit into all this?

I was interrupted by the helpful Matilda from the Tate again. She'd phoned to apologise for a further delay. Because of the outrage at the National Portrait Gallery, both Tate Britain and Tate Modern had closed temporarily for a complete security review and, because of her membership of the safeguarding working party, she was involved and had to put my enquiry on the back burner again.

With the mysterious visitor to Downing Street on my mind I called my contact at the FCO, Leo Somerscales. Leo's precise job is unclear. He has an unusual roving brief and sits on the Joint Intelligence Committee, so he's able to extract information from many sources. Leo refuses to discuss anything vaguely sensitive on a mobile because, since radio transmissions can be intercepted, he prefers to assume *all* mobile calls are listened to. He knows this is beyond the capabilities of GCHQ or the NSA – just about – but he believes following the rule is good tradecraft. Even though it's time-consuming and a pain in the arse.

But Leo is an ace contact. I was at home, so I used the landline. I explained I'd become a temporary SpAd and thanked him for the reference he'd given Tanya.

'Don't thank me yet,' he said. 'It could be a poisoned chalice.'

Disconcerted by Leo's acuity, I paused for half a second. But he picked up my micro-hesitation.

'In the shit already, are you?'

'Don't worry. I'll sort it.' Then I explained I was interested in certain visitors to Number Ten over the past forty-eight hours. Had he access to the CCTV cameras at the rear of Downing Street?

'Don't tell me someone's nicked a painting from Number Ten, or the Prime Minister is a receiver of stolen pictures...' he said laughing.

'If only, Leo,' I said, hoping my own laugh didn't sound too forced.

'I can probably fix something,' he said. 'Who are you looking for?'

'We have no names. There was one principal and two assistants. The main man was wearing a twenty-thousand-dollar suit and thousand-dollar shoes.'

'American?'

'Maybe, but not necessarily.'

'Does Five know about this?'

'Negative. Nor the Met. Nor the PM.'

'Dangerous territory for a Special Advisor.'

'Maybe. What I'd like is an ID on any or all of them.'

'OK. As usual, no promises.'

The call ended and it was time to go to my lunch with Adam Tresize, the Home Secretary. I had no clue what he wanted and I wondered if the lunch was going to be dangerous territory as well. Tresize's name was Cornish and he represented a Cornish constituency, so he liked to play up the fact that he was free-thinking and different. Cornwall had once had its own language and some harboured a dream that the county should somehow be 'independent' from the UK. Tresize supported, or pretended to support, this romantic but unfeasible notion. He backed underdogs and the underprivileged but Tresize himself was plenty privileged. He came from an affluent background and, unlike Spanswick, had never laboured with his hands. Neither did he have a Cornish accent. His tone of voice was cultured and patrician. He wore perfectly cut suits and frequented upper-crust restaurants like Wilton's. We had his 'usual table'.

'Bit of a local, this place. At least for some of us,' he said. 'Discreet, convenient. Chris Spanswick got a good rate for his son to do some filming here. You know he does something in the film business?'

I nodded. 'A location manager, I understand. Though I'm not sure what that involves.'

'Me neither,' said Tresize. 'Not a world I know at all.' He spoke as if watching films and TV was not something he ever considered doing.

We ate well. A crab and lobster starter followed by roast beef. The meat was taken from a huge joint wheeled to our table on a traditional, silver-plated, domed trolley. I watched Tresize's eyes sparkle as the waiter carved and saw him literally lick his lips. Interesting to see that small pleasures still matter to important people.

An hour went by. We finished an expensive bottle of Burgundy. It was time to ask why he'd asked to meet me.

'Quite simply, I wanted a heads up on all this Trastivenia nonsense,' he said. 'You were at the British Museum and the National Portrait Gallery. Did you speak to those responsible? Any idea what they're up to?'

I assumed my chase at the Portrait Gallery had got reported back to the Home Office through DI Bolt, but I was wary of revealing what Helen and Zoe Oxenhope told me. 'I didn't have a chance to talk to the girl at the Portrait Gallery; she ran off. And the three at the Museum were picked up by car and escaped.'

Tresize nodded. 'Yes, of course. Do you think their actions are connected to the Prime Minister's picture? The one you've been looking into?'

Did Tresize know something? I met his eyes but there was no hint of anything apart from curiosity. I hesitated. My hesitation made Tresize fill the silence.

'I only ask because, putting it simply, there are one or two of us in the cabinet who are a bit concerned how he's become obsessed with this problem picture.'

'I didn't know he was obsessed,' I said, wondering if this was another way of describing what Tanya called being tense and under pressure.

'I didn't mean obsessed in any medical or psychological way. In simple terms, something's playing on his mind. I wondered if you had any leads as to what it might be.'

'I've only had one conversation with him about the picture and he didn't confide in me.'

'Not even art lover to art lover?' Tresize smiled in an unsettling way, as if suggesting there was something improper about liking art or even in my relationship with the Prime Minister.

'I'm an art *detective*,' I said. 'I like art, but I'm not a connoisseur and I can't afford to be a collector.'

'Of course. And if you were to uncover anything untoward concerning this picture, I would simply ask you as a former member of the Metropolitan Police to pass on any information you have.'

'I assure you that's what I do. I spent a while on the phone to DI Bolt at West End Central only yesterday.'

'Yes, of course.' He finished his meal and dabbed his mouth with a napkin. 'That beef was simply excellent.'

'Do you have any suspicions about the picture, Minister?'

'Good God, I know simply nothing about art. I've not been into the National Gallery since I was taken by an aunt when I was ten.' And with a sentence, he condemned three thousand years of culture to the trash file.

'Maybe it's not the picture that's distracting the Prime Minister,' I said.

'I can't believe it's simply politics. He's normally as cool as a cucumber. Takes everything in his stride.'

'Does the name Hayden mean anything to you?'

'Hayden? You don't mean Haydn? The composer.' He wasn't a complete philistine. It was obviously okay in his set to be interested in music.

'Hayden.' I spelt it. 'I don't know if it's a person's name or a company.'

Tresize looked me in the eye and shook his head. 'I don't know anybody or any company with that name. I've simply never heard the name in any context whatsoever. Sorry.'

I nodded and smiled. 'Thanks anyway.' Tresize put the word 'simply' into almost every sentence. A meaningless verbal tic or an indicator of nervousness or deviousness?

'Shame about that dealer man. Pilcher,' he said, adjusting his gold cufflinks. 'If only he hadn't had a stroke he could have revealed everything and we probably wouldn't be having this conversation.'

'Or possibly it suited someone for him to die.'

'Good heavens. What do you mean?'

'He might have had information which somebody didn't want revealed. About the Prime Minister. Or someone else.'

'What kind of information?'

'I don't know. But his death seemed… convenient.'

Tresize looked up, concerned. 'Was it murder, then?'

'You said it was a stroke. I assumed you'd got that from the post mortem.'

'No. It simply came from Lyle Brabant. I've had nothing from the police yet. Do you think it *was* murder?'

'There were no signs of violence on the body, and I haven't heard from West Mercia Police either but, circumstantially, it looked like natural causes. A stroke is likely, though probably induced by some shock or threatening behaviour.'

'I see. Thank you.' He paused and I saw him pondering this, thinking it needed an explanation. 'I wonder how Lyle Brabant got to know.'

'You're not implying he's got a connection to the Prime Minister's picture?'

He breathed in hard and raised his eyebrows. He seemed to be implying almost anything. 'Well, you know how close he is to the PM. Bit of a lap-dog at times. I suppose Lyle got it from him.' Tresize fiddled with his cufflinks again.

'Mr Brabant is something of a star,' I said, to see how he would react.

'Oh yes. Simply a national treasure. But whether he's strong enough for the cut and thrust of politics I'm not sure. That probably sounds simply bitchy but it's important to have only the toughest skins at the top.' He paused to let me absorb this, then continued. 'Oh, this Mr Hayden you mentioned. Did you hear the name from your fashionable friend?'

I furrowed my brows. 'I'm sorry?'

Paint It Blackmail

'The chic civil servant, the cutie from the Cabinet Office.'

'If you mean Tanya Brazil, I didn't hear it from her.'

'You surprise me,' said Tresize with what could be an incredulous smile. 'I understand you are close. But let me give you a warning. Don't get sucked in. She's devious and she wants power. Simply nothing will get in her way and she's left a trail of broken men behind her already.'

I didn't react to this and wondered if Tanya had rebuffed him and he was one of the broken men he referred to. I said, 'Thank you. I'll bear in mind what you said.'

There was an alarm tone from his phone. He picked it up and looked at it. 'Oh dear. I've been summoned back. Sounds urgent. So good to meet you, Mr Kite.'

Tresize hurried out to his ministerial car and was driven away. I strolled down Jermyn Street, puzzling over the fact that Tresize's main purpose in inviting me to lunch seemed to be to sow doubts about Lyle Brabant. What did he mean about not having the strength to be a leading politician? Physical strength? Moral strength? Mental strength?

As I headed to pick up my car, Tanya called. She was in official mode. No pleasantries.

'Can you come over?' Her tone was tense.

'I've read all the rumours. You were right about a leak. Did you get called in last night?'

'No. And it's nothing to do with any of that. The PM wants to see you urgently but it's about something completely different. Something more important.'

'More important? Another dodgy painting? Or he's emptying the museums and giving everything to Trastivenia? Or is it to meet the guy in the expensive suit?'

'Kite. Shut up!' She paused. I could hear her swallow and control herself.

'Sorry,' I said. 'Schoolboy stuff.'

'No, no. I'm sorry… I didn't mean… Look, I can't tell you on the phone. But you're needed right away.'

I hadn't heard Tanya so stressed. Fresnel's anxiety must be catching.

I didn't bother to collect my car. It was less than a mile to Whitehall and much quicker to go on foot. Down Regent Street, through Waterloo Place and into The Mall. With Tanya sounding so frazzled, I ran. Not flat out, but a fast jogging pace. I was at the Cabinet Office in six and half minutes.

In the entrance hall a PA was waiting for me with my Special Adviser pass. I hung the lanyard round my neck and she took me up to Tanya's office. It was as I had imagined: a high ceiling, an extravagantly moulded cornice, but poky and cramped because it was a small subdivision of a much grander room. Tanya was standing in front of her desk, waiting for me. She was immaculately dressed as always in another elegant, slim-fitting dress. She had a slash of bright red on her lips and the Edwardian pendant round her neck. From the doorway her poise and aura of control was unchanged. But as I got closer, I saw she was different. Her face was taut, her eyes were tense.

'Thank you for coming,' she said. 'Sorry for the short notice. Sorry for… you know.'

'What's up?'

She closed the door behind me and we both stayed standing. 'What I'm going to tell you is classified.'

'Of course.'

'Have you heard anything about problems with the Government Art Collection? Rumours from the Yard? Old boy network?'

'Nothing.'

'Good. The PM wants a complete news blackout.'

I raised my eyebrows in disbelief.

'I know,' she said. 'A tall order.'

'What's happened?'

'The Government Art Collection provides pictures for government offices and for embassies abroad.'

I nodded. 'Yes. And commissions new work.'

'Correct. Its holding is about fourteen thousand pictures and sculptures. Well, approximately four hundred of those works have been stolen.'

'Four hundred!' It was a grotesquely large number. Mind-boggling. It would be the largest art theft ever. Anywhere.

Tanya nodded. 'They were quietly removed from the places they were hanging in London and from the central store in Westminster and taken away by the official transporters to God knows where.'

I thought of the maroon Tabard & Spurgeon vans I'd noticed recently. Had I seen part of the theft in progress? 'How was it done?'

'We assume some kind of computer hack. Paperwork was all properly filled out, receipts, dockets, whatever; they were all OK. The transport staff just followed the instructions they were given.'

'Where were the pictures taken to?'

I saw her fingers play with the pendant. The jewels looked like emeralds. They matched her eyes. 'To an address in Cork Street. Supposedly for a special exhibition at a private gallery. But it wasn't a gallery, it was an empty shop with some fake signage. Police raided it a few hours ago and found nothing.'

'What happens now?'

Tanya lifted her wrist to check her watch. It was a chunky man's model. 'There's a COBRA meeting in five minutes. The PM wants you there.'

I nodded. 'Of course. Stolen art. It's what I do.'

Tanya gave a grim half smile. 'Finally on home ground. Well, let's get you to the starting grid.'

I followed Tanya out of her office. As usual she walked fast. But there were no swinging arms or swaying hips. Her gait was decorous, graceful, demure. Walking behind her was the perfect angle to admire her legs, her curves, her slenderness.

Going through the maze-like corridors we passed a group of men noisily discussing not government policy but tickets for a forthcoming rugby international. They saw Tanya approaching and the group melted away into an office. The corridor widened so I moved alongside her.

'Interesting watch,' I said.

She held out her wrist. I saw the chunky gold Omega round her slim wrist and beyond it bright red fingernails. 'It was my father's. I had the strap made smaller.'

'Good knuckle-duster as well,' I said.

'Don't think I wouldn't use it,' she said.

We reached Briefing Room A, she led me inside and we found two chairs together. I looked around the room. I recognised Steve Absalom, the Metropolitan Police Commissioner and Mark Boyes, the Assistant Commissioner who headed up Counter Terrorism Command. There were two women in the room apart from Tanya: one, in her forties with short hair and bland, timeless clothes, I guessed was Claudia Tranter, Director General of MI5; the other I didn't know. Tresize was there, adjusting his gold cufflinks; his urgent text must have been to summon him here. Next to him, in total sartorial contrast, was the Foreign Secretary, Rory Featherstone pulling at a loose thread in his jacket. Then Prime Minister Fresnel sailed in followed by the bear-like Spanswick, his deputy, and Lyle Brabant, who looked even more wiry and worried than he had the other evening.

As soon as they were seated the Prime Minister spoke.

'Before we discuss this outrageous attack on the nation's heritage, I'll introduce two people who are unknown to most of you. Mr John Kite, an art investigator who has been working on a personal project of my own. He's a freelance gunslinger with sharp ideas and an independent way of thinking, so I welcome his views. He's a protégé of the estimable Tanya Brazil, so all power to their elbows.'

Across the table I saw the two from Scotland Yard roll their eyes. Beside me, Tanya drew in breath and I sensed her body tense. Neither she nor I enjoyed being singled out in this way.

'Secondly, Julia Frobisher, Director of the Government Art Collection, who I hope will give us, as it were, a victim's-eye view of the affair. Welcome, Julia, and condolences.'

Frobisher shifted uneasily in her chair and stared at the table top, avoiding any eye contact. It was her name written on the wall planner in Zukovsky's office. Why had he gone to see her?

Paint It Blackmail

Fresnel went on: 'Since we discovered the theft there's been a new development. A ransom demand.' A murmur went round the table. 'This is a copy.' Fresnel held up a sheet of paper and passed it round the table. 'The blackmailers are demanding the sum of five hundred million.'

There were gasps, snorts, exclamations from all around the table. I heard someone say, 'Jokers'; someone else, 'Not fucking likely'; another, 'Got to be kidding.'

'Five hundred million,' the Prime Minister raised his voice, cutting through the reactions, 'or they threaten to burn one picture a day until the money is paid.'

There was another loud reaction from several in the room, especially from Brabant.

'Are the pictures worth that much?' Brabant said.

'Good point, Lyle. Short answer is no. Julia, can you expand...' He turned to Julia Frobisher, whose tortured face reminded me of Munch's *The Scream*.

'Thank you, Prime Minister. The collection has few, if any, world class masterpieces. No Picassos or Rubens or Renoirs. We concentrate, as you know, on British art and art which reflects Britain. And British life.' She hesitated, cleared her throat. 'As to value, art is not a commodity, a picture has no intrinsic value like silver or gold, and its price is not calculated on a supply and demand basis like stocks and shares...'

'Just give us a total figure,' said Spanswick who liked bullet points not rambling speeches.

'Yes, sorry,' said the Collection Director, thrown by Spanswick's intervention and fiddling with her notes. 'An approximate estimate of the value at auction of the pictures stolen is forty-five million. Give or take. Plus or minus... say, twenty per cent, or maybe...'

'Why are the bastards so greedy, then?' Brabant said, cutting her off.

'It's aimed at me personally,' said Fresnel. 'They know my passion is art and they think it's my weakness. They think I'll say we can't afford to have a bonfire of four hundred paintings, so I'll pay them the money.' He paused significantly. 'But that's not the case.'

There were the muted sounds of 'hear, hear' around the table. 'The UK's long-standing policy on blackmail and ransom is well known and I don't propose to alter it, however painful it may be to imagine beautiful artworks in flames.'

'What about the demonstrations in the British Museum and the National Portrait Gallery?' said Spanswick. 'All this Trastivenia bullshit. Are they connected to this?'

'There's no reason to connect them,' said Absalom, the Met Commissioner. 'The ransom note makes no mention of Trastivenia, for instance.'

'You don't think the theft is stunt, like the other incidents?'

'No, Minister,' Absalom said.

'Commissioner, what do we know about how the pictures were stolen?' said Adam Tresize.

'The operations manager of the Collection is being interviewed at the moment. He's the person who controls the movement of artworks around the country and around the globe. Most likely someone hacked into the control system. Sent commands to collect pictures from where they were situated and send them into the villains' hands.'

'What kind of person is he, this operations manager?' said Brabant.

'He's been in the job several years. Reliable. Trustworthy,' said Julia Frobisher.

'Or so you thought,' said Adam Tresize.

'I confess I've never had any suspicions...'

'What about all your drivers who simply carted millions of pounds worth of art to an empty shop? Didn't they see anything suspicious?' said Tresize.

'They're not *our* drivers. They're subcontracted.'

'Well, not your fault, then.'

'I was merely pointing out... All the data and paperwork was correct so they did what they normally do. Followed the instructions on their screens.'

'Simply following orders. Yes, we know where that leads,' said Tresize, looking round the table with a smile.

'That's completely unfair,' said Frobisher, no longer looking as if she expected to be dragged away to the Tower, but angered and emboldened by Tresize's cynicism. 'May I ask something, Prime Minister…? What happens if the ransom isn't paid? If they burn the pictures?'

'Let 'em burn, I say,' said Spanswick and there was a chorus of objections from around the table. 'In your own words they're not masterpieces, no Picassos, Renoirs etc., etc. They're second-class stuff. Nice enough to put on the wall in embassies, cover a damp spot in an office, but no one'll miss them.'

'Chris, I'm sorry, but I have to say that's completely fucking outrageous,' said the Prime Minister.

'You think I'm a philistine, then?' Spanswick looked as if he was about to roll up his sleeves for a punch-up.

'Yeah, dead right,' said Featherstone, the Foreign Secretary. And the meeting fell apart briefly as laughter, caustic accusations and insults flew around.

'Ladies and gentlemen, please,' said Fresnel. 'We are not going to let them burn. If they do, then I for one will be finished. Whatever my achievements in other areas of policy – and I hope you agree there have been achievements…' There were nods around the table, murmurs of 'hear, hear' and a general air of support for the Prime Minister. 'But I am lumbered with the frustrating tag of art lover. If we can't get these pictures back they'll say I failed in the area I knew most about, the area which should've been easiest for me. They'll say I couldn't organise a piss-up in a brewery.'

There was no laughter, not even smiles. Just a silent realisation from everyone that the Prime Minister's reputation and career did absolutely rest on the successful recovery of the stolen pictures. One or two in the room might, of course, want him to fail. Any prime minister has colleagues who will stab him in the back if the opportunity for advancement arises. I glanced around. Every face was a mask of serious concern. No hint of treachery anywhere.

'Prime Minister,' said Spanswick. 'I agree with you, but I can't agree with Lyle Brabant. I can't believe it's so serious. I'm sure it's all a bit of a farce, a diversion. Like the messing about in the museum and the Portrait Gallery. We shouldn't sweat too much about it.'

There was another upsurge of protest at this view and the Prime Minister stopped everyone.

'No. I think the demos in the museum and the gallery are far more serious than anyone's been treating them so far. And that includes the media, the general public and, I'm afraid to say, people round this table. It's not student end-of-term pranks, it's our national treasures at stake. Mr Kite, you're an expert in this field, what's your opinion?'

The Prime Minister turned to me. As did everyone else. Some of them – the police – eager for me to make a fool of myself.

'I think the Prime Minister is right,' I began cautiously. 'The main reason criminals steal art is to give them collateral, something they can trade with other criminals for drugs or weapons. Stealing a single valuable painting is easy and, once gone, it's hard to trace. There's no paper trail, no electronic trail. But stealing four hundred lower value pictures is not normal criminal behaviour. You could say bad criminal practice. How do they store them? Who looks after them? And trying to strike a deal with another villain would be difficult. Like buying a car with sacks full of coinage.'

'You say this is abnormal criminal behaviour, so are we looking for someone who's unstable? Deranged?' said Brabant, leaning forward keenly, his forehead deeply creased. And I thought about what Tresize had said.

'I don't know about their mental state, but I suggest the perpetrators are motivated by politics, not money. The ransom demand may be irrelevant. The real blackmail threat may be for something like a change of government policy.'

I felt a general drawing-in of breath around the table. A nervous shifting about as people were rapidly calculating which policies might be threatened, which could be dumped.

'Have you a scrap of evidence for this?' said Absalom, the Met Commissioner, looking unimpressed.

Tresize ignored him. 'What about hostile action by a foreign power? What do you think, Rory?' he said, turning to Featherstone, the Foreign Secretary.

'No hint of that,' said Featherstone. 'Claudia?'

'SIS are on the case but they've no leads. GCHQ have picked up nothing either,' said the Director of MI5.

'On the other hand, if a foreign power wanted to make us look stupid what better way than stealing these pictures?' Spanswick said, thumping a huge fist on the table. 'After all, they've shown that security in two of our most important museums is not fit for purpose.' Spanswick was interrupted by a volley of groans and disagreement. He thumped his fist harder. 'Let me finish. The Russians like causing trouble. Destabilising things. They do it because they can. It amuses them to see western countries get their knickers in a twist. And the Chinese are the same. If they can destabilise the UK government, make us an object of fun, a laughing stock, it'll be one up to them. Because that's what the attacks in the museum and the gallery did. Make us look stupid.'

'Chris, I see where you're going, but it seems very left field for Moscow.'

'I agree. Their approach is more brutal. Unforgiving,' said Foreign Secretary Featherstone.

'Nevertheless, all embassies and SIS should be on full alert for any murmurings,' said Fresnel.

'I think Chris Spanswick has a point,' said Lyle Brabant, surprising the Prime Minister. 'It could well be a plot to undermine the government. To make us look idiotic. I saw the crowd at the National Portrait Gallery on YouTube – they were all laughing. But it's not a laughing matter. Next, they'll be taking stuff off the walls in broad daylight. Taking the Crown Jewels from the Tower.'

'There's simply no need for panic, Lyle,' said Tresize.

'I'm not panicking. But following on from what Mr Kite said, I think the Government itself is in danger.' Brabant's weather-beaten tropical complexion was looking strangely unhealthy.

'That sounds like panicking to me,' said Tresize coolly, adjusting his cuffs again, looking from Brabant to me.

Brabant was annoyed. 'Let's hear your assessment then, Adam.'

'We should simply do as the PM said. Not pay the ransom.'

'That's a given,' said Brabant. 'What else?'

'The police will simply do their job and find the perpetrators,' said Adam Tresize.

'We hope so, but I think MI5 should be actively searching for some... I don't know, home-grown revolutionary cell or militant organisation.'

'That sounds very 1960s,' said Spanswick.

'I don't think so,' said Brabant.

'And what do you know about the 1960s, lad? You weren't even a twinkle in your mother's eye.'

Brabant threw his pen down on the table and leaned back in his chair, pissed off.

'If it's not a foreign government trying to destabilise us it could be a home-grown revolutionary group...' said the Director of MI5.

'Thank you,' said Brabant.

'...but we have no indication of any such thing.'

'Well, keep looking,' threw in Fresnel.

'Are there any leads at all? Any suspects? Any lines of enquiry we should know about?' asked Rory Featherstone, who was tightening his tie, having just realised it was two inches below his collar. I looked at him, but he was looking at the police officers.

'Not yet,' said the Commissioner. 'The blackmail note was sent through normal mail to the Prime Minister. It's clean of any DNA and, as you can see, has been printed not by computer but by some antique process which we don't yet fully understand...'

Just then, the blackmail note which was being passed around reached me. I was shocked at what I saw and reacted immediately.

'Prime Minister, I think I can explain,' I said. 'It's been done on a child's toy. A so-called John Bull Printing Outfit.' Heads turned. 'I'm too young to have had one but they were popular in the 1950s and 60s. Maybe Mr Spanswick had one. You can buy them on eBay or in vintage shops.'

'My God, you're right,' said Tresize, grabbing the sheet from my hands. 'I think my older brother had one.'

'So you're looking for a criminal who likes playing with kids' games,' said Spanswick with a chuckle.

Paint It Blackmail

Claudia Tranter from Five came in assertively. 'More likely a cunning and aware criminal,' she said. 'As electronic detection and surveillance gets ever more sophisticated, criminals are turning back to cruder methods. Typewriters, for instance. Perversely, they're less easy to trace than emails. And unless we actually find someone with inky fingers in possession of this John Bull Kit it'll be bloody hard to pin it on anyone.'

I wondered if I should say more. There was the John Bull Printing Kit at Birchfield Place. I had the address in Finchley. The names of Zoe Oxenhope and her mother and grandmother. The wheelchair and Mrs Plastow. I also had Spenser Duggan. But how did any of it connect together? And I'd passed it all on to Bolt in any case. Before I could say more the Met Commissioner filled the silence.

'You should know that officers yesterday attended an office in Clerkenwell because of a possible link to the leaflets concerning the Trastivenia demonstrations and found two bodies there. Both murdered...'

A chill went round the room.

'... Though we don't know whether these people have any connection with the theft from the collection.'

'It's possible,' I said, thinking of the Post-it note, 'because they were both IT experts. They could have had sufficient skill to hack into the control systems of the collection.'

Fresnel was surprised by my interruption. 'Mr Kite, you know about these people?'

The Commissioner looked at me. 'The original information came from Mr Kite's own enquiries. He had... penetrated the office and passed information to Scotland Yard.'

'Excellent work,' said Fresnel. 'Do you have other leads which the police don't know about?'

'Well... nothing as concrete...' I was squirming with indecision.

'Let me put it another way. Have you any... theories, ideas – even wild, radical ones – which might show us the way forward, help us think outside the box?'

My mind was buzzing. There was the Prime Minister's stolen painting. But surely Zoe's family couldn't have masterminded a mega theft like this.

'I'd like to think so... but ...'

I felt a nudge in the ribs from Tanya. I turned and saw her scribbling a note which she put on the table in front of me: *Don't mention painting.*

'...but they're not fully formed yet...'

There was another buzz around the table and the Met Commissioner intervened.

'Mr Kite, is it true you were involved in an accident at Highgate underground yesterday evening?'

'Correct. A girl... fell on the line. I helped her.'

'You acted bravely, I understand, but you also refused medical attention, in spite of an ambulance being on hand to take you to hospital.'

'Yes. But I felt and feel perfectly well. I didn't want to trouble the doctors and nurses.'

'Are you sure you're fit? Not suffering from shock?'

'Certainly not.'

'I'm sure you know about post-traumatic stress disorder; is it possible you are suffering from that? Even though you believe yourself to be well.'

'I'm fine.'

'Is it true you underwent sessions of psychiatric counselling when you were a teenager?'

'No it's not. I refused counselling.'

'Like you refused medical care yesterday.'

'That's all irrelevant. What are you driving at, Commissioner?'

'Just trying to evaluate how reliable your opinions, theories and ideas may be. Even when they are... fully formed. Whenever that may be.' He and the Assistant Commissioner grinned at each other.

'I think you've made your point, Steve,' said the Prime Minister. 'Mr Kite seems perfectly well to me. Anything to add, John?'

'I won't speculate...'

'Good,' said the Commissioner quietly.

'...but I traced the girl at the National Portrait Gallery to an address in East Finchley. She was the girl who fell on the tracks. Her name is Zoe Oxenhope. DI Bolt at West End Central has the details.' A buzz went round the table. There was no reason not to mention her, but I held back on Birchfield Place. Was I grandstanding? Withholding evidence? The police had more resources than me. They could find her wherever she was. 'And what I'll say further is this threat to burn pictures seems… fanciful. It's play acting.'

Foreign Secretary Featherstone was surprised by this. 'How can you be so sure? There's millions of pounds of art at risk here.'

'Given how cheap high-quality colour printing is, if the criminals want to create some kind of spectacular to unsettle the government, or the country at large, it would be easy to do so by burning prints they've had produced, not the real pictures. And there's a further point. If they do have a bonfire of art, even a bonfire of art prints, that bonfire might remind people of atrocities like book burning in Nazi Germany. Which would put the government firmly on the side of good. Upholding liberal values.'

'Well said. All works of art are unique,' Fresnel said. 'They all say something about us as humans and the world we live in. Even the blandest, most hackneyed work. They are all valuable. Don't you agree, Mr Kite?'

'I do, Prime Minister.'

'Excellent. So, please continue to work closely with the Police Service. And gentlemen, please give Mr Kite every assistance. Solve this case and you'll get a medal,' said Fresnel.

'And if you don't, you'll never bloody work again,' said Spanswick with a grim laugh.

Chapter 15

The meeting broke up soon afterwards. The Prime Minister tried to end on an upbeat mood and expressed confidence that the police and security services would sort everything out quickly. Spanswick, his deputy, was more pessimistic, suggesting lines of dialogue should be opened with the blackmailers. This view was rejected. I was surprised at the lack of concrete decision-making. Few of those present were actively trying to move the investigation forwards.

As we all moved towards the door both the Met Commissioner and Claudia Tranter, the MI5 Director General, steered me into a corner.

'Don't try and be a fucking superhero on this, Kite,' said the Commissioner. 'I know you've got a couple of high-placed friends inside the Service who look after you and who you leech off, though God knows how they allow that, but don't try and go it alone. And if you do get a lucky break and find something, don't keep the information from us. OK?'

'No reason I should.' I kept my voice as light as I could and gave him a half smile. He didn't like that. Nor did the MI5 woman.

'Steve's right,' said Claudia Tranter. You may be Fresnel's blue-eyed boy at the moment, all arty-farty together, but things can change quickly. And even his position's not secure. All these rumours about hare-brained schemes he's considering. Selling the country down the river by the sound of it. I don't see him lasting beyond Christmas.'

They both gave me looks as if I was something they'd brought in on their shoes and marched out.

Tanya was waiting by the door. She didn't say anything, just gave a flick of her head to indicate I should follow her. And back we went through the corridors towards her office. We didn't speak and we went in single file, me in the rear. I took my mind off things by admiring Tanya's backside as she walked ahead in her clingy dress.

Like that royal wedding when the sister stole the show because of the shape of her bum.

We reached her room, still without talking. We went in, she shut the door, then stood only inches in front of me and spoke in a hushed but urgent voice.

'Are you sure you should've said so much in there?'

'You mean the civil service way is to keep your mouth shut and wait for orders?'

'Not at all. But sticking your head above the parapet is dangerous.'

'You mean I'm only a freelance temporary SpAd who ought to know his place.'

'What I'm saying is it's not a world you know. You need to be careful.'

'I can handle the coppers. The Met Commissioner was bloody insulting, asking me about what I did or didn't do when I was nineteen.'

'I didn't mean the police officers.'

I looked at her, understanding the implications of what she'd said. 'Are you saying not everyone in that meeting is on the same side?'

'All I know is there's something odd going on and we need to be discreet. Politicians stick together – until it suits them not to.'

'Is it something to do with the guy in an expensive suit?'

Tanya said nothing.

'Or this Hayden project?'

Tanya said nothing.

'You've got to tell me what it is.'

'I can't.'

'When something explodes, or people are killed, it'll be too late to explain.'

Her eyes turned sharply to mine. They were like lasers, tense, focussed, on guard. Her forehead was creased with tension. She opened her mouth to say something then thought better of it and her head slumped down. Then it shot up again and her eyes found mine. She was breathing hard.

'All I'll say is: be careful, Kite. They don't take prisoners.'

Then she relaxed and whirled away, her long hair flying. She perched on the edge of her desk, shoulders unusually slumped, her head bent towards the ground, breathing hard. Neither of us spoke or moved for a couple of minutes. Her breathing normalised, then still looking down she said in a quiet, casual voice, 'Do you fancy eating?'

Her change of tone as well as subject caught me out. Lunch didn't seem long ago, but it was dark outside. 'What's the time?'

She held up her wrist and pointed the Omega towards me.

'It's a quarter past eight. You may have had a blow-out with Tresize but in the last thirty-six hours I've only had a yoghurt and a cheese and tomato sandwich.'

'And a nice glass of Chablis.'

She smiled. 'I finished the bottle after you left.'

'Three courses for you then.'

We left the Cabinet Office by the main entrance. Tanya strode to the kerb and hailed a taxi. One stopped immediately and Tanya gave an address in Bloomsbury.

The cab set off down Whitehall and we sat without speaking for a few moments then Tanya turned round and looked through the rear window. I gave her a look, but she said nothing. As the cab entered Trafalgar Square and headed for the Strand she turned round again, scrutinising the traffic behind us.

'What's up?'

'You'll think I'm loopy, or hallucinating but …'

'You think someone's following you.'

'How did you know?'

'The way you kept looking behind was a bit of a clue.'

She gave a little gasp. 'You don't think I'm imagining things?'
'Have you taken any counter measures?'
Her face wrinkled. 'How do you mean?'
'Villains call it dry cleaning.' As the cab went into the Strand, I leaned forwards. 'Change of plan, please, driver. We're going to Covent Garden. Could you drop us on Henrietta Street?'

I glanced through the rear window. Behind us was a truck, a moped with one of those big Deliveroo food boxes on the back, and several cars. But neither the Jaguar I followed to Birchfield Place nor any BMWs. The cab turned off into Southampton Street and then went left into Henrietta Street.

'The far end please,' I said to the cabbie.

We reached the junction with Bedford Street and the cab stopped. As I paid off the driver I looked behind. The Deliveroo moped turned into the street and slowed down. He might be delivering a takeaway. He might not.

'We'll run,' I said to Tanya. I half thought about grabbing her hand. But I didn't want to embarrass her and she was keeping up with my fast jog in spite of her heels.

We legged it up King Street then turned into Rose Street and the dark alley that runs alongside The Lamb and Flag pub. It's the one with the sign that tells you about an attack made on the poet John Dryden on that spot in the seventeenth century. Our footsteps reverberated in the enclosed space.

We emerged from the alley unscathed and were in Floral Street. Almost at once we cut through another pedestrian lane, Conduit Court, into busy Long Acre. There was a convenient taxi for hire coming along behind us.

'Shall we?' said Tanya.

'Ignore it,' I said, and she gave me a look.

It's a classic rule of tradecraft – one of Leo Somerscales's favourites – that you should never take the first taxi that presents itself. We slowed to a fast walk and approached Covent Garden Underground. It's an unusual station. There are no escalators. Only lifts and stairs. Choosing the elevator means waiting, then once you're inside the cage there's no way out until you get to the bottom.

The Victorian spiral stairs are wide and spacious, therefore, I reckon, safer. Obligatory health and safety signs warn those with heart conditions not to use them. It's a long way down. 193 stairs.

'Stairs OK?' I looked at Tanya and held out a hand, not offering assistance, just pointing the way.

'Of course.' She started to run down. I charged after her. The Vibram soles of my leather shoes smacked rhythmically on the iron and concrete steps while Tanya's heels produced a sharp rat-a-tat in a similar tempo. Our crashing percussion echoed up the lofty metal corkscrew that is the staircase.

On the platform we took the first eastbound Piccadilly line train. I stood by the closing doors, watching for anyone boarding at the last minute. I saw no one. We stayed on the train for two stops and got off at Russell Square. I led Tanya to the trains going back in the opposite direction.

We got on the first train and I told Tanya to stand by the doors. As the doors-closing warning tone started I touched her elbow and we jumped back on to the platform as the doors slid shut. I looked along the platform. It was deserted. No one had followed us off the train. The train pulled out and as a double check I watched each carriage go by.

'Look,' I said, nodding towards a carriage three behind the one we'd been in. Spenser Duggan was standing by the doors looking out, the white streak in his hair standing out in the harsh lighting.

'The guy with the thick black hair and the white highlights? Yes. I've seen him before. How did he…?'

'It wasn't him on the moped. Though maybe they're working together. But I didn't see him at Covent Garden. He's good.'

'But you're better.' It was a statement, not a question. Tanya's eyes rested on me a moment longer than normal.

I shrugged. 'Let's hope so. But he's dangerous. A killer. And this was first year stuff. Basic tradecraft. The only smart bit was ditching the first cab then crossing into Floral Street. Anyone tailing us in a vehicle couldn't have followed because of the one-way streets.'

We took a taxi to the address Tanya had given earlier. It was Pizza Express in Little Russell Street.

'Let's hope the man on the moped wasn't delivering food from here.' I said.

'Did you know this was the first Pizza Express restaurant in Britain?'

I didn't. But I liked it that Tanya knew.

'I come here quite a bit. I've got a place around the corner.'

'I thought you lived in Hedgerley?'

'Yes, but I've got a *pied à terre* as well. A studio flat for late nights.'

'Classy. But expensive.'

'Courtesy of an inheritance like yours.'

'I hope it wasn't like mine.'

'What?'

'Never mind. Look, if you think you're being followed this isn't the most sensible place to come for a confidential chat.'

Tanya saw my logic and looked cross with herself. 'Yeah. Dumb,' she said, hitting her forehead hard with the palm of her hand.

'Don't worry. I'm sure it'll be fine.'

She picked up my throwaway tone. 'That sounds like a line from a disaster movie... "I wonder what this switch does..."' I smiled.

Even in the casual ambience of a Pizza Express, Tanya kept her straight-backed elegance. Her legs neatly crossed. Her hands resting on the edge of the table. Her table manners were delicate and precise. Her style would not have been out of place in *Downton Abbey*.

The food and drink came quickly and for a while we sat in silence. Then I had to voice a worry.

'I saw some pictures being carried out of Lancaster House yesterday. I might have seen part of the robbery in progress. Trouble was it looked so normal. There's no way I could have intervened.'

'Of course not. The porters and drivers *were* behaving normally, carrying out instructions they believed to be genuine.'

'And the one man who controls all that stuff is the Operations Manager?'

She nodded.

'What about the Director of the Art Collection? Julia Frobisher. Any suspicions?'

'Very solid. Old school.'

'So was Philby. And Blunt.'

'If Julia is bent then I'm Lady Gaga.'

'Who gets to have a picture from the collection in their office or meeting room? Someone like you?'

'Not important enough. Next grade up.'

'The Government Art Collection is an odd target. Not high profile. Most of the public aren't aware of it. It suggests there's someone with specialist knowledge involved.'

'Surely not a senior civil servant?'

'Or politician. Don't know. But tell me more about being followed,' I said.

'The guy we saw on the tube was hanging round near my house in Hedgerley. As you know, it's a village. So I know who lives there and who doesn't.'

'Why didn't you mention it last night?'

Tanya shrugged. 'I know I should have, but I didn't want to…'

'Didn't want to make a fuss.'

'Didn't want to look feeble, I suppose.'

I smiled. I'd never think Tanya was feeble. 'What was he doing?'

'Nothing. Just waiting. Senior civil servants like me get some basic training in security. Nothing fancy. Just common sense. So what I saw made me suspicious. Even though I thought he looked like a policeman. A detective.' She saw a reaction in my face and gave me a questioning look. 'You know him, don't you?'

'He was a detective who used to work with me. His name's Spenser Duggan. He was suspended for corruption and he's served time. I hadn't seen him for years till yesterday. But he's not the kind of guy to be the instigator of all this.'

'Who could be, then?'

'What's confusing is there are two different strands. You know about the concept of piggybacking or tailgating?'

'Like gatecrashing.'

I nodded. 'Gaining entry to an electronic system, or a physical place, by pretending you have authority or in the guise of someone else. The museum and gallery protests are simply the work of Zoe and her family. They have a gripe against the Prime Minister for apparently stealing a picture of theirs. They hung their campaign on the idea that various artworks should be returned to foreign countries. The Oxenhopes saw it as a way of shining a light on their own claim. But their protest is purely personal. Quirky, arty, inventive.'

'Yes, agreed.'

'However, the Oxenhopes are being helped by this mysterious outfit you won't talk about. Hayden. They provide transport and are also holding the Oxenhopes against their will. But Hayden has another agenda. This involves harassing Pilcher so he succumbs to something like a heart attack and murdering the two guys who put together the jokey leaflet on Trastivenia. I don't know what they want to achieve. But they've piggybacked on the Oxenhope protest.'

'You don't think the family are anything to do with the picture thefts?'

'No. It's way beyond their means. And they're supporters of the arts, the mother runs a gallery herself.'

'What about the home printing of the blackmail message? You said that toy belongs to the family?'

'I think the gang just stumbled across it and used it.'

'So it's amateurs and professionals all mixed up. Do they want the same thing or different things?'

'All I know is it's to do with the Prime Minister. If you told me about Hayden it might be a help. Is the guy in expensive clothes part of Hayden?'

Tanya paused. 'You might think that.'

'What about the person you call the Salesman that Lyle Brabant referred to? There was a Chinese diplomat expelled this week. Is that him? Is he part of the gang?'

Tanya bit her lip, uncrossed her legs and put her elbows on the table. Then she lay her chin in her hands. Normal behaviour for many, but extraordinary for Tanya. She stayed like that for a minute at least. Then she took a swig from her wine and resumed her normal straight-backed posture with her hands on her lap.

'He was trying to persuade the Government to adopt various policies which would harm the UK.'

'And make a fat profit for him?'

'Quite probably.'

'Like privatising the NHS?'

'Like that. But not that.' She paused again. 'As for the rest... I'll tell you when I have to.'

'It may be too late then.'

'I'll make sure it's not.'

I looked at her, disappointed. She saw my expression.

'However much I respect you, value your contribution and so on, there are some barriers I can't cross. Does that make sense?'

'Not entirely. But I respect your... loyalty, dedication to the government.'

Tanya pulled a face. 'God, you make me sound a right fucking priggish jobsworth.'

I smiled.

'I also respect your athleticism. That girl Zoe is nifty, but so are you.'

'What?'

'You move fast. Run well.'

She smiled and relaxed. 'You mean I don't run like a girl.' There was a caustic grin on her face. I said nothing. 'If we don't run like men it's because of years of conditioning by wearing long skirts or short skirts and heels.'

I said nothing. What could I say?

She went on. 'Were you testing me?'

'No. Even though you tested me on navigation.' But I like women who can take care of themselves.

'Did it surprise you I could jog a few hundred metres without needing oxygen?'

'A bit. Only because normally you look so serene. So formal. Composed. Like now, sitting in this restaurant.'

'People have told me before not to be so strait-laced. Look like you're having fun, they say. Or, take that stick out of your arse and relax. But it's how I am. If I'm running, I run fast. If I'm dancing, I dance, well... like *Strictly*. If I'm sitting, I sit still and upright. If I'm eating, I don't put my elbows on the table.'

'The only joints on the table should be ones you can eat.'

She smiled. 'Where did you get that?'

I shrugged. 'School maybe. Don't think I'm complaining. Your style is… distinctive.'

'And also good cover. People look at me and imagine I'm delicate. Cut glass or bone china. But I'm not.'

'More… cast iron?'

'Stainless steel, please.' We both smiled. 'Some people say it makes me look stand-offish. Poncey. Snooty. Pretending to be a lady.'

'I think the way you are makes you powerful. Because you're a bit different.'

'Yeah. The freak in the Cabinet Office.' I remembered what Tresize had said about her.

'You're not freakish at all.'

She smiled. 'I suppose that's meant to be a compliment. Am I vaguely normal? On a scale of one to ten, would I rate five?'

I smiled too. 'OK. Try this: you have a great aura of stillness. And there's something sexy in stillness. The Greeks captured it in their statues.'

'You're saying I'm a block of marble?'

I smiled yet again. 'Anything but. Have you seen any Rodin sculptures? Erotic as hell.'

'Really? I've heard of *The Kiss*. I've always thought Rodin was… well, a bit naff.'

'When I was a teenager I was in an art gallery looking at a nude sculpture by Rodin. I realised it was turning me on. And I had to touch it. I waited till the gallery attendant walked away then slid my hand over this bronze woman.'

Tanya's eyes were wide. 'It felt good? You got a hard-on?'

'Well, I'd never touched any real women so it was the best I could do.'

She laughed a warm, genuine kind of laugh. Her mouth opened wide and I saw beautiful teeth and beautiful lips.

Then she composed herself, breathed in deeply and tilted her head to one side. She arched her back a little and pushed her shoulders back, which emphasised the curve of her breasts. She made a serene classical pose with her arms, held it for a few seconds then relaxed and chuckled.

'Not quite Rodin, but artistic nevertheless,' I said.

'Bullshitter.'

The food was finished, the bottle of wine was empty. We were talked out. It was time to go. We paid the bill and sauntered out.

'Which way are you going?' she said.

'I'll pick up a tube at Holborn.'

'We're going in the same direction then.' We started to walk side by side. She turned to me. 'I got the impression you wanted to hold my hand earlier. When you weren't testing me out.'

She didn't miss much. I'm sure she knew I'd like to hold a lot more than her hand. 'It was to... point you in the right direction. Not because I didn't think you could cope.'

'That's OK then.' She smiled.

We walked for a quarter of a mile or so, with a *cordon sanitaire* between us and my hands firmly in my pockets. Then Tanya stopped outside a big Victorian door with numerous bells fixed to the heavily moulded architrave.

'This is my place.' Bell number four was marked Brazil. Her flat was over a shop that sold architectural ironmongery.

'Shall we continue where we left off last night?' Her voice was light and casual.

'You're not being called in tonight?'

'Who knows? But I like you, Kite. And I'm going to embarrass myself now. I'm going to say something I wouldn't say if I hadn't had half a bottle of wine.'

'You had a similar amount last night without embarrassing yourself.'

'Yeah, but tonight I feel like... fuck it, it doesn't matter.' She moved close to me, put her arms round my neck and looked into my eyes. 'Your lovely deep voice makes my insides go *Whiiirrrrrr!* Like a whirlpool.' She giggled.

'Just my voice? You don't care for my face? My body?'

There was a hint of a blush in her face. 'Don't push it, Kite.'

We moved together, wrapped our arms around each other and kissed. Long and deep.

'I hope that bent copper with the hair isn't watching,' she said.

Then we kissed again. And I began to explore her body, as she did mine. Then we broke apart. Tanya's eyes looked deep into mine. 'Have you got some kit?'

I assumed she meant condoms. I told her I had.

'Perfect.' And she opened the door.

Tanya's flatlet was on the second floor.

'Apologies for the mess. I've let the housekeeping go a bit recently,' she said as she led me in. There was no mess at all unless you count a three-day old copy of *The Times* neatly folded on a coffee table and some chrysanthemums in a vase on the verge of wilting. 'Excuse me a second,' she said and disappeared into the bathroom.

The studio flat was a bed-sitting room with a small kitchenette and bathroom. It was as minimally furnished as her house in Hedgerley, but the empty spaces were less apparent because the flat was doll's house small. It was also doll's house perfect. The few items of furniture, a framed print, a large Murano vase in striking colours and the colour scheme itself had been impeccably chosen. The space was an exact reflection of Tanya, an inanimate clone of her, where flesh and blood, clothing and attitude had been transformed into paint and wallpaper, furniture and fittings. The interior was cool, self-assured, fashionable.

The bathroom door opened and Tanya came out. I had half expected to see her partly undressed, even in some cliché Hollywood bathrobe, but Tanya had done her hair, retouched her make-up and was still wearing her emerald pendant and heels.

I smiled at her. 'I thought you were slipping into something more comfortable.'

She smiled, came over to me and put her hands on my waist.

'Some men get off on the unzipping, unclipping, unbuttoning routine. I don't know what you like so I left everything on.' Typical of Tanya to approach sex with the same precision and formality she displayed every day. And then she offered a menu: 'Slow or frantic? Which do you prefer?'

I wasn't expecting her to be like this.

She tilted her head down gave me a femme fatale look through her lashes. 'Surprised?' she said. 'People think I'm hoity-toity but I can also be…'

'Hotty-totty?'

She grinned. 'Possibly even harty-tarty on occasions.'

I laughed and pulled her tight against me. 'What about you? What do you prefer?'

'Just ripping everything off and jumping into bed always feels … vulgar. It's nice to start slow. But sometimes I get so horny I have to rush the ending.' She blushed a little at this admission. I was glad she wasn't always in control.

'We all have the same problem sometimes,' I said. 'But let's start slow.' I reached behind her neck to unclip her pendant.

'That stays on,' she said.

'With pleasure.' So I found the zipper on her dress and pulled it down as gradually as I could. The dress stayed on and I lingeringly slalomed a finger down her back from nape of neck to top of knickers. I felt a thrill tremble through her body.

'Good start,' she said and put a hand on my crotch. 'But I guess it might be quick-quick from now on.'

Chapter 16

I was woken at six next morning by a mind-shattering alarm from Tanya's phone. I sat up to see her, fresh from the shower, doing her make-up in just snow-white underwear and the emerald pendant. That sight would have shaken me awake even if the alarm hadn't. She stood perfectly upright – I nearly said erect, because that was the effect she was having on me – her arms were level with her head and exactly horizontal. One hand held a mirror, the other an eye-liner. I was reminded again of the still concentration of a heron. Tanya's heels were together, feet at right angles. What dancers call first position. I wondered whether she'd done modelling or ballet.

'Why are you up already?' I said.

'The bedside clock goes off at five-thirty. The phone's a back-up.'

Tanya was dedicated, verging on workaholic. I jumped out of bed and reached for her. But she turned and fended me off.

'No time,' she said. But then I watched her eyes travel over my naked body. She lightly prodded my chest. 'You've an ace body, Kite. Rock hard – and I don't just mean… you know. I'd feel sorry for anyone who picks a fight with you.'

'Thank you,' I said, gently stroking her breasts through what looked like an expensive bra.

'Go in the bathroom,' she said, removing my hands. 'I'll be gone by the time you've finished.'

I took a step towards the bathroom but she caught my arm. 'These little scars. They're terrible but… I can't believe I'm saying this, they're weirdly attractive. They look almost designed, like a tattoo.'

'I know. But completely accidental.' Years ago a man I'd been trying to arrest had slashed at me with a vicious oriental sword called a *dadao*. Not life-threatening, but bloody enough. Strangely, the doctor who stitched me up said something similar: 'You can pretend to girls you were in the SAS.'

She let go of my arm and sank down to sit on the bed. She looked thoughtful, a hand smoothing over the duvet. 'I was lying about the clock. I couldn't sleep.' She kept her head down. 'What the PM said in the meeting. It is more serious than anyone thinks.'

'I agree.'

'No one else seems to. Spanswick thinks it's a joke.' She looked up at me. 'You've got to persuade them, Kite.'

I sat down on the bed, next to her, naked as I was.

'Can I, though? It's all vested interests, Buggin's turn, after you my lord...'

Tanya turned to me, suddenly fiery. 'That's not how government works. You know that.'

'It seems like it sometimes.'

'Only if you look at the surface and don't pay attention.' Tanya looked down again, her hand still fiddling with the duvet. 'What you said in the meeting impressed me.'

'I thought it frightened you.'

'It did. That's why I couldn't sleep. You said the blackmail was about forcing a political change.'

'You're thinking of the man in the thousand-dollar shoes?'

She nodded. 'If the country is being held to ransom by the guy I passed in the corridor, that's... well, it's revolutionary. It's also a call to arms.'

I hadn't seen her so worked up, so motivated.

'Yes. And I'm answering the call.'

'You're poking fun again.'

'No.' I held my arms open and clasped her to me. 'I agree with you. It's potentially revolutionary.'

'Yes, I think so.' She rested her head on my shoulder and hugged me back.

'But it's only revolutionary if the Prime Minister or others in the cabinet go with whatever is on offer. They can say no. Chuck him out like the Chinese guy was chucked out.'

She pulled back to look me in the eyes. 'But will they?'

I said nothing.

'That's why you need to keep going on.'

'You trust me more than the Cabinet?'

She shook her head, confused. 'I don't know, at least you don't have any axes to grind. So, keep at it.' It sounded like an annual appraisal. She stood up and continued with her make-up. The calm and contained civil servant again.

I got up from the bed and moved to the bathroom. Having no clean clothes and no razor, I didn't spend long in there. But Tanya had gone when I came out. She'd left breakfast news running on the TV and they were talking about the theft of paintings from the Government Art Collection. The news had broken. It had obviously been leaked because some of the phrases being bandied about were exact quotes from what I remembered the previous evening. For the art-loving Prime Minister to have four hundred paintings stolen on his watch was embarrassing, and it was indeed being compared to someone who 'couldn't organise a piss-up in a brewery'. So much for the secrecy of COBRA meetings.

I watched a report on the operations manager of the Government Art Collection who was taking a lot of flak for failing to prevent the mega robbery, while on Twitter fire-breathing hotheads, who hadn't heard the word libel, were accusing him of active involvement. But he had been interviewed by the police and released quickly. Nevertheless, I wanted to talk to him.

Even if I hadn't got his address it would have been easy to pinpoint where he lived. A posse of photographers, reporters and TV crews were encamped outside the front of his modest Edwardian house in Herne Hill, south-east London. They filled the pavement and overflowed on to the road. Photographers had staked out their positions with camera bags and lightweight step ladders. TV camera crews had set up tripods. A lone uniformed constable stood at the edge of the mob making sure none of the press pack was knocked down by passing traffic.

I walked towards the crowd and recognised someone. It was Lucy Bladon, the TV reporter who'd interviewed me at the museum. She was walking towards the front door, holding a microphone and trailed by a cameraman. She got to the front door, rang the bell and knocked hard. Then she pushed open the letterbox and shouted, 'It's Lucy Bladon, ITV local news. We'd like to hear your side of the story, Mr Vaughan. Record an interview with us and you can say what really happened.' She paused. 'It's a chance to defend yourself, Mr Vaughan.'

She waited. She waited longer. There was no response.

She turned to the cameraman and waved a finger across her throat. The camera operator cut and eased the camera off his shoulder. Bladon turned back to the letterbox. 'I'm putting my card through the door. Just call me. We'll be here.' Then the reporter turned away and followed her camera operator down the front path.

'Should have stuck a wad of fifties through the door, Lucy,' one of the reporters shouted. Lucy glared and gave him the finger.

'She should have stuck her tits through the door,' someone close to me muttered and a couple of his colleagues chuckled appreciatively. I'm glad Lucy Bladon hadn't heard. She'd have stuck her fist through his face. I turned round and saw two photographers equipped for a long wait. They were each munching a bacon sandwich and holding a Costa coffee.

Knocking on Vaughan's door would be a waste of time. I needed a different tactic.

I looked around the street. There were nineteenth- and twentieth-century houses but also more modern blocks of flats. Local authority housing. The nearest block was only six storeys tall but had a feature I could make use of. The emergency stairs at the side of the building nearest to Vaughan's house were encased in glass. If I could access the stairs, I would have a view of the back as well as the front of Vaughan's house. I might see a way to get in and avoid the press.

I walked to the block of flats and saw the entrance to the stairwell was controlled by swiping a key fob. I dug around in my pocket and pulled out a key ring with three different fobs. It's not quite one size fits all for these things, but they're simple devices with few variations. I tried each fob in turn. No result. I looked up to see if anybody was coming down the stairs. They weren't.

'Having trouble?' I looked round. It was a postwoman holding out her own door fob.

'I keep mine next to my wallet. They say the stripe on credit cards can affect them,' I said. The postwoman seemed to accept this and swiped hers. The door opened and she ushered me in. I thanked her and ran upstairs while she delivered post to the ground floor.

From the top floor I had a perfect view. But I'd no sooner got there than I saw movement at the back of Vaughan's house. A rear door opened and a man peered out. He hesitated, looked around, then made a dash for the end of the garden. I could see a gate in the fence which led to a footpath running between the gardens of his row and the houses behind. The man, who must be Vaughan, went through the gate and into the path.

I ran down the stairs, came out of the block and took a pedestrian path at its side which led to the footpath taken by the escaping Vaughan. There he was, only a short distance ahead of me and I followed at a pace which matched his. He looked over his shoulder occasionally but seemed to think I was no threat. We reached a main road with shops and came to a Morrisons supermarket. Vaughan walked across the car park, went into the main door without collecting a shopping trolley and made straight for the in-shop café. I followed, realising the smell of the photographers' coffee and bacon sandwiches had made me hungry. Tanya's flat had been devoid of coffee and anything edible. The only tea was lapsang souchong, which I find undrinkable first thing in the morning. In the café I got a pot of English breakfast and a croissant from the servery. Luckily, the café was busy, so sitting at Dominic Vaughan's table wouldn't feel strange or threatening.

I took my tray over, asked if I could join him and sat diagonally across from him on his table for four. He was about fifty, wearing a blue houndstooth check shirt and a maroon woollen tie with a charcoal V-neck sweater on top. His burnt sienna-colour raincoat was on the chair at his side. He looked nerdy. An older version of Clark Munday. After a few minutes of politely ignoring each other in the usual British way I said, 'I don't want to disturb your breakfast, Mr Vaughan, and I guarantee I'm not a journalist or a police officer.' I passed my card to him.

He said nothing.

'My name's John Kite. I usually investigate art thefts on behalf of insurance companies but I promise I'm not investigating the theft at your place.'

'What are you doing then?'

I explained briefly about the museum and gallery incidents and said I was trying to work out if there was any connection between them.

'Seems unlikely,' he said.

'I agree in principle but there might be some crossovers.'

'How do you mean?'

'Could you tell me how the perpetrators did it?'

'You don't think I…?'

'Of course not. I understand the movement of pictures from the collection is entirely computer controlled. So it seems somebody bugged the system.'

'If it's any use, I'll tell you what I told the police. Couple of weeks ago I had a visit from three men who said they were designing a similar system for a firm in Germany. Not for an art collection but for a company which provided portable toilets to building sites, open-air concerts and so on. They were moving things around in the same way we move pictures around.'

'Who organised the visit?'

'No idea. I was told about it by Julia Frobisher, the Director.'

'I've met her,' I said. 'She seemed very straight. Very pleasant.'

'She is. She'd been asked to organise this fact-finding visit by someone else.'

'Who?'

'She said it came from the top. I assumed she meant a Minister.'

'The Prime Minister?'

'Possibly. She said something like, 'The Government want us to do this.' That was good enough for me. I put my best shirt on.'

'Do you have names for the visitors?'

He shook his head and sighed. 'They all introduced themselves. But you know how it is, people say I'm so-and-so, it sticks for a few minutes but once they've gone... nothing.'

I must have looked let down because he went on quickly, 'I can describe them. Is that any good?'

'Could be.'

'One guy was about forty-five, well built, bit of a beer belly and six foot at least. Not completely bald but not far from it. He was wearing clean, newish jeans and a T-shirt with Charles Babbage on.'

'Charles Babbage?'

'He's the guy – nineteenth century – who had the original idea for a digital computer.'

I smiled. 'Makes sense. He must have had a set.'

'What?'

'He's called Scott Earl. Last time I saw him he had an Alan Turing T-shirt. But with a big bloodstain.'

'Oh, my God. Is he alright?'

'Unfortunately not. What about the others?'

'The guy who seemed to work with him was a similar age but slim and much fitter-looking than his colleague. He had a suit, not pinstripe, one of those business casual things, and a patterned shirt but no tie.'

'His name's Zukovsky. What about the third man?'

'Completely different.'

'Where was he from?'

'Hard to tell. He spoke English well but it was his second language. He might have been Spanish or Portuguese. But he was the one in charge. No question. He didn't say much but the other two deferred to him. And he was wealthy.'

'How do you know?'

'His clothes. A beautiful suit, Savile Row kind of stuff. And his shoes. He looked out of place with the other two. Like he was a film star.'

'You mean handsome?'

Vaughan considered. 'Not particularly. But his hair was smart like his clothes and his skin... well, he looked like a man who pampered himself. Or had people who pampered him.'

'That's helpful. So you described to them how your system worked. Did you leave them alone with your machine?'

He sighed. 'Well, in retrospect, possibly I did. There was a landline call for me and for some reason my extension wasn't working. So I went to another office to take it. Frustrating thing was they'd mixed my name up with someone else and they didn't want me at all.'

'And later you found the reason your phone wasn't working was someone had removed the jack from the socket?'

'Yes. How did you know?'

'You were set up, Dominic. And I'm sure while you were out the three jokers inserted some kind of bug into your system.'

'Which got them in. Yeah, I'm sure that's what happened. They screwed me completely.'

I had to agree.

'What was the name you mentioned first of all?' he said.

'Hayden. That mean anything to you?'

Vaughan thought for a bit, then shook his head.

'Could it be a name you heard, then forgot about?'

He made a sort of guilty-me expression and nodded, seeing my point. 'Possibly. How's it spelled?'

I told him. He thought some more. 'First name? Last name?'

'Could be either. Or a company name. Or nickname'

He thought again and then said, 'Interesting... I can't remember whether any of them spoke the word but I remember *seeing* the word.'

'Where?'

'The man with the Charles Babbage T-shirt had an A4 clipboard, one of those with a PVC cover flap – kind of old-fashioned I thought, for someone in IT, but maybe it was all part of his deception...'

He was rambling like Clark did. 'Go on about Hayden.'

'He opened the flap on the clipboard to take notes and instead of an ordinary lined pad, he had printed letterhead paper. And at the top of the first sheet was a logo. A capital H with the word Hayden in capitals.'

'You saw all this? Are you sure?'

'I said I have good observational recall.'

It seemed too good to be true. Witnesses are notoriously inaccurate on observational details. I worried he was inventing stuff he thought I wanted to hear so I had to be sceptical. Like Tanya's disbelief in my navigational ability.

'Could I test you?' I said.

Vaughan laughed. 'I suppose it will pass the time till the news people get fed up and go home.'

'There was a female TV reporter outside your house this morning. What was she wearing?'

'She's a black woman, late twenties, with ankle boots with a stiletto heel, black knee-length skirt, a white shirt or blouse with a scarlet jacket. She had a gold coloured necklace and gold coloured earrings. Rather lovely brown hair which was well looked after and a wedding ring. Oh... and a radio earpiece in her left ear as well.'

'How could you see the wedding ring?'

'It was on the hand she was holding the microphone with. It was pointing towards my house.' That put a final nail in the coffin of DI Liam Bolt's romantic ambitions.

I felt I'd found a soulmate. Someone with similar memory strengths as my own. 'She called her name out to you. Do you remember it?'

He thought a moment. 'No idea.'

'This logo and letterhead. It seems like it was for show. A visual aid.'

'To persuade me they were genuine? Yes, I guess so.'

Like the Trastivenia flyer. Earl and Zukovsky had been obsessively good at their jobs. But they tried too hard. It was their over-zealousness which led Clark and me to them. And maybe it was the reason they were killed. Hayden, or whoever it was; realised they'd left clues in their work and killed them before they could be interrogated.

I left Vaughan ordering more toast and coffee and headed back to my car. New breaking stories had thinned the numbers of journalists outside Vaughan's house to a rump of the less in demand. Back in the car I opened the laptop and looked for a report by Lucy Bladon to double-check Vaughan's powers of recall. Bladon had done an insert into the morning news show while I was with Vaughan. I found a recording, slo-moed the picture, studied her clothes and saw that Vaughan was spot on, right down to the wedding ring.

Which I took as proof he was right about the Hayden logo on the pad.

On my laptop I clicked to a live news feed and saw a government press conference in progress. Lyle Brabant was standing at a lectern alongside Julia Frobisher, the Collection Director, and they were both having a hard time. The general tone of journalists' questions was that the government had, at best, a laissez-faire attitude to Britain's heritage and, at worst, a fire-sale mentality – in spite of having a prime minister with qualifications in art history.

I was surprised Brabant had been chosen to front the press conference. I understood why the Prime Minister wasn't facing the attack personally and I could see why Spanswick hadn't been chosen, given his 'let them burn' attitude. But Brabant had seemed tetchy in the COBRA meeting and not on top form. Was he ill, as Tresize had hinted? He'd spent years in unhealthy climates: had he picked up some bug?

Then my phone rang. It was Leo Somerscales, my contact at the Foreign and Commonwealth Office.

'Calling on a cellphone, Leo? This must be a first.' My tone was light but his was gruff.

'Sent you a text,' was all he said.

It had arrived while I was watching the press conference and it read: *Can't do on phone. Meet 13:30 St James's Park, southern side / Birdcage Walk. Bring sandwich.*

Wasn't that where movie spies always met each other? I thought that was a thing of the past. But Somerscales was nearly sixty, maybe

Paint It Blackmail

he still lived in the past. Nevertheless, given his concern for security, what he had to say must be hot stuff.

I drove towards central London, grabbed an unappetising-looking sandwich from a petrol station, then found an empty park bench where instructed and was in position by 13:20. I'd known Leo Somerscales for over ten years, having met him when I was seeking a worthy charitable home for some thousands inherited from my parents. I'd funded a development project in Bosnia but had been happy to keep my contribution anonymous and let the British government take the credit. Leo was grateful and, in return, helped my work when he could. Seeing him walk through the park towards where I sat, I noticed how few distinguishing features he had. He was archetypally average. Neither tall nor short, fat nor thin. His hair was a grey-ish brown but he still had plenty of it. His suit was no more than a uniform, dull and chain-store cheap, usually creased. If he was an actual spy, and I was never sure that he was, he was well cast. He was remarkably invisible. Instantly forgettable. Except perhaps to someone with the visual recall of Vaughan from the Art Collection.

'Are you going to eat that?' he said, examining my sandwich in its triangular cardboard with a disgusted face. 'I recommend you double-check the sell-by date.' He then opened a brown paper bag and brought out a tasty-looking granary baguette filled to bursting with salami and Mediterranean vegetables, along with a carton of mango juice, a banana and a large paper napkin.

'If one's forced to picnic, one's got to enter into the spirit of the occasion,' he said, taking the baguette from its wrapper.

Yes, it was all a bit like a spy movie from 1960 and I don't do the play-acting stuff. The debonair insouciance. The extreme understatement. That's what those snobbery with violence heroes did a hundred years ago. 'Just a little local difficulty, old boy,' they'd say, talking about the Russian Revolution.

'You've got an ID for me?' I said, keen to pull his interest away from his overstuffed baguette.

'I have, John. And a warning, too. Stay clear. Don't touch. Highly inflammable. Toxic. As unstable as nitroglycerine. Hazmat clothing to be worn.'

Wow. No understatement there.

'If he's so dangerous why is the Prime Minister meeting him?'

'Several possible reasons. One: because he's too busy thinking about stolen art. Two: because nobody in Downing Street may be across all the information. Three: because he's been pressured into doing so.'

'Blackmailed into the meeting by the threat to incinerate the stolen pictures?'

'I'll leave stolen pictures to you, but you're thinking along the right lines. The Prime Minister is not stupid and could mature into a class act, but someone or something is exerting pressure on him.'

In spite of the autumn sunshine, a chill crept through me.

'You think they're trying to destroy him?'

'Every cabinet contains two or three cut-throat types who are miffed they didn't get the job and think they could do it better. So there are always knives ready to go into backs. *Et tu, Brute* and all that.'

Some more Latin for you. Leo did Classics at university. Naturally.

He went on, 'As to the men on CCTV, I could only ID one. The other two are presumably minders. The one I can name is Clayton Parilla. Known by his enemies – and by his friends – as Gorilla Parilla. He's Venezuelan. Supported Chavez's rise to power and was rewarded with unseemly amounts of the nation's oil profits which went straight to his Cayman Islands bank.'

'Is he anything to do with an outfit called Hayden?'

Leo raised his eyebrows, attacked his baguette with gusto then wiped mayonnaise off his mouth.

'Who told you about them?'

'I just heard the name.'

'Be careful where you mention it.'

'Who are they?'

'They are an amorphous bunch of rich business people, a kind of cartel. Hayden isn't a company name, isn't anyone's name as far as I know. It's a kind of umbrella codename. In the same way COBRA is a changing group of people who only meet when necessary and have no formal structure. These Hayden cowboys set up a new company for each project they undertake, which makes it difficult to track and trace the links. There are one or two billionaire Americans who we think are players, but also a few Russians, certainly some Chinese and Saudis, and probably Mafia involvement. They have no national loyalties and their game is to offer governments what seem outrageously advantageous terms to run sections of the economy. Water supply, let's say, or city buses, or hospitals.'

'Privatisation.'

'It's privatisation, Jim, but not as we know it.' He gave me a grim smile. 'They've undertaken a number of schemes in Africa – running a postal service, or a railway, or supplying electricity – with the result that the services have deteriorated while they rake in big profits. All at a dreadful cost to the nations' citizens and economies. They're also active in Malta where they seem to be trying to take over the entire government.'

'Have they made any deals in the UK?'

'No. And I hope they don't. I'm shocked they've got into Number Ten. But watch your step. Their tactics can be brutal.' Then he indicated my untouched sandwich. 'You haven't touched your lunch.'

'I think I've lost my appetite. But you've given me plenty of… food for thought.'

Leo grunted quietly. 'Think of them as Jaws. A voracious, insatiable appetite. Mind their teeth.'

Chapter 17

As I walked back to my car Tanya texted. The first of the stolen pictures had been burned and a video posted online. Taliban or ISIS tactics.

I sat in the car and watched the pyromania on YouTube. The video started with a small pile of kindling burning quietly on some grassland. Then a pair of gloved hands threw some larger pieces of timber on to the blaze and moved out of shot. The gloves came back in again and held a picture up to the camera so we could appreciate the picture's quality. Then the gloves turned away and put the picture on top of the fire. It started to smoulder at once but to help it on its way the same gloved hands tossed two old-fashioned firelighter blocks on to the picture. Then the conflagration really took hold.

A caption appeared on screen which said: *Sun and Moon, lithograph by Barbara Hepworth*.

I assumed it was a digital copy. A lithograph is a kind of print after all, so it's easier to achieve a good reproduction than it would be with a thickly painted oil. I phoned Tanya to talk about it and also about what Leo Somerscales had told me. His words, like the bonfire, had made an impression and I felt unusually wary. I took a cue from Leo and suggested to Tanya, since I was nearby, it would be safer to talk face to face. In fifteen minutes, Tanya had slipped out of the Cabinet Office and was walking along the Embankment with me.

'So you twisted Leo Somerscales' arm to tell you stuff, and now you want to twist my arm to do the same.'

'No arm-twisting went on. We scratch each other's backs. But he gave me a name – and a warning.'

'Not surprised he warned you. OK, I'll tell what little I know. There was an unofficial, low-key meeting in Davos three months ago. We were invited. We didn't know what to expect. The Hayden people were so obviously toxic we booted them out. And we warned relevant parties like the EU, the White House and Five Eyes SIGINT group that they were looking for an entrée into western Europe and the US. Since then we've learned more about them. They flit about. On multiple passports, I guess. One of them was found to be resident in an embassy in London...'

'The Chinese guy you call the Salesman?'

'Yes. He was at Davos and has now been kicked out of the UK.'

'So how did one of the Hayden team get into Downing Street for a private session with the PM and Brabant?'

'God! When?'

'That secret meeting which meant you couldn't talk to Fresnel about his picture.'

'How do you know?'

'Leo looked at the CCTV.'

'Jesus. Fuck. But the guy I passed in Number Ten wasn't at Davos.'

'His name is Clayton Parilla. Known as Gorilla Parilla.' Tanya made a face. Not her kind of humour. 'Who was at the Davos session from our side?'

'It was a general presentation. There was Rory Featherstone, Chris Spanswick, Adam Tresize.'

'The PM?'

'No. He wasn't there.'

'And you think it's Hayden doing the piggybacking on the Oxenhopes' pictures case?'

'Yes. The next blackmail note might say: We'll incinerate the paintings unless you sell us the National Health Service. Would anyone fall for that?'

'Of course not. But what the hell do they want?'

I had no answer to give and nor did Tanya. Our brief conversation had depressed both of us. We stood side by side for a few minutes, saying nothing and staring at the Thames flowing greyly by. Then Tanya said, 'I'd better get back.' And she hurried away.

The video of the bonfire had no location information. The crooks had naturally disabled that function, but even without, it was a stunning lead. The thieves would not want to transport pictures, or even copies of pictures, around the country so it would make sense for the incineration to be done close to where the pictures were held. The video of the burning picture should let me deduce where it had taken place.

I needed best quality video gear so once again I called Clark and told him I was coming round. Clark's office was much tidier. He must have allowed the cleaners in for their monthly blitz.

He had the burning picture video on screen when I arrived.

'What are you looking for?' he said.

'Anything to give me a lead to the location.'

'Won't GCHQ already have done that?'

'Not necessarily,' I said. 'They're brilliant at aerial shots and satellite pictures, but this was videoed from ground level. Much more difficult. What I want is the big wide shot at the end when the camera pulls right back. Can you fast forward?'

'Hang on,' said Clark. 'There's a brand name visible on the gloves. Right at the start. Interested in that?' He zoomed in on the video to show me. The gloves were a generic kind of protective builder's or labourer's gloves.

'You can get those in any DIY store. I've got some myself. Two ninety-nine.'

He huffed. 'Only trying to help.'

Don't say he was getting moody already. But Clark said nothing else and moved the video on. We saw the fragile picture flare up and disintegrate quickly while the thicker frame remained burning on the ground. After a pause, the gloved hands appeared again and pulled the frame off the fire, broke it into four sections and threw each piece back on to the flames. Then the camera pulled back wider and wider until the fire was small in shot. The owner of the gloved hands had disappeared and we had a wide-angle view of a small fire in the middle of a large grassy field, with the landscape and sky beyond.

There were no buildings visible. No roads. No signage. No obvious clues.

'Just grass,' said Clark. 'Lots of it.'

'Not just grass,' I said. 'Zoom into the field in the background on the left.' Clark did so. 'It's a vineyard. See the rows of vines.'

'Chardonnay? Sauvignon Blanc?'

'No idea. But it means we're probably in southern England. Vineyards are moving further north every year but Surrey, Kent, Sussex, Hampshire are most likely. Can you pan across the skyline?' Clark did so. 'It's strange there are no buildings. We can't be more than fifty miles from London.' I thought for a moment. 'But it could be somewhere like the South Downs National Park. Let's check the sky.'

Clark moved the zoom up to the large expanse of clear blue sky visible in the video. The sun glinted on the wings of a plane turning and descending. Further away another plane was even lower in the sky.

'Boeing 747,' he said.

'Too rural for Heathrow,' I said. 'Too undulating for Stansted. It's near Gatwick Airport.'

'Agreed. Transatlantic planes will come up the Channel and turn left somewhere near Brighton. Planes from Europe will cross the coast a bit further east.'

'Which means that pointy hill there on the horizon is Ditchling Beacon. So we're south of that. Somewhere a few miles from the coast. Somewhere near…'

I stopped abruptly.

'What's up?' said Clark.

'…Somewhere near Lewes. Or near Firle. Which was where Helen Oxenhope lived.'

Clark waved a hand towards the door. 'What you waiting for, Kite? You'd better go and see if she's the one holding the matches.'

I looked at Clark. 'Why her?'

'You know the story of Patty Hearst?'

I didn't. So Clark told me. Patty Hearst was the granddaughter of a US newspaper magnate who was kidnapped in the 1970s by an ultra-left-wing group called the Symbionese Liberation Army. Then she joined sides with her kidnappers and took part in bank robberies. She was arrested, tried and imprisoned but she said she'd been brainwashed by her abductors. This seemed to be true and she was eventually released. Was Harvest Gold or her mother in the same situation?

'And another odd thing,' said Clark. 'People at the time were flummoxed by the 'Symbionese Liberation Army.' They couldn't find any place called Symbio. Just like Trastivenia.'

'And what was it?' I said.

Clark laughed. 'That's your homework.'

An hour and a half later I had left a cloudy London behind and was already on the A23. When I turned off onto a B-road near Hurstpierpoint the cloud had thickened to become that featureless grey canopy called *stratus*. I was aiming for a vineyard that was close to the Gatwick approach flight path, south-east of Ditchling Beacon and on the way to Lewes and Birchfield Place. Was it credible that the Oxenhopes had joined up with Duggan and the Hayden group? Surely not. But in my mind all bets were off.

I found the vineyard – which was on a south-facing hillside, as they always are in northern Europe – and drove round it on minor roads. The ridge of Ditchling Beacon was visible on the horizon and, looking up, I saw a plane emerge from the low cloud on its approach to Gatwick. The narrow roads I was driving on were ancient lanes and over the centuries high banks had built up along them. From time to time I stopped the car, got out and climbed up to look over the hedge tops. I compared the view with a shot on my phone taken from the burning video. The third time I stopped the landscape was similar, but not the same. I drove on further, went uphill, rounded a forty-five degree bend and stopped again by a field gate. I checked the still from the video again: I was getting closer.

I went through the gate, following a bridle path into the field. To my right the land rose gently, while in front of me it sloped down for about a quarter of a mile then turned up again. The fold in the land gave the effect of a secret, hidden valley. Grass was all around me and on the hillside opposite were rows of vines. I followed the path downwards for a few minutes and compared the view once again.

I was there. Away from the path, in the middle of the pasture, was a dark patch. Burned grass, blackened soil and some ash. It looked as if the fire-raisers had tried to clear up afterwards because there were only a few fragments of charred wood left on the ground.

As on the video, there were no buildings visible in any direction so they couldn't have been observed. They had chosen the location carefully. Which suggested local knowledge. I wondered if the pictures were stashed at Birchfield Place and kicked myself for not investigating other rooms in the house when I had the chance.

As I went back to the car, rain seemed imminent. I headed east towards Lewes where I picked up the A26 and saw a brown tourist sign pointing to Charleston. My journey had started with a supposed Vanessa Bell painting and here I was only five miles from the place where it would have been painted. If it was genuine.

My phone rang.

'Kite. Are you near a computer?' It was Tanya. Clipped tones. No warmth. Official business.

'I'm in Sussex. Driving. I've got a laptop. Why?'

'Second picture is going up in flames.'

'Already?'

'This time it's a live feed.'

Events were moving fast. They were ramping up the pressure.

'*Time is running out.* That's what the caption said.'

'Caption?'

'Someone held a piece of paper up to the camera. It looked like it was done with one of those toy printing kit things... John Bull.'

'Where's the fire?'

'It looks like the same location as the first.'

'It can't be. I was at the spot ten minutes ago.'

'You went to where they burned the first picture? How did you...?'

'I worked it out. It wasn't magic. Does the landscape look the same in this video?'

'Almost exactly. It could easily be Sussex.'
'OK. I'm going to find this second fire.'
'How will you…?'
'See you later.' I ended the call and headed back to the highest point in the area: Ditchling Beacon. At eight hundred feet it's only a pimple in global terms but it's high for Sussex. And it's low enough to have a road running right over the top with a convenient car park at the summit.

I scattered gravel as I slid into the car park at sixty and skidded to a halt. There was a three-sixty view and I jumped out with my binoculars, looking for a fire. Or smoke. The sky was leaden but there was no wind, even on the hill top. I saw a thick column of smoke rising vertically into the still air about a mile away. As soon as I put the binoculars on it I could tell it was too big. Too smoky. It was a farmhand or landowner burning hedge trimmings and fallen branches. For some reason I'd watched Rory Featherstone on TV that morning saying that wood burning stoves harmed the environment and fallen timber should be left to rot naturally. But I wasn't there to worry about green issues. I swivelled round. And round. And round again. Maybe the fire had gone out. A picture burns quickly.

Then I felt a light breeze across my face, a passing variation in air pressure. The grass below me rippled and ruffled as the wind blew over it.

Then I saw it. A thin column of smoke where before there had been none. The fire had been roused from near extinction by a new supply of oxygen brought on the wind. I focussed the binoculars. Standing by the source of the smoke were two people, annoyingly unrecognisable at this distance.

I ran to the car and was back on the road in seconds. The wind had brought a change in the weather and it was now raining. I accelerated downhill towards the T-junction with the B2116 and turned right. The fire was maybe a mile and a half away. After a mile I pulled on to the grass verge, got out and looked over the hedge. There it was. A thin column of smoke rising from a field not far from me. I drove on and turned down an overgrown single-track lane where a bent and rusty sign read UNSUITABLE FOR MOTORS. I ignored it: I mean, how bad could it be? I was in Sussex, not Siberia. The lane turned a right angle and up ahead I saw an old Land Rover Defender parked by the hedge. Given the narrowness of the lane and its high banks, the single vehicle was effectively blocking the road. I reversed back around the corner so I was out of sight from the Defender, got out of the car and looked over the hedge.

In the field of pasture, two men were raking the remains of the fire to extinguish it and break up and disperse any potentially incriminating evidence. One of them was Red T-shirt man from Birchfield Place. Duggan had called him Craig. Perhaps he was better at starting fires than getting down ladders. The other man was familiar too. It was my third sighting of him: the man with the Eye of Horus tattoo, the man at Pilcher's house and one of the killers of Zukovsky and Earl. This time he was wearing a camouflage-patterned jacket and a close-fitting woolly hat. His movements looked fit and sharp in contrast to the more lumbering Craig.

I took cover behind the hedge and waited. My plan was to follow them and hope they'd lead me to wherever the stolen art was stored. Trouble was my location was the pits for covert surveillance. Our two vehicles were the only ones on a narrow lane not designed for motors. If the Land Rover made a U-turn I'd be knackered.

The fire was now extinguished and the two men walked back to the Land Rover. Craig got in the driver's seat, started the engine and, as I feared, began a U-turn. I made a dash back to my car, but a thought stopped me. Land Rovers are great vehicles but, whereas a London taxi is said to turn on a sixpence, a Land Rover needs something closer to a football pitch. I crept back and watched Craig make two experimental manoeuvres. Then he realised he would need to go forward and back, forward and back many times to complete the U-turn. Impatiently, or recklessly, he abandoned the turn and went forwards down the lane instead.

I waited for the Defender to disappear around another bend, then followed. I took it slowly, not wanting to show up in their rear-view mirror. At each bend in the road – and there were many – I stopped, got out and looked around the corner and waited until they disappeared from view. It was slow and frustrating. Like those early days of driving when a man with a red flag had to walk in front. The third time I stopped I saw the Land Rover ford a stream which crossed the road. It looked straightforward but when I got to it, I found it wasn't a ford as such, just a gulley across the road through which a stream ran. Fine for farm tractors and high ground clearance vehicles. Not fine for an ordinary saloon.

I abandoned my car in front of the stream and waded through the knee-deep water. Then I broke into a jog. I do marathons so I can go for ages at ten miles an hour. It would be fast enough on this rough track but hopeless when they reached a main road. But going on foot gave me advantages, too. It was quieter, easier to keep myself concealed.

The surface of the lane became even more broken. Shattered tarmac gave way to uneven concrete interspersed with gravel and grass. Someone had tried repairs: house bricks had been chucked into potholes, but the surface was terrible. I had to concede that the highway engineer who'd placed the sign at the top of the road knew what he was talking about. The Defender should have coped fine because it had the advantages of four-wheel drive, a variable differential and a dual-ratio gearbox but Craig's driving was worse than his ladder work. Like he'd not read the manual. Or if he had, hadn't understood it.

The Land Rover halted. A fallen tree blocked the track and further progress was impossible. Eye of Horus Man got out, walked a short distance back in my direction, then dragged open a field gate.

The Land Rover reversed, jerkily. Eye of Horus Man got back in and they drove through into the field, fast. I ran forwards and saw a steeply sloping field of pasture, at the bottom of which, another gate led to a proper tarmac road. A good shortcut but Craig was handling it wrong. The rain had made the grass wet and the correct method of descent on a steep incline is to zig-zag, like a skier. Otherwise there's a danger of the vehicle sledging down the hill, its own weight overcoming the poor adhesion of tyres to wet grass. Craig was pointing the Land Rover straight down the slope aiming directly at the bottom gate. He was also going too fast and hadn't engaged the lower ratio gearbox.

I saw brake lights come on and I imagined Eye of Horus telling Craig to slow down. The wheels stopped turning but the vehicle's speed didn't change. Gravity took over. With wheels locked, the slide downwards got faster and faster. Then the vehicle began to fishtail, veering from side to side as the contours dictated. Its uncontrolled descent continued until it reached flat ground at the bottom and was stopped by crashing into a barbed wire fence.

I ran down the grassy slope, went to the driver's door and pulled it open. Neither man was hurt and Craig recognised me at once from the previous night. Before he could say anything, I grabbed the keys from the dash with one hand and his shirt collar with the other. I yanked his collar tight.

'Where are the stolen pictures? I watched you burn the second one – or a copy of it. Are they all stashed at Birchfield Place?'

Craig said nothing and struggled to release my grip.

'Who's behind the ransom demand?' I said. 'Is it Clayton Parilla? Are you working for him?'

Craig's colleague was already out of the Land Rover and coming round to tackle me, brandishing the heavy stick Duggan had used before. Eye of Horus swung it at me. I released Craig and stepped back. He swung the stick again with a scything motion and I moved back further. He shouted back to Craig.

'Go for the fence post. The Land Rover will take it out.'

'He took the keys,' Craig said. I held them up and rattled them provocatively.

'There's a spare set in the glove box,' Eye of Horus told Craig.

'What does Parilla want?' I said. 'It's not money. He's a billionaire already. What's he after?'

Craig had the engine going and manoeuvred the Land Rover back and forwards to line up on the nearest fence post.

'And use the low-range gears, for Christ's sake,' said Eye of Horus over his shoulder to Craig while keeping me at bay, swishing the cosh around. There was grinding from the dual gearbox as Craig selected the right ratio then the vehicle lurched forward and made heavy contact with the fence post. The post tilted over forty-five degrees but did not fall, held up by the barbed wire nailed to it.

'It's no good, Lee,' said Craig.

'Give it more welly, for God's sake,' the man called Lee yelled.

Craig reversed and tried again. He drove at the post faster this time and there was a loud clunk as contact was made. The post tilted further but still did not fall. The wire stretched and twanged but still held the post up.

'Give it more,' said Lee. Craig put his foot down. The post moved back another few degrees and the wire, under huge tension now, started to sound almost musical. It emitted a high treble, like a violin or guitar string tightened to breaking point. Craig gunned the Land Rover and its wheels slipped on the muddy surface. The gearbox whined painfully, smoke poured from the exhaust, the barbed wire zinged an ever higher note.

Then three things happened at once. With a sound like a gunshot, the wire snapped. Released of its support, the fence post was flattened at once by the Land Rover, which charged forwards. And Lee screamed in agony and clutched his face.

The snapped wire had whiplashed back and ripped across Lee's face. Blood was already dripping down on to his jacket. I thought about stories of cables snapping on fishing trawlers and crewmen losing fingers, arms, even legs. Lee was lucky. He could have lost his head.

Craig had seen what happened and chickened out of hanging around to help his mate. The road was only a couple of hundred feet away and the last remaining barrier was a scrawny-looking hawthorn hedge. He aimed the Land Rover towards it and charged.

I reasoned Lee could get himself to the road and find help so I raced after the Land Rover. Craig went for the hedge confidently, but it was stronger than it looked. Again he had to have several attempts. As he finally broke through the foliage on to the road, I was behind him and running fast. The Land Rover had a short, galvanised ladder fixed to the rear to give access to its roof-top cargo rack. I grabbed the ladder and heaved myself aboard, steadying myself with one foot on the towing hook and one arm round the rear-mounted spare wheel.

Craig saw me in the mirror at once and tried to throw me off. He began swerving wildly across the road, but a thirty-five year-old

Land Rover wasn't made for fast manoeuvring. In any case there was traffic ahead of us and he had to slow down. Then a gap appeared in the oncoming traffic and he pulled out to overtake. I was flung sideways against the bodywork, my foot slipped off the tow-hook but I held on to the spare wheel. Craig powered past three vehicles but an approaching truck forced him to swing back to his side of the road, cutting in front of a Toyota which was forced to brake hard. The Toyota blasted its horn. Then the driver saw me hanging on the back of the Defender and flashed his headlights and leaned on the horn.

The rain was now only drizzle but, with the wind-chill, my exposed and cramped fingers were turning numb. Looking ahead over the roof I saw a crossroads with traffic lights. The lights were green: Craig accelerated. Close to the crossing, the lights changed to amber. Craig accelerated again. But fifty feet away, the lights changed to red. Craig had an abrupt loss of confidence and hit the brakes. I was slammed forwards against the metalwork. Then, fatally, Craig changed his mind again. He accelerated hard and my body was wrenched back as the Defender surged forwards. We reached the crossroads still accelerating and I saw a Transit van coming from the left. Craig saw it too. He hit the brakes once again. Then he veered left, then right.

His last move threw me off. My frozen fingers were no longer in control. As I hit the tarmac and tried to roll away I heard the hollow, thudding clank of an impact followed by lighter, tinkling sounds as broken shards of glass, plastic and trim tumbled down on to the roadway.

Chapter 18

After what felt like a pleasant nap, I was aware of someone talking to me.

'Are you all right? Are you all right?' The female voice was urgent but not panicking.

Slowly I regained consciousness and opened my eyes.

'He's opened his eyes. He's opened his eyes,' the voice said.

All I could see were some strange black and white shapes, like giant jigsaw pieces. The jigsaw pieces were moving, moving towards me. I lifted my head.

'Don't move, don't move,' the voice said. Why did they have to say everything twice?

My vision cleared. I found myself lying on a muddy roadside verge next to another barbed wire fence. Through the fence the black and white jig-saw pieces resolved into black and white Friesian cattle who'd come to the fence to investigate the unusual activity. Then I remembered what had happened and sat up.

'Careful. You had a nasty fall.' The voice belonged to a Mother Earth type in a big skirt with a bold pattern, a mud-coloured jumper and chunky trainers. Her Citroen C4 was parked at the crossroads.

The Land Rover was embedded in the side of the Transit van and I saw Craig's body in the driving seat slumped over the wheel. No airbag in a vehicle that old.

I stood up and flexed myself. I was bruised, grazed and painful but all the bits seemed to work. I checked the time. I couldn't have been out for more than a minute or two.

'Your clothes are a terrible mess,' the woman said. It was though Tanya had materialised next to me. Apart from being wet from the rain, one jacket sleeve had been shredded as I slid across the road surface and the back was ripped almost in two. My trousers were smeared with mud and what looked like the remains of a roadkill.

But my phone was in good order. It was ringing.

'Kite, you're needed.' It was Tanya. On duty.

'That's nice... it's, um... nice to be needed...'

'Kite...?' Tanya knew at once I wasn't sounding normal. 'Are you alright? You sound half asleep.'

'Well, I am half asleep...' I explained what had happened.

'God. Are you all right?'

'I'll live. There's a nice lady by the roadside looking after me.' I smiled at the Citroen driver and she gave me an encouraging smile in return. 'Have you got a slot for us,' I said. 'A slot to see...' I broke off, aware of my good Samaritan standing close by. 'To see the... principal... ask him what the hell's going on?'

'Other way around. The PM wants an urgent update from you. Can you make it? Where are you? I can hear birds. And a siren.'

It was an approaching ambulance, but it wasn't for me or Craig. It drove straight past the crash site and on down the road. I imagined Lee, the Eye of Horus man, had called for help or else flagged down a motorist. Not such a lucky charm, that Eye of Horus.

'I'm still in Sussex. Near Lewes,' I said to Tanya.

'So a couple of hours before you can be in Westminster. Let me ask what they want to do and I'll call you back.' And she ended the call. Tanya ringfenced her private life from her work. It was a Mexican Wall, a hardened frontier with tripwires, mines and watchtowers. No access at any time. It was remarkable, admirable even. But a bit disconcerting.

The woman in the jumper handed me a can of Coke. 'It was in my car. Thought it might help.'

I thanked her, opened the can and took a long swig. I put her down as a care worker or a nurse.

'Were you crossing the road when the crash happened,' she said. 'Only I couldn't otherwise work out how you got to be where you ended up.'

Well, nobody would expect idiots to be surfing Land Rovers. It was easier to agree with her. So I did.

'The police and ambulance will be here soon. The man in the Transit called them first thing.'

I nodded acknowledgment and finished the Coke. Then Tanya phoned again.

'Plan B,' she said. 'Lyle Brabant will stand in for the PM. His constituency is not far from where you are and he's down there today. He was opening something and there was a lunch afterwards. He's at the Piltdown Golf Club.'

'We need to speak to the organ grinder, not the monkey, Tanya.'

'But you're not in London. The PM's got the country to run.'

'He might not have it much longer if he doesn't sort things out. We must see him.'

'We will, but we can't today. So, the Piltdown Golf Club. I take it you don't need the postcode.'

'I'll find it. It's about ten miles from me. What does Brabant want to know?'

'Just an update the PM said, that's all.'

And off she went.

'You're not walking ten miles in your condition.' It was the Mother Earth woman.

'What?'

'You said you had to go ten miles.'

I was about to say I had a car nearby. Then I realised it wasn't nearby but a few miles down the road, across a field and up a single-track lane which was unsuitable for motors. So I paused in mid-sentence and that must have made the woman, who told me her name was Ruth, think I'd lost it or was suffering from concussion because she told me she would drive me. I protested, but she was adamant.

Ruth talked a lot. She was a health visitor, a rare breed she said, like Soays or Gloucester Old Spots. I wasn't going to ask what she meant but she told me anyway. Soays are a rare breed of sheep which originally came from the Scottish island of the same name. She said they were tough as old boots. Not to eat; she meant they were hardy in all weathers. Gloucester Old Spots are of course pigs with spots. Ruth wasn't from a farming family but her duties included visiting an old gentleman with Alzheimer's who owned one of the local estates where they farmed these rare breeds.

The monologue continued as we passed the place where Craig had driven out of the field on to the road and there was the ambulance I'd seen earlier. Lee was lying on a stretcher.

We reached my car. Ruth was reluctant to let me drive since I'd had a 'shake-up'. I insisted I was fine and pulled out my keys. Except they were not my keys. They were the ones I'd grabbed from the Land Rover. I looked at them with a puzzled expression as they lay in the palm of my hand.

'Look, there's an Old Spot,' said Ruth pointing to the key fob in my hand. Attached to the keys was a brightly coloured fob from some pig breeding association. On it was a picture of a happy-looking Gloucester Old Spot pig. 'You should've said you were into pigs.'

I invented a story as to how I had come across the keys which seemed to satisfy her. 'Any idea who they might belong to?' I said.

'If you found them round here it'd most likely be my old gentleman with Alzheimer's,' she said. 'He's a member of this association.'

'Perhaps you'd like to return them to him. Since you visit regularly.'

'Be my pleasure,' she said. 'Not that he can drive any more, of course.'

'Of course. And what's the gentleman's name?' I said.

'Mr Brabant. Peregrine Brabant, he's called. He owns a lot of land here about and his son's a doctor. And in the government.'

'Really?' I said.

'I've seen Mr Brabant playing with these key fobs. He likes looking at the pictures on them. He can't get out to the farm any more.' Then she looked at the time and said she would have to fly. Then she gave me some glucose sweets from a tin she had in the car, told me to take care, gave me her card in case I felt queasy later and finally gave me a little hug.

I gave her a little hug too and a kiss on the cheek. The least I could do.

She did a better U-turn than Craig could have managed in the narrow lane and drove off. I was about to do likewise when I remembered the burner phone I'd located at Birchfield Place. Both Duggan and Craig had been in the house but there had been only one phone signal. I'd assumed at the time the phone was Duggan's but Craig's lack of competence with the ladder and the Land Rover made me think again. Duggan wouldn't have left his phone on when it wasn't needed. I set up my scanner and searched. The burner was within a few miles of where I was and the triangulation from local masts was persuasive. The centre point of the overlap put the burner pretty much at the crash site. The burner must be Craig's. He and his phone were out of action for the foreseeable future but that left me no tab on Duggan. And he was more formidable opposition.

Piltdown. Its name is pretty much forgotten now but it was the site of the biggest fraud in British archaeology. Over a hundred years ago, before the First World War, someone claimed to have discovered human bones there that were half a million years old and would provide the evolutionary missing link between apes and modern man. The discovery was accepted as true. Fame and fortune followed for the archaeologist. But later, after the Second World War, the bones were found to be much younger and not even totally human. It had all been a clever fake. An ironic place, then, for a serious meeting about national security and potential terrorism.

I drove fast to Piltdown and got there with time to spare. Brabant's lunch wasn't due to finish until three. For my lunch I sucked on the fruit sweets Ruth had given me. And very refreshing they were.

How had Peregrine Brabant's Land Rover got into the hands of the villains? If Brabant Senior had Alzheimer's then any involvement he had in the plot must be involuntary. But what about Lyle Brabant? Was he the source of the leak about the stolen pictures?

Whatever his guilt or otherwise, I couldn't meet the minister in my torn and dirty clothing. I rummaged in the car and dug out an old

Barbour waxed jacket which wouldn't look out of place on a golf course. I shook it out and dusted it down. Then I sprayed some water from the windscreen washers on to a sponge, dabbed at my trousers and removed some of the muck. I still looked like the scarecrow Worzel Gummidge but it would have to do.

Then I called DI Liam Bolt and updated him. I suggested that, if Craig had survived the crash, Sussex police might want to throw an attempted murder charge at him. Then I told him about Lee, the unlucky Eye of Horus man, who could be picked up for his role in the killing of Zukovsky and Earl.

'Hang on,' he said. 'Let me get that sorted first then I've got some info for you.' I heard him asking one of his DCs to trace the hospital where Lee had been taken, then get down to Sussex pronto. He was back on the phone within a minute. 'This man Lee... didn't you say he was responsible for the death of that art dealer? When you were down in Broadway.'

'You could say he was responsible, but Pilcher died of natural causes. The post-mortem said a stroke.'

'Hang on, hang on. You may think I'm getting soft in my old age, but I was kind of interested in what you told me about the painting and the dead dealer and I did a bit of unpaid overtime. I put a call in to West Mercia and I asked about the post-mortem. They haven't got the results yet.'

'When did you speak to them?'

'Today. There's some kind of bug going round among their pathologists. Well, cutting up dead people isn't healthy is it? Anyway, there's a delay because staff are on sick leave. Who told you it was a stroke?'

'It was someone from the Home Office.'

'You know what civil servants are like. They got their files mixed up or something.'

I knew that wasn't the case with Tresize. He'd told me he'd heard it was a stroke from Lyle Brabant. But to Bolt I said, 'Maybe.'

'When I hear back from West Mercia, I'll give you a call.'

'Thank you.' Bolt's attitude had done a turnaround since we first met. He now did some more unpaid overtime and made various suggestions for places in and around London where the missing four hundred pictures might be secreted. They were sensible suggestions, up to a point, but a bit like a list of 'the usual suspects': none of them had what marketing people call a USP. A Unique Selling Point. He detected my lukewarm response.

'Nothing grab your fancy? Well, I'm flying blind there. Anyway, back on the ground: Shawn Cussons. I found him. He's a DCI in SCO7 and if you want to speak to him you better get in quick. He's on the verge of retiring. He's done over thirty years.' He gave me a direct office number.

'That's great, Liam. Thank you.'

'Why do you want to talk to him?'

'He plays bridge with someone I've come across.'

'Right…' Bolt paused a moment, wondering if I would add anything. Then, when it was clear I wouldn't, said, 'OK. It's your secret. I won't ask again.' Bolt laughed. 'But I'm hearing things from Downing Street. Word is it's either the House of Lords or the Tower of London for you. Peerage or prison.'

'Those meetings are supposed to be secret,' I said, realising I was sounding fuddy-duddy.

'They say that to all the newbies, but Number Ten leaks worse than the Yard. Anyway, good luck. I put a fiver on you to be the next Commissioner of the Met. Just remember your old mucker when you're Lord Kite; put a line in the autobiography or something.'

And he ended the call.

I was grateful that Bolt had tracked down Shawn Cussons but before I contacted him, I wanted to nail down how Lyle Brabant had known Pilcher died of a stroke before the post-mortem had been done. I called Tanya.

'Did you speak to Lyle Brabant about Pilcher? After we got back from Broadway?'

'Not at all. I've not told anybody. Why?'

'Are Brabant and Adam Tresize close?'

'I wouldn't say so. Why?'

'Which of them would you trust to tell the truth?'

'Kite? Tell me what's happened?'

'I will when I've worked out the logical possibilities.'

'God, you're not compiling syllogisms are you? I was hopeless at that. All Cretans are liars, all that sort of stuff...'

'I don't know what you're on about,' I said. 'Look, I'll call you back when I've thought it through.'

I did vaguely know what Tanya was on about. If Tresize was telling the truth to me then Brabant must be involved with Pilcher and Lee, the Eye of Horus man. Otherwise how could he have known about the stroke? If Tresize was *lying* to me, there were two options: either he himself was involved with Pilcher and the others, or he heard the stroke story from another person and was trying to implicate Brabant for some reason. So either Brabant, or Tresize, or someone else could be involved with the Pilcher case.

That didn't get me far. More questions than answers.

There was still no sign of Brabant finishing his lunch, so I called Shawn Cussons. SCO7 is organised crime so Cussons would have dealt with some of the worst villains around and would have been a credible source of information for William Havers about my past. Not that my father ranked high among Britain's worst offenders. He just made crime a profitable career. Weeks, months go by without me consciously thinking of my dead parents, but the memories are always standing by, waiting to make an appearance. Sometimes in dreams, sometimes out of the blue in broad daylight. I was keen to know how much Cussons knew.

Cussons answered himself and I gave my name. He took a moment to place me so I said, 'My father was Roger Broughton.'

'Yes,' he said, trawling through his memory. 'You changed your name.' I did indeed. In my late teens after my parents had been killed and I had discovered the scope of what they'd done. 'What can I do for you?'

'I understand you play bridge with William Havers.'

'Correct.'

'I understand you may have given him some information about me.'

There was a pause. He was trying to remember. Wondering if I was right.

'I don't think so,' he said.

'Chief Inspector, could we meet?'

'Would that be useful?'

'It would for me. Basically, I would like to know what you know. There may be things I don't know. And it would help me.'

'You mean… psychologically?'

'Yes. And personally. To get a full picture of my parents.'

He grunted. 'Alright. But this is my last week in the job. Leaving party tonight. I can see you tomorrow. Meet in the Black Friar, Ludgate Circus. Say, eleven o'clock. I might need a pick-me-up.'

He ended the call and I felt my heart thumping. Fifteen years after my parents died, I might be getting a few more pieces of the jigsaw of their lives.

But then I saw movement outside. It was the minister's driver getting out, preparing for Brabant's return. Then a group of men in smart suits came out of the golf club's main door, with Brabant among them. Hands were shaken and Brabant walked to his car. He spoke to his driver then came towards me. I got out and went to meet him.

'Mr Kite, thank you for coming. As we were both in the area the PM thought it convenient for me to stand in.'

'Of course. What would you like to know?'

'Shall we walk and talk? There's a footpath to a bench by the fifth green I think.' He looked at my messy clothes, but made no comment. Perhaps his years ministering to the poor in developing countries had made him blind to how people dressed.

We had only taken a few steps towards the course when a government car came into the car park at speed. As soon as it stopped, Chris Spanswick jumped out from the back and his protection officer got out of the front. The officer stayed by the car but Spanswick came towards us, moving quickly despite his bulk.

Brabant was as surprised as I was. 'Chris, what brings you here? Not golf, surely?' he said.

'Lyle, could I have a word, old son?' said Spanswick, putting one of his hefty arms round Brabant's shoulder and dwarfing the smaller man. They walked away from me and spoke quietly for some minutes. I could see Brabant nodding and agreeing to something without any apparent conflict. Then I heard Spanswick say, 'Good man,' and Brabant walked away from me towards his own car while Spanswick came towards me.

'Change of plan,' Spanswick said.

'Is Mr Brabant all right?' I said.

Spanswick was surprised by this. 'Yes, of course. Why do you ask?'

'With you suddenly taking over... I wondered if he was ill.'

'The PM thought it better if I talk to you instead.'

'And you were in the area, too?' I said.

'Yes,' Spanswick smiled. 'You'll think it's a suspicious set-up but it's genuine happenstance. There was an RAF thing I had to appear at.' I remembered he was Minister of Defence as well as Deputy PM. 'Let's go, shall we? Lyle says there's a path to a quiet place by the fifth green. Wherever that is.'

I looked around at the flags flying from the hole pins. 'There's four,' I said. 'The next one should be five.'

'Well done. Don't play golf myself.' We set off towards the fifth green and Spanswick went on, 'Someone mentioned you organise charity golf matches for the police.'

'I help a bit with that kind of thing.'

'You play much?'

'For the charity matches I just stay on the sidelines.'

'You mean in the clubhouse with a stiff drink?' He smiled.

'Usually in the rough with an umbrella.'

He laughed. 'You had a tragic time as a teenager, I hear,' he said.

WTF? Is that why he'd taken over from Brabant? To delve into my past and dig up something suspicious?

'Well, it wasn't so bad,' I lied.

'So, bring me up to speed on what's happening with these blooming pictures. Time was when government was about economics, education, employment and the occasional war. Now we're bogged down with protests about bloody antiques.'

I gave him a look and then, as we walked across the course, I told Spanswick everything that had happened. Well, almost everything. I avoided mention of the Prime Minister's picture altogether and the Oxenhopes' allegation against him. But I told him about Birchfield Place, that Helen and Zoe Oxenhope were virtual prisoners, about Duggan's role and my observation of the picture burning and my chase of Craig.

'You did all that?' said Spanswick, openly impressed. 'Brave lad. No questions about your dedication to the cause. How are you feeling? A bit bruised?' He looked me up and down. 'That explains why you look all raggedy.'

We sat on the wooden bench. There were no players on the green. No one in sight. Just the flag flapping at the top of the pin.

'Got any idea where these pictures are?'

I breathed out hard. 'If I had, I wouldn't be sitting here. It was a bit odd that the second picture was burned so close to the site of the first which made me think they could be hidden away nearby. Somewhere in Sussex. But we know they're a clever team, so it could be a double bluff.'

'You mean the pictures are actually hundreds of miles away?'

I nodded. 'Oxenhope has a base in North Yorkshire, but the police have searched it already. It's clean.'

'No one can deny you've done a thorough job, but you know senior management at the Metropolitan Police and the security services are not happy.'

'They want me off the case? Is that what you've come to say?'

'Hold your horses. The situation is urgent because the public is becoming agitated. They've got the collywobbles, think the government's lost control. We must calm things down before there's mass panic.'

'And how to do that?'

'You find those fucking pictures, that's how.'

'You don't want to fire me?'

'No. We feel you're doing OK and we should let you get on with it. Fuck what Scotland Yard thinks. If they can do better, let them.'

'I see. Well, thank you.'

Spanswick shrugged. 'Bloody pictures.'

'And the Prime Minister agrees with you on this?'

'As far as I know.'

'You've not discussed it?'

'That's not for you to know, son.'

I gave him a look. Was he doing this without Fresnel's agreement? Flying solo? I took a gamble.

'I've been worried about what the Prime Minister told me about his picture – the one by Vanessa Bell. I don't think he was completely honest.'

'Really?' Spanswick didn't look surprised, or particularly interested.

'I'm sure he didn't get the picture from the dealer, Pilcher, and I also think…'

'Hey, there are more important things to sort out than one bloody painting.'

'You were at the meeting in the flat with us.'

'I'm at lots of meetings where I don't want to be.' He paused. 'You think you're close to finding out why someone stole those four hundred pictures?'

I paused as I decided what to say. 'I think it's to do with a group called Hayden.'

'Who?' Spanswick's face was impassive.

'You haven't heard of them?'

'No.' He was looking straight at me, unblinking.

'I think you may have met some of them when you were in Davos earlier this year.'

'Really? Well, I met a load of people in Davos. Most of them boring twats. But there was nobody called Hayden.'

'It's likely they go under various assumed names. Does the name Clayton Parilla mean anything to you?'

He shook his head. 'Absolutely not. If he's a criminal, the Home Secretary will have the gen. Ask Adam Tresize.'

My eyes were on his. He didn't turn or look away. If he was lying he was highly skilled at it. I changed tack.

'What about Mr Brabant? Did he want to fire me? Is that why you spoke to me in place of Mr Brabant?'

Spanswick looked at me coolly and calculatingly. 'He seemed to have some gripe against you which I couldn't understand.' He paused and looked around. 'He was born near here, you know. Village called Firle. His father has a big estate.'

'So I understand.' Was Spanswick suggesting something? 'Firle is close to Charleston House. Where Vanessa Bell and Duncan Grant lived.' Spanswick looked at me as if this information was irrelevant. I paused a beat. 'One of your colleagues suggested to me that Mr Brabant was unwell in some way.' Again he gave me a dead kind of look.

'I couldn't comment on that. I'm not a doctor.'

'Do you think the Prime Minister's in danger?'

'Do you?'

'Yes, I do. I think there's a faction within the government that wants him out.'

Spanswick laughed. 'That's been true of every government for the last two hundred years.' Tanya had said something similar.

'But this faction has got allies outside government.'

'So you agree with what I said at the meeting? It's the Russians or the Chinese making us look stupid.'

'It's more than that. Something that will damage the country.'

'That's what Brabant suggested. People thought he was panicking.'

'Maybe he knows it's true. Maybe he knows who's organising it. Who do you think could be behind it? Anybody in the government?'

Spanswick gave me the blank, no comment look again.

'Or in Whitehall.'

'I don't think you should joke about things like that,' he said.

'I wasn't joking. I think there's involvement.'

He leant towards me, his face set and serious and said quietly, 'I'd advise you not to repeat such allegations. To anyone else. Anywhere else. But if you're such a hot-shot gunslinger, lone wolf – whatever the PM called you – track 'em down, bring me the proof.' Threat or promise? We were eyeball to eyeball but his politician's face was inscrutable.

Paint It Blackmail

Down the fairway, two golfers were lining up their approach shots to the green. A 5-iron, perhaps; they were both well positioned. Spanswick watched the players take their shots. One of them made the green, leaving a doable fifteen-foot putt.

'Let's walk back,' he said. We walked back in silence. By his car we shook hands, he thanked me for coming and said, 'Don't forget what I said, son. Do nothing without proof or you'll be fucked.'

I watched his ministerial car leave then got into my own. I couldn't work out what Spanswick thought. Had he spoken honestly or not? And what was his attitude to Brabant? Spanswick's arrival out of the blue was odd and I wondered what Brabant's message would have been if he'd been allowed to deliver it.

To many people in the UK and abroad, Brabant was a brave surgeon, a fighter for human rights, a hero. But being a national treasure could be great cover for self-aggrandisement. Look at those Third World leaders who sweep to power on a popular vote to bring freedom and equality to a poor and subjugated nation. So many become kleptomaniacs and continue to rape their country just as their predecessors did but with dancier music, faster cars and wilder clothes. Perhaps Brabant was going that way.

I started the car and headed homewards.

I had gone only five miles when I saw a police car in the rear-view. Lights flashing. Siren on. I slowed and pulled over to let it past. Then it swerved in sharply ahead of me and pulled up. Forcing me to stop.

Two uniforms got out and walked back to me.

'Mr John Kite?'

I agreed I was.

'Mr Kite, you are under arrest on suspicion of an offence against the Official Secrets Act. You do not have to say anything, but it may harm your defence if you do not mention when questioned something which you later rely on in court. Anything you do say may be given in evidence.'

I was gobsmacked.

And I said it out loud. 'I'm gobsmacked.' And I watched while one of the uniforms wrote it in his notebook. 'I suppose you want me to come with you,' I said.

'If you would, Mr Kite.'

Chapter 19

I wasn't taken to the Sussex Police HQ but into London. To West End Central. This was a Met Police job.

I'd been in plenty of cells in my time in the police service. But never on my own. In the past I'd heard several prisoners tell me they'd be released as soon as their brief got there, as soon as I believed what they told me, as soon as everybody understood a mistake had been made. I always ignored them because it was always bullshit. But now I naturally thought the same. That I'd be out soon.

Two hours passed.

My cell door opened and I was taken to an interview room where I was confronted by DCI Aidan Salt and DI Wes Cannon. Being interviewed by an inspector and a chief inspector meant somebody was treating the case seriously. The formalities were over quickly. I agreed I had signed the Official Secrets Act and that I had been present at the COBRA meeting in question. And I denied I had revealed any information from that meeting. Had I contacted Sky News? I hadn't. Did I know Hester MacFarlane? I had never heard of her. She worked on the newsdesk at Sky and had received a call from a man identifying himself as John Kite who then passed on information about the COBRA meeting. I denied I had made such a call and added that if I were to leak information to a news agency I wouldn't be so stupid as to give my name.

'Newsdesks apparently ask for names,' said Salt. 'They don't like anonymous tip-offs.'

'So I can imagine,' I said. 'But I might have been bright enough to give a false name.'

The questions then became repetitive, covering the same ground but from different angles. Had I spoken to any other journalists? Had I spoken to any other media organisations? And then, curiously or ominously, had I received any large amounts of money recently?

I invited the officers to investigate my bank account. They had already done so, they said.

'Your bank balance is substantial,' said Salt.

'My current account has around five thousand, but there is a larger balance in the savings account.'

'Why is that?'

'My parents died some years ago. I inherited money from them.'

'You haven't spent it?'

'Not all of it. Some I gave to the Police Benevolent Fund.'

That surprised them.

It was apparent they hadn't any evidence against me and were trying to make me incriminate myself by essentially asking the same questions over and over. I relaxed a little. Someone must have phoned Sky pretending to be me. Then someone had tipped off the police. But the information given must have been vague otherwise they would be asking me more specific questions.

The to and fro continued for some time. I gave them nothing because I had nothing to give. The officers became frustrated at the lack of progress and were scratching around trying to think of questions to ask.

'May I ask something?' I said.

'You want to know what's for supper?' said DCI Salt. It wasn't especially funny but his remark had the effect of breaking the tense stalemate. He and his sidekick laughed. I'd probably done similar in my time with an uncooperative suspect.

'Do you know ex-DC Spenser Duggan?' I said.

The two detectives reacted slightly to the name and looked at each other.

'Friend of yours?' Salt said.

'On the contrary. But I saw him around recently. He was acting suspiciously. Is he involved in this?'

The two detectives exchanged glances again. I saw a hint of uncertainty.

'Have you any reason to think he is?' said Salt.

'Several reasons. He pursued then assaulted a young woman at Highgate tube station which resulted in her falling on the track. He was following a senior civil servant from the Cabinet Office and kept observation on her house. His associates were involved in burning the paintings stolen from the Government Art Collection. There is also evidence associating him with the murder of two men at the Trieste House office block in Clerkenwell.'

The inspector made a note.

'Who tipped you off about me?' I said.

Two pairs of eyes angled hard on me. But they said nothing.

'I guess the information came from someone high up, otherwise two senior detectives wouldn't be spending so much time on me. I also guess that apart from my name you've got no evidence of any kind. Because of course there isn't any. Whoever tipped you off did it to get me off their tail. To keep me quiet for a bit. And they're wasting your time.'

Salt sighed. 'Shut it, Kite. You're not here to make fucking speeches.' He stood up abruptly. 'Interview terminated,' he said and stomped out of the room.

The arresting officers knew exactly where I'd be. They hadn't even needed to track my phone. Someone had told them. But who had wanted me arrested? Who would benefit? The Met Commissioner and MI5 had an axe to grind. Had the Prime Minister suddenly tired of me? Been persuaded that I was a liability not an asset? Like Thomas Becket who had to be got rid of?

Tanya had been worried by my outspokenness and asked if I should've said what I did. I remembered her adding, 'They don't take prisoners.' Well, she was literally wrong on that.

Back in my cell, I listed everyone who'd been at the meeting. There was Prime Minister James Fresnel; his deputy, Chris Spanswick; Adam Tresize, the Home Secretary; Lyle Brabant; Rory

Featherstone, the Foreign Secretary; Julia Frobisher, the Director of the Government Art Collection; Steve Absalom, the Met Commissioner and Mark Boyes, the AC for Counter Terrorism; Claudia Tranter, the Director General of MI5 and of course Tanya and me.

If someone had given my name to the police it had to be one of these, or else a person linked to one of them. If they wanted to get rid of me for a while it meant they were involved in the blackmail threat, the theft of the paintings and the incidents at the museum and the Portrait Gallery. Were they also trying to foment trouble in the country? Trying to get rid of Fresnel? If this was true, what they were doing was treason. There was no other word for it.

It seemed preposterous that any of the men and women round the table in COBRA had a secret agenda to topple the government. Yet, someone in Downing Street had invited the man from Hayden to a meeting there and got him access to the Art Collection. Someone had also arranged for the crucial phone call which distracted the operations manager while his systems were compromised. Was the Collection Director, Julia Frobisher involved? Lyle Brabant had a gripe against me, according to Spanswick, but was Spanswick telling the truth? Spanswick seemed the most likely person to be behind my arrest since he knew at what time I left the golf club. Lyle Brabant was under attack from both Spanswick and the Home Secretary, Adam Tresize. And finally, at the top of the pyramid was the Prime Minister, who had lied about his painting.

Plenty of questions, but no answers. Time passed. A meal was brought to me. I ate it. It got late.

If the shadowy Hayden group had stolen the four hundred pictures, what they wanted was leverage on the Prime Minister. Leo Somerscales thought the group was trying to take over Malta, were they trying to do the same here? Not a revolution with weapons and tanks but a subtler takeover that may not even be apparent to the average voter.

I was woken from a disturbed sleep by the cell door being unlocked. I was taken out not to the interview room but to the custody sergeant. I stood blinking under the unforgiving fluorescents as he produced a manilla envelope full of the belongings which had been removed from me when I was taken in. Then he pushed a clipboard across the counter.

'Sign, here,' he said.

'You're releasing me?'

'Why else would I want your autograph?' I signed. 'Have a nice day, Mr Kite.'

I checked the time as I put my watch back on. Ten past five in the morning. Then I stuffed my wallet and keys into my jacket and pushed open the door to the public area. There I saw a familiar shape. Head erect, back straight, hands in lap, legs crossed and angled at forty-five degrees. Tanya.

She stood up as I came out.

'You look pretty shit,' she said.

'It was the car crash did this,' I said, exhibiting my ripped jacket. 'And you should have seen the trousers before I wiped them.'

She raised her eyebrows.

She was immaculate as usual. In another chic and close-fitting outfit with straight-from-the-salon hair and make-up and the emerald pendant round her neck.

'Why do you look so good at this time in the morning?' I said.

'I get up at half five most days. For the gym. I got the call about four this morning, so not much difference.'

'Is this how you dress for the gym?'

'Of course not. When I've dropped you I'll go straight to the office.'

She led me out to the street, Savile Row, and the pre-dawn cold September air. A government car was waiting and as we emerged from the police station the driver opened the rear door for us.

'This is nice,' I said, indicating the car. 'Some kind of compensation? Has it got a TV inside? A cocktail cabinet?'

'You can walk if you like,' she said, not happy with my teasing.

Then I remembered. 'Actually, one of the uniforms drove my own car back.'

'Well, if you don't want a lift...' Tanya was deflated. Her gesture rejected.

'Sorry,' I said. 'I'm looking a gift horse in the mouth.'

'Don't worry. You obviously need your car.'

Then I realised it could wait. 'It'll be in a pound somewhere. I can't be arsed.' I got into the back seat and Tanya followed. The driver closed the door and we set off.

'Do you know who was behind it?' I said. 'Who tipped off the police? Fitted me up?'

She shook her head, looking away from me out of the window. Something was bothering her. Or maybe Tanya didn't do conversation this early.

'You heard about the meeting with Spanswick?'

Her head shot round ninety degrees to face me. 'Spanswick! What happened to Brabant?'

I explained what Spanswick had told me. 'I reckon Brabant wanted to fire me and Spanswick wanted to keep me on board.'

'If Brabant wanted to fire you, that suggests Fresnel did as well. Brabant was meant to be there as the PM's messenger boy. But are you sure Spanswick was telling you the truth?'

I thought for a moment. 'I'm not sure if any of them are telling the truth. Which one is more loyal to the Prime Minister, Brabant or Spanswick?'

'God. Just hearing that question makes me feel sick.' Tanya leaned forward and supported her chin in her hands. A sign of how disturbed she was. She stayed as she was for some minutes. Then she lifted her head from her hands and resumed her normal upright posture. 'Adam Tresize told me something yesterday. About you.'

'What about me?'

'Some not very nice things.'

'Did you believe him?'

'Like you, I don't know what to believe.'

'But you still came to meet me.'

She shrugged with an ironic smile. 'Someone had to.'

'I guess no one else was up early enough.' She gave me a smile. 'Tresize told me some not very nice things about you, too,' I said.

Tanya looked aghast.

'The kind of things a jealous lover might say…'

'I've honestly never…'

'I didn't think you had. So I ignored what he said. As for me, I've no idea what he told you but, for the avoidance of doubt, as lawyers say, I'll give you a quick resumé. I've never killed anyone, though I have damaged a few to stop them committing crimes. There are things in my past I don't want to boast about, but there's nothing I can be arrested for. On the other hand, my father should have been arrested and sent to prison but never was. He, and probably my mother too, were full-time criminals. When I discovered this, in my first year at university, I pulled out of the course and joined the police. The money I inherited from them I've mostly redistributed to worthy causes, including law enforcement charities.'

I turned and found she was studying my face with something approaching wonder. What I'd said was all news to her. 'That's the stuff your vetting didn't reveal. Tresize didn't mention any of it?'

Tanya shook her head. 'No, it was all character assassination, but without any hard facts.'

'Same as he told me about you.'

Tanya didn't move, she sat there looking at my face for a long time. There was water in her eyes. Then she turned to the front and I saw her lip tremble ever so slightly. Then she swallowed hard and breathed in deeply. She clutched my left hand with her right. Her hand was wintry cold. She squeezed my hand then turned to look out of the window, gazing into the middle distance.

'These people at the meeting… they should all be above suspicion,' she said.

'I know. I was thinking things over in there. Wasn't much else to do.'

'We should talk about it. As soon as.'

'What about work?'

She checked the oversize Omega that circled her wrist. 'I'm OK.'

'Come back to mine and I can cook you breakfast. Or will that mess with your gym routine?'

'My stomach's churning. Not sure I could face the gym. Or a fry-up.'

'How about scrambled eggs and smoked salmon?'

Chapter 20

The government car dropped Tanya and me outside my house thirty minutes later. I hoped I would find some reasonably fresh eggs in the fridge and some bread that hadn't grown fungus. I hadn't any of Tanya's lapsang souchong and wondered whether she drank ordinary tea. And did she have full-fat milk, skimmed or semi-skimmed? Or maybe a non-milk milk. Almond, or whatever.

But when I put my key in the lock I forgot all about breakfast. Something was wrong.

The snib was down on my front door Yale. It's something I never do. I rely on the six-lever Chubb below it.

'What's up?' Tanya had seen my reaction.

'Not sure. You might want to stay back. In case of... anything.' I moved out of the garden, stood on the pavement and surveyed the front elevation. The house was how I'd left it. No broken glass. No windows open. No lights on. No drawn curtains or blinds.

I walked down the road and turned into the footpath that, like the one at Dominic Vaughan's house, runs behind the properties on my side of the street. Tanya followed.

'Mind your clothes on the brambles. And there's probably dog shit somewhere.'

'I'm fine,' she said.

We reached the back of my house and went through the gate that separates my excuse for a back garden from the footpath.

My back door was wide open. It had been clumsily forced with a crowbar. I went inside and Tanya followed. Everything was tidy. The

TV was still there, the audio gear and the only two pictures I have which are worth more than a cup of tea. The only item missing was my PC. It had been neatly unplugged. There was a rectangle of dust-free carpet to show where it had been standing.

Tanya looked at the trailing cables. 'Someone really wants to fuck you over, don't they?'

I couldn't put it better myself.

The eggs in the fridge were fresh, so was the bread and Tanya drank builder's tea with whatever milk was available. She said the Chinese stuff had been a present and she'd never got round to opening it. We sat at the kitchen table. I was in my torn, grubby and sweaty yesterday's clothes, unwashed and unshaved like any jailbird. Tanya smelled of exotic fruits and spices courtesy of some fabulous perfume, wearing a crisp white jacket over a silk blouse and dark pencil skirt, with perfect hair and make-up. There was only one tiny imperfection I noticed.

'You snagged your tights on the brambles.'

She was unconcerned. 'I always carry spare,' she said.

We ate the smoked salmon and scrambled eggs on toast and drank tea. And we chewed over the events of the last twenty-four hours.

'What about Brabant?' I said. 'He was the only one with Fresnel in that meeting with Clayton Parilla. Spanswick dropped the fact that his family home was near where the women are being held and I felt he was hinting at something. And I believed Spanswick when he said Brabant had something against me, then Tresize talked about him being unwell.'

'But he also told you lies about me. No, I can't believe Brabant has gone rogue. Working undercover for someone else... a spy?'

'He's worked abroad a lot. In places with no proper government, no law and order. You form strong friendships in those situations, to ease the pressure. There must be Russian doctors and nurses there, and Chinese. They could have taken advantage of his do-gooding, his ethical beliefs, his desire for a better world.'

Tanya was still unconvinced.

'All those classic British traitors who spied for the Soviets, they didn't do it for money. They did because of their political beliefs.'

'What about your old detective? Spenser Duggan. Isn't he more likely? I asked an old friend about him.'

'Really? Who?'

'George. He was a major in the SAS. Now runs an international security and close protection company.'

I raised my eyebrows at the width of Tanya's circle of friends.

'We met at Oxford. Both in the OTC.'

I gave a puzzled look.

'Officers' Training Corps.'

Tanya was full of surprises. 'So you were considering the army as well as MI5 and the civil service?'

'Well, not really. Anyway, my friend George knows of Duggan. He remembers the hair. He interviewed him for a job, but rejected him outright. George says he's the dregs. And dangerous. He says Duggan has established himself as a fixer for illicit operations around the world. No questions asked, no accountability, payment in Bitcoin.'

'So he could have been working with Parilla for a while.'

There was a ping from Tanya's laptop and I saw her immediately give full attention to the new mail in her inbox. She started tapping a reply. 'You'll want to get to work,' I said.

'It's only five past seven. I'm good for a little while. And it's still quiet. Only six emails since I picked you up.' She looked at me. 'How are you going to research without a PC?'

I still had my laptop but the PC had access to data sources that your average Joe Blow isn't supposed to have. 'I have a contact,' I said, grabbing my phone and standing up. 'Very reliable. With some of the sexiest software available. I'll call him and freeload. But before that I need to shower and change out of this grunge.' I glanced round at the broken door. 'But before *that*, while I'm in these filthy clothes, I'm going to fix the door. Are you OK here?'

Tanya said she had plenty to keep her busy.

I found a sheet of 18mm plywood in my shed, cut it to size and nailed it over the broken rear door to deter anyone who fancied nicking my non-existent valuables.

Then I showered, shaved and cleaned my teeth then, still in the bathroom, I called Clark. His phone went to voicemail. I called the main number at Maskelyne Global, which had a human on the switchboard from 07:30, and enquired about Clark. The woman, who was Scottish, told me Clark had collapsed in his office the previous evening and been taken to hospital. The theory was he'd been overworking and doing without sleep. Blimey. Did I feel guilty or what? He was probably doing without proper food as well. He didn't expend much energy sitting in front of his screens but he needed more than a vegan burger every second day.

I made sympathetic, condoling noises and suggested Clark pushed himself too hard. She agreed and said he'd looked peely-wally recently.

I smiled at the Scottish phrase. 'That's an expression Fiona MacIver uses,' I said.

'Did you work for Ms MacIver?' she said. I explained how I'd sorted a case for her involving a fake da Vinci.

'I remember you,' she said. 'Mr... Kite.'

'So you must be the lady with flame-red hair who sits to the left of the receptionist.'

'Aye. It's Roisin. Nice to talk to you, Mr Kite.'

'And you. I think the trouble with Clark is he lives on his own.'

'Does he, now?' she said. This was news to Roisin. Welcome news. 'He'll be wanting someone to look after him.' I could almost hear her brain plotting a campaign. 'He's such a bonny lad I'm surprised he's not got a lassie.'

'Perhaps I could point him in your direction?'

'Now that would be a thing...' Roisin giggled, embarrassed now, but wanting to tell me yes. 'What d'you think he'd say?'

'I'm sure he'd be delighted.' I said, crossing my fingers and hoping Clark would forgive me. I had no evidence of Clark's sexual orientation let alone his taste in women. I'd always thought of him as married to his computers. But it was time to cash in. 'The reason I wanted Clark was that he was going to send me something but was obviously taken ill before he could do so.'

'Where is it?'

'On one of the computers in his office. I was wondering if…'

'If you could go up to his office and get it? Yes, of course. Will you be in this morning?'

'I certainly will. If it's OK with you.'

'All fine with me, Mr Kite. See you later.'

Better result than I could have dreamed of.

I left the bathroom and walked naked to my bedroom to get some clothes. The first thing I saw was a pair of tights and some wispy underwear on top of a pile of neatly folded clothes on a chair. Then she sat up. Tanya was in my bed, naked but for her emerald pendant.

'I thought you were just changing your tights.'

'I watched you sawing that wood and hammering those nails. You were so macho-man, virile and red-blooded that I had a better idea.'

I smiled. 'Absolute brainwave.'

We didn't hurry. But we didn't linger. It was still only twenty past eight when Tanya was once again unruffled, immaculate and with perfect hosiery. I would have given her a lift to work but my car was still in the possession of the Metropolitan Police. So it was a taxi job and I stood on the doorstep waving. Tanya waved back, but discreetly, serenely.

The police car pound at Perivale was my first destination. By the time I had repossessed my vehicle I realised I would have to postpone using Clark's kit at Maskelyne Global. I had to meet DCI Shawn Cussons, Havers' bridge partner, at Ludgate Circus.

From an architectural and design point of view, The Black Friar is one of the most unusual pubs in Britain. Its style is art nouveau, not uncommon for a bar in Brussels but probably unique in London. The interior is made more eye-popping by low-relief plaster friezes of jolly friars drinking and disporting themselves.

The pub was quiet so early in the day. I walked through the bar until I saw a man in a grey suit slumped on a banquette in a corner by the pub's spectacular inglenook fireplace. He was sleeping, his face unshaven. As I approached, his eyes snapped open, took a second to focus, then he said, 'John Kite?' He sat up and held out his hand.

'Chief Inspector,' I said shaking hands. 'Are you all right?'

'I will be. Big send-off last night. Great party. I've not been to bed yet.' He grinned happily. 'Haven't done that for a few years.'

'It's good of you to meet me.'

He waved away my thanks.

'Would you like a drink?' I said.

He hesitated then said. 'I'd like to say a pint of beer, but my brain says no. I'll break the habit of a lifetime and have a sparkling water please.'

I got the same for myself and sat down opposite him.

'So, William Havers...' he said with surprising animation and enthusiasm. The prospect of discussing crime had made him feel better already. 'Shall I crack on?'

'Please do.'

'He'd found your name and said he wanted to hire you for an easy job and could I dredge anything up to persuade you, because he thought you'd say no.'

'He was right,' I said.

'So I looked you up, saw your record in the police – shit-hot, if you don't mind the compliment...'

I nodded my head.

'... But I couldn't find anything before the police. Then a little bell rang in my head. *Broughton*, it went. *Broughton*. And I remembered a story from somewhere that you'd changed your name. So there was a little something I could give him, something to twist your arm with.'

'Any backhander involved?'

'I'm not answering that.'

'Fair enough. Did he have a hold over *you*? Did you owe him one?'

'I'm not answering that either.'

'OK. And that was all you told him?'

'Pretty much. I didn't mention your father.'

'How much did you know about my father?'

'You writing his biography?'

I laughed. 'Maybe when I'm your age. You never know.'

He took a sip of his water and made a face. 'The first time I came across him he was about to be charged and knew there was enough evidence to put him away for a few years. So he offered to become an informer. I was running a couple of undercover operations and I got to hear about it. Your dad had been around the block, knew his left from his right, he was a good candidate. I took him on. There was a gang we wanted to bust which was doing big numbers in VAT fraud, importing and exporting precious metals. They were making millions. Your dad infiltrated them and I was hopeful of a few good collars. But...'

'There was a bent copper in on the gang.'

'Two bent coppers. Your dad was told to go to Manchester in the middle of the night...'

'And he took Mum.'

'Yeah. And up the M6 a big tractor unit forced him off the road and into a bridge support.'

I nodded. It was exactly what I'd heard before. 'Did you get them? The bent coppers?'

'In the end. But it took time. We compared paint scrapes off your Dad's car with an abandoned tractor unit and put a case together.'

'They were sent down?'

'Yeah. But not for long enough.'

'I'd like you not to mention any of this again to anybody.'

Cussons nodded. 'I won't. I shouldn't have done to William Havers, but he has a way of persuading you. Even an old bruiser like me.'

I smiled. I knew what he meant. He took a swig of his sparkling water and made another disgusted face. 'Got no flavour.'

'Water generally doesn't.'

He nodded as if learning this for the first time. 'Just one other thing... a journalist came knocking a few months back. A woman. She had half the story, she was persuasive, very persuasive. Said she knew you.'

'Her name's India Paine. She knew me at university.'

'Well, she got no more off me. I played shtum.'

'Thank you,' I said. 'Did William Havers talk to you about his divorce?'

'Maybe. In passing. Why?'

'Did he mention a scam he was pulling on his wife? Something to do with a painting?'

'You mean with the fake attribution, or whatever? Yes. I told him he'd end up in trouble if the lawyers found out. He's a rich guy. No need for penny-pinching.' Cussons turned and gave me a look with suddenly wideawake eyes. 'Is that what this meeting's about?'

I put on an innocent face. 'Who else do you play bridge with?'

Cussons gave me a guarded look. 'Better be careful what I say now. I play with some actors: they get a lot of practice while they're waiting to go on set. Apparently acting means hanging around all day. Sounds a piece of piss.'

'Anyone else?'

'Couple of politicians…'

'Any ministers?'

Cussons gave me a knowing look. 'Anyone in particular you're interested in?'

'Anyone in the cabinet?'

'I play with Chris Spanswick sometimes. You wouldn't think he was a bridge man but he's keen. Like a terrier.'

I sat back. That was the link I'd been looking for. William Havers – Cussons – Spanswick – the Prime Minister. Spanswick knew that Fresnel had a problem with a picture and must have heard by chance from Cussons about the scam Havers was playing on his wife. So he suggested the same trick to the PM. Except… Spanswick had made it clear several times he wasn't interested in art. Why would he have suggested this to the Prime Minister?

Cussons saw my expression. 'Got what you wanted?'

I just smiled. Then I had an idea from left field. 'Final question. Then I'll let you get home to bed. Do you know ex-DC Spenser Duggan?'

'He's a piece of shit.'

'Was he…'

Cussons was awake enough to read my mind. 'Was he involved with any of this VAT scam crowd?'

'Was he involved in killing my parents?'

Cussons looked straight into my eyes. 'I can't prove anything. But I reckon he organised it. Trying to make a name for himself, prove himself to the gang leaders, that kind of thing. Sorry I can't be more definite.'

I said nothing, just nodded, wondering what I could do about the man who killed my parents. When this gig was over I would try to put a case together against him. Then Cussons looked at me appraisingly. 'He was brave, your dad. Made a stupid career choice but, in the end, he was brave and strong-minded. Bit like you, from what I've heard.'

We shook hands.

'Have a good retirement,' I said.

'Two days left and nothing to do but tidy the office,' he said, taking pleasure in a huge yawn. He was a man looking forward to a well-earned rest.

Half an hour later, I walked into Maskelyne Global and crossed over to Roisin behind the reception desk. She was pleased with the bottle of Prosecco I'd brought to thank her and gave me the key to Clark's office along with a handwritten note for him. On the envelope she'd drawn an ornate, curly frame round his name. I bet she also put little circles instead of dots over her i's and had drawn a heart next to her name at the bottom. If she could put up with Clark's obsessions they might get on well.

I went upstairs to the eleventh floor. Clark's office was back to being a public health hazard. Takeaway food trays lay around, the waste bin overflowed while discarded wrappers, napkins and coffee cup lids formed a corona around it. The air was hot and stale with his machines all powered up and burning kilowatts. I remembered that Clark never turned them off and – which was great for me – had tweaked them to remove the need for passwords. Although inputting a password takes only seconds, Clark reckoned that at least once in five start-ups you mistype the password. Which doubles the time taken. He also took into account the time wasted between the machine being ready for your password and you inserting it. His calculation was he could save over five hours a year by not employing passwords in any of his machines. He wasn't careless of security, but he saw his computers as research tools not data storage facilities. As soon as he reached a conclusion on a fraud case he sent all he'd discovered to the executive concerned.

I sat down in Clark's chair and noticed at once how extraordinarily comfortable it was. Somehow, he'd persuaded MacIver to buy a state-of-the-art ergonomic seating machine for him. Given the hours he spent there he probably deserved it. But however good the chair, I could hardly see my fingers on the keyboard. Clark liked to imagine he was in a cinema and set the lighting accordingly. I wound up the levels and got to work. His gear was primarily set up for motor vehicle enquiries, so the Land Rover Defender registration was the place to start. I quickly confirmed that Peregrine Brabant, father of Lyle, was the registered owner. From the Land Registry data I discovered how much property the family owned. It was a substantial estate with several tenanted farms as well as Birchfield Place. The land where the paintings were burned was also owned by him.

I moved from Peregrine Brabant to Lyle. On Facebook many of his friends and correspondents were medical people rather than politicians. There were also soldiers and ex-soldiers. I noticed references to PTSD and that Brabant was a member of a PTSD Facebook group. Then I spotted a name that was neither medical, military nor political. Helen Oxenhope. She had liked many of Brabant's posts and commented on them. I checked her Facebook page and found *she* was a medical person. Helen worked as a clinical psychologist and had a surgery address in Hertfordshire. It was her medical practice which paid the bills, not the art gallery in Staithes which was run long-range and looked after by a local manager.

Attached to her practice website was a blog she wrote about mental health. I scrolled through it. One patient she wrote about – called 'Dr A' – was a medical practitioner whose career had taken him abroad and put him in stressful situations. He had worked in war zones and areas of famine and natural disaster. Although always a skilful and competent doctor, his experiences had caused him to develop Post Traumatic Stress Disorder. Dr A's career sounded spookily close to Lyle Brabant's.

Helen Oxenhope gave birth to Zoe when she was only eighteen and married Neil Oxenhope, presumably Zoe's father, when she was twenty-four. They divorced five years later but she preferred to keep her married name. Her grandparents, the Plastows, and her mother, Barbara Turner, all lived at Firle and must have known both Peregrine Brabant and Lyle Brabant. If Helen Oxenhope ever visited her grandparents before they moved away from Firle to East Finchley, it was possible she had met the Brabant family too.

The links between Brabant, the Oxenhopes and Mrs Plastow suggested he was involved in, or at least knew about, what Helen and Zoe were doing. If he was the patient with PTSD it was being kept secret, and that made him open to blackmail.

Clark's gear was producing results and it was a shame not to go further. I started to dig into the lives of Brabant's cabinet colleagues: Spanswick, Tresize, Featherstone.

Chris Spanswick made no secret of his differences with Fresnel. They worked together well enough but Spanswick had no time for the 'arty-tarty' stuff which Fresnel supported. According to an interview he had been 'knocked for six' when Fresnel was elected party leader, having fully expected to win the top job himself. Was he bitter, resentful? In public he seemed to support the Prime Minister, but Spanswick had been around long enough to be a skilful player, more skilful and Machiavellian than Fresnel. My meeting with him at the golf course still puzzled me and I couldn't rule him out as being the person who got me arrested. He came on like someone with no side, a plain-dealing, honest broker. But the longer I knew him the more devious he seemed.

Adam Tresize was certainly a smarty-pants operator and had been keen to interrogate me as soon as he got the chance. In the same way Spanswick played on his northern roots, Tresize played on his Cornish background and would say things like, 'We Cornish people know what it's like to be neglected and ignored.' Cornwall isn't the wealthiest part of Britain, but Tresize was certainly in the wealthiest one per cent of the population. He took expensive holidays and he'd reported one holiday to the House of Commons Members' Register because it had been funded by an overseas company. The holiday was to Malta. His entry on the register stated that the holiday had been in return for 'security advice' which, as Home Secretary, he was well qualified to give. According to Leo Somerscales, Malta was the place where Hayden were exerting their power. I wondered which side he had given advice to.

Rory Featherstone had a different background from Tresize, Brabant and Spanswick. He had been a student activist, not for his current party but for the Greens. He'd even been arrested at an environmental demonstration against building a new motorway. He'd been a member of Greenpeace then – and it seemed he still was. He was a vocal supporter in Parliament of various bills and initiatives to combat global warming and had been one of the UK delegates at several international climate change conferences. Featherstone also stood against Fresnel and Spanswick in the race to be party leader but had withdrawn after the second round of voting, having come third. Thereafter he had urged his supporters to vote for Fresnel in the final ballot.

I moved on to Fresnel himself, where the number of search results was naturally ten times those for the others. I wasn't interested in his political views: it was his background I wanted to uncover. So I looked through magazines, gossip columns, blogs, memoirs. In one of those country-living-style glossies I found a retrospective of Fresnel's time as a student. There was a direct quote:

Manchester is a great city. Very vibrant. Very of the moment. But it was also great to get away in the long vacation. I remember some idyllic times at Lyle Brabant's father's place in Sussex...

So Fresnel had been to Firle as a student. Did that help? It meant that Fresnel could have met Helen Oxenhope if she were visiting her grandparents at the same time. Very much a long shot, I thought. Too many ifs.

Then another, older, result caught my eye. It was from a student arts magazine from Manchester University. One of those short-lived publications that exist for a few years then disappear as student editors graduate and freshers arrive with new ideas. It was a series on students who were interestingly unusual in which Fresnel was featured. The article described his collection of paintings at length and one section jumped out at me.

On the mantelpiece is a gilt-framed sketch of a strikingly attractive young man. He looked my type. 'Have you got his number?' I asked James Fresnel jokily. 'You wouldn't like him,' Fresnel replied, 'at least I hope not. He's dead.' A comedian as well as an art collector. He explained that he believed the sketch was of the gay artist and Bloomsbury Group big cheese Duncan Grant. But he had no way of proving it. He also would like to think that the picture was by Grant's good friend Vanessa Bell who lived in the same Sussex house. 'If that were so, I'd be minted,' said Fresnel. 'But as I only paid loose change for the picture in Levenshulme Antique Market I think that's unlikely.' And he laughed.

I read it twice. Then sat back in my chair and breathed out. Here was red meat. I read it again slowly. There was no mistake. Fresnel had not bought the Vanessa Bell sketch recently. He'd owned the picture as a student, twenty years ago. And he was playing down its quality even then. Doubting it was genuine. Saying he'd bought it cheaply. I didn't miss his use of 'loose change' either: the term he'd used about my payment at our first meeting.

Levenshulme Antique Market was where Pilcher had a stall in the 1990s. Did Fresnel buy the picture from him in Manchester? But the Oxenhopes said he'd stolen it from them. When was this theft supposed to have happened?

Fresnel had lied about this picture ever since he'd got it. He'd lied to a student journalist. He'd lied to me. This quotation from a defunct magazine convinced me Fresnel's picture was a hundred per cent genuine. And the fact he continued to lie about it suggested he felt guilty about it.

I called Tanya, explained what I'd found and asked to meet again.

'Come over. I'll meet you in Whitehall Gardens. Thirty minutes.'

Another outdoor meeting. What was the fascination with horticulture? At least I didn't have to get a sandwich this time.

Paint It Blackmail

Whitehall Gardens is a well-tended small park overlooked by the hulking Ministry of Defence building, whose forbidding architecture seems aptly appropriate for what goes on inside. I looked up and wondered where Spanswick's office was. Would our supposedly covert meeting be observed? In the park, gardeners were hoeing, weeding and removing the spent summer bedding plants. While I waited for Tanya, I read the words on the monument to William Tyndale. He was the first translator of the Bible into English and was burned at the stake for his trouble. Nevertheless, within a year of his death, Henry VIII had a change of heart and every church in the country had to have a copy of the Bible in English. History can be depressing at times.

Tanya arrived, as usual, thirty seconds before the time she'd specified. We sat close together on the edge of a hard bench near the Tyndale monument. I adopted her straight-backed posture, my knees adjacent to and matching hers. It wasn't a time for lolling.

'Isn't the Vanessa Bell picture irrelevant, now there's something so much bigger to sort out?' she said.

'No, I think it's fundamental. In some way the Prime Minister's picture has been the catalyst for everything that's followed.'

Tanya thought about this a moment and looked at me intently. The autumn sunshine made her eyes and the matching emerald pendant sparkle. 'Go on.'

'I think his lying about this little picture has somehow festered away for years. Like an infection or a cancer it starts small, but if it's not treated the problem gets bigger and bigger and takes over the whole body. Bang, suddenly you're dead. Suddenly the country blows up.'

Her brow creased. 'Isn't that a bit dramatic?'

'I don't think so. It's the bad apple analogy.'

'Something rotten in the state of Denmark.'

'Never mind Denmark, it's this country I'm worried about. I was talking to a senior detective today about corrupt officers. He knew my Dad and it was corrupt officers who killed him in the end.'

'But he wouldn't have been involved with the corrupt officers if he hadn't been a criminal himself.' She broke off, looked at the ground and her voice softened. 'I'm sorry to be blunt, Kite.'

'No, you're right. All I'm saying is one thing leads to another. Once upon a time, the Prime Minister stole this picture and has been lying about it ever since. Now, that error, that misdemeanour…'

'Crime?'

'Well, yes. That crime has come back to bite him in the bollocks and it could well knacker him forever. That's why he got me involved to try a desperate, last-minute stunt with Pilcher. But by the time Pilcher died Duggan and the Parilla mob had got involved. What started as a family protest from the Oxenhopes became much bigger. Four hundred pictures stolen, Zukovsky and Earl murdered, the Oxenhopes under house arrest, blackmail threat to the government. None of the villains care about the Oxenhopes' picture. It's been a way to get under the Prime Minister's skin.'

Tanya considered. 'We still don't know what they want.'

'But somebody back there does.' I waved a thumb in the general direction of Whitehall and Downing Street. 'There must be an inside person. Otherwise Parilla would never have got into Number Ten.'

Tanya considered again. 'What's your next move?'

'I've got to talk to Fresnel. He made me a Special Adviser. I need to advise him.'

'You can't just burst in.'

I pulled my ID out of a pocket and put the lanyard round my neck. 'Why not? I've got this.'

'That'll get you in the front door but not into Fresnel's office.'

'Is the Prime Minister in Downing Street?'

Tanya confirmed he was.

'What about the others? Spanswick, Tresize, Brabant, Rory Featherstone?'

'The Foreign Secretary is out of London, meeting ambassadors at Chevening. Spanswick's at Aldershot with army people, Tresize is visiting a prison. Brabant's in his office, as far as I know.'

'But maybe he can't rely on Brabant,' I said. 'So Fresnel is vulnerable. No senior ministers nearby.'

'Vulnerable?' She paused a beat and her eyes held mine. 'You mean to being attacked?'

'Yes. Definitely.'

Tanya looked shocked. 'What do you think could happen? I mean, no one's going to kill him, are they?'

I said nothing and her emerald green eyes bored into mine.

'Are they?'

Chapter 21

We went into Number 70 Whitehall and walked through the Cabinet Office into Number Ten and went straight to Tom Daubeney's office.

'Tanya, John... can I help?'

'We need to see the PM urgently,' I said.

'What's it about?'

'The matter you called me about last week and also...'

'National security,' said Tanya, instantly trumping me. 'It is urgent, Tom. We're not being melodramatic.'

'Of course not,' said Daubeney, calmly consulting his screen. 'He may have a window around 5:45 but he's due in the House at six.'

'We can't wait that long,' I said.

'I'm sorry...?' Daubeney looked affronted.

'What's he doing in the next hour?' I said. Daubeney gave me a dark look.

'Sorry to press you, Tom,' said Tanya, 'but we must talk to him.'

Daubeney sighed. 'He's got the Chief Whip and Leader of the House at twelve, the Slovenian president at twelve-thirty for a working lunch, the Chancellor and the Governor of the Bank of England at two, a deputation from the Confederation of British Industries and the Department of Trade at two forty-five. At three forty-five the Minister of Health, at four o'clock he goes to the Palace for his weekly audience of the Queen, then at...'

'What's he doing at the moment?' I said.

'Mr Kite, please may I ask you to be patient?'

'What's he doing at the moment?'

Daubeney gave me another filthy look. I returned his stare. He then looked at Tanya who, I was pleased to see, said nothing and also looked straight back at him. 'He's with Lyle Brabant,' Daubeney said finally.

I had visions of a final tragic showdown between them. The old friend, Brabant, perhaps mentally challenged, finally revealing his true self and stabbing the man who trusted him in the back.

'How long has he been in there? What are they talking about?' I said.

'I see no reason why I should tell you, Mr Kite.'

'Oh, for God's sake. Brabant is a sick man. He's got PTSD.'

'I don't think so, Mr Kite.'

'I know so. He's been having treatment. He could be trying to harm the Prime Minister.'

Daubeney smiled. 'Now that does sound melodramatic. Why don't you calm down, Mr Kite. I can't believe things are as bad as you say.'

'For Christ's sake!' I thumped on Daubeney's desk and turned to Tanya. 'We're wasting time here.' I stormed out of the door, into an outer office past a pair of female assistants who must have heard most of our conversation but pretended not to have done, and then into the corridor. Where next? I realised I had no idea which of the many doors led to the Prime Minister's office. Presumably there'd be more assistants, more private secretaries, more Special Advisers in offices clustered around Fresnel.

Then I heard a door open and a familiar voice.

'Rendezvous by the postern gate in five.' Then another door opened and closed again.

It was Fresnel. I hurried back into the outer office with the two assistants.

'Where's the Prime Minister?' I said.

'Where do you think?' one of them said, nodding her head to an unmarked door. I went to it and pulled it open. There was a small tiled vestibule and then another door which I opened. The Prime Minister was standing at a urinal.

'Sorry to barge in, Prime Minister...' I began.

'There's room for two,' he said, looking over his shoulder. 'Mr Kite, how goes it?'

'Very briefly, Prime Minister, I think you're in danger. Possibly from one of your own cabinet ministers.'

'Why do you say that?'

'I've heard about the Hayden organisation and Mr Parilla. They have a number of criminals working for them who I've met. I think they are behind the theft of the four hundred pictures and...'

'John, please. Now is not the time for this. I have an appointment.'

'Yes, of course, Prime Minister. But this is vital. I know about the fake letter you gave me to research and I'm sure your Vanessa Bell picture is a hundred per cent genuine. I know you obtained it many years ago and almost certainly not from the dealer called Pilcher. I believe you probably came across it illegally...'

'What?!'

'Yes. I don't know how or why but it involves the Oxenhope family. The people who have been demonstrating recently. They certainly have some grudge against you and they are being used by villains, maybe the so-called Hayden people, to attack you in some way. You've resisted giving in to the blackmail demands. You must continue to resist them.'

'Mr Kite, this all sounds exciting and engrossing, but it's quite fanciful.'

Fresnel zipped up and turned away from the stall to wash his hands.

'Prime Minister, you must admit the truth. You must face the past. My father was a criminal. I only discovered it when I was at university, but I confronted him, I left home, left university and changed my life utterly. He was the reason I joined the police. I don't choose to tell everyone this, but I long ago faced the fact that my father was a thief. He stole stuff. If, as I suspect, you have done something similar in the past – even in a minor way – you must face up to it. You don't have to broadcast it to the nation, but admit it to those you wronged. Admit it to yourself.'

Fresnel finished drying his hands.

'If you'll excuse me, I have to meet Lyle Brabant in the rose garden.'

I had made no impression so far but I had to make one last throw. 'Are you sure you can trust Mr Brabant?'

Fresnel looked at me. His face showed astonishment, incredulity and what I took for pity. 'You have no idea what you are talking about,' he said. He turned and left.

I had failed. Hopelessly. The Prime Minister thought I was a raving idiot. Or drunk. Or high. He was probably revoking my Special Adviser status at that very minute.

I leaned on the washbasin, turned on the cold tap and splashed water on my face. I had tried direct confrontation. I needed a plan B. I walked out of the toilet and came across Tanya in the corridor.

'There you are,' she said. Where have you been?'

'Talking to the Prime Minister in the gents. He thought I was loopy.'

'You didn't shout at him? Swear at him? Stamp your foot?'

I looked at Tanya levelly and exhaled a despairing breath. 'Have you ever seen me stamp my foot?'

'Where is he now?'

'In the rose garden with Lyle Brabant. Why don't you have a go? Say I got over-excited if you like. Say I didn't get all the facts in the right order. Say whatever you like.' Tanya didn't move. Just looked at me. 'Go on. He trusts you.'

She thought about it. Looked at the floor. Looked back at me. She looked glum.

'Sure?'

'Am I sure he trusts you? You know he does. Am I sure you should go and see him? Too bloody right.'

Tanya nodded slowly, then turned and walked away towards the famous rose garden at the rear of Number Ten. I slumped down in a convenient chair and wiped some remaining drips of water off my face with a handkerchief.

In no time at all Tanya was back.

'He's not there.'

'He told me he was going there. And I heard him say, to Brabant I think, "see you at the postern gate" or something. A postern is the back door of a castle.'

Tanya looked at me and gave a puzzled shrug.

'I'm not making this up,' I said.

'Nor am I. He can't have vanished.'

'Zoe Oxenhope did in the Portrait Gallery. Let's go have a look,' I said, and we walked out into the garden, a lovely backdrop for occasional press conferences and photo shoots. It was, as Tanya said, empty of anybody, let alone the Prime Minister. We stood on the grass, bemused. Then I noticed that, outside the back gate leading to Horse Guards, the armed police officers on duty seemed agitated. I went to the gate and was aware of much radio chatter. I called out to one of them.

'Officer, this may seem a silly question, but have you seen the Prime Minister?'

'Yes sir, that's the problem. He came out of here with another minister, Mr Brabant, and they got to a car and were driven away.'

'Where to?'

'No idea, sir.'

'Who was driving?'

'Again, no idea, sir. It wasn't a government car.'

'Was his protection officer with him?'

The officer hesitated and looked at the ground, embarrassed. 'We don't know where he was, sir.'

At that moment, a man in a suit ran at top speed out of the rear door of Number Ten and came towards me at the gate.

'Open the gate, Nick,' the man shouted to a colleague and I recognised him as one of the PM's close protection officers. One of the uniforms opened the gate and Tanya and I followed the protection officer out to Horse Guards.

'What the fuck...?' said the protection officer to his uniformed colleagues.

'It's like this, Gerry,' said the sergeant on duty. 'About ten minutes ago, the PM and Brabant come out, just the two of them. We were taken unawares. Weren't expecting any traffic here today. They stood where you're standing and I said, "Are you going somewhere, Prime Minister?" and he said, "Just for a drive, officer. Nothing to worry about." With that, this big limo drives in. I say, "Where's your protection officer, Prime Minister?" and he says, "Don't worry about that. I'll be back in a trice."

The protection officer was horrified. 'Jesus. The PM stood me down before lunch. He said he was going nowhere till he went to the Palace at four o'clock.'

'Have you tried to call him?' I said.

Gerry, the protection officer, showed me his phone. 'Just done that. His phone's switched off. And Mr Brabant's. I'll set up tracking on their numbers.'

'Did you follow the car?' I said to the uniforms.

The sergeant looked embarrassed again. 'Tried to, but our mobile got stuck immediately behind an RTA on Birdcage Walk.'

I frowned. 'An accident? There?'

'Yes, sir. Suspicious.'

'Too bloody right. It was a set-up, officer. No doubt about it. So you lost the limo?'

'We're tracking it on CCTV…'

One of the other officers interrupted. He was listening to a message on his phone. 'They've gone into a multi-storey…'

'Switching vehicles,' I said. The other officers nodded agreement. 'No visual contact. No radio contact. That's the Prime Minister lost, then.'

Chapter 22

Fifteen minutes later, Daubeney came out of his office to find Tanya and me in the hallway. 'I've scheduled a meeting…' he said.

'That's always a good start. When's it for? A week on Tuesday?'

'Kite, don't make things worse,' said Tanya.

'Mr Kite, you understand these are exceptional circumstances…'

I nodded a sort of apology.

'We'll meet as soon as the key ministers can get back into London. An hour. Two at the most.'

'OK. I'll stand by.'

'And I'll go to my office,' said Tanya, rolling her eyes at me as she walked off.

'I'm sorry I can't offer you a place to wait in my office,' said Daubeney, picking up on Tanya's reluctance to do the same. 'But there's a little ante-room round the corner.'

I left Daubeney and found the place he'd indicated. It was more of an alcove in the corridor than a room, but a satisfactory place to think things over. I'd barely sat down on one of the red leather chairs when I heard hurrying feet in the corridor. The Foreign Secretary, Rory Featherstone appeared. 'Am in time?' he said, seeing me.

'Yes, Minister. Tom Daubeney is waiting for the Home Secretary and Mr Spanswick to get back.'

'Good. My driver was doing ninety down the motorway. I didn't think we'd make it.' He blew out and loosened his shirt collar. 'Are you hanging around waiting?'

'That's right.'

'Well, shall we have a chat? I've not had a chance for a one-to-one with you. You can brief me so I'm on top of my game for the meeting.'

'By all means.'

'Shall we go to Briefing Room A? Then we'll be ready for the others.'

He led the way and I followed. I was flattered he wanted to pick my brains but was also guarded. I no longer knew who to trust in Downing Street. We sat down in the meeting room, across the table from each other like Tanya and I had done a few days previously. As usual, Featherstone's tie was at half-mast and I noticed there were more loose threads hanging from his jacket. Perhaps he did buy second-hand clothes.

'So the Prime Minister's absconded?' said Featherstone. 'Off for a jolly with Lyle Brabant. At least that rules out him going off to see his mistress, not that I think he's got one.'

His light, almost dismissive tone worried me. 'It's more serious than that,' I said. 'Abduction is the word I'm thinking of.'

'What? You need to take what Tom Daubeney says with a pinch of salt. He does get flustered.'

'The police and the PM's protection officer were flustered too. And they had a right to be. I think the Prime Minister's in danger.'

'You don't think he's had a bit of a breakdown? Found he couldn't cope and had to get away. It does happen. Didn't Stephen Fry walk off stage in the middle of a show in London, leave the theatre and never came back? Just because he was depressed or something.'

There was circumstantial evidence about Brabant being depressive, but surely not the Prime Minister. Then I wondered if Brabant could have engineered Fresnel's disappearance as part of his PTSD. Featherstone was looking at me, waiting for my reaction.

'You don't agree?' he said.

'You think Mr Fresnel's depressed?'

'It's a tough job, being PM. It gets to the strongest people.'

'Do you think he *isn't* strong? Just because he's got an unusual background doesn't mean that he's not up to the job.'

Featherstone smiled. 'I see… you're a loyal supporter. All art tarts together.'

'It's nothing to do with training or education.' I shrugged. 'I'm not a pal, if that's what you're implying. He certainly has his faults.'

Featherstone narrowed his eyes and looked intently at me. 'And what would they be?'

'There are certain things I've uncovered, but I think I should keep them confidential.'

Featherstone made a face. He didn't like being excluded, not trusted. Rather than give in, I went on the attack. 'May I ask what you think of him?' I said.

'Why should I tell you?'

I persisted. 'Were you surprised when he became leader of the party? Disappointed?'

And he gave way. 'Of course I was disappointed. And so were Chris Spanswick and Adam Tresize. We wouldn't have stood if we didn't want the top job.'

'You think you could have done a better job?'

'Yes, I do. Fresnel is a middle-way man. Likes to keep everyone happy. Balance the left wing and the right wing. The result: his policies are vanilla. Nothing intrinsically wrong with them, but they're not radical enough. A government mustn't pussyfoot about, it needs to make big, bold changes. Like the Labour government did after the Second World War or, in a completely different direction, Margaret Thatcher in the 1980s.'

'What bold policies should Fresnel introduce?'

'The area where he's weakest is the environment. It's a big, glaring void in his policies. Everyone's green these days but he doesn't seem committed. Brabant is a good Lincoln green, so is Adam Tresize. Even people like Chris Spanswick, who burns up a lot of petrol driving his big car round his son's film locations, even Chris is a sort of spring-green, light emerald. Fresnel is only pale eau-de-nil or pistachio.'

'Artistically put.' It revealed a passion he normally kept hidden. 'How about you?'

'I'm the darkest forest green. One of those greens that's so dark it's almost black. I cycle everywhere – except when I have to come down the motorway at ninety to get to a meeting.' He laughed again. 'And we need to price all cars off the road.'

This was new – way outside the party's manifesto. Was it only a dream or did he believe it could be accomplished? I gave him a questioning look. 'You used to campaign against road building.'

'Yes, and I haven't changed my views. I still believe to save the planet we have to find a replacement for the internal combustion engine and power generation must be a hundred per cent either nuclear or renewables. And that's in every country in the world.'

This seemed utopian but unachievable. I wondered if he shared Brabant's ideals and asked him, 'What do you think of Mr Brabant?'

'Should have stayed a doctor. He'd be doing more good than being Fresnel's pet.'

'That's a bit harsh.'

'It's how Fresnel uses him. Like a mascot.' Or maybe a crutch, I thought.

'Does the name Helen Oxenhope mean anything to you?'

'Ah, it's interrogation time, is it?' He said with a laugh. 'Well, Inspector, I'm afraid it doesn't. Should it mean something to me? Who is she?'

I ignored his question. 'Do you play bridge?'

He laughed again. 'I see! The suspect is a bridge-playing friend of this lady, Heather… I mean, Helen Oxenhope. No, I don't play bridge. Poker sometimes. Texas hold'em for preference, but not bridge.' He paused a moment. 'So if you don't think the PM's collapsed under the strain and hidden himself away in some funny farm, you would also rule out suicide.'

'I think that's highly unlikely.'

'I agree. So let's consider what you said first. Abduction. Why would somebody abduct him?'

'To force him to do something he doesn't want to do. The stolen pictures are leverage.'

'I see. And who would be doing the persuading?'

'A foreign power?'

'Reds under the beds? Yellow peril? Surely not. Got any other suspects?' Featherstone looked at me in a tense, almost combative way.

'I don't have a suspect as such.' Featherstone's face relaxed and I got the feeling he'd been expecting me to name somebody. 'But there must be someone close to him involved.'

'How close? You mean one of the cabinet?' Featherstone looked shocked. 'That's outrageous. I hope you're going to stop them.'

'I hope so, too.'

His eyes locked on mine. Neither of us spoke for a moment, then he stood up, thanked me for the chat and excused himself with a 'see you later', and wandered off. Our conversation unsettled me. Until now I had considered Featherstone an unlikely suspect. But I recalled a chance remark of Fresnel's at our first meeting; how he'd had a 'set-to' with Featherstone over an Environmental Bill. How big was the rift between them? Even with his put-down of Brabant I wondered if Featherstone and he could be working in a strange partnership against Fresnel.

The key players returned more quickly than anticipated and within thirty minutes we were assembled in Cabinet Office Briefing Room A. Apart from Daubeney, Tanya and me, there was Adam Tresize, the Home Secretary; Chris Spanswick, Deputy Prime Minister; Rory Featherstone, Foreign Secretary; Steve Absalom, the Met Commissioner and Claudia Tranter, Director General of MI5.

I gave the Commissioner and Claudia Tranter a nod. 'You don't mind me being here, then?'

'We were outvoted,' said Absalom with a sour smile.

In the absence of the Prime Minister, Chris Spanswick chaired the meeting and opened in his usual blunt style by saying, 'It looks like we're up shit creek without a paddle.'

'Graphically put,' said Tresize, 'but accurate.'

'Has anyone round this table got a paddle? Or a lifeboat?' said Featherstone.' How about the police? What's the latest?'

'No sightings yet,' said Absalom. 'We interviewed people in the multi-storey car park but no one could give a description of the car the Prime Minister and Mr Brabant left in.'

'Any news on the phones?' I said.

'Both are still switched off,' said Claudia Tranter. 'We've found mobile numbers for both Helen Oxenhope and Zoe Oxenhope but there's no response from theirs either.'

'And who are these women?' said Featherstone.

I answered him. 'Helen was involved in the demonstration at the British Museum. She's the mother of Zoe, who did the demo at the National Portrait Gallery. They are associated with a gang that may be holding the Prime Minister and Mr Brabant. The women themselves are victims of false imprisonment.'

'Why do you think they're involved?' said Tresize.

'Helen Oxenhope has a relationship with Lyle Brabant.'

There was surprise from everybody. 'Have you proof?' said Absalom.

'If you raid Helen Oxenhope's surgery in Hertford I'm sure you can find some. She's a psychologist who has been treating Mr Brabant and it's possible their relationship goes beyond the simply medical.'

'Lyle Brabant gone off his rocker?' said Spanswick.

'That's simply crass and insensitive,' said Tresize, who could sound gay on occasions. 'Brabant has some kind of depressive state.'

'Sorry, I'm sure. But I didn't know,' said Spanswick.

'Nor me,' said Featherstone.

'Oxenhope is treating him for PTSD,' I said. 'She's written him up on her blogs.'

'Fucking hell,' said the Commissioner. 'Is he behind the picture thefts too? Together with Oxenhope?'

I paused. How much should I incriminate Brabant? I had no evidence that he was mixed up with the thefts but there was a lot of circumstantial. I gave Tanya a look. She nodded encouragement and I decided there was no point holding back. Things were critical. 'I don't know. But there's a lot of evidence pointing in his direction.'

'Tell us,' said Featherstone.

'The police have most of this already,' I said, looking at Absalom, 'so apologies for going over old ground.' It wasn't strictly true but I said it to spare his blushes. Absalom's jaw was clenched, an insincere smile on his face. Being given hints and advice by an outsider is excruciating.

'Sussex seems to be a centre of interest for the picture stealing gang. The two pictures destroyed so far were set alight near Lewes. And a house called Birchfield Place near Firle is of particular interest. It's owned by Peregrine Brabant, the father of Lyle Brabant. The house was being used by Duggan and other members of his gang to imprison the two women, Helen and Zoe Oxenhope.'

'My God,' said Featherstone, who looked sincerely shaken. 'How dreadful.'

'Also, a Land Rover belonging to Brabant's father was being used by two of the criminals involved.'

'We know the Prime Minister left Number Ten with Lyle Brabant,' said Tresize. 'Does anyone know what they were doing immediately before? Or indeed over the last few days?'

'They had a private meeting this morning,' said Tanya. 'Just the two of them.'

'Yes,' said Daubeney. 'I confirm nobody else was present.'

'What was being discussed?' said Spanswick.' Anyone got a clue?'

'Theft of the pictures?' said Daubeney.

'Maybe Lyle Brabant was confessing to his girlfriend's involvement,' said Featherstone, who looked pale. The strength and bravado he'd shown when talking to me had vanished and was now visibly distressed by events.

'Asking to resign, do you mean?' said Spanswick. 'But the PM persuaded him to stay on?'

'It's credible,' said Tresize.

'It's also credible that the Prime Minister was confessing to Brabant,' I said, 'if Brabant didn't already know.' Beside me, I heard Tanya clear her throat in a warning kind of way.

'What?' said Spanswick. 'Confessing to what?'

'I have evidence that the Prime Minister has also been involved with the Oxenhope family. They accuse him of stealing one of their paintings.'

'Stealing? Even if that's true, what's that got to do with anything?' said Featherstone whose worry was showing as impatience.

'It's irrelevant,' said the Met's Absalom. 'Can't we stick to the point at issue?'

'Yes, forget bloody paintings,' said Spanswick.

'It is relevant,' I said, 'because the Oxenhopes' grievance was the starting point for their demonstrations. If the Prime Minister had been more honest years ago we might not be sitting round this table now.'

'I see no point in digging over the Prime Minister's past life,' said Featherstone, still twitchy, playing with a loose button on his jacket.

'I agree,' said Tresize.

'On the contrary, I think it's vital,' I went on. 'His past errors have opened him up to blackmail from an international group of shady businessmen who run under the codename Hayden.'

'What is this?' said Spanswick with a laugh. 'The plot of the next James Bond film?'

'Unless you've anything more concrete to contribute I think you should withdraw,' said Featherstone, looking directly at me, his voice strained.

'This *is* concrete,' I said. 'Claudia, you and SIS know about these people…'

The Director General of MI5 looked at me and paused before replying. 'This is classified material of the highest sensitivity…'

'We need to know,' said Tresize. 'Spit it out.'

'We are aware of this group codenamed Hayden who have been seeking to lobby the Prime Minister. We're also aware that one of them had a brief informal meeting with the Prime Minister earlier in the year and subsequently telephoned Tanya Brazil to press his case further.'

Tanya nodded at Claudia Tranter. I remembered her long call in the garage at Pilcher's.

'And another member of the group, a Venezuelan national called Clayton Parilla, along with two associates, had a secretive meeting with the Prime Minister last week,' I said.

'I can confirm that,' said the Director General of MI5.

'Was that the huh-hush meeting? Secretaries and Cabinet Office staff excluded?' said Daubeney.

'Yes,' said Tanya.

'Are you suggesting that the Prime Minister has gone rogue? Joined up with this simply odious group?' said Tresize.

'I'm suggesting that *somebody* has,' I said. 'I don't know if it's the Prime Minister but somebody at a senior level in the British government is plotting something with this group.' There were outraged protests from round the table. 'The other person in the meeting with Clayton Parilla was Lyle Brabant,' I said.

Tanya and Daubeney both confirmed this.

'What would Brabant's motive be if he had turned against the PM?' said Tresize.

'I'm not saying it's definitely Brabant. But I do believe the Prime Minister has been kidnapped.' There was an outcry from Daubeney and the ministers. I felt Tanya's restraining hand on my arm. 'It's possible Lyle Brabant is the perpetrator, but it's also possible Brabant has been kidnapped with him. I think the Prime Minister is being held incommunicado until he agrees to whatever his captors want.' There was shocked silence for a whole second, then an outburst of protests, incredulity and questions from everybody in the room except Tanya.

'Listen, please…' I tried to quieten them. 'The theft of the four hundred pictures is part of the leverage they have against him. It's a serious attack on the democracy of our nation and the Prime Minister is in danger. The people behind this may be in Parliament, they may be in the police or the armed forces, they may be in this building, they may be in this room.'

There was outrage. Spanswick stood up, banging his fist on the table and shouting at me. Featherstone's face was white. Tresize was talking to Tranter from MI5, Absalom from the Met was asking for hard evidence.

I stood up. 'Quiet, please! 'If you don't want to listen to what I believe is the truth then I'm happy to resign as a Special Advisor.'

'Yeah, I should have let Brabant fire you the other day at the golf course, like he wanted to,' said Spanswick.

'That's very significant,' I said pointing at Spanswick. 'And, given the closeness of Mr Brabant and the Prime Minister, it suggests the PM wanted to get rid of me too, because he knew I was near the truth and it would be embarrassing for him. Maybe that's why he got me arrested.'

There was another outcry, but I carried on. 'When the Prime Minister hired me to validate a simple piece of art work he lied to me. It was because he thought he could get away with something he did wrong many years ago. It wasn't a big thing but it's something he chose to ignore rather than confront and sort out properly.

'That was his mistake. And it's what could bring him down. If you don't believe me, tough. But I've told you and the police all I know and I'm not wasting any more time in this room with its infighting and bureaucracy. You can sit here talking but I'm going to find the Prime Minister and try to help him.'

With that, I left the room.

Chapter 23

I walked upstairs to the hallway of Number Ten and the doorman pulled it open for me – just as the Downing Street cat appeared from nowhere and walked out proudly into the street with me. The cat stalked off up the street towards Horse Guards looking for prey while I marched towards the police barrier and went through into Whitehall.

As I reached my car, I had a call from the helpful Matilda from the Tate. She sounded even more like an innocent sixteen-year-old and I imagined a useful sideline for her in telephone sex lines. She said now the safety review had been completed she'd had time to delve down into the Charleston archive. She was excited to report a reference to Vanessa Bell giving a picture away as a present to someone called Peggy. No one knew who Peggy was, but she was presumably a friend or relation or one of the locals. There was no record of what the subject of the picture was and no indication of its present whereabouts.

'But it could be the one you're interested in… the one of Duncan Grant,' Matilda said.

'I know it is,' I said.

'How can you be sure?'

'Isn't Peggy a pet form of Margaret?'

'It certainly used to be,' said Matilda.

'Right. I'll come over in a few days with the evidence and you can add a footnote to your archive.'

Paint It Blackmail

It was a call I'd been waiting for, but now things had moved on. It wasn't the Prime Minister's picture I was trying to save, it was the Prime Minister himself.

But it seemed walking out of the Downing Street meeting had turned on a tap of information. Next, I got a video message from Zoe Oxenhope.

I touched play, stared at the screen and soon forgot all about Charleston.

It was a shot taken from inside a moving car showing landscape rolling by. The phone was being held against a window with part of the car door visible at the bottom of frame. The shot bounced up and down with the motion of the car and it was obvious the video had been shot surreptitiously, the phone being held low to escape detection. The fixed shot ran for several minutes, then there was a man's voice asking, 'What's she doing?'

Another voice said, 'She's filming. Get the phone. Stop her.' I saw fingers cover the lens of the phone.

Zoe shouted, 'No. Let go.' The picture went black as Zoe struggled to retain the phone while someone tried to get it from her. Then there was the sound of a slap. A cry from Zoe and the picture resumed. There was a brief flash of Zoe's face, then blurred images of faces inside the car, someone's trousers, Zoe's legs and more fingers.

Someone said, 'How does it turn off?' Another voice said, 'Just chuck it out.'

The picture cleared again and there was the briefest flash of another face before the picture went bright white, over-exposed. Then the exposure settled and there was a confused spiral of blurred images, a loud clunk on the soundtrack and a scraping noise which reminded me of the tube train going over me and Zoe. I guessed this was the phone hitting the road and skidding along the tarmac. Then the phone was finally still. The shot was of a clear blue sky and the tops of trees. There was traffic noise. A car approached, the picture went dark and then the sky appeared again. The wheels had gone either side of the phone. There was a long pause, with only birdsong on the sound track, then I heard the throaty, diesel roar of an approaching heavy goods vehicle. The picture went black and transmission ended as the truck went over the phone and smashed it to pieces.

Zoe was sending me a cry for help. An ingenious move. Was her mother with her? The Prime Minister? I played the recording twice. Zoe was unmistakeable but I wanted to identify the others in the car. One of the voices was Duggan. The other I couldn't place.

I transferred the video to my laptop, slowed it down and muted the sound. I wanted to identify the brief shot of a face after the phone was wrenched away from Zoe. At half speed it was still unidentifiable. At a quarter speed it was the same. Then I watched it frame by frame. Some of the frames were themselves blurred because the subject was moving as well as the phone. Finally I found a single frame with a clear, sharp image. As I supposed, it was James Fresnel, the Prime Minister.

I realised the video she sent wasn't identified by location. Her mother had made her turn her phone's location function off and she'd not turned it back on again. But even if I found out precisely where the video had been shot, it didn't tell me where Zoe and the Prime Minister were being taken to.

I phoned Roisin at Maskelyne Global and heard that Clark was back.

'He's looking so much better, Mr Kite, after a good night's rest and a proper meal. And Ms MacIver said he must go home at six o'clock tonight. Not a moment later.'

'Good. That's excellent,' I said, checking the time. 'Tell him I'll see him soon.' It was a few minutes to five when I knocked on Clark's door and went in.

'I go away for a single day and come back to find someone's fucked about with my room,' he said.

'Really? It looks a lot tidier.' I kept a straight and sympathetic face.

'Yeah, the cleaners came in. That's usual, but someone screwed with my light settings, opened half the windows, and put the blinds up.'

'That's sacrilege,' I said.

Clark paused and turned away from his monitors to give me a hard look. 'Are you taking the piss?'

'Never,' I said.

'I think it was one of the girls that did it.'

'Which girls?'

'The office girls. One of them left a note for me. Like a Valentine. I don't know what to do. It's from someone I've never heard of. Girl called Roy-zin.'

'It's pronounced Ro-sheen. It's a Scottish name.'

'You know her?'

'She's on the switchboard. Next to reception. Red hair.'

Clark thought a moment. 'Oh, yeah…' He thought again and nodded. 'Nice tits.'

'I hear you've got to go at six. So you could ask her out.'

'Sod that for a game of soldiers,' said Clark. 'I mean… going home at six, not the other.' He considered a moment. 'I may say hi, or something. Anyway, what you got for me?'

He loaded the video from Zoe's phone and saw the problem at once.

'I get it. You want to know where they're going?'

'Well, let's start with where they *were*. Then I'll try to work out where they're going. We'll need to go through it frame by frame.'

'Frame by frame? Really?' he repeated with an amused, incredulous look. It runs fourteen minutes nine seconds. That's…' He paused, doing the maths in his head. 'More than twenty thousand frames. And you want it done by six o'clock?'

'I was thinking of you, Clark. Your health. Your sex life.'

He gave me another dubious look. 'Very kind, I'm sure. Let's get going.'

The video played from the start. The scenery was rural and dull. Fields of crops. Occasional houses. The road was straight and level. Featureless countryside.

'Very flat,' said Clark.

'Looks like East Anglia,' I said. 'Lincolnshire, Cambridgeshire, Norfolk, Suffolk.' The video showed the typical big skies you get in those areas. The skies that filled the paintings of Constable. Or indeed of John Sell Cotman. It would be ironic if I was being taken back to Norwich where the case started. The road crossed a railway line via a level crossing.

'Stop and roll back,' I said. 'Tell me about the railway, Clark. You're the transport expert.'

Clark rewound the video then forwarded it and stopped it in the centre of the railway lines. The tracks stretched away, straight, level and undeviating until they appeared to meet and vanish a mile or so in the distance. A perfect demonstration of perspective.

'Unmanned level crossing monitored by CCTV, remotely operated by a signalman,' said Clark. 'Common in East Anglia because the land is so flat. Overhead electric cables. Just two tracks, so it's not the east coast mainline. So you've got the lines to Norwich or Kings Lynn, then cross country services from Norwich to Ely, March, Peterborough.' Clark looked at me for approval.

'Great. Play on.'

The video moved forwards. The fields continued. Then there was a flash of water as the car went over a bridge.

'Stop and roll back. Let's look at that river.'

The video showed a waterway as dead straight as the railway line. No boats. No anglers. No people. The distinct feature of the waterway was high dykes either side of it and the water level in the channel looked higher than the land beyond the dykes. I got Clark to zoom in on the land surface. It *was* lower than the waterway level. We were in Fen Country. The waterway wasn't a river, it was one of the hundreds of miles of drainage channels which keep the area liveable and workable.

The video moved on. More fields. A few houses. Another land drain. Then there was a sudden noise and a flash on the video.

Clark rewound, turned the volume up and played it frame by frame. The sound was high-speed aircraft at low level. What I thought was a flash was two distinct images. First the briefest shadows on the field nearest the car, caused as the planes were overhead, then a flash in the sky as the aircraft that had caused the shadow passed overhead in vision.

'There's Lakenheath and Mildenhall up there,' I said. Both nominally RAF stations but primarily bases for the US Air Force.

'Mildenhall is special ops, tankers and intelligence,' Clark said. 'But they're fighters. F15s from Lakenheath.'

'We know the general area but I need something to get us closer.'

'Doing my best,' said Clark, aggrieved he was being underestimated.

'Yes, of course. I meant we could do with a road sign or something.'

'What's that?' Clark said, stopping the video and rewinding. 'There's a sign.' Attached to a telegraph pole near a farm track was a Day-Glo yellow sign only four inches wide and a couple of feet long. It was pointing down the track and read 'DIG LOC'. 'Digital something?' said Clark.

'It's to do with a film or TV shoot,' I said. 'They put up signs to guide crew to where they're filming.' I thought about Spanswick's son who worked as a location manager. 'LOC is short for location. They're supposed to take the signs down when they're finished.'

'What's DIG then?'

'An abbreviation for whatever the programme or film is.' I turned to him. He was the TV and video addict.

'*Dig For Victory*,' said Clark. 'It's a rural thing. Second World War. I've seen it.'

'Not my thing,' I said. 'But they're obviously making some more.'

'Even if you found exactly where the phone was dropped, they might have driven another hundred miles.' Clark had suddenly turned grump.

'If they were going a long way north from London they'd have gone up the M1, but they're on smaller roads. As if they're near their destination. I think Zoe thought so. That's why she started filming.'

Clark nodded, conceding my point.

We had got to the point on the video where Duggan noticed Zoe filming and took the phone off her. Looking at the video on Clark's systems it became clear for the first time that the car wasn't an ordinary saloon; it was a people carrier with three rows of seats. Zoe was at the back, which was why it had taken some time for anybody to notice her filming. As the phone camera moved around inside the car I could piece together who was where. Helen was sitting beside Zoe at the back. In the middle row of seats was Fresnel with an unknown member of Duggan's team next to him. Duggan was driving with nobody in the front passenger seat. Duggan had spotted Zoe filming via his rear-view mirror and alerted his colleague. The guy had made a grab for the phone but Zoe had moved back and held it out of his reach. He then had to unbuckle his seat belt and half climb into the back to grab the phone. He then had trouble switching the phone off so Duggan told him to throw it out. Which he did.

The Prime Minister hadn't intervened at all and now I saw why. He was handcuffed to the door handle.

The phone sailed through the air and landed on the road. I noticed that the shot from the road surface included more than sky. The phone had come to rest not quite horizontally, in a pothole I guess, and a building was visible at the edge of frame. It looked like a pub.

Clark zoomed in and cleaned up the image. It was a pub. The White Horse. It took only seconds to locate it. It was near a village called Stow Fenney.

'Now you know exactly where they *were*,' said Clark, 'how are you going to find out where they *are*?'

Chapter 24

I'd been convinced that the Firle area was the key to whatever was going on. Brabant was born there. The Prime Minister had visited him there as a student. Oxenhope's family came from the area. And Vanessa Bell and Duncan Grant lived and painted nearby. I'd been convinced, but I'd been wrong. How much else had I been wrong about?

I jogged down the stairs at Maskelyne Global, keen to get to East Anglia and on the trail of the Prime Minister. Coming up the stairs, I met Fiona MacIver, Head of Investigation and Fraud. We hadn't seen each other since I worked for her investigating the violent theft of a sixteenth-century German painting.

'Kite! Good to see you,' she said in her gentle Hebridean accent. 'Freeloading off Clark Munday?'

'That's about it,' I said. 'And easier when he's off sick. Did you mind?'

'As long as you don't hack into the Pentagon.'

'That's beyond my level,' I said. 'Still doing the stairs?' She was a great hill-walker and I'd previously suggested she walked up and down the stairs as a way of training.

'Twice a day, and sometimes again at lunchtimes. The trainers are getting a bashing.' She held up a leg to show her footwear. 'I've done three more Munros since I last saw you, but it's harder to get away. I go to bridge classes now on a Friday evening.'

'Bridge?' This didn't sound like MacIver.

'Aye. For my retirement.'

'You're not retiring yet?'

'Another eight years. But it'll take me that long to get to a decent standard. And you meet interesting people. The Foreign Minister was at my club the other day. Rory Featherstone.'

'Featherstone? Sure it wasn't Lyle Brabant?'

'My eyesight's still twenty-twenty, Kite, thank you very much. Does Brabant play too?'

'Apparently.' I wondered whether everybody did apart from me. Featherstone had categorically denied he played bridge. What reason could he have for that? Unless he played with Havers and was the one who told the Prime Minister about the painting scam.

'Your sudden interest in politicians must mean you're working on the Government Art Collection theft,' she said. I agreed I was and she gave me a look which was both sympathetic and cautionary. 'However brilliantly you do, you'll get no thanks from them.'

And she continued up the stairs.

On the way to my car I called Tanya to update her on Zoe's video so she could pass it on to Daubeney and everyone else. She answered the phone in her normal cool fashion and I tried to pre-empt her giving me a bollocking for storming out of the meeting by saying, 'I've got something new. Let me explain.'

So she said, 'OK,' and listened while I told her about Zoe's video. Then she surprised me. 'Can I come with you?' she said.

'I was expecting you to say you'd never speak to me again.'

'Why?'

'Because I went over the top in that meeting.'

'Well, yes. But you were kind of right as well.'

'Why do you want to come?'

'Why not? I could be useful. Ride shotgun.'

'Have you got a shotgun?'

'Don't be daft.'

'Aren't you needed in Whitehall?'

'If someone's planning a coup I think that takes precedence. If it's not sorted I may not have a job and there may be no government. And we're wasting time chatting.'

She was right. I told her where to meet me and I ran the rest of the way to the car.

She was at Tufnell Park tube station before me. She swivelled elegantly into the front seat and once again I admired her thighs as she adjusted her skirt hem. I raced north up the A1 but at the Hatfield Galleria exit I turned off the motorway into the shopping centre.

'Why are we stopping?' Tanya said.

'I want to buy you something.'

'A shotgun?'

'Wait and see.'

I led her into Mountain Warehouse.

'Why do we need climbing gear? Where we're going is dead flat.'

I said nothing but took her to a changing cubicle.

'Take your clothes off,' I said.

'Interesting location, but have we time for that kind of thing?' she said, quirking her eyebrows. I closed the curtain on the cubicle and went to the women's section of the store. I chose quickly and returned to Tanya's cubicle where she had removed her skirt and jacket.

'Try these for size.' I handed her a shirt, a padded gilet, lightweight hiking trousers and a waterproof jacket. I checked her shoe size and went to find some boots and a pair of socks.

'Comfortable?' I said as we walked back to the car, carrying Tanya's office clothes in a bag.

'Fine, thank you.' I looked across at her. She looked as sexy in the check shirt and the rugged trousers as she had in the silk blouse and short skirt. I guess Tanya would look sexy in a plastic bag.

'Does the new kit mean you're expecting serious opposition?'

'Whatever happens I thought it'd be a shame to mess up your Bond Street stuff.'

'If we're in trouble I can use some Tai Chi.' I gave her a surprised look and she went on. 'I did evening classes for about ten years. That's how I learned good posture.'

'I thought you may have been a dancer.'

'I wish. Though I guess it's similar training. But Tai Chi's also a martial art. In some disciplines they use weapons.'

'Sorry they didn't sell swords in the hiking shop.'

She smiled, then as I looked ahead, I saw a man rising up from the far side of my car. I put a hand on Tanya's arm and stopped her. Tanya followed my gaze.

'Bloke in the zip-up leather jacket?' she said.

'Exactly. He was doing something to my car.'

'Like what?'

'At best, sticking a tracker on it. At worst…'

Tanya turned to me. 'Something that goes bang?'

I nodded and looked around the huge car park. Among the hatchbacks and family saloons one vehicle stood out. Peregrine Brabant's old Land Rover Defender, hardly damaged after smashing into the Transit van. Built like a brick shithouse those old vehicles.

I called Clark. When he answered I heard pub noises in the background.

'Having a night off?' I said.

'Anything wrong with that?' He was oddly defensive. Then I heard a familiar Scottish accent saying, 'There you are,' and the sound of glasses being put down. Fast worker, Clark. In spite of his earlier shrugs and disinterest not only was he out with Roisin but she was buying the drinks.

'Transport problem,' I said. 'I know it's late but I need a car. Got any contacts near Hatfield who owe you a favour?'

'Sure,' said Clark. 'What kind of thing are you looking for?'

'Anything with four wheels and a full tank.'

Forty-five minutes later night had fallen and two identical, showroom-new Ford Focuses arrived from a local rental depot.

'Which do you fancy?' said the guy in charge.

'They look exactly the same,' I said.

'They are,' the man said. 'Except for colour. One's red, one's blue.'

I had noticed that. 'Anything else?'

The man shook his head, waiting eagerly for my choice. 'Thought you might have, you know, a lucky colour or something. Clark is fussy about that kind of thing and if you're a friend of his…' I shook my head. He looked at Tanya and tried again. 'Does Mrs Kite have a favourite?'

She gave me an amused look and zipped up the front of her waterproof jacket to cover her nose and mouth.

An hour later, in the blue car – we tossed a coin, if you're interested – we were about thirty miles south of the pub that appeared in Zoe's video.

'It's nearly nine o'clock,' I said. 'Are you happy if we hole up somewhere till daylight?'

'You don't mean a bivouac? Sleeping under a hedge?' she said, sounding worried.

'Just because I bought you hiking clothes doesn't mean we can't go to a hotel.'

'Of course not. Good plan.' She smiled and gave my thigh a squeeze.

At 8:30 next morning I picked up Zoe's run-over phone from the middle of the road near the village of Stow Fenney in Norfolk. It was comprehensively shattered. A piece of roadkill itself. The White Horse pub was nearby but was boarded up and for sale, something that wasn't apparent on the video. Like many other rural pubs, there wasn't enough trade to make it a viable business.

We drove northwards from the pub; the direction Duggan and the others had taken. What were we looking for? I wasn't sure. I assumed that the Prime Minister, Brabant, Zoe and Helen Oxenhope had all been taken to the place where the stolen pictures were. Which suggested the pictures had never been in the south of England at all. The bonfires had been a decoy.

'If it's really a takeover or coup, what are we talking about?' I said. 'The army on the streets? Tanks in Whitehall?'

'God. Don't,' said Tanya. 'Changing a Prime Minister can be remarkably simple in this country. You don't need an election. Look at the way Margaret Thatcher went, and Theresa May and others.'

'But it's not being organised in some London club over a decanter of claret. Parilla's involved for a start.'

'He can't be the organiser. Just the catalyst.'

That was true. 'So whoever it is who wants to take over from Fresnel must have backing from others.'

Tanya nodded. 'Senior MPs and maybe people outside Parliament. Do you know about Mountbatten in 1968?'

I didn't.

'There's a theory that Lord Mountbatten tried to organise a coup to get rid of Prime Minister Harold Wilson. He's supposed to have had retired army people with him and a couple of business moguls. There could be something similar in place now.'

'A historical precedent. That's made me feel a whole lot better.'

I drove on and we scanned both sides of the road for anything that didn't look right. For anything unusual. We stopped to investigate a large empty house that was set well back from the road. But it was nothing more than an empty house. I climbed to the top of a fence by a field of root vegetables and scanned around with binoculars. This part of Norfolk is thinly populated and not prosperous. The land is flat and bleak, scarcely above sea level. Five hundred years ago it had been mostly swamp and marshland which flooded regularly. Now it's farmland, kept usable by the drainage systems first engineered by the Dutch. I could see miles in all directions but saw nothing of interest.

We went on. We came to another of the film company signs I'd seen on Zoe's video. This one read 'DIG LOC2'. A second location. The fact that our route was following film locations felt significant. Spanswick could have come across a good place to store the pictures because of his son's work. But that wasn't a motive to stage the robbery in the first place. And someone else, knowing his son's involvement in location work, could have tapped him discreetly for advice.

We stopped to check out LOC2. It was disappointing. Nothing more than a field. There were multiple vehicle tracks, ground flattened by foot traffic and an area where the field had been ploughed. But the ploughed area stopped unrealistically in the middle of the field and some of the plough lines wandered drunkenly. The tractor driving looked as bad as Craig's Land Rover handling. Then I recalled what Clark had said about *Dig for Victory*.

Paint It Blackmail

'I think they were filming ploughing,' I said. 'Actors doing it for the drama.'

Tanya nodded. 'Which is why it's so haphazard.'

We left the location, underwhelmed.

In the car Tanya got a text from Daubeney telling her that a TV channel was announcing an exclusive live interview with the Prime Minister in which Fresnel was going to reveal startling new policies. The interviewer was to be none other than Lucy Bladon. I stopped the car again and phoned the newsdesk of the firm Bladon worked for.

It took a while to get through to anyone who was anything other than a gatekeeper but finally, reluctantly, the duty news editor took my call.

'Jeff Peachey speaking,' he said, sounding like he wished he was somewhere else. 'What's the problem?' I put the call on speaker and explained I was a Special Advisor working for the PM and wanted to know where the interview was happening.

'Why are you asking me? Why don't you know?'

'I didn't fix the interview up.'

'Well, it sounds like a right shambles. I've had someone else from Downing Street asking the same question. Can't you walk along the corridor and ask whoever it was who had the bright idea?'

'Downing Street called you?'

'Yeah. You need to get yourself together.'

'Are you sure you're not being pissed about? Are you sure it's not all a hoax?'

'Absolutely sure. I was phoned by a senior member of the government who is known to me. And before you ask, no it wasn't some comic faking his voice. We talked about personal things as well. He told me he'd set up the interview.'

'Which senior member of the government?'

'If you don't know I'm not fucking telling you. You could be calling from the BBC for all I know. Trying to screw our exclusive.'

'This senior man, he gave you the location, did he?'

'No. I don't have the location myself. It will be communicated at six o'clock this evening so we can get a truck there with our reporter and set up a link.'

'Were you suspicious of all that?'

'No. As I said, I know the man. Now, I've got a programme live on air in twenty-four minutes so I'll bid you farewell. Don't forget to watch the interview – you may learn something.'

Duty Editor Peachey may not have been suspicious, but I was, and so was Tanya.

I drove on. In a couple of miles we came to another of the film company signs. This one said 'DIG BASE'. Which we assumed meant it was the production base camp, whatever that was. If it was suitable for a film production with all their trucks, lights, make-up and hundreds of actors and extras then it could be a suitable hiding place for four hundred pictures – and a Prime Minister.

The sign pointed to a closed-down budget hotel, an ugly three-storey building from the middle of the last century. It had evidently been closed for some time. A sales agent's board fixed above the entrance was faded, bird shit-stained and the plywood it was made from was splitting. A large neon sign – Fenland Hotel Bed & Breakfast – had been removed from the frontage and lay on the ground covered in moss and dead leaves. The property looked a sad victim of recession, mismanagement or lack of trade, like the pub we'd seen earlier.

I left the car in the empty front car park and we set out to explore. The main entrance was boarded up and a sign sent callers to the back of the building. We walked round and looked through windows into an empty dining room. Tables had been up-ended on top of others, and chairs stacked in piles. A plastic box held dozens of salt and pepper sets.

As soon as we reached the back of the building I knew we had found the right place. Parked in a yard near the hotel's rear entrance was Peregrine Brabant's Land Rover Defender. Next to the Defender were smarter vehicles, rental cars like those used as getaways by the Oxenhopes. Beyond the yard was an expanse of grass and a steep embankment, behind which ran one of the major rivers of the area, the Ouse.

Incongruously, in this semi-derelict place, a rostrum had been erected, complete with chairs, table and a lectern. There was also a backing screen behind the rostrum to mask the tatty hotel. It looked like the setting for a political rally or a press conference. But the rostrum faced not rows of seats but the empty yard where weeds and grass poked through tarmac. This, it seemed, was the location for the advertised policy speech by the Prime Minister.

The most ominous feature in the yard was unmissable: a tall pyramid of lumber fifteen, twenty feet tall. On the pile were fragments of ex-hotel furniture: legless tables, backless chairs, half a bedside cabinet. There was also an ancient window frame, a door with its panels missing, a wooden cable drum and innumerable tree branches. Telegraph pole-size timbers had been laid vertically over all this, meeting together at the top like the ribs of a teepee.

'Like those piles of rubbish kids put together on waste ground for Guy Fawkes bonfires,' said Tanya as we surveyed the heap.

Unless the Prime Minister agreed to the demands put to him, this was where the blackmailers were going to burn the paintings. I hoped they didn't intend to follow the Tyndale precedent and burn the PM as well.

Chapter 25

Near the bonfire-in-waiting stood a heavy-duty truck-mounted crane with an extending jib. We circled past its six-foot tyres and saw the yellow-jacketed driver dozing high above us. Then we heard a car approaching at speed from the main road. We concealed ourselves behind the fire heap.

A limo with blacked-out windows appeared. A Bentley Mulsanne. The sort of car that's tailored to a billionaire's personal specification. It was sleeker, more attractive than the US President's Beast but would have a similar defensive and protective function.

It drew up by the hotel's rear doors. A heavyset man with buzz cut hair, in a black check sports coat over a black T-shirt and jeans got out from the front passenger seat. A bodyguard. He scanned around the deserted yard and opened a rear door. A tall man in his fifties with a bronze complexion got out the other. I'd never seen a twenty-thousand-dollar suit or thousand-dollar shoes in the flesh, but what Bronze Face was wearing fitted the description. He looked around deprecatingly at the closed hotel, the stack of timber and the overgrown yard.

'I sure get taken to some exotic places,' he said. 'Is the whole of England rotting away like this?' And he laughed. His accent was Spanish. Venezuelan, I guessed.

The minder simply said, 'This way in please, sir.' As they walked towards the hotel door a gust of wind shook the fire heap and picked up a piece of plywood. It soared briefly in the wind then fell back and cartwheeled down the pile and rolled across to where cars were parked.

The two men turned back, alerted by the noise, but then strode on into the hotel.

'Clayton Parilla,' I said to Tanya.

Tanya nodded. 'He's the man I passed by in Number Ten.'

We made our way to the back door of the building through which Parilla had gone. It was unlocked and there was no sign of Parilla or anyone else. It was the service end of the hotel. There were staff toilets, clothes pegs with hard hats and yellow jackets on, then a laundry room and a small office. Next was a wash-up area, with huge stainless steel sinks, leading into the long-disused catering kitchen with more stainless steel in the form of work and preparation tables.

On one of the tables was a metal tray with some hypodermic syringes in sealed sterile packages and ampoules of some kind of drug. Tanya and I looked at each other, wondering what their grim purpose might be. Tanya shivered but said nothing. Whatever Parilla's plan was he seemed ready to carry it out with extreme ruthlessness.

We moved on and passed a row of huge fridges and freezers, all switched off, an eight-burner cooker, two fryers and a large grill beneath a fat-encrusted extractor hood. The floor was sticky with dirt and grease too. When operations had ceased and staff were fired, cleaning up was the last thing on anyone's mind.

There was a rhythmic clanking noise from the extractor as the wind flapped its exterior vents, but no other sound. No footsteps. No voices. Where was everybody? We moved through a swing door into the dining room we'd seen from outside. The carpet was thick and we moved noiselessly across the room, past the silent rows of tables and piles of chairs.

At the far end of the dining room were double doors. I pulled one of them gently towards me and looked through the gap. I saw the hotel's reception area, which was also deserted. Nobody to check in now. Tanya and I went through the doors and listened again for sounds. Still nothing. Next to the reception counter was a staircase. I made an upwards gesture to Tanya and we started to climb. On the next floor, signs indicated directions to bedrooms and to something called the Ely Suite. A banqueting and function room, presumably. We followed the sign and came to a pair of closed double doors.

We listened and could hear the mutter of voices, but words were unintelligible. A function suite would be big, empty and echoey. A poor acoustic. Then one voice came across louder than the rest and we clearly heard the phrase 'absolute perfidy'. Fresnel's voice and choice of words were unmistakeable.

Then we heard a different sound. The swish and crackle of someone approaching wearing protective clothing. We hurried away, following the corridor round a corner and flattened ourselves against the wall. We heard the person go up to the function suite, knock on the doors, then open them.

'Sorry to disturb,' we heard. 'I'm Dan. Crane driver. Just checking the timetable.'

Someone inside asked him to go in and he did so, shutting the doors behind him.

'We need to get ears on what's happening,' I said.

We carried on down the corridor. The first door past the suite was locked; the next, marked 'staff only', was open. We went in. The room had served as a drinks storeroom behind a bar. We walked round to the bar servery where a fireproof metal screen was down over the bar counter itself.

We heard the low voices again. They were still indistinct but seemed to be coming from above where we stood. I looked up and saw the source of the sound. One of the panels in the suspended ceiling was missing.

I climbed on to the bar counter and put my head through the gap in the ceiling. The light was dim but I could see the ceiling extending far in front of me. The voices from the function room were louder now but still hard to interpret.

I extended a hand to Tanya and pulled her up onto the bar beside me.

'What do you think?' I whispered.

She put her head as far into the ceiling void as she could.

'Can we get any closer? Crawl over there, maybe?'

I looked doubtful. Suspended ceilings are not load-bearing, not designed to hold much more than the weight of the ceiling tiles. The wires holding up the ceiling were thin and the alloy frame into which the tiles fitted was far too weak to support either of us. Then, in the gloomy light, I noticed trunking for the air conditioning system. I removed another couple of tiles from the bar's ceiling and moved over to investigate it. Air con trunking is lightweight for a good reason but the supports which held up this rig looked unusually rugged. I grabbed hold of the fixings bolted into the concrete floor above us and tried to move them. They held firm. Over-specified by the architect? Or maybe the construction firm had used leftover stock to save money. The trunking was wide and suspended low enough below the concrete floor to enable us to slide along it.

Tanya had watched what I did.

'Looks good,' she said softly. 'I'm lighter. I'll go first. You stay a good few feet behind so we distribute the weight.'

Exactly what I would have said. I put my hands round her slender waist, she angled her tai chi-honed body with skill and in a few seconds was lying flat along the top of the trunking. There was a creak from the metalwork as it sagged under her weight, but the metal supports held firm. She slid forwards along the trunking, disturbing decades of dust, spiders' webs and builders' leavings. A screw which a construction worker had abandoned fifty years previously rolled off the trunking and fell on to a ceiling tile. *Clunk.* The sound it made was soft but, like a pea on a drum, it would be audible to anyone directly below.

When Tanya was twenty feet away from me I sprang up into the void and climbed on to the trunking behind her. The metal surface crumpled a little under my weight and the support rods groaned and creaked, but I pushed carefully forwards. As did Tanya. In this way, maintaining what we hoped was a safe gap between us, we moved about thirty feet along the trunking until the voices from the function suite below us were clear.

The Prime Minister sounded tense, even scared. '…life imprisonment is the penalty for what you're doing. Did you know that? And it's no good pretending you've got some immunity or you'll not be extradited. The Americans will want to put you in Guantanamo and I'll do everything in my power to help them. Extraordinary rendition? I'll make sure it's extremely extraordinary rendition. I'll drive you to the airport myself.'

'I'm doing this for the good of your country.' It was the bronzed voice of Clayton Parilla.

'For the good of your bank balance, you mean. Overthrowing a legal government is treason – or in your case an act of war. How dare you say it's for the good of the country? You'll destroy the country, bleed it dry.'

The trunking beneath me complained again with a louder clunk. I hardly dared breathe.

'We'll save it. Raise revenue. Reduce toxic emissions.'

'I can't understand how you persuaded other good people to join you.'

'I'm doing it at the invitation of one of your colleagues.'

'Mr Parilla... I must intervene here,' it was Rory Featherstone. 'That's not strictly correct, what you said. Prime Minister, I must assure you this is not the outcome I intended.'

'But you obviously instigated it by talking to this... gangster. This racketeer.'

'Don't go all shaky on me, Rory,' said Parilla. 'I thought you wanted to be prime minister.'

'I do. But not like this. You can't threaten the Prime Minister.'

'Well if you've got cold feet, maybe when Mr Fresnel resigns, I'll support one of your rivals to take over his job.'

'I'm not resigning,' said Fresnel. 'If you want to get rid of me, you'll have to shoot me.'

'That can be arranged.' It was Parilla, with a laugh in his voice.

'No. Mr Parilla,' said Featherstone. 'This was meant to be a day of discussion, debate and making agreements. Deals, not threats and violence. Your people have got guns.'

'Of course,' said Parilla.

'Rory,' said the Prime Minister, 'There's an old proverb: he who sups with the devil needs a long spoon. You've been so naïve. I can't imagine how you thought you could agree a deal with this terrorist.'

'All I said, Prime Minister, was, if I became prime minister, I would put his scheme to cabinet...'

'My *excellent* scheme. That's what you called it. So don't start reneging now, Rory.'

'I may have praised it. And it would work. But I made no deal. You've got to believe me, Prime Minister.'

'Lack of the right stuff, that's the problem. None of you are decision makers. Plenty of debate and discussion, but no decisions. The Prime Minister's up in the clouds with art. Mr Featherstone wants to save the world but is frightened of drastic policy changes. What the fuck use is that mentality in today's world? What insanity while Europe's in decline and...'

With a loud clang, one of the metal rods holding the trunking to the concrete above us sheared off. The bolt which had held it in place dropped on to the ceiling tiles below with a dull thud. The rod itself fell on to the trunking with a loud clang, rolled sideways and then it too fell on to the ceiling tiles.

Parilla had stopped in mid-sentence. He started talking again but now his tone was different. I could hear his voice change as he moved around beneath us. '... Europe in decline and the East, especially China, is in the ascendant.'

I could imagine him stalking round the function suite, working out where the noise had come from. He stopped talking and all was quiet below. Unnaturally so. What was going on?

Tanya looked at me and screwed up her face in an 'oh shit' way. I silently echoed her. A minute passed. Two minutes. Nothing happened apart from the occasional groaning complaint from the trunking. Then I heard footsteps and furniture being moved. There was the noise of something hitting the ceiling tiles and a fist appeared from below, the tile was moved out of the way and Duggan's head appeared through the ceiling, followed by the beam of his flashlight.

'Two intruders,' Duggan called down.

Then more heads popped up through the ceiling from the bar servery area. Then guns were pointed at us.

We were pulled out of the ceiling void by force with the result that a large section of the ceiling collapsed completely. We were dragged into the function suite where Parilla was standing up straight and proud as if he'd just won the third world war. Duggan and the black check-jacketed minder were standing beside him. Rory Featherstone was close by; he looked strained. The Prime Minister was sitting down next to Lyle Brabant, who looked pale in spite of his permatan. They were both handcuffed to their chairs.

'Mr Kite! Thank God,' Fresnel said. 'Rescue me, if you can, from this deranged person and his thugs.'

I was being gripped firmly by the two muscle-men who'd dragged me from the ceiling. Rescuing Fresnel was on hold for a while.

'What's going on?' I said to Featherstone, whose tie was loosened and his top shirt button undone.

'We wanted a quiet, discreet place for confidential negotiations. This old hotel seemed ideal.'

'Lyle Brabant and I got into a car to go to a brief meeting at a hotel in Knightsbridge yesterday afternoon. Instead we were kidnapped and brought here.'

'Why is the Prime Minister a prisoner?' I said.

'He is free to go any time,' said Featherstone.

'Any time I resign and let him take over,' Fresnel said.

'That is what we are negotiating about,' said Featherstone.

'We didn't hear much negotiation. All we heard were threats. You invited this man here?' I said to Featherstone, pointing to Parilla.

'I'm assisting in the negotiations,' Parilla said.

'He's trying to take over the country,' said Fresnel. 'Mr Parilla is dangerous, corrupt and has associations with organised crime. He should be arrested and deported.'

'That's my understanding too. He's known as Gorilla Parilla.'

'Hey! Less of the lip,' said Parilla, waving a be-ringed finger at me.

'Yeah, shut it,' said Duggan.

'No. You shut it,' said Fresnel, red in the face with anger. 'I am still your prime minister, even though kidnapped.'

'Ah, he wants respect,' said Parilla in a cynical drawl.

'Yes, I fucking do,' said Fresnel. 'What's going on, Mr Kite and Tanya, is that *Mister* Parilla and his associates from China, Russia,

Malta and God knows where else has been invited to take a slice of the nation's wealth. By my Foreign Secretary. By Rory Featherstone. Essentially, he's organised a coup d'état against me. A revolution. An uprising.'

'No, Prime Minister, you've got to believe me. I made no deal. I didn't intend for him to kidnap you.' Featherstone looked desperate.

'You've behaved stupidly, recklessly, treasonably. You've let this oaf into the sweet shop and he's helping himself to all the goodies. You're finished, Rory.'

'Not if he becomes prime minister,' said Parilla.

'Which of Hayden's shit-brained policies have you gone for, Rory?' said Tanya, who was being held captive as I was.

'Hey, lady. There are gentlemen present,' said Parilla.

'It'll be something green,' I said. 'Or something that's supposed to be green but shovels money into the syndicate's pockets.'

'It wasn't the crazy road scheme, surely?' said Tanya. 'Say it wasn't the road scheme, Rory.'

'The road scheme's brilliant, Tanya,' said Featherstone. 'A real winner. It ticks all the boxes.'

'What's the road scheme?' I said.

'It's something they floated at that Davos meeting. They don't want to privatise the NHS,' said Tanya. 'It's roads. Privatised roads. It'll be like going back two hundred years to a turnpike system where you have to pay tolls to use the roads. Every road. Motorways, A-roads, B-roads, everything except suburban roads. They'd charge journeys at so much a mile. London to Bristol would cost a hundred pounds, say, or two hundred or whatever they want to charge.'

'It would raise billions in revenue,' said Featherstone.

'And stop people travelling about because they couldn't afford to,' said Fresnel.

'That's a plus. It'd reduce greenhouse emissions overnight. It's a win-win.'

'This is environmentalism gone mad. You're curbing people's liberty. Stopping free movement,' said Tanya.

'Nobody ever had an inalienable right to drive around the country,' said Featherstone. 'We have to reduce car usage. Reduce emissions. Reduce dependence on oil.'

'You'd lose revenue from fuel tax,' Fresnel said.

'But save money on oil imports,' said Featherstone and the two of them began an argument as if they were sitting round the cabinet table.

'Prices for everything would rise because of extra transport costs.'

'Roads would be maintained to a perfect standard. No more potholes.'

'But only the rich could afford to use the roads.'

'Less reliance on the car will mean people will exercise more. They will walk to schools and shops, not drive. We will construct thousands of miles of cycleways, proper ones, fit for purpose. More cycling and walking will increase fitness, reduce the occurrence of obesity and diabetes, scourges which cost the NHS dear. No government in this country has had the courage to grab the car problem by the throat. Every government gives in to the road lobby by building wider roads, and more roads. Which only increases car ownership and car mileage.'

Parilla started to clap his hands. 'Nice speech, Rory. I couldn't have expressed it better myself.'

Tanya joined the debate. 'You may believe all this, but why involve a shady cartel of foreign tycoons and organised crime?'

'I dispute there's any link to organised crime,' said Featherstone. 'It's a classic private-public partnership and Mr Parilla and his colleagues are in a position to provide cash to get things going.'

'You can't believe that,' I said. 'You heard what MI5 said about this group.' Featherstone looked sheepish. He'd been whistling in the dark and he knew it.

'Why do you want to hand over control of a basic national infrastructure like roads to a foreign consortium?' It was Fresnel again.

'We've done the same with the water supply, electricity, gas, and parts of the rail network. What's the difference with roads?' said Featherstone.

There was a pause.

'Q and A session over?' said Parilla.

'What happens next?' I said.

'The Prime Minister will resign this evening in a special TV transmission and will appoint Rory Featherstone as successor. I'm told hardly anyone will notice.'

Fresnel snorted a derisory laugh.

'Why will the Prime Minister resign?' I said.

'Because if he doesn't, four hundred paintings from the Government Art Collection will be burned in the yard outside,' said Parilla.

'They think I won't allow that because of my feelings for art,' said Fresnel. 'So they think I'll resign to prevent it. But I'm on the horns of a dilemma. If I refuse to resign and say to hell with the pictures, they'll brief the press that I was trying to negotiate with the blackmailers on my own at this remote place, and was double-crossed. They'll say I paid the five hundred million and still allowed the pictures to burn.'

Then Duggan turned to Parilla. 'What do you want to do with these two?' He pointed at Tanya and me.

'My boys have plenty of firepower,' said Parilla.

'No. You can't. You're not in Miami or Irkutsk now,' said Featherstone loudly, becoming agitated. 'I cannot countenance murder. This isn't a police state. It's a democracy.'

'Glad you think so,' said the Prime Minister. 'You're Foreign Secretary, for God's sake. Phone the police, have this man arrested and put on a plane out of the country tonight.'

Featherstone seemed to be considering this. 'Would I have immunity from any kind of censure, or prosecution? Would you keep me on?'

'How fucking dare you...' The Prime Minister tried to get up and physically attack Featherstone but he was held back by his handcuffs. 'Just do as I say.'

'Cool it,' said Duggan, advancing on Fresnel. Then he remembered his manners and said in a taunting voice, 'Sorry... cool it, *Prime Minister*.'

'I've an idea,' Parilla said, then he turned to Brabant. 'You're a doctor. Time for you to do some work.' He had a word in Duggan's ear and Duggan sent another man out of the room while he unlocked Brabant's handcuffs.

'So convenient having a doctor around when you need one,' said Parilla.

'If I refuse to do what you want?' said Brabant, plainly nervous in spite of, or because of, his battlefield experiences.

Duggan held a gun to Brabant's head. 'I'll pull the trigger then put your body on the bonfire with the paintings.'

'No,' said Featherstone. 'Please, Lyle, do what they say for God's sake.'

Duggan's colleague returned with the metal tray of medical gear we'd seen in the kitchen. A syringe was put in Brabant's hand, Duggan pushed him towards me and pulled up the sleeve of my shirt.

'Go on, doctor,' he said.

I struggled to get away from the two heavies who held me, but their grip was vice-like.

'No,' said Brabant. Duggan flicked off the safety on his gun and pressed it against Brabant's head.

'Stop this!' said Featherstone, who was looking increasingly ineffectual.

'Doctor, give him the injection,' said Parilla, as calm as anything.

Brabant was so close to me I saw perspiration on his brow. He started to tremble. Was he having an attack of his stress syndrome? He screwed up his eyes and turned his head away from Duggan and the gun. But Duggan gripped Brabant's hand, stabbed the syringe into my arm and pressed down the plunger.

'I'm sorry,' I heard Brabant say. 'Sorry…'

Then everything went fuzzy at the edges.

When I woke up everything was dark. Not night-time dark, when there's always light from the street or the moon, but absolute dark. A complete absence of light. Like it is supposed to be in deep space. I could see nothing. No glimmers, no reflections, no pinpricks of light. The dark was so intense it took me some time to work things out.

Paint It Blackmail

Was I still unconscious? Was I asleep but dreaming I was awake? Had I suddenly lost my sight? I felt my eyes, my face, my body. There was no wounding, no blood, no pain – except a minor ache in my arm where the needle had gone in. I reached out a hand to feel around and touched something warm. A body. The body moved. And groaned.

'Tanya?'

I sensed, rather than saw, her moving around.

'Where am I? Kite? Is that you?' Her hand touched me. 'Why can't I see?'

'I don't know.' I felt around. I could feel a smooth, solid floor and further away a smooth solid wall. 'We're in a box, a chamber, some kind of container.' I explored further with my hands and felt nothing but smooth surfaces. Then I became aware of a faint odour. I sniffed the air and sniffed again. It was the smell of food, stale and fatty. I remembered the same smell in the hotel kitchen and saw in my mind's eye the row of disused commercial fridges.

'I think we're inside one of the kitchen fridges.'

'Oh God. And my arm hurts.'

'They injected us. With an anaesthetic.'

'So next they're going to freeze us to death?'

'The fridge isn't on. The temperature feels normal. Warm, in fact.'

'So we'll suffocate…'

I said nothing. I felt a rising tension within me. A rising dread. Not panic. Just a sense of severely limited options. I stood up, slowly, feeling the air around me. Where were the walls? Where was the ceiling? How big a space was I in? I touched the ceiling, then I found a wall. And I remembered something. 'All these big walk-in fridges have a handle on the inside to open the door. It's a compulsory safety thing. We'll be able to let ourselves out.'

'Well, let's find it, for God's sake,' said Tanya.

I moved my hand and found the nearest wall. I swept my hand along it until I came to a right angle, and then a hinge.

'I've found the door.' I sounded exhilarated. I moved along the door feeling for the device that would open it. 'I've found where the handle is.' I rubbed my hands over it. I could feel a circle of small holes, with a larger diameter hole in the centre of them. 'Hang on…'

'What is it?'

'There's no handle here,' I said.

'What do you mean?'

'I can feel screw holes where it was fixed but the handle, the knob you press to open the door, it isn't here. It's been taken away.'

'Then how do we get out?' Tanya's hands brushed against me as she groped around. I took hold of them and pulled her towards me. She lumbered into my arms and flung her arms around me. I felt her body shaking with fear.

'Kite, how do we get out? Tell me that. How do we get out?'

Chapter 26

We had no way of measuring time. Even if Tanya's big Omega hadn't been removed, along with our belongings, the total darkness would have sapped the power of its luminous hands.

I must have spent an hour exploring every inch of our prison. First I crawled over the floor, feeling for something, anything, that could help us. I found nothing. Then I stood up and began to sweep my hands across the walls, one by one, from side to side and top to bottom. Tanya wanted to help but I said it would be easier if she stayed sitting down. That way we wouldn't collide with each other and we wouldn't miss bits out.

As I worked on the walls, Tanya tried to keep our minds off the worst-case scenario. 'I went to what's called a black restaurant once,' she said. 'Everywhere was dark, blacked out, not a glimmer of light. Some of the waiting staff were actually blind so they were hunky dory.'

'Was that the point? To replicate what it's like to be blind?'

'I think it's to do with savouring the taste of food without being influenced by the colour or shape of what's on the plate.'

'Weird.'

'Completely. And wrong as well. Eating something without knowing what it is… it's disconcerting. You stab your fork into something – could be a prawn or a potato – and you bring it to your mouth almost frightened to eat it. Is it something I like or not? The whole experience was utterly ghastly. The pleasure of eating doesn't only come from taste. It's from appearance as well. And the anticipation. That sirloin looks beautiful, you think, and you start to salivate. Then it's in your mouth and you appreciate the flavour more.' She paused. 'Sorry, that's all irrelevant. And there's no food in here.'

'I'll remember what you said next time we have dinner.'

I looked at her, or rather looked towards where I thought she was, because I couldn't see her. But I felt her looking at me and I knew we were thinking the same: if there *is* a next time. I tried to reach for Tanya's hand, but I had no idea where it was and I flailed about without making contact.

We had to stay positive. We had to avoid despair. I changed the subject. 'Did you have any suspicions about Featherstone?'

'He's always been ultra-green, wanting a radical environmental policy. But I didn't think he was so gullible as to fall for Parilla's sales pitch.'

'How did they make contact?'

'He must have kept in touch after the Davos session. And then set up the meeting at Number Ten between Parilla and Fresnel.'

'You think Fresnel will resign?'

'He won't allow those pictures to be burned; he loves art so much and it would end his career. The only way he can stop them being burned is to resign.'

I had shuffled around the walls and floor for what seemed like hours and found nothing except smooth metal surfaces. No openings, no cracks, no useful left-behind tools.

I sat down, feeling light-headed and afraid I was losing it. The utter darkness was disorienting. I was losing my sense of direction and my sense of space. I couldn't tell whether Tanya was in front of me or behind me. To my left or to my right. Distance was distorted too. Was our prison six feet long or sixty feet? It seemed at the same time both infinitely big and claustrophobically small.

I said nothing to Tanya but she must have been feeling the same because she said, 'It's weird in here. It's not just pitch black but silent too. We could be in a mine or a cave.'

'Sensory deprivation,' I said. 'It's a form of torture.'

'How can we combat that? Keep talking? Make some noise?' Then she clapped her hands together loudly. The sound was strangely explosive in the enclosed space. 'Sorry,' she said.

'Don't apologise.'

'Which part of our cell haven't you checked?'

'The ceiling.'

'Well, crack on then.'

Her attitude made me smile. Not that she could see it. I found a corner and started to feel my way across the ceiling. After a moment she said, 'Were you... smiling?'

'Have you got ESP?' I said.

'You sort of breathed out, like a tiny sigh, that's all. Not that there's much to smile about.'

I continued exploring the ceiling, then I smiled again.

'And another,' she said. 'That was bigger. More of a grin. What's going on?'

'I've found something.'

'Not a trap door?'

'No. But it could be useful.'

In the middle of the ceiling my hands had come across a light, one which would come on automatically when the door opened. It wasn't the light itself which interested me but the rectangular metal frame which held a glass cover over the bulb. The metal frame was screwed to a base plate and the frame was loose. Two of the screws which should have held it to the baseplate were missing. The glass itself was no use, but maybe the metal frame could be fashioned into a makeshift tool.

I dropped to the floor again and crawled toward where I thought the door was. Crawling there was simpler than walking, less danger of crashing into Tanya. I got to the door and found the hole where the knob or handle had once been. I pushed my index finger into the hole as far as it would go. Which was not far.

'Tanya, can I borrow you?'

'What for?' I heard her shuffle over on her bottom towards the sound of my voice.

'Your fingers are thinner than mine. Reach into here. Tell me what you can feel.' I took one of Tanya's hands and guided her index finger in. 'Push in as far as you can.'

'There's something metallic.'

'Can you depress it, push it forwards?'

'Only a little. It feels like it's on a spring.'

'Good. It'll be the lock mechanism. If we can push it further in, we can open the door.'

'But how do we do that? And what are you doing with my fingers?'

I was holding Tanya's hands, feeling her fingernails. 'Your nails are long, but are they strong?'

'My manicurist seems to think so. Has to sharpen his clippers whenever I go.' I smiled again. This time she put a hand to my face and felt my lips. 'Thank you for the appreciation,' she said.

I held her hand, felt along the ceiling until I found the light. Then I led her underneath it. 'I want to use your nails to unscrew this.'

'Is that possible?'

'I don't know, but the screws are the old slotted type, not Pozidriv. They're small and some are loose.' She stood behind me and I held one of her fingers as if it were a screwdriver, guiding it towards the slot in one of the screws.

'Feel the screw?'

'Yes. I'll try to turn it.' She winced as her nail bent under the pressure. And winced again. 'I'll use my thumb. It's stronger.' Then, 'It's moving. Yes!' Slowly, painfully, she undid the screw and took it out. 'How many more?'

'Four.'

'God.'

The next one was loose and came out easily. As did the next. The third was difficult. Tanya broke both her thumb nails and another nail.

'I don't think I can do this,' she said. 'I've no nails left. Is there anything else we can use?'

Then I had an idea.

Paint It Blackmail

'What are you doing?' she said. 'You're moving around, flapping something. And I can feel the heat of your body. Are you undressing? And if so, why?'

'I'm taking off my shirt. It's got stiffeners in the collar. Little brass things.'

'I've heard of plastic ones but never brass. You must shop in the same place as Parilla.'

'I get shirts online. Twenty-five quid each. Maybe they think brass is more eco than plastic.' I removed the brass stiffeners from the collar, held them together for added strength and offered them up to the screw in the ceiling. The two pieces of brass fitted into the screw slot and I tried to turn it. Nothing happened except the brass bent a little.

'Is it working?'

'Not yet.'

I pressed the tiny metal strips hard into the slot and tried again. The screw turned a few degrees. I tried again. I could feel the brass bending further but I pressed it hard into the slot and the screw turned a little more. I tried again and the screw turned again, more easily now. I re-angled the pieces of brass and turned the screw until it fell out on to the floor.

That left one screw holding the metal frame in place. The head of the screw felt damaged; there were bits of rough metal protruding from its surface. I tried again with the bits of brass but couldn't get them to grip and they slipped out of the screw slot.

'Time for some brute force,' I said. With only one screw holding it, the metal frame was loose. I slid my fingers under one edge and pulled down. As I'd hoped, the metal was thin enough to bend under pressure. It bent almost ninety degrees, then I worked the metal back up again. And down again, creasing the metal where it was still held by the final screw. Up and down. Up and down. I bent it repeatedly until I felt the metal softening. At last it snapped. I now had a broken rectangle of metal in my hands.

Had the doorknob still been fixed on the fridge it would have been a simple push-in device which pressed against the lock mechanism on the other side of the door. My plan was to insert one of the longer sides of the broken light frame into the handle socket and push against the lock to make it open. Was the metal alloy strong enough, or would it bend under the pressure? Using one of my feet as a vice I bent the metal over on itself lengthwise, so instead of a rectangle I had a shallow, flattened U-shape. Then I bent one of the arms of the U back against the longer side to strengthen it further, giving me a L-shape. Crude, but it might work.

I inserted the end of the homemade tool into the handle socket and pressed against the mechanism. The lock was old and stiff, no doubt caked with dirt and grease like the rest of the kitchen. I pressed harder, the metal end cutting into my hand. I could feel my improvised metal rod bending under the strain and I was despairing of it ever working when I felt the lock's spring mechanism give slightly. I pressed harder, my feeble metal tool bent further. Then there was a click which seemed deafeningly loud in the enclosed silent space. The door moved and a crack of light appeared. I pushed against the door. It opened. The cannibalised electric light in the fridge roof came on.

We dragged ourselves out into the kitchen and leaned on one of the stainless steel tables. Neither of us said anything for a few moments. Then Tanya said, 'Every time I get milk out of the fridge at home I'll remember this.'

I put an arm round her shoulders. 'Don't let it get to you.'

'What do you suggest?' She looked forlorn. 'Take my coffee black?'

I smiled. I caught one of her hands and examined her nails.

'A big sacrifice. But they'll grow back.' She gave me a rueful look. 'And as they grow back, so your memory of the experience will shrink and wither.'

'What's with the cod psychology? Are you taking the piss?'

'I was reading Helen Oxenhope's website. That's the kind of thing she does.'

Neither of us had thought about her for a long time.

'Do you think she and her daughter are here?'

'Zoe sent the video. They must be.' I paused. 'But…' I didn't want to say it.

'But what?'

'But what use are they to Parilla? Do they need them anymore? They've no interest in whether the Prime Minister stole a picture from them. No interest in their quirky demos.'

Tanya saw my point. 'Surplus to requirements.'

In unison, our eyes turned to the row of six fridges beside us. Five of them, including ours, had their doors open. Only one had its door shut.

'When we first walked through here weren't all the doors open?' said Tanya.

I nodded.

We both walked slowly over to the closed fridge. Tanya reached out for the door handle. She touched it. Her hand was trembling. She pulled back and turned away.

'You do it,' she said.

I took her place, reached for the handle and yanked the fridge open. The interior light came on. The fridge was empty. Tanya gasped with relief.

'Sorry,' she said, leaning against me. 'Sorry I was so stupid.'

'Doesn't matter. And you weren't. But we must find them,' I said. 'Before anything does happen to them.'

I led Tanya out of the kitchen, avoided the stairs leading up to the function suite and searched for a secondary staircase which I knew had to exist in a hotel. We found it and went up. From windows on the stairwell we paused a moment to watch the crane driver moving his crane to a new position.

'Not much time,' I said.

On the top floor we went into a long corridor with bedrooms on both sides, typical of hotel design all over the world. The bedroom doors were all unlocked and empty of furniture. Then we came to one that was not only locked but had a hastily fixed padlock on the door as well. Another prison cell.

I banged on the door.

'It's John Kite. Who's in there?'

There was no reply.

'Zoe? Helen? It's me, Kite.' I banged on the door again and listened. Tanya put her ear to the door, then shook her head.

I went down the corridor into the room next to the locked one and tapped on the wall. It was a standard partition of wooden studs and plasterboard. I came out of the room and went back down the corridor to the staircase.

'What are you doing?' said Tanya.

At the top of the staircase, by the fire alarm call point was, as there should be, a CO_2 fire extinguisher. I grabbed it and hurried back to the empty room. I held the extinguisher up and rammed it against the partition. My first blow punctured a hole in the plasterboard on our side of the wall. I pulled the shattered material away from the wooden studs and aimed the next blow at the plasterboard on the far side. I smashed through the second skin of plasterboard, pushed the fragments out of the way and looked through the hole into the next room.

Zoe and Helen were sitting in chairs bound and gagged.

Chapter 27

It took only a few minutes to smash a big enough hole in the wall for me and Tanya to get through. The two women were frightened but unhurt.

'You got the video, then,' was the first thing Zoe said when we ungagged her. 'And you worked out where we were. Cool or what!' Zoe seemed to be strangely enjoying herself.

'What's this about the Prime Minister stealing a picture of yours?' said Tanya as we untied them.

'It was my grandmother's picture,' said Helen.

'The lady in the care home in Ruislip,' I said.

'Margaret Plastow, yes. She lived near Charleston. I don't know whether she did work for them, but she certainly became friends with them. Vanessa Bell, Duncan Grant and the others. It's isolated there. Not many neighbours. And one day, maybe as a present for services rendered or for Christmas or something, Vanessa gave my grandmother a sketch she'd done. Of Duncan Grant. I remember it on her wall when I visited as a child.'

'She was called Peggy, was she? Your grandmother.' I said.

'Yes. Christened Margaret but always Peggy to her friends.'

'How is the Prime Minister involved?' Tanya said.

'He wasn't the Prime Minister then, of course, only a student. He had a friend, Lyle Brabant, and Brabant's father has a big estate. In fact he owned the house my grandparents lived in. James Fresnel would come down and stay with his friend Lyle occasionally. Somehow he got to hear about the picture my grandmother had.

She's senile now but she was getting feeble even then, giving up a bit on things. And she certainly had no idea of the value of things.'

Zoe butted in. 'Mum's sugaring the pill. Aren't you?' Zoe gave her mother a look which I couldn't interpret and her mother looked embarrassed. 'The truth is my great-grandmother was easy prey. Lamb to the slaughter. All the clichés. Her husband was dead and Fresnel... wormed his way into her confidence. Chatted her up. Groomed her. Isn't that right, Mum?'

Helen nodded, still looking strangely embarrassed.

'Fresnel was a hot-looking guy. Clever. Loaded. Friend of her landlord's son. Talked about art and pictures he'd seen all round the world. She was flattered by his interest in her. Infatuated, seduced even. He got her to do just what he wanted. Sold him the picture. She was trying to clear stuff out, downsizing. He probably said he could take it off her hands, suggested he was doing her a favour. Gave her five quid or something for it.'

Helen came back. 'He paid a hundred, I think. It seemed a lot to my grandmother. But obviously a fraction of what it's worth. He ripped her off. Quite blatantly. He unashamedly took advantage. Raped her, you might almost say. He was selfish and greedy. No thought for anyone but himself. I hate him.' Helen's voice was shaky with emotion, her eyes were burning and her body trembling. I remembered her behaviour at the British Museum. I'd thought she was nervous but what I'd seen was twenty years of pent-up passion about to be released. I'd spoiled her moment, stolen her thunder. That was why her slap across my face was so hard. She imagined she was slapping the Prime Minister and she gave me the full fury of her anger.

Zoe continued, 'When we heard the Prime Minister seemed to approve of sending exhibits back from museums to the places they originally came from we thought we could use that. Mum wrote to him. A nice straightforward letter. We waited ages but there was no reply. So we sent another. Again we waited and again there was no reply. That's when we had the idea of those little demonstrations. We hoped a journalist or somebody would be intrigued and we could tell the whole story.'

Helen had controlled her emotions and took up the story again. 'That was the idea, but then we got an approach from Mr Duggan, who said he could help us. We didn't know who he was or whether to trust him, but it seemed too good a chance to miss.'

'If things seem too good to be true, they usually are,' Tanya said.

'We know that now. But he introduced us to Mr Featherstone, who had seen one of the letters we'd sent to the Prime Minister, and we seemed to have almost won already. I mean, Foreign Secretary, how good was that? Only one step away from Fresnel himself.'

'He agreed for you to do the demos?' I said.

'Yes. He thought they were... a bit strange, but he agreed they could help.'

'And undermine Fresnel's position,' I said.

'Yes. He said our demos would be a way of putting pressure on the Prime Minister and attracting publicity. I had no idea he wanted to get rid of the Prime Minister. Then things went pear-shaped when you thought we were anarchists or something. My poor brothers got beaten up. I had to do something to get you back on track, Mr Kite. To make you see what our real point was.' I looked at Helen and it struck me what she was referring to.

'You mean Pilcher the dealer? You were involved in that?'

Tears welled up in Helen Oxenhope's eyes. 'I'm so sorry. It was all my fault. Mr Featherstone told me the Prime Minister had employed you to try to prove his picture – our picture – was a fake and was going to see this man in the Cotswolds who had been set up to agree with Fresnel. If this dealer told you what the Prime Minister had asked him to say, you would have gone away and never thought about that painting again. So I wanted to give you something to think about. A problem. A puzzle. Something that didn't look right.'

'Well, it worked,' I said, watching Tanya shake her head in disbelief. 'Or we wouldn't be here now.'

'The idea wasn't to kill him, Mr Kite. You must believe me. One of Duggan's friends went down to ask him to say something different to you. It seems he had a heart attack or stroke.'

I nodded. 'He was in his seventies. Having a tattooed thug bursting into his bathroom and threatening him was probably too much.' I paused. 'And why did your two IT friends have to die?'

'I honestly don't know. That was nothing at all to do with us. Poor Richard and Scott. They did the brochure thing for amusement more than anything.' Helen started to cry.

'When Zoe threw the flyers around the National Portrait Gallery why didn't you explain the truth then?' I said. 'You had an audience, you had your pamphlets.'

Helen was wiping her eyes. Zoe answered. 'Duggan told us to hold off. He said there was a thing called the rule of three.'

'What?' I looked at Tanya, who shrugged, as mystified as me.

'It's a thing in advertising, or maybe in film-making or books. I don't know. Anyway, he said we had to do three events and only on the third should we reveal the whole truth.'

'But he was lying,' I said.

'Yes. Completely,' said Helen, sniffing. 'They never intended to allow us to do any more. They wanted to shut us up. Get rid of us, probably. It's all gone terribly wrong. I wish we'd never started this.'

'What about Lyle Brabant?' I said. 'You've been treating him? How much did he know?'

'He wasn't involved at all. I never spoke to him about the picture until a day or so ago and he wasn't aware of how Duggan and the others took advantage of his father. His father's ill, you know?'

'Yes. With Alzheimer's.'

'One of the guys in Duggan's gang works for him. He stole the keys to the big house where they kept us, stole the Land Rover. The old man knew nothing about it and nor did Lyle Brabant.'

'Is there anything else?' I said.

'Yes, there is,' Zoe said.

'That's enough for now,' Helen said, taking another tissue out of her bag.

I was about to press her for more but Tanya, who was standing by the window, called me over. In the yard a forklift driver in a fluorescent yellow jacket was moving a large packing case out of a storage shed.

'What do you think?' she said.

The wooden crate was big enough to contain fifty pictures.

'I think the show's about to start,' I said. The forklift trundled across the yard and deposited the packing case next to the crane then drove back to the outbuilding for another load. The truck crane had deployed its stabilising outrigger legs and the driver, Dan, was on the ground arranging a chain sling from the crane's hook.

As we watched, another man doused a rag with petrol, lit it and threw the flaming cloth on to the fire heap. The old, dry wood ignited quickly. Within a minute flames were leaping up, licking hungrily at the timber stack.

Time was running out.

Chapter 28

Tanya and I slipped out of a fire exit at the bottom of the secondary staircase and saw the pile of timber was well ablaze. Dried-out bits of old furniture burned ferociously. Green timber spat and crackled. Oil paintings or watercolours would burn even faster.

The forklift came out of the shed again with another packing case. As it took its load towards the crane Tanya and I slipped into the shed. There were six more packing cases, each about six-foot by four.

Industrial premises always have a few tools lying around. Hanging inside the door, on a six-inch nail banged into the brickwork, was a crowbar. I grabbed it and applied it to the nearest packing case. I didn't want Parilla to con Fresnel with boxes containing nothing more than old hotel furniture.

The first box opened easily. I lowered the plywood side and revealed a similar sight to what I'd seen in the truck outside Lancaster House. Forty or fifty pictures, carefully wrapped and secured.

'That's them?' said Tanya.

'Certainly is.' I looked around. 'Eight cases, each with fifty or so pictures.'

'What are you doing?' It was the guy in the zipped leather jacket we'd seen at Hatfield interfering with my car. He had a chunky, gold chain round his neck.

'Hi,' I said. 'We're with Hayden.'

He said nothing for a moment, his eyes going from me to Tanya and back again. He kept his eyes on us as he pressed a number on his phone.

Paint It Blackmail

'There's a bloke here and a woman. Say they're with us. I wasn't expecting no more and certainly not a woman.' He listened then said, 'Right. My pleasure.' Then he put the phone down and spoke to us. 'I don't want no trouble...' he started.

'No trouble? That's fine by me,' I said with a smile. 'But I'm not leaving here without these packing cases. They contain government property. Stolen pictures.'

Leather jacket laughed. Then he stopped laughing, and advanced on us, his face set.

'Get out,' he said.

'We'll go when we're ready.' I said.

'Like fuck you will.'

'You'll get hurt if you try anything,' I said.

He let out an exaggerated roar of laughter, took something out of a pocket, pressed a button and held a flick knife out towards me. 'This'll change your mind.'

'I don't think so,' I said.

He was standing about twenty feet in front of me. Instead of advancing slowly as I expected – as anyone would expect – he ran towards me, knife hand extended forward, as if he was an old-time cavalryman charging with a sabre. He thought he'd frighten me. But he'd made a mistake. He'd committed too soon. I only had a second or two before he'd reach me, but that was plenty. In a cricket match a batter facing a ninety mile an hour bowler has only half a second to react. The crowbar was my bat. The head of the man rushing me was the ball. I turned sideways, my right foot sweeping back and across for a better angle, did a short back-lift, swivelled my hips fast to the left, at the same time bringing the crowbar round in a circle to hit Leather Jacket hard on the head as his blade passed my left shoulder. I finished with a neat follow-through. A perfect hook shot. Not four runs but one semi-conscious man.

Tanya and I bent over Leather Jacket to make sure he wasn't going to trouble us again when we heard:

'Don't move.'

We whirled round. One of Leather Jacket's colleagues had appeared behind us. A real man-mountain, six-six at least, approaching three hundred pounds and with forearms bigger than Tanya's thighs. But even more important, he was pointing a gun at us.

'Come over here,' he said. An invitation I didn't want to accept. I was holding the crowbar against my right leg and he hadn't seen it. But a crowbar isn't a match for a gun. Making as if to comply, I took a step towards him to gain leverage, then hurled the crowbar at him underarm. Tanya was sprinting away even before the lump of iron hit him. I didn't hang around to see where it struck but, from the sound of his cry and the clatter of the gun on the concrete floor, I reckoned it got him in the chin or the neck.

Tanya and I legged it fast. We ran further into the shed, hoping, assuming, there was an exit on the far side. We hadn't gone far when there was a shot behind us. The bullet whistled past, punched a hole in the metal skin of the shed and went on going into the countryside. We came to a back door. The kind of push-open lock that there should have been inside the fridge. I rammed my fist on the knob. This one worked. Tanya and I ran out of the shed, leaped off a loading bay on to the yard and sprinted towards the river embankment.

I risked a glance behind and saw the big man at the door to the shed with his gun raised and aimed. He pulled the trigger, but we were over a hundred feet away and it was becoming a difficult shot. I heard the crack of the detonation and bits of tarmac were kicked up six feet to our left. He fired again and more tarmac was damaged.

We got to the twelve-foot river embankment – a forty-five degree incline – and surged up it. We went over the top of the dyke and down the other side, running along the flat ground of the narrow flood plain beside the water. We came to a smaller watercourse, feeding into the river through a piped culvert which ran under the steep embankment. I grabbed Tanya's hand and pulled her after me into the culvert. A brick arch supported the main embankment and there was just room for us to hide within it, out of vision to anyone walking on the dyke above.

We soon heard the sound of heavy breathing as our pursuer approached. A big guy but not so fit. The gasping got nearer and nearer and then it seemed the gunman needed a breather. He stopped.

Paint It Blackmail

I edged out of concealment and saw a pair of trainers standing above me. I leaped out of hiding, hooked my hands round one of his ankles and yanked hard. He tumbled to the ground, dropping his weapon on the grassy bank. Then I was on top of him, putting a couple of punches into his face, trying to pin him to the ground. He wasn't an athlete but he was big and powerful. He brought his knees up under my stomach and pushed me off. I fell back as he scrabbled for the gun lying on the ground only three feet from him. He got to the weapon, picked it up, turned round and aimed. He couldn't miss me.

A booted foot shot out of nowhere. It hit the man's gun hand and sent the weapon flying into the river.

'Next time it'll be your head,' Tanya said.

Next time it *was* his head. But it was my fist that made contact not Tanya's boot and he toppled over in the same direction as his weapon. The current was strong and within seconds he was in mid-river being swept downstream. I guessed he'd soon be netted by a weir.

We went back to the top of the dyke to see what was going on. The forklift driver was continuing to move packing cases of pictures towards the crane. Five of the large boxes now stood ready and the crane driver had two of them slung from the hook. I looked around and counted four others in hi-vis clothing. Two of them were the heavies who'd held me immobile while I was injected; one was Duggan, who was now toting a handgun; the other looked as big as the guy we'd dispatched into the river. There was still Parilla's black check-jacketed minder, and probably others.

We were seriously outnumbered.

'We could do with some help,' I said. 'And a phone call to the police. Let's find Brabant. We could use him.'

We crept back towards the hotel. We used the massive crane and the blazing fire as cover and timed our run back to the fire exit to avoid the to-and-fro of the forklift. We slipped back in and went along the ground floor corridor which led to reception.

Halfway there, Tanya was a pace ahead of me when she stopped dead and put her hand on my chest. There were voices approaching. We heard Parilla, Duggan, Featherstone, Fresnel and others coming down from the function suite area. Were they heading towards the exit we'd just come through? Where we stood there were no doors. No places to hide. No concealment. Moving would attract attention. So we froze, pressing ourselves against the blank wall, trying to be invisible.

The voices and footsteps continued through the reception area and into the dining room. We heard the door to the kitchen swing open and the sounds disappeared.

'Will they check the fridge?' Tanya whispered. We hadn't moved a millimetre; her hand was still pressed against my chest.

I shook my head with a show of confidence. But how could I know?

We moved on. Reception was deserted once again. Still nobody to check in. We moved up the stairs to the function suite and saw as we got to the landing that the double doors were wide open. I peered round the door jamb. The room was empty. Except for Brabant, unguarded, but still handcuffed to the arms of a dining chair.

In the bar lounge area, amid the wreckage of what had been the suspended ceiling, I selected a thick metal support that had broken off from the air con system. Using the metal rod as a lever, I worked to prise off one of the chair arms and at the same time released a torrent of anxious explanation from Brabant.

'James only told me about this picture the other day. I urged him to confess everything and give it back, but he said it was all too late because Parilla's gang was now involved.'

'They stole the pictures to make him agree to the roads plan?' I said.

'Yes. Originally the PM was going to meet them on his own. But it seemed a good idea if I was there too. Support. Evidence. That kind of thing. Parilla was aggressive, threatening.'

'I'm not surprised.' One of the chair arms snapped off. I began to work on the other.

'It was after that meeting the pictures were stolen. James was irate. He didn't know what to do. I told him to talk to Helen, see if she could influence Parilla, but he wouldn't. Then yesterday, when we snuck out of Number Ten, we thought the situation was resolved and we'd only be away an hour at most. But Parilla lied.'

'Gangsters tend to,' I said as the second chair arm broke off. 'I can't unlock the cuffs, but at least you're free to move. And we need your help.'

'Anything,' Brabant said. 'What's our strategy?'

Where did he think we were? In a cabinet meeting? It was a time for ingenuity and improvisation. As we went downstairs Brabant explained why he had wanted to fire me at the golf club meeting. Spanswick, Featherstone and Tresize all envied and disliked him because of his closeness to the Prime Minister and had a habit of briefing journalists against him. They all told him I was suspicious of him – which was true, mainly because the other ministers had suggested it to me. He had then persuaded Fresnel I was no longer an asset, but Spanswick had got wind of this and stepped in as my supporter at the last minute. Brabant assumed it was Featherstone who had got me arrested.

We went through the dining room, and into the kitchen. Coming into the service area, I stopped by the coat pegs where there were still some hi-vis yellow waistcoats.

'Put one of these on,' I said. 'People in yellow jackets are always invisible.' Then I pointed to the tray of medical equipment Duggan had used before: syringes in sealed bags and a few ampoules of colourless liquid.

'Is this what we were injected with?' I said, picking up one of the ampoules.

'Propofol,' said Brabant. 'It's an anaesthetic.'

'Grab them. We've no other weapons.'

We went back through the kitchen and dining room, turned right at reception and took the long corridor to the distant fire exit. We went outside, where it was getting dark and the hotel's exterior floodlights were on. But the fire upstaged the electricity and cast the whole scene in a menacing red glow. Flames leaped high in the air and threw distorted shadows. We concealed ourselves behind a return wall as we took in what was happening.

A camera and microphone had been set up in front of the podium where Parilla and Duggan stood conferring. Featherstone was by himself, his face blank, looking like a man who'd heard the cry 'iceberg ahead,' but carried on steering his ship towards it. The Prime Minister was sitting down. Still handcuffed to the dining chair. There were two identical chairs placed either side of it. On camera, the Prime Minister's handcuffs could be concealed and it would look like any other press briefing with Parilla and Featherstone flanking him. Parilla would film Fresnel agreeing to let the pictures burn or agreeing to resign. He had to do one or the other. If he let the pictures burn and did not resign he would be toast himself in a matter of hours. Then the news film crew would arrive at nine o'clock to record a statement for the ten o'clock news.

On the podium, Parilla sat down in one of the seats by Fresnel. He seemed to want to warm up. Rehearsing, you might say.

'Mr Prime Minister, let me ask you first …' he began, and was immediately interrupted by a furious Fresnel.

'If you have any aspirations to play a part in this country's future you should learn once and for all that is the wrong form of address. This is not the United States; we do not say *Mister* before the title of our nation's leader.'

'I am so *terribly* sorry,' said Parilla, smirking at Featherstone.

'Are you filming all this?' Fresnel said, apparently seeing the camera and mic for the first time. Parilla nodded.

'In that case I want to make a statement.'

'We're recording. It's not going out live,' said Parilla.

'Doesn't matter.'

'We'll cut what you say.'

'Doesn't matter. It will be there for someone. For posterity.'

Tanya and I exchanged looks, our brows furrowed. This was surreal. We were in an overgrown yard behind a closed budget hotel. The Prime Minister was effectively a prisoner of a billionaire South American oligarch and he wanted to make a speech. He was acting like there was an audience of thousands. Instead there was a crane driver, a handful of criminals and us. But politicians like making speeches. However difficult the odds, however bad the situation.

The fire burned more strongly. Sparks flew overhead. I remembered the memorial to the tragically innovative Tyndale in Whitehall Gardens.

Fresnel continued resolutely. 'I want to put it on record – for whomsoever may discover it – that I and my friend and fellow Minister, Dr Lyle Brabant, have been kidnapped by this man, Clayton Parilla, assisted by, I am sad to say, my minister, Rory Featherstone, a man in whom until today I had absolute trust. What they have done is an attack on the legally appointed government of the United Kingdom. It is therefore treason. They are attempting a coup d'état. Apart from being treasonable, it is also madness.'

I nudged Tanya. 'I'll head for the crane operator first,' I said. 'If he's out of action then the paintings are safe.' The three of us moved away from the building, behind the blazing fire, slipping out of range of the lighting and into the gloom.

'Their plan to privatise the entire road system of the nation and introduce tolls is supreme folly. It will raise billions in taxation and make Parilla here even wealthier, but it will bleed our citizens dry. Like the National Health Service, the nation's roads are free for all to use. Nobody in the UK would have thought of this madcap scheme but for the influence of an international conspiracy of criminals.

'It is to my eternal sorrow that they have persuaded, or bribed, one of my ministers to join them and also, I understand, other notable but deluded personages who have signed up with them include a duke, a former head of the Royal Navy and a number of backbench MPs and–
–'

'That's enough, Fresnel.' Parilla interrupted. 'Listen to me now.'

We were close to the crane now. The driver was facing away from us, watching Parilla, waiting for a cue, but I could see he had the typical heavyweight look of crane drivers. People who spend the working day sitting down pulling levers. He looked at ease. A pro. Not someone Duggan had dragged out of a cell somewhere.

Two packing cases of pictures were slung from the crane hook but still rested on the ground.

'Get a syringe ready,' I said to Brabant.

'Shame it's not a gun,' Tanya said. I gave her a sharp look. 'I can shoot,' she said. 'Used an SA80 in the OTC.'

I should have guessed. Her precision would have made her brilliant on the parade ground too. The drill sergeant's favourite.

'We can do this the easy way or the hard way,' Parilla was saying. 'To speed your thinking along, I'll start a ticking clock.' He made a sign to the crane driver.

The crane's engine revved, fumes belched from its exhaust and the hook rose, lifting the two packing cases up. When they were ten feet off the ground the crane cab rotated slowly around towards the fire until the crates were in front of it, in line with Fresnel and Parilla. The packing cases swung from side to side, close to the fire but not yet in serious danger.

I started to climb the ladder which gave access to the crane cab as Parilla continued: 'The easy way is for you to resign. I understand you have to tell the Queen first. Well, you can invent some illness. Say you are too sick to continue and Rory will take over from you. He tells me the Queen can't object.' Parilla gave another signal to the crane driver. The crane rotated further towards the fire. The dangling packing cases swung underneath and, as they swung, they were in range of the searing heat of the flames. Fresnel's face was anguished.

I reached the crane cab and knocked on the side window. The driver turned round, surprised. I gave him a thumbs up, opened the cab door and climbed into the cramped space.

'Hi,' I said, 'it's Dan isn't it?'

'That's right,' he said, wondering how I knew.

'Sorry to interrupt. I was nearby and I heard a fire was involved on this job, so I thought I'd look in to make sure nothing was damaged. I was worried about the hook getting burned.'

The driver was struggling to catch up. 'You're from... the office?'

'That's right.'

'I thought this was a hush-hush, nudge-nudge, under the counter kind of job.'

'You're right. It is. But they had to run it past me.'

The driver seemed to accept this. 'So what's in the crates? I thought they'd be empty but they're heavy.'

'No idea, Dan. Probably just ballast to stop them blowing around too much.'

I looked towards Parilla, who was speaking again. 'Now, the hard way,' he said, 'is for us to set fire to all these pictures which are so dear to your heart and we release the video of them being turned to ash with you standing by watching. That won't go down too well with the British public. They may not care a shit for art but they will see you as a liar, a charlatan.'

Parilla signalled again to Dan the driver and he swung the cases of pictures closer to the fire. The biggest flames were now in reach of the edge of the packing cases as they swung under the crane hook. There was a smell of scorching wood in the air.

'That geezer's a dead ringer for the Prime Minister though, isn't he?' Dan laughed.

'Yeah, good casting,' I said, thinking how reality is becoming harder to recognise in our world of fake news, CGI, phishing and hoaxes.

'What are they doing here anyway?'

'Some sort of film shoot,' I said, continuing the fiction. 'Low budget. Maybe a commercial, I don't know.'

'Low budget all right. There's no catering. Usually the food on film shoots is ace.'

On the podium the Prime Minister was getting desperate. 'Rory, for God's sake, can't you stop this madman?' said Fresnel.

Featherstone looked pale, nervous and embarrassed. But his game wasn't over yet. 'If you hadn't stolen a painting all those years ago, or if you'd confessed and given it back, or if you hadn't tried to wriggle out of it by lying more and hiring that detective, Kite. If you'd been honest about your past, we wouldn't be here now.'

And I thought back fifteen years to my father and how I'd tried to hide the past. Should I have changed my name, cut myself off from friends, given up my university course? It seemed right at the time. And I thought it was a way of making amends for what my father had done.

I looked out of the cab and checked that Brabant was ready below. I gave him a sign to stand by. 'Tanya down there has got something for you,' I said to the crane driver. 'Cash bonus. From the hirers.'

Dan looked out of the cab window. Then he screwed his face up. 'Cash bonus? I don't think so. And who the hell is the dolly bird?'

'Tanya's my PA.'

That lie tipped the balance for Dan the driver. 'PA?' he said. 'There's no PAs at the office.' He got up out of his seat, eased his bulk around the cab and came towards me. 'Just who are the fuck you? You're sure as hell nothing to do with this firm.'

I opened the cab door then stepped back away from the opening. 'If you get down we'll explain.'

He stood there with a half-smile on his face, knowing he was in the right. 'No, mate, you get down. Out of my cab.' He took a step towards me but I put a foot to his stomach and shoved hard. He staggered back, tripped and fell clean out of the cab door. There was a solid thump as he hit the ground. Tanya leaped forwards, sat on a shoulder and pulled up a sleeve of his shirt. I jumped down and pinned him to the ground as Brabant whipped out the syringe and sank the needle into the man's arm. He yelled and screamed and struggled, but between us we had him under control and the fire's roaring and crackling covered his noise.

Dan's struggles stopped and his body went limp. We left him where he was and Tanya and I climbed back up to the crane cab. I looked over towards the podium where Parilla was waving at me.

'Closer!' he shouted. 'Closer to the fire.'

I put my hands on the crane controls.

'Can you work it?' Tanya said.

'My dad had a building business. It was a front, of course, to hide how he really earned his money but, when I was about fifteen, I went on a site visit with him. There was a crane there like this. My dad let me have a play.'

'And you've remembered it all?'

'We'll see, won't we?' I said, pressing one of the foot pedals. The hydraulic jib extended further upwards, taking the packing cases closer towards the fire. Not what I wanted. I grasped one of the joysticks on either side of my seat and pulled it towards me. The crane body revolved on its base, swinging the big cases in an arc towards Parilla.

'Stop, stop,' he yelled. 'Other way.'

I stopped the rotation abruptly but of course the packing cases continued to swing back and forth like a pendulum. I noticed one of Parilla's yellow-jacketed toughs had been stoking up the fire. He was carrying another huge piece of timber that looked like one of those cabers they toss at the Highland Games.

I lowered the hook until the packing cases were only a few feet above ground. Then lined up the angles as best I could, waited till the cases were at the end of their arc of swing and pushed the joystick away from me to rotate the crane abruptly in the opposite direction. My amateurishly violent handling of the crane propelled the swinging crates forward at speed.

My aim was true. The crates hit the pole-carrying man squarely in the back. The force of the impact was so strong I heard the plywood of the packing cases crack and I saw the man shoot forwards twenty feet to the edge of the fire. He screamed as he landed in the red-hot embers. The pole he'd been carrying tumbled on to the side of the fire heap, but it didn't lodge there and slid down, ending up half in and half out of the fire.

Parilla's black check-jacketed minder rushed to help his comrade and dragged the screaming man out of the fire. His clothes were ablaze. Duggan and another man ran to help but I swung the crane boom away from the fire and then back again towards Duggan. He was quick enough to see the packing cases coming towards him and he flattened himself on the ground as the crates whizzed overhead. His colleague was slower and the boxes hit him so hard I heard again the splintering sound of plywood. The thug lay unconscious on the ground. Then I extended the boom to its furthest extent and lowered the packing cases as far from the fire as possible. I let the boom descend until it touched the ground. Not a normal operating position, but I hoped this barrier would stop anyone escaping by road.

Then a bullet smashed into the crane cab.

Duggan was aiming at Tanya and me, indicating for us to get out.

Parilla was waving a gun towards Fresnel. Tanya and I exchanged looks. We had come to save the Prime Minister, not get him killed. It seemed we had no option but to comply. At least the pictures were safe for the time being. We climbed down from the cab and walked towards the group on the rostrum, leaving Brabant concealed behind the crane.

'Close, but no cigar,' said Parilla with a sneer as we approached. He turned to the Prime Minister. 'Ready to record the resignation speech? We have a TV crew arriving shortly.'

Fresnel said nothing.

'Don't resign, Prime Minister,' I said.

'You got to,' said Parilla.

'I do not,' said Fresnel. 'Rory, stand up to him.'

Featherstone looked anguished. Parilla turned to his black check-jacketed minder who had returned from the injured man. 'Persuade him,' he said.

The minder drew out a pistol and held it to Fresnel's head. In the shadows, I saw Brabant creep out from behind the crane, then use the grounded boom arm as cover and run in our direction. He was holding something in his hand.

'Do as I say,' said Parilla.

'I refuse,' said Fresnel.

'Mr Featherstone, it could be life imprisonment,' I said. 'Or else a fugitive forever.'

Suddenly Featherstone was galvanised. 'You can't do this,' he said, grabbing Parilla by the shoulder. 'You can't hold a gun to the Prime Minister.'

'You can where I come from,' said Parilla.

'I won't allow it. This was not how it was supposed to be. It has to be a voluntary resignation, not at gunpoint for Christ's sake.'

'You invited me here,' said Parilla. 'You knew how I work.'

'Tell your man to put the gun down.'

Parilla ignored Featherstone and turned away. 'We're waiting, Prime Minister.'

Fresnel said nothing. I looked at Featherstone, who was looking even more tortured. He looked at me. I caught his eye and held up a finger, trying to suggest he bide his time for a good opportunity. Black Check Jacket held his gun to Fresnel while Parilla covered me.

Duggan returned from attending to the burned man. 'He needs a doctor,' he said.

'We've a doctor here,' said Parilla. 'Go get him from the function room.' Duggan turned towards the hotel building as Brabant himself ran out from behind the grounded crane boom holding a syringe and charged towards us.

At the same moment a large baulk of timber slipped from the fire and crashed to the ground, sending a welter of sparks towards the parked cars.

There's something magnetic about the sight of a fire. Children, mystics and romantics see shapes and portents in the flames. Fire authorities say that one of the causes of death in fires is that, instead of running away, people stop to look at the flames and are then engulfed. Now, for just long enough, everyone turned to look at the fire. I took advantage of the double diversion.

I threw myself at the pudgy, unfit Parilla and wrestled him to the floor. Following my lead, I saw Featherstone grab Black Check Jacket and struggle with him while Tanya lashed out with her foot at Duggan. Maybe tai chi, maybe instinct. Her foot was well aimed and hit him in the balls. He crumpled over and she followed it with a second kick to his gun hand. The weapon tumbled to the ground and Tanya made a grab for it as a gunshot rang out and Featherstone collapsed from his struggle with the minder, blood already seeping through his shirt. Tanya pointed the gun at Black Check Jacket as Brabant rushed in with his syringe and sank it into the gangster's arm. For all his bulk, a few seconds were enough to render him comatose. Brabant then turned his attention to the badly wounded Featherstone.

I had subdued Parilla and was searching his jacket for a weapon when Tanya yelled, 'Kite!'

I dodged away but not before Duggan, back on his feet, hit me a glancing blow with a plank of timber and I rolled off Parilla.

'There's keys in the Land Rover,' Duggan shouted, dragging the dazed Parilla to his feet. Parilla ran off. Duggan ran after him. I got up and ran after both. 'I'll drive,' Duggan called after Parilla. But it was Parilla who got into the driving seat. Perhaps he'd forgotten which side we drive on in the UK. This threw Duggan. I saw him stop by the vehicle, think about Parilla changing seats, then realise it would take too long. So he had to run round the front of the vehicle. The two-second delay gave me an opening.

I leaped on Duggan and dragged him to the ground.

'You killed my parents,' I said. I hadn't meant to say that. It just came out.

Duggan was so shocked he stopped struggling and looked at me. Did I take advantage? Of course I did. I got in hefty blows to his face and stomach. I hit him like Helen hit me in the museum – with years of pent-up fury. My fingers were round his neck and I was pressing down hard. We were on the ground in front of the Land Rover when I heard its engine start. Parilla revved hard. There was a grinding sound as he engaged gear and the Land Rover shot forwards towards Duggan and me. I rolled out of the way, but Duggan didn't. The Defender drove right over both his legs and he cried out in pain.

The Defender lurched forwards, straight towards the fire, but Parilla swung the wheel towards the exit from the yard. Then he found the grounded crane boom was blocking his way out. He swung the wheel the other way, the Defender scraping past the giant tyres of the truck crane.

I ran after him. As I did, I heard a shot. And another. Tanya had retrieved Duggan's weapon and was aiming at the Defender. She was using a target shooting stance, standing side on, holding the gun in one hand and using her arm as a sighting device. Elegant and classical. Like she was at some Olympic Games of yesteryear. I hoped she was accurate enough to miss me. As I chased the Land Rover I heard her fire three times more. The first two shots sank into the bodywork, but she was aiming for the wheels and her third shot shredded a tyre. The blow-out made the Defender swerve, but Parilla corrected. What he didn't do was change gear. Either he couldn't work out the dual gearbox or he thought it was automatic, but the high-pitched engine whine was terrible. More like a circular saw than an auto. The rev counter must be well into the red but the vehicle was still travelling slowly, slowly enough for me to catch it. For the second time in two days, I got a hand on the tailgate ladder. Once again, I hauled myself up. It felt like catching up with an old friend. As I climbed, I saw fuel weeping out of the side panel. Tanya had holed the tank.

I climbed up on to the rooftop luggage rack and clambered forwards. Parilla had driven round the outbuildings looking for another way out of the yard but had discovered there was no other exit. Once again, he swung the wheel and did a U-turn. At the front, I leaned down and opened the passenger door. This spooked Parilla and the vehicle swerved again, which swung the passenger door wide open. I took advantage of his loss of control to lower myself down and jump into the seat next to him. Talk about life repeating itself. But I didn't have time for the déjà vu feeling. He was holding a gun in his right hand. I made a grab for the handbrake. He transferred the gun to his left hand and beat at me with it. Which meant both his hands were off the wheel and, since he was looking at me, both his eyes were off the way ahead.

Too late, he saw he was driving straight towards the fire. Before he could hit the brakes, the Defender crashed into one of the big poles that had formed the skeleton of the teepee-shaped fire base. A ten-foot flaming log crashed on to the cab, crushing metalwork which the Transit crash had failed to do. At the same time I saw flames licking around the back of the vehicle. The leaking fuel had ignited.

I opened the door and jumped. Flames were around my legs, my feet were in red hot ashes. I ran. My trousers were alight, my shoelaces were alight. My shirt was smouldering. My head felt hot. My hair must be alight. I ran to the river. I went up the embankment, over the top, down the far side and jumped.

The water was a beautiful relief. The river was still in flood and moving fast, but I held on to an overhanging branch to steady myself and put my head under the water. As I surfaced I heard a massive explosion. Smoke and flames shot up into the air.

I climbed out of the river and went back up to the top of the embankment. The Land Rover was a wreck of twisted metal. Of Parilla there was no sign.

I squelched my way back towards Tanya and Fresnel. Duggan was still lying badly injured on the ground. Featherstone was dead.

Tanya had found some cutters somewhere and freed the Prime Minister. Then Brabant led Helen and Zoe Oxenhope out from the hotel.

Fresnel sat down again on one of the seats on the podium, his head in his hands. 'God,' he said, pale-faced, trembling a little. 'Thank God this nightmare is over.'

'Not over yet, Prime Minister,' said Zoe.

'Sorry. Of course you will have your picture back. I apologise for trying to pretend it wasn't genuine. And for misleading you, Mr Kite. It was foolish to try to be as slippery as Havers, the man I was told about.'

'All we wanted was the picture,' said Zoe. 'We wanted what was rightfully ours. And Mum and I wanted you to know what was rightfully yours.'

Fresnel looked blank.

Helen went on, 'I was just sixteen when you chatted me up and seduced me. Persuaded me to have sex for the first time. You were glamorous and smart, but I thought you cared for me, at least a bit. But the only reason you were so passionate was to use me to get close to my grandma. And chat *her* up. To swindle her out of the picture which she had been given by the artist herself.'

I saw Fresnel nodding.

'So what's rightfully yours is Zoe here. You're her father. You bastard.'

Fresnel was open-mouthed. He muttered something about 'being in touch' and 'putting things right' but wandered away from the two women towards Brabant and Tanya.

I guessed that was the source of Zoe's therapy sessions. She had been told the story of her mother's seduction and reacted badly.

Brabant had called the police as soon as he'd recovered his phone and a local armed response team arrived quickly. They were followed an hour and a half later by a team from Scotland Yard led by Detective Chief Inspector Cussons.

Paint It Blackmail

'Thirty-six hours to go,' he said to me. 'That's all I had. Just clearing the office. And you bugger up my retirement.'

The TV crew duly arrived and got the world exclusive Featherstone had promised them. Their camera panned over the stolen pictures that had been hidden in the packing cases and the Prime Minister announced how proud he was to have rescued the art and thwarted the blackmail attempt. He praised additional help from his old friend, Dr Lyle Brabant, who was now appointed Foreign Secretary, following Rory Featherstone's most distressing accident. Fresnel also thanked an unnamed Special Adviser and an equally unnamed civil servant from the Cabinet Office.

Fresnel won the next general election with an increased majority, riding on the back of what was called the Art Rescue Factor. The role of Featherstone in nearly destroying the government was hushed up and a secret report about it will not be released for at least thirty years.

TV journalist Lucy Bladon rose to become the anchor of a weekly networked investigative TV show and attempted to put together a one hour special on 'Gorilla Parilla'. She asked me to take part and I declined. As did Tanya, Fresnel, Brabant and other members of Fresnel's cabinet.

Tanya was promoted. To a rank sufficient to choose her own wall art from the Government Collection. I was flattered that she asked my opinion about what to have, but sadly, if predictably, that was the last time we communicated. I never got the medal the PM mentioned, nor even some alphabet soup. Well, what use would a few letters be?

######

If you've enjoyed this book you might like to leave a review. Reviews help authors like me and also help readers like you find books they'll like. Leave a review on Amazon – and by all means on Goodreads and Bookbub too, if you wish.

*You also might like to join my Readers' Club. If you join, I'll send you a **free John Kite story** immediately – a story you can't get on Amazon, or anywhere else! Just go to:*
https://stuart-doughty.com/freedownload/
I promise I won't pass your address on to advertisers and you can unsubscribe whenever you like.

If you enjoyed this book you will like other books in the John Kite series.

THE ART OF DANGER

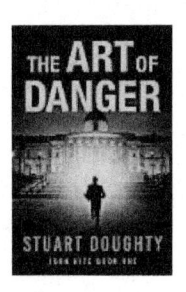

Can a painting be dangerous? You'd better believe it! PI John Kite's job is to recover stolen art but when three men are murdered to get a painting by a forgotten artist, he knows it's not a regular heist. It's far more sinister: a foreign spy is planning mayhem, not an art show. Our hero is tough and sparky, like the dialogue. And he finds the sexy young woman tailing him to be both kooky – and a tough cookie. An entertaining, fast action thriller full of twists, thrills and a bit of wit.

PICTURES TO DIE FOR

Mayhem in Florida and murders in Europe. If a billionaire wants something badly enough, who can stop them getting it? Especially when his accomplice is an obsessive criminal. In this fast action thriller – with a touch of wit – it's art detective John Kite's job to nail the dangerous and mystifying thieves who steal paintings – then destroy them. Kite criss-crosses the world to save millions of dollars' worth of art from destruction as a beguilingly sexy, and kooky, ex-cop re-enters his life with problems of her own she wants him to solve.

KILLING ART

"China is killing art," a woman tells PI John Kite, "You must stop them." Then she is killed in a hail of bullets. Is the bizarre message connected to the flood of robberies Kite is investigating? Or to the dead auctioneer found floating in the ocean? Or is it evidence of a world-wide conspiracy? Being shot at with a flare gun is just the start of this action-filled adventure for ex-cop John Kite. His quest for answers takes him on a 1500 mile road chase, and a speedboat pursuit across the Mediterranean. A girlfriend tells Kite he is "too dangerous to know", but his signature sense of humour is undimmed. With a volcano ready to blow its top, can Kite stop the conspiracy before it causes western economies to go into melt-down ?

Join my Readers' Club for updates, news and chat about books and things by going to my website – https://stuart-doughty.com

Author's Notes
The "Elgin Marbles" which I refer to in the book are sections of ancient Greek statuary and carving from the Parthenon in Athens. The Parthenon was constructed from 447 BC on the Acropolis as a temple to Athena. Greece was part of the Ottoman Empire from the mid fifteenth century and the Parthenon became a mosque. Later, in the 17th century, it was used as an Ottoman ammunition dump and badly damaged by a Venetian siege.

The Earl of Elgin was British Ambassador to the Ottoman Empire from 1799 to 1803. At that time the Parthenon was a military fort and the structure and carvings were in a poor state of preservation. It was thought that some pieces of statuary were being ground up to make cement. With the permission of the Turks, Elgin employed artists to draw the Parthenon sculptures and make casts of some of them. He then began to remove sections of the frieze and carvings and transported them back to Britain, claiming that he had permission from the Turkish Sultan to do so.

The sculptures and carvings have been in the British Museum in London ever since.

There has been debate about the rights and wrongs of what Elgin did almost from the beginning and Greece has been asking for the return of the statuary for many years. In the 1980s the Greek Minister of Culture, the actress Melina Mercouri, was a vociferous advocate of return. The British Museum claims that more people are able to see the statuary in London than could do so in Athens.

The arguments continue.

The Bloomsbury artists Vanessa Bell and Duncan Grant did indeed live at Charleston near Lewes in Sussex. Their house is open to the public and you can see some of their original furniture and how they decorated it.

If you want to know more about me – what I've done, where I live, how much hair I have – you can do so at my website https://stuart-doughty.com. *And you can write to me at* stuart@stuart-doughty.com

And there's also my Readers' Club of course – Did I mention that? The address once again is https://stuart-doughty.com *Go on, you know you want to!*

© Stuart Doughty 2020 All Rights reserved

This is a work of fiction. Names, characters, places, events and incidents either are the products of the author's imagination or are used fictitiously. Any resemblance to actual persons, living or dead, businesses, companies, events, or locales is entirely coincidental.

Printed in Great Britain
by Amazon